A Question of Conscience

Stevens' breath stank. "Know why I'm quitting?" he asked Damion. "Because nobody gives a shit anymore, Captain. They can get the Vietnam box score every night from Walter Cronkite. The latest kill on the same plastic plate with their TV dinner."

"You'd better go, Stevens."

He began to laugh. A nasty sound. "You're a registered U.S. hero, Captain. That's what the Navy Cross is for, isn't it? Now, don't tell me you're having regrets."

"I don't know what to tell you."

"You're no hero," Stevens snarled. "You're a goddamn fraud." It was something that Captain Paul Damion, USN, would have to decide for himself.

Other Pinnacle Books by Martin Dibner:

The Deep Six
The Admiral

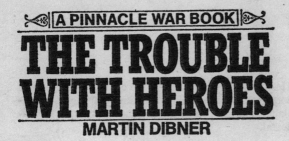

A PINNACLE WAR BOOK

THE TROUBLE WITH HEROES

MARTIN DIBNER

PINNACLE BOOKS   LOS ANGELES

THE TROUBLE WITH HEROES

A Pinnacle Books edition, published by special arrangement with Doubleday & Company, Inc.

First printing, October 1976
Second printing, May 1979
Third printing, September 1980

ISBN: 0-523-41007-7

Cover illustration by Ed Valigursky

Printed in the United States of America

PINNACLE BOOKS, INC.
2029 Century Park East
Los Angeles, California 90067

For Noah

Quiet now, no cries of triumph.
It is not decent to exult over
slain men.

HOMER
Odyssey

THE TROUBLE WITH HEROES

I

The two men met again, this time by chance in Hiroshima. Eric Stevens was a war correspondent too long in Vietnam and now on his way home. Paul Damion was the skipper of the Navy's newest nuclear-powered cruiser, *Chesapeake,* tied up at Sasebo. The year was 1968. It was a very hot day.

They met in the Peace Memorial Museum. People stared. Few Americans visited here, overreacting perhaps to the myth that a murderer always revisits the scene of his crime. They shook hands. Damion looked pleased. "You're fat, Chief." It was an official reprimand.

"And bald," Stevens growled. "So what?"

"No need to snap," said Damion surprised.

"Just don't call me Chief." Stevens felt trapped and angry. The sweat-stained shoulders of his fatigue shirt sagged under a heavy load of camera gear. His soiled slacks were tucked into the tops of muddy worn boots. He studied Damion in spotless dress whites.

Damion had not changed much. Tanned and trim at

1

forty-two. A touch of silver at his temples. The submariner's gold dolphins dominated the rows of bright campaign ribbons on his chest, one ribbon for the Navy Cross. Stevens had been there when Damion won it. The memory made him a bit sick. So did the resplendence. *The hell with all that*, he told himself. *Nobody got out of a uniform faster than I did*. All he wanted was to be on his way. After a few words he said so.

Damion would have none of it. He'd buy the drinks, he said.

"Sorry," said Stevens and hitched up his load.

"I'd not insist," Damion went on in an oddly quiet way, "if there wasn't something on my mind."

And blood on your hands. An edge of pleading in Damion's voice puzzled Stevens. He rubbed his stubbled jaw. "Just one," he said, "but not for old time's sake."

They left the sleek place of grisly reminders. Stevens' boots made loud slapping noises like the wood block *geite* of the locals. His shoulder load bounced awkwardly. He needed a shave and a hot bath a hell of a lot more than he needed Captain Paul Damion. The title stung. Eighteen years ago at Inchon, Damion had been a lousy jaygee. His annoyance swelled. The quicker he ditched this cold-blooded killer, the happier he'd be.

They crossed the vast Peace Square. Holiday was in the air, shining in the eyes of the proud people. Hiroshima was their newest shrine. Brightly painted buses disgorged tourists. They came in droves, packed in compact cars to see the sights. They came from everywhere, it seemed, to share in the fun. Stevens cursed softly. Damion glanced at him, not turning his head. He had been watching children playing near the fountains where doves splashed.

"Idiots," Stevens said.

"Why?" asked Damion surprised.

"Who the hell are they fooling?" He scowled. "Doves! Fountains! In Hiroshima!"

"It would be lovely anywhere," said Damion.

2

In the cool bar Stevens drank thirstily and ordered another. Damion sipped slowly, absorbed in his thoughts. After somewhat aimless conversation, Damion abruptly called for the check. Stevens carefully set his glass on the hard plastic table top. "You said you had something on your mind, Captain."

Damion shrugged. "Forget it."

Across the park small people in floppy shorts and sports shirts snapped pictures of the A-Bomb Dome, the Children's Memorial, the Epicenter. All the shining monuments. Stevens cursed again. Damion's smile was steady. "What brought you to Hiro?"

"A gung-ho managing editor." He drained his glass. "Stupid bastard thought there was a story here."

"What kind of story?"

"The *hibakusha*."

Something happened to Damion's face and Stevens' quick eye caught it. "You know about the *hibakusha?*"

"Yes. The living victims of the A-bomb."

"If you call that living."

"And you're here to do a story on them?"

"I started to. I quit."

"Why?"

"Too gruesome."

"You're supposed to be a reporter," Damion said with some of his old arrogance. "I'd expect you to do your job."

Stevens sucked the dregs from his icy glass. *Why the hell do I take this crap from the snotty military? Year in, year out, rain or shine. Yong-hung-do to Khesan and Hue. And two days ago in the bomb-splintered waiting room of the airport at Tan Son Nhut. No story's worth it. . . .*

"I'm serious," Damion was saying. "What made you quit?"

"Forget it." He grabbed a waiter's arm and ordered another drink.

"I want to know," Damion persisted.

"You'd never understand, Captain."

"What the hell's that supposed to mean?"

"What it meant at Inchon, on the island."

3

"I don't get it."

"I quit because if finally got through my thick skull there's no end to the killing. Ever. Thanks to types like you."

"You mean career officers?"

"Career something."

"We're no different from other men."

"The hell you're not." He welcomed his fresh drink with a loud belch. "Men with opposing ideas—I'm referring to civilized men—can discuss their differences rationally." He swallowed some of his drink. "But not us. That's the one difference, my friend, that makes us hopeless enemies of men."

The sun poured through a high window. The whiteness of Damion's uniform was dazzling. "I don't believe your ideas about life are much different from mine."

"They were different as hell when you murdered those three prisoners on Yong-hung-do."

Some of the color left Damion's cheeks. "I've grown some since then."

"I doubt it."

"I think I have."

"If you'd really changed, Captain, you'd have dumped that Graustark uniform for sackcloth and ashes." He got to his feet and felt the drinks grab him. "You bastards don't change. Only the battlefields change. And the body count." He gathered his gear. "Thanks for the drinks, Captain. Have a fun weekend. Kill a few Japs. Rape a few geishas."

Damion was on his feet. Stevens tensed, expecting Damion to hit him.

"Before you go," Damion said, very easy.

"Yeah?"

"I came here for a personal reason."

"Like I said."

"One of your *hibakusha*."

"You expect me to believe that crap?"

"I knew her when she was nine. A year before Korea, Stevens. Before Inchon. She was five when the Bomb fell. Since then, I've helped with her doctoring, her education. I've just been to visit her—"

4

"Dropped in to see how the keloid scars are progressing?" He thrust his face close to Damion's. "How sweet, Captain. How kind. And the other eighty-nine thousand nine hundred and ninety-nine? Who's holding their lumped-up, scaly hands?"

Damion sat slowly. "I should have known better."

"You guys'll never know better until it's too late."

"Fame's made you bitter, Stevens."

"Not fame, Captain. Senseless killing. Your dishonorable profession."

"You made as decent a living out of it as any other camp follower."

"You're goddam right I did. But I'm no ordinary whore. I know when to stop. Which is something you boys don't know and never will." He hooked a crooked finger round a gold button on Damion's tunic, thrust his sweaty, stubbled face close to Damion's. His breath stunk. "Know why I'm quitting the *hibakusha* story? It's ancient history, Captain. Like Guernica. Rotterdam. Buchenwald. Nobody gives a shit anymore what happened to Hiroshima. They can get the Vietnam box score every night from Walter Cronkite. The latest kill on the same plastic plate with their TV dinner."

"You'd better go, Stevens."

"Can't take it, Captain?"

"You're drunk."

"Drunk my ass. I'm scared. That's the trouble." He began to laugh. A nasty sound. "You're a registered U.S. hero, Captain. That's what the Navy Cross is for, isn't it? Now don't tell me you're having regrets."

"I don't know what to tell you."

"You're no hero," Stevens snarled. "You're a goddam fraud. A lousy goddam stinking fraud." He spat on the floor and reeled out.

Stevens in his hotel room wearily flung his gear aside and sprawled across the bed. His nerves were shot. He knew it when he left Saigon. He knew damned well the shape he was in and he should not have baited Damion as he had done.

The year in Vietnam had stripped him of strength and hope. An honest war reporter's life among the

5

grunts, slopes, and the CIA spooks was hectic enough, raddled with sweat and dust and grinding frustrations. Back in Saigon the press corps had swollen to several hundreds of accredited characters, too many of them with uncles in the Pentagon who paved the way. They sat around the terrace bar of the Continental ruining their livers and bragging about last night's boom-boom. The only things they filed were their fingernails. It was a disgusting sight to Stevens. Not that hard-working professionals thought of themselves as an elite corps. They were concerned only with getting the story straight and staying alive, in that order. The phonies left them no choice but to band together, a few wire service hands and photographers, the few big city newspapermen with the solid novel inside they'd never write, and an occasional well-paid feature writer from the slicks.

They all had heard of Eric Stevens. A few knew him. They were flattered to be around him and didn't mind that he did both the reporting and the taking of pictures. Being a little older helped, although he bawled the hell out of one well-meaning magazine writer who referred to him as the "dean of." They were a cheery carefree lot just the same, whether or not they had gone to journalism school or had no uncles in the Pentagon. They went out when they could where the shooting was and got their stories and pictures, always scared inside and bolstered by booze or pot, and sometimes one or two wouldn't come back.

Stevens was seasoned and lucky and a perfectionist in his work. His editors got what they asked for and a lot they didn't ask for, hot off his typewriter, the fiction sifted from fact in the canned command releases doled out to him.

He was at his best picking up the pathos of violence, revealing the new look of war, the agonized eyes of bewildered old men in black pajamas, weeping women and children, country dust and fat flies on the hairless bodies of dead obedient sons.

He rode the shuttling "choppers" from Khesanh and hit the landing pad at Dong Ha with his camera steady on the flying bullets and the skinny legs of the frightened rice farmers who caught them. He crawled with Navy corpsmen through rain and mud to unload the wounded and carry them into the tin quonsets of, say, Med Company D, for first emergency treatment. Then with notebook and pencil he would sit, mute with pity and horror, while the doctors, must of them nice young guys barely out of their internships, worked around the clock to piece and sew together the torn flesh before the kids could be evacuated to the larger safer hospitals in Phubai and Danang.

"What's your home town, son? Your father's name . . . ?" Thinking, *Can this bandaged and bloody piece of meat be the same brute kid killer, the Zippo Squad burner of hootches who showed me the fake leather folder of atrocities he had personally snapped? Is this how it will be for my own two sons?*

He hacked out his stories with two fingers by candlelight in a foul-smelling press bunker on a vintage Empire *Aristocrat* that, carrying case and all, barely weighed nine pounds. Gravelly drippings mixed with candle wax and the thump of shell fire. He typed savagely in the forlorn hope that this time the readers would get to read what he wrote the way he wrote it. It was a long-running battle with his editors, and a losing one. They wanted the facts, not his opinions. It was war itself he no longer believed in. Not this particular war. Any war.

No more of that. He was out of a job and on his way home. The side trip to Hiroshima was his last good-by. Running into Damion was the last sad straw.

His harsh denouncement of Damion still rang in his ears. Now the words dismayed him. Why Damion? Why not all those generals and admirals he had privately detested in Saigon and Danang and Cam Ranh Bay? Decent men and loyal, doing nothing more than their duty.

He was wasting his time. That was the hell of it. The thousands of words he had written and pictures he had taken would do no more to reveal the tragic idiocy of this war than the non-nuclear weapons being used would win it. He had shown the world how things truly were, brutal or tender, trusting the people to listen, to

7

be deeply moved, to act. But no one did anything about it and the time would pass and be forgotten and he would find himself off again to another Vietnam.

But he had quit now. No more Vietnams. Or Waterloos. He would say what he had to say in another way, not to be read once and kept only to wrap fish and garbage.

Too bad he had not given Damion a chance to say what he wanted to say. Or had he? It was decent of Damion to blame it on the drinks. It wasn't the drinks at all. It was the way things were. Everywhere. Damion just happened to be at the wrong place at the wrong time. Like that time on Yong-hung-do . . .

He had met Paul Damion in the late autumn of 1950. Stevens was a staff photographer then, with a chief petty officer's rate. He was attached to Navy Headquarters Photo Lab, Tokyo. His duties consisted mostly of supervisory darkroom processing with occasional flurries of rush jobs for military brass and junketing congressmen.

It was dull work for Stevens. In New York he had established an on-the-ball commercial photography studio and it was making money. He had got started as a free-lance photographer when he was still in high school. There was no chance for college. He never knew his father. His mother had died in violence. He supported himself. At eighteen he felt older and wiser than his high school friends who had gone on to college. He had a small reputation for doing good work for a reasonable fee and delivering the finished prints when promised.

In five years he had a floor-through studio in a midtown walkup, an outside man, a lab assistant, and a shapely studio-secretary-bookkeeper who doubled in styling and sets. Stevens did all the camera work. His agency accounts and department store assignments gave him more business than he could handle.

The Korean situation worsened. Following an unnerving confrontation with his draft board, he sold the studio to his employees, put the money in a savings bank, and made his talents known to the Navy. A ten-

8

week refresher course at a Navy photography school taught him how much the Navy did not know about his profession. A few weeks later he found himself in Tokyo with a photographer's mate, first-class rating. In six months he was advanced to chief petty officer.

His superiors sent for him one autumn morning. There was a request for Stevens to appear before the headquarters intelligence officer at once. Stevens loaded his equipment and headed downtown.

A Marine sentry checked his identification and led him to a door marked *Private—No Admittance*. Inside, he faced a trim, beaknosed Navy three-striper erect behind a scarred desk. "Commander Fogarty," the man said with a show of small stained teeth. "Sit down, Chief."

Fogarty wasted no time. He put Stevens through an inquisition on photographic techniques, his high school football record, the reasons why, during his childhood, his mother had moved around so much. He asked his questions in a rapid, clipped monotone, pure Texas with no drawl. Stevens had the feeling Fogarty had done this many times.

Fogarty pressed most sharply on the subject of flashless night photography. Stevens had studied advanced techniques of infrared and ultraviolet picture taking with a refugee German during night sessions for two years in a New York art school. He knew the answers.

Fogarty relaxed. "You're the man we're looking for, Stevens."

"What's it all about, Commander?"

"Operation Choptank." The teeth gleamed like dirty tombstones. "You're a lucky man."

"Why?"

"You'll come out of this mission a Navy hero."

Alive or dead? Stevens wondered.

Fogarty led Stevens along a corridor to a door marked Operations Officer. "They're waiting for you inside. Good luck, Chief."

Stevens watched his small straight back recede in the dim corridor. He was relieved to see him go. Fogarty made a man feel like his dreams were bugged.

9

It was a small, badly ventilated cubicle crowded with officers. Introductions were made by the mission plans officer. He was a tired-looking, moon-faced Army colonel with rimless glasses and a pale scar like a sickle blade across his bald head. His shirt was drenched with perspiration. He was flanked by a Marine colonel and several flag rank Navy officers. Stevens sat alongside Damion and a wiry South Korean army officer, Lee Sung Nam, with broad pockmarked cheeks. The three of them faced the officers across the table. Stevens was the only enlisted man present, except for a bored-looking Navy yeoman who took down shorthand notes of everything said.

The air, clouded with tobacco smoke, was almost impossible to breathe in the crowded room. Everyone seemed hostile and faintly suspicious. Stevens assumed this to be standard practice in joint military conferences. Two inadequate electric fans pushed the moist air around. The officers with the exception of Damion wore short-sleeved open-collar shirts and khaki shorts. Damion, looking very young, was dressed in the full regulation Navy work uniform. He smoked a small cigar and seemed quite at ease. His cap on the table in front of him bore a salt-encrusted gold-and-silver embroidered device, well worn and in need of stitching. He looked to Stevens like the run-of-the-mill trade school type, the kind with chicken guts on their shoulders who play equerry to admirals.

The staff operations officer proceeded to explain the background of Operation Choptank and then the mission itself. It would be the only briefing before the mission got under way.

The Communists from the north, he said, had already swept southward across the thirty-eighth parallel. Seoul had fallen. In bitterly contested, inch-by-inch fighting, the American and ROK ground forces had been pushed back to a tiny perimeter around the port of Pusan. The situation was critical. To the dismay of his expert advisers, the Supreme Commander proposed an amphibious assault at Inchon.

The military professionals had balked. Inchon was impregnable. Such an assault could only lead to dis-

10

aster. The general himself blandly quoted the odds at 5000 to 1. He then undertook to convince them of its strategic, psychological, and tactical feasibility.

It will work, he said, because we will move in on the optimum tide. Each detail of the invasion will be painstakingly planned. And finally, the enemy will be taken by complete surprise because he regards such a landing impossible and insane and will not dignify its possibility by preparing for it.

Inchon's tides, the operations officer explained, are among the greatest in the world. They rise to a maximum of thirty-three feet, reaching their peak in about six hours. In Flying Fish Channel, its main approach, this change creates a dangerously swift five-knot current. Ebb and flow over the centuries have deposited mudbanks around the harbor that stretch to seaward at low tides for more than three miles.

The approach through Flying Fish Channel is narrow and hazardous even for daylight passage. The North Koreans had destroyed all navigational aids and mined the waters. A single miscalculation could mean a foundering vessel that, at low tide, would trap the vessels ahead of it, cut off their escape route, and bring disaster to an entire invasion fleet.

Twenty-nine feet of water was the minimum needed to keep assault landing craft afloat during the six-hour rise and fall of tide. The optimum time in any month of the year in which such an invasion could be undertaken was limited to a few nights. Even then, the availability of high water was never more than two hours.

Inchon itself was a fortress protected by stone sea walls and the fortified island of Wolmi-do. Wolmi-do was joined to the mainland by a narrow causeway some eight hundred yards in length. Its topography and location gave it excellent command over the sea approaches in all directions. Several of its nearby islands, including Taebu-do, were garrisoned and patroled.

The operations officer asked for questions. There were none. The room was still, the heat forgotten.

"Of course," he went on, "the enemy's as wise to the tide tables as we are. A leak in our planning'd give him time to pinpoint our invasion effort to the few nights of

11

high water. Everything hangs on absolute secrecy at the outset, and surprise. Not to mention all the breaks."

He spread his hands. "Anyway, that was how the general himself put it to his advisers. They told him it wouldn't work. He said it had to work or they'd lose Korea. He pointed out that a successful landing at Inchon would reverse the course of the war. Its boldness would capture the Oriental imagination and revive the sinking prestige of the West. And of course it'd serve our basic purpose, which is to block the spread of communism in the Far East."

"What'd the advisers object to, specifically?" someone asked.

"Too many details, any one of which could go wrong and mean disaster." He leaned back and rubbed his eyes. "The general, being senior in rank, won them over, of course. The operations's in the works and the old boy will either wind up his career with a brilliant victory or with his scrambled eggs all over his face."

The group recessed for lunch. When they reconvened for the afternoon session, the operations officer told them the invasion date was set for September 15.

The basic plan was to neutralize Wolmi-do with naval gunfire, invade Inchon by assault landing craft through Flying Fish Channel, take the airfield at Kimpo, and capture Seoul.

There were problems. The amphibious assault commanders faced a shortage of seasoned personnel and time in which to train any. Details on Inchon waters and defense were inadequate. There was an urgent need for up-to-date intelligence. Air support and navigational charts were unreliable. Most current ground information was provided by a sheaf of badly worn copies of Japanese World War II maps.

Command decided that a reconnaissance mission was needed to gather necessary intelligence data at the walls of Inchon itself and Operation Choptank came into being. The Bureau of Personnel in Washington was asked to produce a Navy officer qualified to lead such a mission. The man they came up with was Paul Damion. It was a wise choice, the operations officer told them, glancing at Damion. He took a few minutes to explain why.

Damion had spent most of his childhood and youth in the Far East. His father, Stark Damion, had been a career naval officer, Annapolis, Class '19, his mother a Washington diplomat's daughter. As an ambassador's naval aide and later on diplomatic missions of his own, the elder Damion served in numerous Asiatic countries. Paul was born in Hong Kong and raised in mission schools in Korea, Indo China, and Japan. Most of his childhood playmates were Asiatic. He spoke Japanese and a variety of Asiatic dialects as easily as he spoke English.

On graduating from the Naval Adademy, he turned down the diplomatic corps and chose to become an officer of the line. When Operation Choptank was conceived and BuPers caught up with him, he was a gunnery officer aboard the light cruiser *Worcester*. Luckily, she was in Korean waters. Damion was immediately transferred and he reported to Headquarters Tokyo within twenty-four hours.

Damion sat through the thumbnail review of his career with no comment, puffing on his cigar. The officers present regarded him with renewed interest. To Stevens, he still looked too young, too cocky, and unrelentingly trade school.

The mission's purpose, as the staff operations officer explained it, was primarily to secure accurate information on the tidal nature and conditions of the mud flats, and the strength of the enemy's garrison defense. Damion had a two-week deadline in which to get there and back. His party would be put ashore on one of the islands somewhere off Inchon. The exact location was being withheld for security reasons until the last moment. Stevens would take pictures when possible. Damion would send daily reports and film via native messengers, some of whom Lee knew, to headquarters in Tokyo for evaluation. Radio transmission had been considered and vetoed because of the risk of discovery. The reports were to cover the tractional quality of the mudbanks at different points and their ability to support landing craft, vehicles, and assault troops. The

13

men were to measure the heights of the sea walls, determine the nature of their surfaces, and suggest techniques for scaling them. Damion was also directed to gather what information he could on the suitability of unloading areas along the beaches and nearby islands and the movements of patrols and sentries.

The colonel mopped his face and arms and neck with a huge handkerchief. That was it, he told them. Lieutenant Damion would lead the mission. Did he have any questions?

Damion crushed the butt of his cigar. "Some questions, Colonel. One request."

"Shoot."

"How reliable are the charts?"

"Out of date, naturally. Best we could come up with on short notice."

"Any local fishermen we know to be friendly?"

"Our ROK friend here—" The colonel pointed. "Ah, Lieutenant Lee—ah?"

"Lee Sung Nam, Colonel." He turned to Damion. "Hard to say. I'm counting on the two guys I really know. The messengers."

"Do you know the waters and weather, Lieutenant?"

"When I was a kid I fished every one of those islands. I've been back as recently as two years ago."

"How do you know these people?"

He shrugged. "I used to fish with them. But who knows what's changed since then?"

"The request, Mr. Damion?"

"I'd like to have the radio transmitter."

"Too dangerous," someone said and the others nodded.

"It's the only means I'll have to pass along anything of an urgent nature."

"You'll have those messengers."

"Too slow in an emergency. I'd prefer the transmitter."

"You might just blow the whole mission. It's too damned risky."

"I'll keep it in standby condition except for an emergency."

"Can you operate a radio transmitter, Lieutenant?"

"Yes, sir."

The operations officer sighed. "I'll try to clear it for you."

The meeting broke up. The three men were left to work out details of supplies, weapons, and equipment. They went through repeated drills of the operation using wall charts and the old Japanese area maps. Lee Sung Nam proved in short order he knew the waters well, giving prompt answers to Damion's sharp questions. Stevens felt better, having the amiable Korean along for company. He learned that Lee had been a schoolteacher in Seoul for several years and a locally famous wrestler. Until a few days ago, he had been working as a liaison officer for the ROK ground forces.

The colonel's review of Damion's background had helped, but Stevens still felt he was too junior for such a dangerous mission. Damion was a few years younger than he and had graduated from the Naval Academy only three years before. He was married and the father of a baby girl.

That evening Damion put Stevens through a thorough grilling on his professional capabilities. When it was over, he seemed satisfied that the technical end of the photographic mission was in good hands. Stevens found him to be stiff-necked and his lack of warmth irritating. After all, they were going to spend a nasty two weeks together. He brought up the matter of photographic materials. He told Damion he'd need another twenty-four hours to go through the regular requisition channels.

"The hell with the channels," Damion snapped. "Cumshaw what you can and steal the rest. You've got all night."

II

There was no sleep that night. Stevens scurried around Tokyo borrowing every spare piece of photographic equipment he could lay hands on. In the morning they were flown to the Navy facility at Sasebo. Camouflage clothing, rations, foul weather gear, arms and ammunition were issued. A compact radio transmitter brought the first glint of approval to Damion's eye. At midnight they boarded a decrepit British trawler and were transferred at dawn to an even less seaworthy Korean frigate. It smelled of grime and salt sweat and rotted fish. They were put ashore on the island of Yonghung-do the night of September first.

Yong-hung-do is a six-mile island, three miles wide. It lies about fourteen miles south and slightly west of Inchon in shallows uncomfortably close to the island of Taebu-do, a well-garrisoned enemy outpost.

Damion chose the campsite in a thick growth of stunted pine and hardwood. Lee made contact with his friends. Damion talked to the village chief. The island people were friendly and eager to help. The messengers were given their instructions. Damion organized a group of teen-age boys into watch-standing parties.

One of the three men was on duty at all times. Damion trained another group as a reconnaissance party for work at night on Inchon and Wolmi-do. A routine was established. The first two days passed slowly.

Stevens still had deep misgivings. He had not volunteered for this mission. So much could go wrong. Damion's willingness to depend on a handful of teen-agers for critical information, for example, seemed risky to him. And it seemed foolhardy to take orders from someone younger than himself, when his own skin was at stake. Yet Damion never failed him. With irritating self-confidence he would plunge ahead long before Stevens in his own mind believed it was safe. In establishing their hideout and setting up the sensitive procedures for the mission, Damion had moved with a boldness Stevens envied but did not always share. Yet his judgments always proved sound in practice.

He commandeered the only power boat on the island. It was a run-down motorized sampan that belonged to the two friendly fishermen messengers. They kept her near the camp, under a heavy camouflage of boughs that Lee rigged. Damion spent the second night tinkering with the old engine until it ran smoothly and quietly. He stowed rations and arms on board and worked with the fishermen replacing much of the rigging with fresh manila and wire. Lee also camouflaged the emplacements around the hideout and mounted two light machine guns with their muzzles trained on Taebu-do. That night Stevens slept easily for the first time. They had been on the island four days.

They remained in hiding during the long daylight hours, closely covering the movements of enemy patrols on Taebu-do. An hour after dark Damion would dispatch a small party of the native teen-agers with Stevens to Inchon in two small innocent-looking fishing boats. Damion and Lee, heavily armed, would follow in the sampan to cover them until they were clear of Taebu-do. The boys would make their way into the city and measure a section of mud flats and the heights of the sea walls. Stevens, put ashore, would shoot countless exposures from different angles using infrared and a telephoto lens. The boys would return by a different route, bringing with them estimates of the number of troops defending the city and charted positions of Inchon's coastal guns, observation posts, and ammunition storage.

They returned to Yong-hung-do well before dawn. The messengers carried the exposed film and Damion's reports to a pickup point at a remote end of the island. A south Korean patrol boat met them and delivered the film at sea to an American destroyer, where they were developed and flown to Tokyo.

One afternoon while Lee had the watch outside, Damion seemed in a relaxed, almost friendly mood. Stevens asked about the salty old insignia of the embroidered cap device Damion wore.

"It belonged to my father, Chief."

"Is he still on active duty?"

"No."

"Retired?"

"He's dead."

"Sorry, Lieutenant."

"He was killed in Savo Strait."

His whole manner had changed. He abruptly arose and went out to the emplacements and checked the machine guns. He ordered Lee inside and took up the binoculars to watch Taebu-do. The boys slept. Stevens joined Damion who still seemed offended by what had been a casual and quite harmless question. He ignored Stevens' presence, darkly silent, and after a few words, Stevens left him. *The hell with it,* he thought. Yet it was almost exhilarating to see Damion's cool reserve shattered.

By evening he was his old poker-face self. Nothing more was said. Stevens decided they were all beginning to get on each other's nerves under the strain.

They gathered the information in bits and pieces, slowly and, so far as they knew, without detection. The village fishermen reported no suspicious actions on Taebu-do.

One moonless night Damion took the big sampan into Flying Fish Channel. The hull slid almost silently

18

through blackness with Lee well forward indicating with hand signals the course Damion should steer. Stevens stood watch astern. The tide had ebbed. A rank humid smell permeated the still night. Flying insects were everywhere.

Damion directed the boat to an area of mud flats close to Wolmi-do. He idled the motor. The boat drifted broadside to the beach until her bottom scraped. Damion removed his shirt and trousers and ordered Lee to the helm. They lowered a small skiff over the side. Damion took off his shoes and socks and, with Stevens, boarded the skiff. He rowed close to the towering walls of Inchon, skillfully feathering the oars. He nodded to Stevens and slipped over the side. Stevens began taking pictures. Damion wallowed about with what seemed to be pure delight, almost naked and calf-deep in the mud flats. Stevens shot frame after frame until Damion wriggled aboard. Stevens expected him to be grinning like a kid who had just climbed out of a tree full of apples. Damion's face was dead serious. He scraped the mud from his legs and took up the oars and rowed back to the sampan.

"A military necessity," he explained. "To prove to Joint Command that no Marine, no matter how light and small, and certainly no vehicle of any kind, can navigate through this muck."

Luck was with them the last night before the planned invasion date. Returning from the mud flats, they explored an abandoned lighthouse on the tiny island of Palmi-do at the entrance to Flying Fish Channel. The enemy had damaged the rotation mechanism and extinguished the wick. After an inspection, Damion determined that it could be repaired and suggested the possibility of using the radio transmitter to pass along the word of this discovery to Tokyo. The reactivated light could help guide the invasion fleet through the tricky channel.

"How about using messengers?" Lee asked.

"They'd never get word back in time for us to activate the light. Radio contact's immediate."

"The minute we open up," Stevens said, "Taebu-do will get a fix on us and move in."

19

"It's a risk we'll have to take."

An hour later, the word went beaming to Tokyo. Joint Command came back with a *Well Done* and instructions to activate the light exactly at midnight the eve of the invasion. Stevens slept uneasily that night, hoping the duty radio operator on Taebu-do had missed the brief transmission.

The boys' work was done. Damion dismissed them in the morning with instructions to return to their families. They had served their country well. They would be rewarded. The three men were alone.

They packed most of their gear. Damion shifted the watch to double the lookout duties. Each man now stood eight hours on and four off, the watches overlapping. Stevens stood the first half of his long watch from midnight to four with Lee. Damion relieved Lee from four to eight.

A faint breeze from the east came up with the dawn in Damion's search sector. During the night they had been startled by the sound of heavy shellfire. It was the American Navy, pounding Inchon and Wolmi-do to rubble in the pre-invasion air and surface softening-up. Damion looked pleased and Stevens felt relieved.

Stevens had been having trouble staying awake in the last hour of his long watch. His eyes ached from the unrelieved tenseness. Damion's voice snapped at him. He was pointing toward Taebu-do.

Stevens adjusted his binoculars. An enemy launch was headed their way. It carried at least two men, possibly a third. Damion awakened Lee and swiftly outlined a plan. They crept from the hideout and circled southward toward the landing beach where the launch was headed.

It was halfway across the open water between the two islands. Damion chose a post hidden in the thick tangle of bushes flanking the path that wound from the beach to the rise of land where the camp lay. Damion cradled a .30-caliber Browning machine gun in his arms. Extra rounds of ammo were in a bandoleer slung across his chest. Lee and Stevens held automatic rifles and each carried a .45 automatic in his belt. Damion

20

stowed several coils of manila in the undergrowth nearby.

For the first time, facing the flesh-and-blood enemy, Stevens experienced real fear. He was a photographer, not a killer. His mouth went dry. His insides churned and for a moment he thought he might be sick. His eyes met Lee's. Lee winked and signaled victory with his stubby brown fingers. Stevens understood what Lee meant. This guy Damion was infallible. How could they miss? Some of the tenseness drained from him. The enemy boat came on steadily, faint blue smoke sifting its wake.

He tried to think of other things. Manhattan streets sticky in summer heat. The noon hour crush along the avenue. The RUSH RUSH print orders from Saks and Bonwit's for the bulldog edition of the Sunday Times. The deadlines—*deadlines!* What the hell was this—

Damion's elbow jolted him from his insane reverie. "I'm moving up the path," he whispered. "Drop back from here about ten yards. Stay out of sight. Send Lee across the path, same distance, both of you out of sight. Let them pass you. I'll stop them up the line. When I do, come out fast and cover any retreat. They may panic and try to make it back to the boat. Shoot to kill. We can't let 'em get away."

Damion crawled up the path and disappeared. Stevens crawled to Lee and passed along Damion's instructions. He tried to sound calm when he said *Shoot to kill.* Lee touched Stevens' hand and moved off. Stevens watched him, head and backside, a small brown friendly creature. Then a rustling of branches and leaves. Then nothing.

Shoot to kill. He was alone for the first time in two weeks. His head throbbed. He began to wonder where Damion and Lee were. Nothing stirred. Nothing showed. My God, if he shot wildly, if he hit one of them—? He raised his head cautiously and searched the beach.

The enemy patrol had reached the narrow strand and was wading ashore. He counted three of them and estimated the distance at two hundred yards. Their voices carried clearly. His grip tightened on the automatic rifle.

21

They had pulled the boat closer to the beach and buried the anchor in the sand. A heated argument ensued and finally all three started up the path. Stevens crouched low with the rifle muzzle trained on the leader. Early morning insects crawled over him. He thought of the island's pit vipers and lizards and shuddered. For a stricken moment he lost sight of the search party as the path wound around the side of the slope.

The leader's head appeared. He passed Stevens no more than ten yards distant. He wore an ugly scowl. The other two followed, still arguing.

Damion's clear voice rang out. The leader's head snapped up. Stevens leaped from cover and almost ran head on into Lee charging from the other side of the path. He shouted. The last two in line had turned to run but stopped and dropped their rifles when they saw Stevens and Lee.

Damion stood at the head of the path, legs planted apart, the .30-caliber piece pointed at the leader's middle. He snapped orders. They fell to their knees. He kicked the rifles aside and stripped the leader of his holstered pistol.

Lee meanwhile had recovered the coils of rope. Shoving the three prisoners before them, he and Damion started up the path with Stevens covering from the rear. They kept up a steady barrage of harsh words, shouting and poking the backs of the three men with rifle muzzles. It seemed quite unnecessary to Stevens. The prisoners seemed meek enough and quite willing to do whatever Damion demanded.

They were led blindfolded to the coarse growth surrounding the camp. Damion ordered them to strip and take sitting positions. Lee bound them, kicking them brutally from time to time. Their ankles were tied and staked and they sat with their backs against tree trunks.

Stevens, still charged with excitement, retrieved their weapons and unloaded them. He asked Damion about the enemy launch.

"Don't go near it. They're probably watching it from

Taebu-do." He hesitated a moment, then grinned. "They must've picked up our signal last night."

"Think they'll come looking?"

Damion took his time lighting a fresh cigar. "We'll take 'em as they come, Chief."

Lee had been questioning the prisoners. He looked angry. "That leader's a mean bastard. Won't talk."

"What'd you ask?"

"How many men on Taebu-do. What guns they got. What boats." He shrugged. "Name, rank, serial number is all I get."

"It's all he's required to give. He's a prisoner of war."

Lee grinned crookedly. "Give me a few minutes. I'll get it out of him."

"You'll leave him alone, Lieutenant. That's the law." He looked to the tree where the men were tied. "What about the others?"

"From the north, too. But nice kids. Scared shitless. He warned them to keep their mouths shut."

"You two keep a sharp eye for any movement from their island. I'll talk to those two."

Damion spent several minutes with each of the two prisoners. He told them they would not be shot and it made them happy enough to talk freely. The leader from his tree cursed and warned them. They jeered him. He had been giving them a hard time all morning.

They told Damion a shore-based direction finder had gotten a radio fix the night before and instructed the garrison commander on Taebu-do to investigate. He was vain about his coverage of the area and touchy about outside advice. He refused to believe an enemy was anywhere within miles of Inchon. Only when his superiors ashore demanded a search of the nearby islands did he undertake to send a party. Three men were all he deemed necessary for this silly mission.

The two soldiers, new recruits, were delighted to get off the island for a few hours. The argument on the beach had been over the leader's decision not to leave a sentry with the launch. Each man wanted to remain there rather than hike around in the hot sun. There might even be a chance to catch a nap. The leader

23

himself was a petty officer uncertain of his ability to handle men, yet eager to do a good job. He finally decided they must both walk, for discipline and punishment. Now that he had been ambushed and captured, he realized his mistake. An alert sentry would have had an even chance to run the boat back and give the alarm.

Damion tried to talk with him, with little success. The Navy bombardment continued through the morning without letup. At noon Lee fetched canned rations and relieved Damion, who was guarding the prisoners. No action was forthcoming from Taebu-do.

At three o'clock, Damion ordered Stevens to take pictures of the prisoners. The leader tried to hide his face. The others posed and made faces and joked with each other and Lee. They were not much older than the boys who had worked for Damion. Stevens felt sorry for them and took a roll of pictures and relieved Damion on the Taebu-do vigil. They did not relax until dusk. Lee suggested that there had been no action because the garrison commander refused to lose face and still hoped to prove his superiors wrong.

They had loaded the gear into the sampan for the night run to Palmi-do and the lighthouse. Stevens fed the last of their rations to the prisoners. The leader refused his. When Stevens tried to force some food through his clenched teeth, the man spit a mouthful directly into Stevens' face.

By eight o'clock it was dark enough for them to get under way for the lighthouse. Damion checked the camp area carefully before they abandoned it. The weather had turned freakishly cold. A hard wind lashed in from the northwest. Trees and bushes bent and groaned with its force. Lee double-checked the prisoners' bonds.

Damion seemed more tense than usual. He kept snapping orders at them until they left and headed for the sampan. Damion remained for a final look at the prisoners.

Stevens helped Lee remove the camouflaging boughs for the last time. He was beginning to feel marvelous. The Taebu-do garrison had not detected them. In a few hours the mission would be over. Any day now he'd be sitting in a hot bath with a tall cold drink in his hand and a jolly Japanese miss scrubbing his back.

The steady barrage of Navy gunfire had stopped. The quiet seemed wonderful. The sky over Inchon to the north flamed crimson and orange. The sampan was clear now. Stevens was stowing the last item of his photographic gear when the shots rang out. A dozen shots in three rapid bursts, seconds apart.

Lee cursed. "That's the .30-caliber." He grabbed a rifle and began to run.

They raced up through the dense growth. Damion was striding back, pushing his way through the foliage, the weapon in one hand. Stevens' long legs got him there first.

"You okay?"

Damion pushed past him, his lips gray as stone, past Lee to the boat. Stevens, confused, pushed on a few yards and stopped in his tracks. The prisoners were dead, each body strained awkwardly against its bonds. Bits of wet food still clung to the leader's lips. In the failing light the spreading stains of blood looked like dark wine.

"What for?" Stevens asked, horrified.

Lee avoided his eyes and after a moment started down the path. Stevens stood there until Damion shouted his name. He turned and went down to the sampan, twisting his fingers.

Lee ran the boat in absolute darkness. No one spoke. It was a rough crossing, wind and sea against them, the bow flung skyward or buried deep into a wave. The sampan, listing badly, finally made Palmido. Lee beached her and they unloaded the gear they needed. Stevens followed Lee up the ladder with Damion behind.

It was a cramped space, fouled with years of sea bird droppings. The wind swept through the rotted roof timbers in whining blasts. They could clearly see the fires now over Inchon's walls several miles to the north. The night smelled of wood smoke and the wind lashed their faces with cinders.

Damion hoisted himself aloft and stuffed thin blan-

25

kets into the eaves. For a moment Stevens caught a surprising look on Damion's face, reflected in the flames ashore. His mouth was drawn tight, as though he were in pain.

Lee wiped the thick glass of the Fresnel lens. Stevens stood the lookout watch. Damion busied himself with the rotation mechanism. He wound it and checked the oil level in the bowl and trimmed the wick. At twenty minutes before midnight, everything was in readiness.

Lee and Stevens settled against the wall, huddled together for warmth. Damion sat apart, his form hazy in blackness, bent over his wrist watch. At five minutes before midnight, he unstrapped the watch and handed it to Lee. "Give me *'Mark!'* at two minutes before the hour, Lieutenant."

"Yes, sir."

"Prepare to take your pictures, Chief." He moved to the south end and searched the blackness of the channel where the first invasion ship was due to appear.

Stevens did not move. His fingers were stiff with cold.

"Two minutes, Lieutenant." Lee's voice, steady as ever.

"On your feet, Stevens."

Stevens rose slowly, wanting to disobey, somehow captured by his sense of duty, hating it. He saw in Damion's face, in the uneven flushed glow of Inchon's fires, the same suppressed pain seeming to tear at the lips. "I want pictures, Stevens," he said in a pinched voice. "The first ship's bow that enters the channel. Understood?"

"Did you have to kill them?"

"Pictures, Stevens. That's an order."

"Sixty seconds, Lieutenant."

Lee's words were lost in a blast of yellow gunfire. Stevens grabbed up his Speed Graphic and had it pointed down the channel before he knew it. Nothing showed. The gunfire seemed uncomfortably close. "What the hell are they shooting at?"

"Mines." He tapped Lee. "Give me a ten-second

26

countdown." He stationed himself alongside the wick, matches in hand. "This'll help your pictures, Stevens."

"Stand by," Lee said. "Ten. Nine. Eight. Seven—"

Damion struck the match. The wick sputtered and flared and Lee shouted *"Mark!"* and the place exploded into blinding light. It blazed a path beyond the Fresnel lens, bathing the sea and channel and bursting shapes of land in its brightness. Its beam caught the lead destroyer bearing down on them, her bow wake live with phosphorescent sheets of spray tossed by the wind and sea. Beyond her gaunt bridge structure the shapes of many ships took form. Stevens' spirits soared and his eyes filled and he began shooting pictures.

"Right on station," Damion said, buckling his watch to his wrist.

As though he never had doubted it. As though this was a routine midshipman exercise in Chesapeake Bay.

By daylight's first gleam, Stevens had hundreds of exposures. Rocket ships, support vessels, small craft. Destroyers anchored close to Wolmi-do. The F4U Corsair fighters from the carriers beyond the channel strafing the target beaches to clear them for the Marines. Two waves of eight LCVPs and three LSUs slapping beachward. Green Beach on Wolmi-do. Red Beach west of Inchon. Blue Beach below. He had never had such a field day of shooting pictures.

The Marines landed and scaled the shattered slopes of Wolmi-do and dug themselves in for the next drive to the walls of Inchon. It was too bad the general was not around to see it. It would have warmed the cockles of his heart. The least it did was keep his scrambled eggs where they belonged.

An American flag cleared the flames and fluttered in the breeze. Stevens in spite of himself felt a welling of tears and was tempted to cheer.

"We can go now," Damion said.

Eighteen years . . .

Stevens got off the bed and went to the window and stared gloomily at the Peace Memorial Museum. Had the good Captain Damion gone back and was he still getting his jollies out of the macabre exhibits? Or had

27

he rushed back to dig the crooked furrow of his pitiful *hibakusha?*

Why the hell can't I let it go? he wondered sourly.

The Operation Choptank team broke up immediately after Inchon. Damion got his Navy Cross. Stevens won a Distinguished Service Medal but never went round to collect it. Lee Sung Nam got his medal posthumously. He had rejoined his unit of a ROK division a week later and in the street fighting to retake Seoul he was killed by sniper fire.

The native kids who had helped out on the island and at Inchon received a hundred American dollars which they soon lost, and a letter of commendation from the general, which they could not read.

Stevens got out fast when his time was up, and headed eagerly for New York. He got no further than San Francisco. Her name was Julie, a rosy peach, pure Renoir American from a small Wisconsin village, studying Oriental painting techniques at Berkeley. Stevens ran into her one afternoon at the DeYoung Memorial Museum, up to her elbows in rice paper and sumi-e brushes and ink. They took long walks, exchanged views on seafood and Sartre, discovered Sausalito and laughed a lot. They were jealously cautious about their careers, but nature ran its course. They tried living together for a few months and it worked out fine, both matinal people, outdoorsy and flexible. The city clerk married them. Their honeymoon was a midsummer Yosemite nightmare which they both miraculously survived.

Stevens found a job with the *Chronicle,* moved on to free-lance assignments, and wound up with the Orient as his bailiwick. Two sons came along in good time and the love of Julie was a splendid and enduring thing for him. He never went back to New York.

New York, he decided, was a can of worms.

III

The streets of Sasebo in the brittle rain had an ominous air about them. Paul Damion first noticed it at the outskirts of the city. He had driven the rented Toyota hard south from Hiroshima to this harbor city where his ship lay, reaching the shabby suburbs with the first light of dawn. The number of people up and about at this early hour surprised him. Everyone seemed headed for the center of the city. They walked purposefully in the bleak morning light, singly and in groups, some pedaling, some riding motor bikes.

The downtown streets were jammed. Damion was forced to slow the car to a crawl at the approach to Hirase Bridge. He checked the door locks and glanced at his watch. A phone call from his executive officer had sent him racing back to Sasebo. His orders were to get under way for Yankee Station no later than 0700. The yard gates lay on the other side of the bridge not a hundred yards away. There was just time enough to make it and none to spare.

The bridge was packed with people shouting slogans. Rain streaked the words on the hand-painted placards they carried. A river of helmets and umbrellas surged through the narrow streets. The signs rode the crest like the sails of tossing boats. The Toyota inched ahead until a clot of chanting demonstrators hemmed it in. Hostile faces were thrust against the car windows, each for a brief moment, then swept along with the current. It was impossible to move ahead. After a futile honking of the horn, Damion cut the motor. Fists hammered the car's sides. A stone bounced off the hood and nicked the windshield.

He sat marooned but not afraid. *I'm a fortress of gold braid in a violent sea of peace lovers. For all their honest outrage none will lay a hand on me. The Japanese more than any other race hold duty sacred. They hate neither me nor my men. They hate only these reminders we bring of their defeat. They hate the pity of the world and the shame.*

Two harassed and angry-looking policemen clubbed their way to the beleaguered car. A glance at the gold on the visor of Damion's cap was all they needed. Orders were shouted. More police arrived brandishing fire hose and canisters of tear gas. They formed a cordon round the car and Damion started the motor. The crowd yielded slowly.

Across the bridge the demonstrators looked younger. They seemed better organized and fiercer in their shouts and their defiance of the police. Damion had seen them in Tokyo. They were the *Zengakuren*. The hard core fanatics.

Having just seen Hiroshima, Damion reflected, *can I blame them? Given another time and place I might have joined them.*

Through the misty rain and beyond the gates where the students fought, he spied the familiar superstructure of his command moored in the channel. He breathed easier.

On *Chesapeake*'s rainswept quarterdeck, her executive officer also breathed easier. Commander McKim was a burly career officer, a worried-looking, brow-furrowed man with early signs of good muscle going to fat. Since dawn he had kept abreast of the shoreside activities, with understandable anxiety, by telephone, blinker signal, and binoculars. Now with the captain's gig clear of the Navy landing and making for *Chesapeake*'s side, he issued orders for the signal bridge to stand by the Captain's absentee pennant. Everything was in readiness for getting under way.

McKim revered Paul Damion. Like Damion he had come to *Chesapeake* from nuclear submarines. Like Damion he belonged to the elite corps of men who had skippered a nuke sub under the polar icecap. It would have been a most painful duty for McKim to depart Sasebo harbor without his friend and commanding officer on board. But orders were orders. Duty was the name of the game—a responsibility that a dedicated officer like McKim could not by the remotest chance ignore. In another ten minutes he would not have hesitated to issue the underway order, skipper or no skipper.

The gig came smartly alongside the accommodation ladder. Captain Damion stepped aboard. The officer of the deck ordered the gig swung to her chocks and the boat detail secured. Precisely at 0700 *Chesapeake* slipped her mooring and made for the open sea.

McKim followed Damion to the captain's cabin. He carried a thick folder of papers which he placed on the captain's desk. Damion's steward, a trim Filipino named Cesar, served coffee and retired to his pantry. Damion changed to a khaki work uniform. McKim sipped his coffee, slouched in a deep leather chair.

"You had me worried for a while."

"Told you I'd make it."

"An all-night drive on lousy Jap roads in the rain. And your little holiday blown to hell."

"Just as well."

"You had me over a barrel, you know. Another ten minutes and you'd have missed ship."

"A regular Captain Bligh, aren't you?"

"Orders is orders, Cap'n, and I'm a stickler for the rules."

"So I'd have grabbed a helo and landed on your fantail. And put you under hack."

"After what you did to my ulcer? Why?"

31

"Deserting an old buddy." He grinned and tucked in the tails of his khaki shirt. "I must admit, it looked rough for a minute or two at the Hirase Bridge."

"How'd you get past that mob?"

"Prayer. Clean thoughts. A judo chop or two."

"The harbor master swore you'd never make it. He said the cops were cracking Commie student skulls like walnuts."

"At the gates, yes."

"Wish I was there." He rubbed his knuckles.

"Most of the people I saw were ordinary citizens, Mac. Not kids. Mad as hell. Waving signs. Yelling slogans. But middle-aged. Middle class. Not beatniks or hippies."

"What are they trying to prove?"

"They don't want us around. Our nuke subs and ships are polluting their water with radioactivity."

"You believe that crap?"

"It's possible."

"Hell, Paul. You know the cobalt 60 level in the harbor here. It's nil. You can't believe those lies."

"*They* believe it. They came all the way from Tokyo to protest it."

"So what? We licked 'em, didn't we? To the victor, I say—"

"It was their fathers we licked. Twenty years ago, Mac. We're facing a different crowd now."

"You want my opinion, it's Commie propaganda. Our pulling out like this is losing face. We're too damned soft on this crowd. If it was up to me, I'd give 'em a taste of the old mushroom again."

"If I thought you meant that, Mac, I'd rewrite your last fitness report." Damion poured some coffee. McKim watched him narrowly, sensing for the first time a change in Damion. Damion yawned. "Anything urgent in that stack of papers?"

"Just that big baby on top. From Com Seventh Fleet."

Damion picked up the envelope marked SECRET: COMMANDING OFFICER'S EYES ONLY. He broke the seals and read the contents.

"Neat, Mac. A shore bombardment."

32

"Where?"

"En route Yankee Station. Singly, before we join Task Force One."

"That should make the missile boys happy. They've been itching for a live target since we left Pearl."

"Looks like they have one." He seemed preoccupied. "Set up a meeting with department heads. Noon briefing. Meanwhile I'll check out the details."

"Aye, Captain."

"Advise weapons and operations officers now. They'll want time to get ready." He walked with McKim to the door. "I'll run through the mail and division reports and grab some shut-eye."

"You look a bit bushed."

"How's the crew?"

"All on board."

"No AWOLs?"

McKim shook his head. "Just the usual bitching about losing a liberty. They dig Sasebo, you know."

Damion nodded. "Dig. Yes. I remember the VD reports last time in here."

"How'd it go in Hiroshima?" He grinned. "Before we cut it short for you."

"Not bad."

"Any action?"

Damion took his time unwrapping and lighting a thin cigar. "I spent the time with this girl I knew as a kid."

"A swinger?"

"A social worker, Mac."

McKim grinned. "You got to be kidding."

"One of the *hibakusha*."

"Please, Professor?"

"A victim of the A-bomb."

McKim stared at him. "What for?"

Damion smiled faintly. *You'd never understand,* Stevens had said. "Ever been to Hiro, Mac?"

"Not personally. A bunch of the junior officers flew up for kicks once."

"For kicks."

"They dig the ball club."

"Dig it."

33

"Yeah. The Hiroshima Carps. In the cellar most of the season but the boys tell me they got the hottest fan club in Japan. Like the Mets. Built themselves a brand new stadium. You get to see the stadium?"

"From the outside is all."

"Personally I never made it to Hiro. They tell me it's a real swinging town. Sex joints, pachinko parlors. Geisha parties. One of these days I'll give it a go."

"You can't afford not to, Mac." Now curiously animated, he opened his suitcase and removed a handful of brightly colored brochures and picture postcard folders. "Take a look at this. You'll hardly believe your eyes." Damion spilled them on the table. "Here—*'Views of Hiroshima,'* Mac." His eyes were bright. He flipped over a postcard. "How about this one? *'Night Life on Hachobori Street.'* How about that?" He punched McKim's arm. "Swinging, man?"

"Looks like Broadway." McKim's face had a faintly bewildered look.

"Look at that Peace Memorial Museum. I was in it. A body shop, Mac. Beats burlesque. Beats the Seagram Building. Beats the lunch hour parade on Park Avenue. This one. *Statue of the A-Bomb Children.* Licks Disneyland a mile." He flipped open a larger folder. "You ought to be ashamed of yourself, Mac. Neglecting Fun City."

McKim started to say something. Damion waved his hand and began to read. " *'Mecca of World Peace, Hiroshima. Hiroshima, well-known as a town of water, is the biggest center of politics, economics and culture in the Chugaku district. The dropping of the A-bomb on the 6th of August in 1945 made this town a memorial of our hope for world peace.'* Here we go. Shukkei-en Garden. Dig those swans, Mac. Are you digging those swans?"

"Real pretty," McKim said.

"And the Light of Peace. You dig that, Mac?"

"Kind of grabs you." He glanced sharply at Damion. "Makes me sorry I've missed Hiro, Captain. Next trip to Sasebo—"

"Listen to *this*. And I quote: 'When the Atomic Bomb made its historic debut'—Get that fancy word,

34

Mac? *Debut?*—'in Hiroshima 22 years ago, it was rumored that vegetation will be nil for the coming century. Today the city has revived with a population exceeding half-million and the green seen in all parts of the rehabilitated city. Hiroshima gained world fame both as the atomic-bombed city and the peace city. 900 thousand visitors yearly. We are now collecting impressions of the visitors who have seen the exhibit—' "

He stopped abruptly. His eyes glowed. "Mac, you have got to promise me one thing. You'll go to Hiroshima and give them your impressions of the exhibit. Will you do that? Will you do that for your old skipper?"

McKim's taut expression relaxed a little. He laughed nervously. "You had me scared there for a minute. Like you'd gone off your nut."

"You don't want to miss it, Mac." He laughed harshly. "They've done wonders, these Japs. Turning an atrocity into a Disneyland." He handed McKim some of the folders and brochures. "Take 'em along, Mac. Study 'em. You've been to Disneyland, haven't you?"

"Who hasn't?"

"Coney Island?"

"Once. Before I was married."

"Then you can't afford to miss Hiroshima."

McKim patted the brochures. "All in here, is it?"

"Oh yes."

McKim winked. "We'll do Hiro together, Captain. Next time in." He edged toward the door.

"Nothing would give me greater pleasure, Mac. I mean that. I mean it from the bottom of my heart." He winked back. McKim sort of saluted and turned to go. "One thing, Mac."

"Sir?"

"Dig."

"Dig, sir?"

"When I went to school it meant to turn over earth with a shovel."

"Well, the way the guys use it, sir—"

"Guys." Damion shook his head. "Unnautical, Mac. Like dig. Pass the word round the wardroom. Dig and guys. Those two words are *verboten*. That means for-

35

bidden. Loose terminology encourages sloppy discipline. Take care of it for me, Mac."

"Aye, sir." He saluted and with a baffled expression left. He climbed to the chart room abaft the bridge and tossed the brochures on a leather settee and stared morosely at Wilcox, the navigator. Wilcox handed him a mug of coffee and nodded his head toward the brochures. "Planning a vacation, Commander?"

McKim sipped noisily. "Willie, something's bugging the skipper and I don't like it."

"So you're taking a vacation."

"Knock it off, wise guy. I'm really worried." He stared through the thick glass at the enlisted men on watch in the pilothouse.

"He ream you out or something?"

"Something I can't put my finger on, just since he came aboard this morning."

"Sure. He shacks up in Hiro with a beautiful chick and we send him this emergency wigwag to get his butt back aboard. Who wouldn't be teed off?"

McKim looked hurt and said nothing.

"Why not?" Wilcox demanded. "Makes sense. What else could bug a guy as steady as the skipper?"

"Don't use that word."

"What word?"

"Guy. It's not nautical. Or dig. He gave me the order not five minutes ago. So help me God. Tell the wardroom not to use words like guy and dig, he tells me." He glared at Wilcox. "And if you think Paul Damion was shacked up you just don't know the kind of man he is."

"I'm beginning to wonder," Wilcox said.

"He's plenty man. *Mucho*."

"He hasn't chased a piece of ass in the nine months I've been aboard."

McKim slammed the mug down, spilling coffee across the charts. "Watch yourself, Willie." He jerked his head toward the pilothouse. "Every word'll be all over crew's quarters."

"Mac, you're jumpy as—" He grinned foolishly. "It's going to be hard to say an honest word around here."

36

McKim wiped the charts with his sleeve. He handed the mug back to Wilcox. "Your coffee stinks."

"Ah, ah! Naughty word!"

"You got a dirty mind, Willie, and a foul mouth. How you got this far I'll never know." He stared at his soiled sleeve. "I'm going down and slit my throat."

"Be my guest. There's a fresh blade in my razor."

McKim heaved a sigh. "Wish I knew what's with the skipper." His worried eyes sought Wilcox's. "No kidding, Willie. I don't like it one damn bit."

After McKim had gone, Cesar served up a bountiful breakfast. Damion could touch none of it. He sat brooding over the color photos in the promotional material from Hiroshima. He returned to his desk and lighted a cigar and tired to concentrate on the work before him. He finally gave up and went into his bedroom and took off his shoes and stretched out on the bed.

Lucky Mac, he thought. All that fun in Fun City. The bar girls and the gentle geishas and the sake-and-sex teahouses. Even pachinko, if you can stand loud music and the endless clink of steel balls. It's my own bloody fault for going back, he reflected. What did I expect this time? Dreamland Revisited?

He had seen Hiroshima once before. That time in 1949. He was a junior grade lieutenant, two years out of Annapolis, and aboard a light cruiser serving with a carrier group in Japanese waters. On his first three-day leave he heard there was a festival in Hiroshima. He left at once. He never understood what made him go.

Twenty hours by train from Tokyo through green countryside fresh as a spring salad. Rice paddies, vegetable gardens, arching bamboo, forests of red pine. Factory chimneys rebuilt and belching smoke once more. On the right through the train window a rhythm of sweeping ridges. On the left, the sea. Past Odawara through citrus groves and Fujiyama swathed in clouds.

Workers bent with the weight of years toiled in the paddies. Some worked on all fours, crippled or too old to stand erect. Windbreak trees hemmed the trim rectangles where squash vines bore golden-yellow blossoms. Laundered kimonos stretched to dry on bamboo poles rippled in sunlight. The ditches were choked with huge round lotus leaves.

Children walked in bare feet along the narrow dirt roads with smaller children strapped to their backs. Farmers drove their carts stacked crazily with firewood and brush and bowed their heads to the passing train. There were many bicycles and small birds.

A curious quality marked the celebration in Hiroshima, sadness and festivity spiked with a touch of bravura. Young Damion drifted where the crowds took him. He felt conspicuous in his wrinkled white uniform. No one else seemed to mind. They were honored to meet a foreigner, an American who spoke their tongue so well.

He found himself with a serious and dedicated group of American volunteers who had come to build homes for the homeless. A token of regret and humiliation, their gray-haired leader told him. Damion listened gravely to their dreams and plans. The air smelled like May wine and no one complained of the heat.

The city and prefecture officials had guaranteed the citizens a full-scale celebration and kept their word. After the speeches there were fireworks and confetti and much ringing of bells. The feature of the festival was the crowning of Miss Hiroshima 1949. She was small and fragile and wore a long white dress, American style, with a blood red rose. She appeared entirely lovely and unreal to Damion. Nor had Damion's eyes missed the quiet ones who came and celebrated in a rather subdued way, bearing their keloid scars and crippled limbs like swords.

One of these was Mizu Yokaga.

Mizu was nine years old. She sat with her grandfather in the cool shadows of the Dome and placidly watched the celebration. Her grandfather told Damion that Mizu was much better now. She had been shy and frightened for several years after the family was destroyed. Mizu had been the youngest of four and in a nursery school when the A-bomb fell. Her exposure was minimal but it left her face and hands permanently disfigured. After the blast, the old man hurried to the center of the city from his small farm in the suburb of Koi to search among the living, dying, and dead for his son's family. He found their house buried in a mountain of rubble. The scene was one of total horror and the violated air was rank with the odor of burning flesh. Even now, he told Damion, he could hear the screams of the injured and bereaved.

"I ignored them all," the old man went on, "seeking my loved ones. They were gone. I found only Mizu cowering among torn and bleeding bodies near the ruins of the Hiroshima railway station. She does not remember how she got there. It is a long way from her nursery school. All she remembers is the *pikadon* and her shame at being naked."

Several people had come over and were listening while the old man talked. They were silent and polite, fascinated by what he was saying, as though they were hearing such things for the first time.

"The *pika* I remember," Mizu said. "A sudden blinding flash. But not the *don*. I did not hear the *don*."

"She was too close to the hypocenter to hear the boom," the old man explained. "But from Koi I saw and heard both flash and boom. My first thought was that this was hell—the Buddhist hell we are taught about, where sinners go. I carried Mizu home. Her hands were badly torn and one leg broken. For weeks she would eat nothing. I had to force her. All her hair fell out and her skin—well, you can see for yourself."

"There were others much worse than I," said Mizu.

The old man nodded. "Many strangers came to us, silent, broken in spirit. They asked to stay. They no longer could face their ruined city or their ruined lives."

"You took them in."

"All who came. They soon grew restless and left, or ill and died. Huge sores first, and vomiting." He smiled sadly. "They're all gone now. Dead, I hope. Mizu and I are alone but alive. *Iiunmei.* Our special luck." He stroked her head fondly. "Her hair has grown back. I find it quite beautiful."

"Mizu is beautiful," Damion said. "I would be honored if she and her honorable grandfather would join me for dinner when the celebration is done."

They did. Mizu told Damion that quite definitely she would be a nurse someday, or a social worker. She spoke with dignity and tried to hide her limp when she walked. Damion told her she could not have chosen a nobler profession for herself.

Later everyone agreed that the festival, the first of its kind anywhere in the world, had been such a financial and spiritual success, it must become an annual event. Rather than weep for his fellow men, Damion got gloriously drunk. He embraced everyone and toasted his new friends many times and talked too much. They put him on board the last Tokyo train and he slept most of the way back.

A day of leave still remained but Damion spent it on board in quiet meditation. Later that day he wrote a long letter to his wife and made arrangements for an allotment to provide for Mizu's education and future.

At sea he thought often of Mizu and her people and the dedicated missionaries who had befriended him. He prayed for all the *hibakusha,* lucky or not, who had survived the Bomb. He still did not understand what had sent him so impulsively to Hiroshima, but he knew he must go there again some day.

He rose and washed his face and rubbed it briskly with a coarse Navy towel. The chance meeting with Stevens still haunted him. Could Stevens have been right? Had something morbid and unhealthy, some aberration of nature, compelled him to go back? Was there something more than fascinating about Mizu's keloid scars?

Because something terrible and completely fascinating had happened when he did go back. A small accident, nothing more. But he would live with each detail of it all of his life. Mizu had greeted him warmly, a slim smiling woman of twenty-eight. Her good grandfather had passed on a year ago. She lived alone now. Roommates were hard to come by. Living with an obvious victim of the Bomb could spoil a girl's chances for marriage.

She sat with Damion in her tiny modern apartment and served him Japanese scotch and chatted about her world. Hiroshima had changed, of course. It was a boom town now, very tourist-conscious. Everyone had a job and was making a decent living and the city was as good as new. Mizu was the nurse and social worker she had dreamed of being. She was grateful to Damion for his help and proud that she had learned to live with her misfortune where so many others had failed.

His limp was barely noticeable and she had a way of angling her face so that her scars were less visible. She wore a smart cotton dress, American style, and a pair of polished leather loafers. Her nails were lacquered with a silvery gloss but neatly trimmed, and she smoked a cigarette. Her English came quaintly fresh to his ears. Sometimes their conversation lapsed into Japanese, and she would speak animatedly of her busy hours in the hospital wards and how grim life was with the poor she visited and cared for.

Damion felt proud of Mizu and truly loved her. He did not shrink from her scars. He thought of them as he did his own campaign ribbons. He did not see the scars. He saw only the lovely human being Mizu had become.

Until the small accident.

It happened while she was describing a tourist curiosity—a human shadow imprinted on a step stone of the Sumitomo Bank by the heat rays of the Bomb about three hundred yards from the hypocenter. He sniffed the odor of scorching meat. Mizu was too absorbed in her story, it seemed, to be aware of it. He saw with horror that her cigarette had burned a hole into her flesh and only then, seeing his eyes, did she realize what was happening. She put aside her cigarette and with the end of her handkerchief calmly brushed the hole clean. She apologized to Damion, explaining she had not felt it, and he assured her it was quite all right and after a terrible silence she hid her face in her hands and quietly wept.

Soon it was time for Mizu to go to work. Damion walked with her to the bus stop. She was limping, he noticed, and her old scars in sunlight gleamed like

41

shiny plastic scales. They both seemed relieved when the bus came. Mizu said again she hoped he did not mind what had happened. She had felt nothing, really, and was sorry he had to witness such an unpleasant thing. It had marred the pleasure of his visit and she could scarcely forgive herself. Would he come again, please? Perhaps she should give up smoking.

He said he would come again. He helped her into the bus and watched her go. He did not believe he would ever see her again. She had already left him with too much to remember.

It was then, when Mizu's bus had gone and he was alone and badly shaken, that he walked the long walk to the Peace Museum.

IV

Damion put aside his thoughts of Mizu and Hiroshima and his chance encounter with Eric Stevens. He drank a glass of orange juice and two cups of coffee and ate a piece of buttered toast. He lighted a long cigar and settled down to read the details of the new orders.

Chesapeake's missions was designated Operation Wipe Out. Damion studied the operation plan until his Marine orderly announced the arrival of *Chesapeake*'s departmental officers. He gathered up the papers and rose to greet them.

"This is our present situation, gentlemen. We're on a southwesterly course." He indicated a penciled track on a large chart hung from the bulkhead. "We will pass through the Ryukyu Islands chain and Bashi channel, thence westerly on various courses and speeds to arrive at Point Alpha here, off the DMZ. We will undertake a dawn bombardment using Terrier missiles. We plan a port and a starboard run. Our objective: to destroy the village of Ha Loi Trung." He pointed to the village. "No resistance or counterfire is expected. Following the order to cease fire we will resume our course to Yankee Station and rejoin Task Force One. Any questions?"

"Yes, Captain. This village. Any people in it?"

"Negative."

"What's our reason, Captain? I mean, why are we destroying the village?"

"Viet Cong heavy gun emplacements and bunkers are known to be in the vicinity. Operations will have the exact details as to the location."

"Will there be air coverage?"

"Weather permitting. If air coverage is not provided, you will be so advised. Any other questions?"

There were none. A brief discussion of ship's business followed and the meeting broke up. Damion asked his weapons, operations, and navigation officers to remain. Commander McKim, who had other pressing duties, would be advised later of the second meeting's details.

"The details, gentlemen," Damion began, "seemed to me to be too complicated and of secondary interest to the others. But you three are primary to the plan. Here's the pitch: Since last May the Navy's been conducting amphibious heliborne assaults against the enemy in northern Quang Tri Province. These are amtrac teams working the coast, with helicopter units providing air support from our assault carriers off the Vietnam coast. The Marines who ride these amtracs are a rugged lot. Call themselves amgrunts and they operate south of the DMZ on search and destroy missions.

"A few days ago the 3rd Marine Battalion Landing Team from the Seventh Fleet's Special Landing Force began predawn operations in a new zone along the coastal plain about six miles northeast of Dong Ha . . . here . . . and should have been put ashore at night at Cuat Viet . . . here. Tanks, tractors, landing craft. They had a bad time of it. Monsoon storm and winds raised hell with their night navigation. Some of the craft smashed up. Two men were lost. It was midmorning before they got organized and got word back to their command base on where they thought they were and what was what.

"The foul-up was especially galling to this bunch because ten days earlier the landing had been smooth and undetected. They had swept the dunes and captured almost a hundred Chinese 122-mm. rockets, complete with launching ramps, that had been zeroed in on our Marine forward positions a few miles south. Anyway, this outfit wasn't about to quit. They made a fast run north, their objective being the enemy artillery emplacements stashed out in caves just over the DMZ."

"Do you mean," the navigator asked, "they actually crossed into the demilitarized zone?"

"Didn't intend to. But with the lousy navigation and all, when they clanked to a halt, the Marine CO checked his maps and landmarks and figured they were well over the line."

"That's a violation of the Geneva Pact, isn't it?"

"Technically yes. But it's tough to establish an accurate fix in the boondocks. These poor guys were working along a mine-infested beach with limited visibility in unfamiliar and hilly terrain in wet weather with mud up to their eyeballs. Not like you, Willie, with well-charted seas and a chartroom and bridge full of electronic gadgets."

"Sorry, sir." Wilcox grinned.

"Anyway, it's officially denied and has nothing to do with what we're talking about."

"Wasn't there helicopter cover to guide them?"

"Weather was too dirty to launch helos. Also a communications foul-up, don't ask me why. Incidently, these amgrunts are hand-picked volunteers and very gung-ho. The Marine CO hated to quit but he knew he had overshot and swung his column around and headed south. You know, these amtracs run with one tread in the surf and the other in the sand, to avoid mines. Just their luck to hit two. The mines blew 'em both apart. Another got stuck in the guck as the tide came in and had to be abandoned." He poured some water and drank it and went on.

"The CO had another headache. He was in radio touch with his base ship and any minute the VC might pinpoint his transmissions and open up. And he was running out of time to make his landing craft rendezvous to the south for the return to the ship.

45

"He got one break. The enemy's artillery fire control was also fouled up by the storm and had no contact with his forward observation posts south of the DMZ. So the VC never found out about the amtrac landing team. On the way south the Marine CO picked out the shapes of a few beached fishing boats and collared the fishermen. They told him their village was just over the ridge. Ha Loi Trung. Our target. Smack on the southern border of the DMZ.

"The Marine CO knew from intelligence that all those villages had been evacuated and then destroyed by our heavy barrages. He took aboard the fishermen and made a swing west to investigate. The village was intact. Wives, kids, nets, the works. The fishermen explained that they had hidden in the jungle for a few days after the evacuation order was dropped. This was their home. They did not want to leave it. The rest of the villagers had gone south as ordered, but this bunch had opted to stay, preferring the risk of being bombed to life in a strange and distant refugee camp."

"Not unreasonable, Captain."

"Not to me, either. But the cagey Marine CO didn't like it and wasn't about to buy it. He figured if the huts stood and people lived there, they had to be working with the VC. He radioed for permission to run a reconnaissance sweep in the area. His command ship denied permission and ordered him to make his scheduled rendezvous with his LCMs. So he headed south. He hadn't gone a thousand yards before his group was taken under heavy artillery fire and blasted. A handful made it to the rendezvous, including the Marine CO, badly wounded. They reported ninety per cent casualties to equipment, eighty percent to personnel."

Damion poured fresh coffee for himself and relighted his cigar. "The Marine CO and the rest of the survivors swear the shelling came from a point perhaps five hundred yards due west of the village of Ha Loi Trung. This all happened maybe forty-eight hours ago. The information the survivors brought in has been carefully evaluated. Except for the location of Ha Loi Trung, it doesn't tell us much. The whole area was a sea of mud. The storm wiped out the few recognizable

46

landmarks. We've flown recon from our helo carriers but they show no signs of heavy artillery emplacements anywhere around the village. So our orders, gentlemen, are to destroy the village and everything around it."

"What about the women and kids you mentioned?"

"Today and tomorrow, evacuation leaflets are being dropped over Ha Loi Trung. That'll give 'em time enough to get out. If they had followed orders and gone to the refugee camps, none of this would have happened." He stood. "We plan to fire Terrier missiles from a range of ten miles, making two runs. Any questions?"

Some minor points were raised and after several minutes, the officers left. Damion dispatched his orderly to request the executive officer to stop in at his first opportunity. He felt better now. The rhythm of sea routine had caught him up again. He ate the lunch Cesar had prepared, and rose to resume the work piled on his desk.

"One moment, Captain." Cesar carried a small birthday cake in his slender hands. It held two lighted candles.

"How did you know, Cesar?"

"I read your mail, Captain." He grinned.

"Only two candles?"

"Old Oriental saying, Captain. Life begins at forty." Grinning, he carried the cake to the small table. The two candles flickered, gained strength, flamed anew. "Now you make a wish, Captain. Then you blow out the candles."

Damion made a wish and bent over and blew out the candles. "Thank you very much, Cesar." He was deeply moved. "What would you have done if I hadn't made it back aboard?"

"I never give that a thought, Captain."

"You just knew I'd make it."

Cesar nodded and grinned.

"How old are you, Cesar?"

"Forty-seven, Captain. An old man."

"You look half my age and you know it."

"In two years I retire. Thirty-year man."

47

"Back to Cebu and the wife and kids."

"Yes, sir."

"You're a lucky one, Cesar."

"I thank the Lord each day for my blessings."

"You were in World War II, right?"

Cesar nodded. "A stewards' mate, Captain. U.S.S. *Missouri*."

"In Tokyo Bay?"

"I watched the whole surrender, sir. MacArthur, Nimitz, Bull Halsey. All those Japanese."

"Ever been to Hiroshima?"

"One time, Captain. That same year during the occupation."

"Why'd you go, Cesar?"

He looked bewildered. "Don't know why, Captain. But to this day I'm sorry—"

The Marine sentry knocked. "Commander McKim, sir."

"Hi, Mac." He watched Cesar retreat to his alcove. "Grab a seat, Mac. Sing me a Happy Birthday."

"How much, Paul?"

"Forty-two." *I'm always twenty-four,* he thought, *and still on Yong-hung-do. And why is simple Cesar sorry?*

He cut two fat slices and sat with McKim and they ate it with their fingers. "Take the rest of it to the wardroom," Damion said.

McKim wiped his lips. "They'll go ape. This is cake we don't often see there."

"When you're forty-two, Mac, I'll have Cesar bake you one." He reached for a cigar. "How goes the stout ship?"

"Four-oh." McKim consulted his notes. "Your elevator'll be out of commission from midnight for two hours. Weekly maintenance check. Tomorrow 0900 we run VD films for the First, N and OS Divisions, Crew's Lounge; Second Division in the forward top hat area; Third Division in the aft top hat area; Marines in the detachment spaces. That's it for the clap-happy—"

"Locking the barn door—"

"I know, I know. Somebody should invent a pill.

That's pretty much tomorrow's Plan of the Day except for regular drills and the weekly inrush controller test."

"Okay, Mac. Print it up."

"Aye, sir. How'd the briefing go?"

Damion gave him the details. McKim left and the captain spent the balance of the afternoon clearing his desk. He dictated a dozen official letters, all brief, informative, concise. After the lonely evening meal he lighted a cigar and read through a pile of the routine directives and reports that plague all commanding officers ashore and afloat. He spent a quiet hour on the bridge and at ten retired to his sea cabin abaft the pilothouse, where he wrote up the night orders and turned in.

He savored each rustle and soft-spoken word and the hum of instruments that filtered through the bulkhead. *Chesapeake*'s underway throb and murmur soothed him. It meant a vast improvement over her predecessor, the prototype cruiser *Long Beach,* in which he had served a tour of duty as executive officer before taking command of *Chesapeake.* Advanced reactor design gave her much greater cruising range without refueling. A redesigned hull did away with the fantail rumble. Her superstructure had been streamlined to modify the top-heavy bulkiness that typified the *Long Beach* silhouette.

Like all nuclear-powered warships she carried no fuel oil, no stacks, she blew no tubes. She was clean and swift, smokeless, barely visible at night except for running lights, and as quiet as so complicated a mechanism can be. One of two identical nuclear propulsion plants drove a single shaft and propeller thrusting a thousand men, munitions, armament, supplies and her own fifteen-thousand tons easily through the night sea. The responsibility no longer awed Damion. The astronomy of costs had become meaningless.

You have got to look at it this way, he told himself. It's a business like any other business. I run an ultramodern electronics plant. It cost half a billion to build and another hundred thousand every day it's operating. It's got its headaches like any other business and it has its rewards. Had I chosen private industry I'd be earning five times the take-home pay I'm getting now. I'd have a piece of the action and a few fringe benefits not in the contract, like weekends off and the non-Navy luxury of time with my family at least a few evenings a week. But I'd be slave to a desk and checkbook, paying back huge chunks of the dough to Uncle in taxes and barely solvent keeping my family abreast of the Joneses.

Family? His wife, Martha, had surprised him with a divorce four years ago—the grounds: mental cruelty. A bit farfetched, he had thought, since he was at sea most of those years. He was shocked to learn that it was Mizu's allotment that had decided Martha. He had explained Mizu's circumstances to her a long time ago and assumed she would believe him. He was deeply hurt, but he went along with the divorce, submitting without complaint to the indignities her attorney deemed necessary to make it stick.

He had taken Martha for granted. He had been too young when they married and not deeply in love, not even clear what love implied or demanded. Martha was eager to marry and drove him, pampering him, showering him with attention until she had won him and they were into the business of crossed swords and dress uniforms and the old Navy rituals. The divorce came as a stunning surprise.

He felt sorry only for his daughter, Angela. She was the true loser. Martha remarried a Coddington, of the old Monterey Coddingtons, the solid, socially prominent type she believed she needed. Angela was sent to the right schools and shipped off to college. She and her father wrote to each other. From the letters she sent, he knew she was still in love with her war hero dad. For Martha he felt nothing but pity. There was no loss, no sorrow. Martha was a misfire.

And had I chosen academe? With my nuclear expertise, I could add a string of impressive initials after my name, leather elbows on my tweed jacket and ivy in everything. I could indulge my ego before the adoring eyes of a classroom full of nubile female physicists with contact lenses, unsatisfied father fixations, and an adequate supply of the Pill. How long could I take their protesting? Their innocent inanities? And could I suffer the orders of the absentee trustees?

And how much would I miss the sea?

So here I am and in a couple of mornings it will be Tonkin Gulf and Ha Loi Trung.

He had never heard of Ha Loi Trung. The chart placed it not too far north of Hue, and oh yes, he had heard of Hue.

Once with a school companion, an older French boy whose sophistication fascinated and ensnared him, he had visited a brothel in Hue. Fifteen then, and the occasion the successful completion of midyear exams. It could have been a disaster, that first time in Hue, for a fifteen year old lad operating mostly on nerve. But the girl, a French Indo Chinese, had wisdom and understanding beyond her years. The experience proved astonishing and instructive and he went back again, always to the same girl, much to the disgust of his jaded companion, who already had a taste for Gallic variations.

In those young years it seemed a marvelous way to grow up. He took it for granted other kids had just as much fun. He was enrolled in the Lycée Quoc-Hoc in Hue, a well-run progressive school attended largely by children of the wealthy families living in the imperial capital. He studied French, English, Vietnamese, and Vietnamese culture. He took naturally to the study of foreign languages. Before Hue it had been Tokyo and before Tokyo, Manila. He learned the knack of dialects, the key phrases and intonations, often surprising and delighting foreign visitors in his father's home with phrases in their own tongue.

Brief periods of Stateside residencies broke up the extended missions abroad. America was a strange land to young Paul. His family would rent a house in Georgetown or take a place for a few months in the Virginia countryside, but none of these stays were of long enough duration for Paul to feel at home.

Home was a word he would find hard to describe.

His mother, Alice, had been a Maryland beauty, the languorous daughter of a widowed, land-rich diplomat,

51

living out his retirement on bourbon and Chesapeake Bay bug-eyes. She had met Stark Damion during his last Annapolis year and invited him to her father's place on the Eastern Shore for a sail down to Tilghman, and to Oxford for a crab feed. The old man admired his good manners and was impressed by his seamanship. When he learned of Damion's New England ancestry, he served up his best brandy. He was weary of his daughter's indolence and shrewd enough to know she was ripe and ready to drop. He had a mistress of his own in a sagging cottage on the Wye, whose patience was wearing thin. He urged Alice with paternal tenderness and a touch of diplomatic guile to get on with it.

They were married on a sweltering day in the family chapel and blessed by waving fields of corn. Alice moved out and the wilting mistress moved in. Paul came along in the proper time allotted by nature and society, give or take a few days. The ambassador, in gratitude for his new role of grandpapa and in-home lover, opened the doors for Stark's career in the foreign service of his country.

Alice Damion rejected the challenges of mother-hood. She considered herself too ladylike to engage in the indignities of diaper changes and breast feeding. Her dismay at the prospect of childbirth almost broke up the young marriage. The event came to fruition only because her husband, as brave and indomitable as John Paul Jones engaging *Serapis,* turned a deaf ear to her pleas for abortion and stoutly withstood her trau-mas through to the delivery day. She never forgave him though her hips measured no wider than before.

Alice Damion tolerated the existence of her newborn son with less concern than she held for the house cat. Her servants despised her. She remained aloof from the household, slept late, scattered her clothes everywhere, and was impossible to approach before noon, at which hour she permitted a tray of chocolate and *petit beurre* to be placed at her bedside. By teatime she was blos-soming, phoning friends, writing gushy letters in a large backward script to friends in London and Rome and sometimes Madrid, but never to Paris, which she loved and where her mother had died in a horrible boating accident. The sight of the written or printed word was too much to bear.

Most evenings were devoted to her husband's commitments, receptions and functions of state, a routine quite naturally familiar to her. His abilities were soon evident to his superiors and his assignments often took him abroad. Alice sometimes accompanied him on these sudden secret journeys, but most of the time she remained at home.

She would amuse herself in these absences with intrigues of harmless dalliance. She lavishly entertained her social crowd, a loose-living, duck-shooting menagerie of fascinating failures who were rarely invited to her husband's parties. She was a selfish woman of rare beauty and grace, a witty and flirtatious hostess much admired by those who did not know her too well. She was utterly incapable of an enduring love and devoid of sentimentality, desirable qualities in a diplomat's wife and daughter, perhaps, but certain hell for a lone child in a household that shifted and changed like the characters and settings of some frenetic stage play.

If she failed as a mother, it was lost upon Paul, who loved her, remembering only marvelous scents and softness and never a harsh word. He accepted the world of governesses, amahs, and tutors as naturally as he did the plane and train journeys and the steamships to Hong Kong, the single black valise that was his alone, packed and ready to go anywhere on short notice.

That time in Hue, in 1940, his father was a Navy commander attached to a State Department intelligence team working behind the scenes with the French Colonial Command. The team's mission was to establish escape routes for downed American fliers should war break out between the United States and Japan. By then, young Paul had learned to live with himself, a quiet, self-reliant, young man of fifteen, who moved with grace and with a faintly challenging look in his deep-set gray eyes.

He carried with him a small portfolio of tender memories, secret and personal, of his father, who by

53

now was rarely present and under constant pressures. Fifteen is an awkward age, a time when sons need fathers most. All that Paul could turn to were these memories.

A game of catch in the tiny garden of their suburban Tokyo house, with a birthday ball glove, made in Japan of plump tanned leather, the pocket oiled and pounded with his fist so long he thought his knuckles would split; his father in white shorts, tall and grinning, catching the new ball barehanded; his mother asleep in her dead white bedroom of screens and whining fans.

A tour with his father and an admiral through the Navy establishment at Cavite and luncheon in the palm garden of the flag officers' club; his heart swollen with pride in his father's crisp and elegant world of uniforms and snappy salutes.

A hydroplane ride in the public park at Ueno, surrounded by lanterns and black swans. His father had asked if he'd like a career in the Navy and he had only nodded, too full of the image to speak.

That picnic at Enoshima when his mother had decided not to come with them. His father made it seem like fun but both of them knew it was not.

And once in America, painting a wooden plaque with a motto for the mantel of the stone fireplace in a rambling white house in Virginia, the words indelibly painted in that memory.

From Hue he was shipped off to Severn Academy to prepare for Annapolis. His parents followed to Washington a year later. War with Japan seemed inevitable. It was all anyone talked about in the Damion house. Stark Damion, now a captain, had been hurriedly detached from his diplomatic duties and assigned to Navy Intelligence, where his firsthand expertise in Far East affairs was sorely needed.

He spent anxious weeks analyzing the intercepted secret dispatches between Tokyo and its Washington agents, now decrypted and translated. He had his own file of reliable information on the temper of the Supreme War Council held that September in Tokyo. He had copious notes of private conversations held with Japanese officers who were his friends and whose opin-

54

ions he trusted. He consulted with his aides who knew the Oriental mind as well as he.

He submitted a detailed report to his superiors, warning of the Japanese determination and plans to strike with force, at either Hawaii or the Philippines or both, sometime during the first week in December, give or take a few days. They pretended to listen but he sensed their disbelief and hostility. The entrenched military professionals disliked this suntanned Asia duty dandy in his Hong Kong tailored elegance. He was too polished for the tastes of his trade school peers and too much the cosmopolite. They resented his easy entrée to the upper echelon of Washington society and even more his meddling in a brewing war they regarded as their personal affair. Hadn't they been sitting on this Japanese firecracker while he was out in the boondocks fiddling with chopsticks?

His efforts to convince them of the danger were scorned. His informed opinions were ignored. His tacit recommendations were tabled or rejected. He realized the futility of trying harder. Washington in a war scare was a jungle of raw nerves, each office a snake pit of false rumors. Its heightened social pressures became a crashing bore and he asked for a transfer of duty. A command at sea would have pleased him, but he was hardly qualified. A return to his attaché duties in the Far East seemed highly unlikely now, though his treatment, even by the enemy, would be more courteous.

Paul had come in from Severn to spend that Sunday with his parents when the bombs fell on Pearl Harbor. The reunion was marked with sadness but charged with an unprecedented affection. Paul saw to that, drawing the three of them close to each other in a warmth it seemed they had never shared before, sensing in some mysterious way that it was the last time they would be together.

He returned to school bemused by love and sadness. The war was on and he was too young to fight in it. His mother surprisingly involved herself at once in USO work and Red Cross driver duties. His father was rushed to the Pacific with orders to a cruiser division for sea duty, attached to an admiral's staff. He was

55

glad to get out of Washington. No one around the department could look him in the eye.

Captain Stark Damion was lost in the narrow passes of Savo Strait during the November battle for Guadalcanal. Along with six American warships, two rear admirals, and hundreds of officers and men. In morning darkness. On Friday the thirteenth. Paul Damion added that to his portfolio of memories. Almost as though he had been there.

His mother? She withered and died, brave thing. Not out of grief for her lover's passing. It was cancer.

Annapolis then, Class of '47. His grandfather hung on until the graduation ceremony, then violently passed away. All that he had not squandered on bourbon and boats, he left to the widow who had waited so long in the cottage on the Wye.

The years between Inchon and command of *Chesapeake* were the most trying years of Paul Damion's life. He was selected for the Navy's fledgling nuclear power program soon after the Korean War and devoted himself with single-minded intensity to its challenge. He was the first man in his class to skipper a nuclear-powered submarine, the first to gain the rank of captain. The breakup of his marriage drove him to achievements that ended in the coveted command of the nuclear ship, *Chesapeake*.

He was as good as the Navy made them. In forty-eight hours, off Ha Loi Trung, he would test how good that truly was.

V

It was almost midnight before McKim, full of antacid pills, felt satisfied he had done a full day's work. He turned the penciled Plan of the Day over to his prize yeoman, Howie Morgen, for typing and mimeographing. The command duty officer dropped by for a preview of the next day's schedule. McKim went topside to the bridge and memorized the captain's night orders. He chatted with the OOD on the open starboard wing of the bridge and learned that the aerographer's forecast for the next twenty-four hours indicated the possibility of heavy weather as they moved southward toward the area of Operation Wipe Out. He settled in the chartroom for a cigarette and after a few minutes of gossip with the duty nav officer, went below. Sprawled in his cabin chair, he reviewed the day.

The pressures of getting underway after an extended liberty stay in port invariably left him in a highly charged state. McKim enjoyed his duties. He went about them with the same brutal enthusiasm that had made him an All-American guard his last year at Annapolis.

Working parties had stowed the last case of stores below. The liberty boats were secured, the binnacle list compiled, the captain's gig properly swung to its davits and cradle. It was all routine, all in the day's work. Only the last-minute doubts about the captain's arrival had kicked up the commander's ulcer and he was not about to forget it. Reports of civilian unrest in the area did not help matters.

Word to leave Sasebo for Yankee Station had come directly from the area command in Tokyo. The order had originated in San Diego with ComCruDesFor, U.S. Pacific Fleet. It carried the endorsements of Com-PacFleet in Pearl Harbor and ComTaskFor One, Admiral "Fife" Pfeiffer, commanding the carrier attack force in Tonkin Gulf. McKim, after agonizing delays, had reached his skipper at his Hiroshima hotel by phone, no easy matter in Japan outside Tokyo. Damion assured McKim he would depart at once and arrive in ample time for the 0700 departure deadline. McKim waited until midnight for a progress report, then left instructions at the quarterdeck to be notified at once of any message from Captain Damion.

At 0500 with Damion not heard from, McKim took his first two milk of magnesia pills and debated the consequences of requesting a delay in departure from his area commander in Toyko. The image of the inter-command complications that would ensue drove McKim to two more antacid tablets. He held off until 0530, at which time his sense of duty overcame his loyalty for his commanding officer and he radioed Admiral Pfeiffer for permission to delay departure, omitting his reasons. ComTaskFor One snapped back demanding cause, length of delay requested, and inquiring authority of *Chesapeake's* executive officer to originate operational messages. Forty minutes and four pills later McKim had put together a message stating that his commanding officer was unexpectedly detained en route Sasebo from Hiroshima. However, *Chesapeake* was prepared to depart Sasebo harbor at 0700 as scheduled. He read it over and finally notified the radio officer that he had a message for transmission to ComTaskFor One. His ulcer dug in. He was waiting in pain for the messenger

58

when the yard signal bridge opened up by blinker. *Chesapeake*'s commanding officer had just cleared the yard gate and was headed for the Navy landing. Radio shack's messenger arrived. McKim happily deleted the first part of the message and went to the quarterdeck to meet the captain.

Now he thought of the alibis he could have presented to hold the ship until Damion was on board. But he knew himself too well. He sure as hell would have shoved off on time because that was what the orders said. He wondered what Damion would have done with the roles reversed. He did not like the look in Damion's eye when he had come aboard. Nor did he see the humor in Damion's light remark about flying a helo aboard and putting McKim under hack. After eight milk of magnesia pills nothing seemed funny, not even a silly crack like the one about his fitness report.

The wild harangue on the beauties of Hiroshima had scared the hell out of McKim. Damion never slipped out of character. He was solid, predictable, admirable. The nuke sailor's nuke sailor. Steady and sharp. The fair-haired boy of the Navy's crusty old nuclear god-head in Washington, who no one else seemed able to please. The Navy's Numero Uno. That was Damion. Not the stranger of this morning.

McKim undressed and lay in his bunk. The ulcer pain had eased but he could not sleep. At the Academy they had called him JoJo the Dogfaced Boy and he had made a hell of a reputation as a defensive guard. He had graduated in the first quarter of his class. He was good, he knew, but he was no Damion. No one had ever handed *him* a Navy Cross at twenty-four or told him he was an engineering genius at thirty.

He was damned glad Damion had made it back aboard. Just as he said he would. McKim sure as hell would have hated to shove off without him.

He hoped Damion was all right. He knew damned well there wasn't enough radioactive waste in the harbor bottom sediment to give a baby diaper rash. Why the hell the Navy's running scared he'd never know. Why an ace like Damion would swallow that Commie crap he'd never understand.

Commander McKim sometimes read a page of his Bible before he slept. Tonight he could not concentrate on the meaning of the words. He lay uncovered with the open Bible face down on his chest in the gentle rise and fall of his bunk, uneasy and discomfited.

It's this new Navy, McKim reflected sourly. Ever since we pulled World War Two out of the fire by licking the Jap, everybody's tried to cut us down. The Pentagon politicians and the left wing do-gooders moved in and took over and tore the old Navy blue to shreds. So that you can't go near an officers' club and not find some wop or yid or jig in Navy gold braid pushing up to the bar like he belonged there. To call this lash-up a band of brothers is a slap in the face to the sacred old Union Jack. God alone knows what's happening to this great nation with its riots and strikes and long-hair hippies. If it wasn't for the oath I took to defend my country and the uniform I wear, I'd be back there doing something about it.

He clearly remembered the page of *Naval Leadership* from his midshipman days, quoting the example of a destroyer skipper who always gave his officers a 4.0 rating in loyalty on their fitness reports, reasoning that there could be no compromise in one's loyalty and hence only two marks—either 4.0 or zero. An officer who rated a zero of course would be dropped from the service. McKim never forgot that and often quoted it to his men. When he had taken his midshipman oath he had vowed loyalty to the President and to the Government of the United States. He meant it. He had fervently promised himself he would uphold that oath with his life if it came to that.

He wished he understood what it was that bugged the Old Man. He had never known Damion to act so strangely. Maybe not being able to shack up with that scabbed-up Jap social worker did it. God knows he isn't getting any poontang I know of, McKim thought. Could be it got to him and he left a little piece of his mind back there in Hiro. Could be the strain of command. God, I hope not, not him.

Things like that were known to happen to the best of Navy men. That was exactly what he was here for.

Second-in-command. He put his Bible aside, marking the place with the red silk ribbon, and snapped off the light. It had been a long hard day for McKim. His thick body tingled with fatigue. It was a heavy burden, duty. It took all day and sometimes all night. In the dark his eyes filled. Claudius F. McKim of Garden Grove, California, loved God & Country fiercely.

So did his prize yeoman, Morgen, but for different reasons. Nights at sea were Yeoman Howie Morgen's finest hours. He ranked fifth in the exec office's pecking order, but he carried the brunt of the work load. Morgen's immediate superior was a chief petty officer named Gurney. Over the chief were the commissioned officers of the department—the exec, the administration officer, and the chaplain. Morgen respected all of them except Chief Petty Officer Gurney. And with good reason. Gurney was lethargic and potbellied, a worn-out China duty sailor with twenty-eight years in, faking out the last two years before retirement. He passed much of the time on board swapping salty exaggerations or playing acey-deucey with the other chiefs in the CPO lounge. The remaining hours were spent in the sack dreaming up improbable do-it-yourself projects for his paid-up two-bedroom shake-shingled and termite-infested bungalow in Redondo Beach.

Howie Morgen welcomed the extra responsibilities. In addition to God & Country, he loved his parents, his ship and duties in that order. And he particularly loved order. Disorder offended him. The grinding pressures of the office routine would often continue late into the night, bolstered by much black coffee, with Morgen typing, cutting stencils, handling the flow of requests and orders and through it all maintaining a calm worthy of a battle admiral. He often made the comparison himself, but only to himself. With the work load done, he would dismiss the duty strikers, lock the metal Dutch door, and take over the office for himself.

The first hour was devoted to a thorough clean-up fore and aft. Desks, files, office machines, waste baskets, damage control, and emergency gear. All would get dusted and neatened. Nothing missed Morgen's

61

sharp eye or soft dustcloth. His world had to be squared away before he could indulge the single pleasurable pursuit that was not an official duty. Howie Morgen was a compulsive letter writer.

He would plan the night's batch of letters during his meal hours. Morgen usually ate alone in a corner of the first-class mess. It was known as Morgen's Corner. No sailor dared challenge his right to it and its privacy. Morgen carried too much power over their shipboard lives for anyone to risk his disfavor by challenging him. Occasionally he held brief court to release a choice tidbit of scuttlebutt to which, through his office duties, he had prime access. It was a privilege he never abused. Any information he revealed, he felt the crew was justified in knowing.

Morgen had been writing his letters since he first left home to join the navy almost six years ago. Home was Cleveland Heights, Ohio. Morgen had never been out of Cuyahoga County except for the senior-class autumn trip to the nation's capital. For Morgen, this was a pilgrimage to Mecca, a spiritual experience that would sustain and inspire him for the rest of his life. Because of it, and with his father's blessings, he dropped out of school before Christmas and enlisted in the Navy. The Vietnam war was on. It was the least a patriotic boy could do to serve his country.

From boot camp at Great Lakes, Howie was ordered to Yeoman School at Bainbridge, Maryland. He was an outstanding recruit. He typed ninety words a minute. He broke the school speed record for shorthand. Howie was assigned to the nuclear-powered cruiser *Long Beach* and served in her during a Mediterranean tour of duty. He was transferred to new construction and became a "plank owner" of the new supernuclear cruiser, *Chesapeake*. He re-enlisted when his four-year hitch was up, earned a good conduct medal, and made his first-class stripe a year later.

Now at twenty-three, with five and a half years of service to his country, Howie Morgen believed he had found a way of life well suited to his temperament. He would have liked to finish high school and college.

Now it was too late and it no longer mattered. He was content with his shipload of duties, his unique prestige, his letter writing. If he seemed somewhat odd, he was also a rather nice, quite harmless, and well-meaning young man. He neither smoked nor drank. He led what he wryly described as a clean Christian life. Many young men in the navies of the world do so in spite of the dull or suddenly violent nature of their duty and the crudities of the environment. That they survive in such a dichotomy is a miracle of character and upbringing.

Morgen did not deny himself the company of women when it was available, but he lacked the stamina for lengthy involvements. He had no sweetheart worth remembering. The available favors of liberty port prostitutes were adequate for his low-key needs. He regarded such departures from his puritan routine as necessary as teeth brushing and haircuts. They were followed as soon as possible by sick bay prophylaxis and hot showers. If his conscience troubled him, it was evident only in the renewed vigor with which he attacked his shipboard duties.

He engaged in no religious ritual on board except a patriotic one which involved the twice-daily devotional of raising and lowering a small silk American flag which he had purchased in Tokyo. There were several Jewish men in *Chesapeake*. Morgen avoided them. Yet it amused him to drop a Yiddish or Hebrew expression now and then, to see the reaction it invariably aroused. Who would expect a sailor with straight blond hair and blue eyes, named Morgen yet, to be a Jew?

He was a Jew and a proud one. Long before Howie was born, his father, Chaim Morgenschein, a slave laborer, had seen his parents and sisters herded into the gas chambers at Buchenwald. Chaim helped bury their corpses. He escaped in 1943 and was brought to America in time for the Jewish New Year in October. He kissed the soil in gratitude and vowed undying devotion to his new country, the homeland of freedom and democracy. He regained his health, moved to Cleveland, worked in a laundry, studied English at

63

night, and saved his money. He shortened his name, became a citizen, and married a placid, farm-raised *shiksa* from Ashtabula who had been his floor nurse during an appendectomy at St. Vincent's Charity Hospital. They opened a modest laundry and dry-cleaning establishment with a generous bank loan. The shop on Mayfield Road never failed to observe a national holiday with a lavish display of red, white, and blue bunting, and American flags. A loudspeaker blared "God Bless America." The laundry bundles were plastered with leaflets of Chaim's original patriotic platitudes. Customers were in a mood for it then and, anyway, no one washed cleaner or gave better service than the Morgens. With war's end, he became something of a bore. Some of the second- and third-generation Jews from Chaim's synagogue privately deplored his overt chauvinism, but, knowing his tragic background, none doubted his sincerity.

The business prospered. Chaim contributed generously to the United Fund and the Bellefaire Model Orphanage. He took long walks in the peace and quiet of Cleveland's lovely parks and dutifully visited James A. Garfield's tomb (a nice Sunday walk) and the burial vaults of John D. Rockefeller and Mark Hanna. He switched from the orthodox synagogue to a conservative Heights temple, moved his family into a neat brick home on Blanch Road, and urged his friends and customers to call him Harvey. Harvey Morgen opened two branch stores in the shopping centers of South Euclid and University Heights. He gave generously to the veterans' organizations, and became a popular speaker at the Sunday morning bagel-and-lox breakfasts of the temple brotherhood.

Howard was born the day the war in Europe ended, surely a sign. He was raised in the apartment over the shop surrounded by the red, white and blue artifacts of his father's infatuation with his adopted country. As the firstborn grew, his father never allowed him to forget the Morgen debt to America. Howie had memorized the Pledge of Allegiance when he was five and at eleven had won his school's first prize for a composition entitled: "The Fourth of July—What It Means To Me."

The war in Vietnam provided Chaim with the first opportunity to repay his debt in a truly meaningful way. He was the proudest father in the Heights the day Howie at seventeen quit high school to enlist in the Navy. ("School you can finish anytime, Howie, but a war don't wait.") It was written up in the Cleveland newspapers. Three news services carried the item. The local post of the American Legion presented Harvey Morgen with a testimonial, hand inscribed on simulated parchment, praising the Morgens' selfless act of patriotism. Harvey had authentic copies made and blown up and displayed them in the windows of his shops. Much to his surprise and embarrassment (because it was not at all why he had urged Howie to volunteer), his business more than doubled. From time to time, he posted a blow-up of one of Howie's letters in the window. It never failed to attract interest or business. Everyone agreed you could not find anywhere in Cuyahoga County a more ardently patriotic family than the Morgens. The Morgen success story was an avowal of the American Way.

Howie Morgen at sea went his well-meaning, well-ordered way. He was the exec's right arm. During GQ he was on the bridge as the skipper's JA phone circuit talker. With diligence and good behavior he would make chief within a year. He looked forward to the promotion. It would make available to him new duties and added authority and privilege. He would wear uniforms that closely resembled the uniforms of the commissioned officers. His cap would have a plastic visor and three color changes. He would share chief's mess, the best in any ship. He would sleep in chief's quarters and have the use of the lounge when he tired of his office domain. It would open new worlds for Howie to write home about.

He dwelled on these thoughts for a few moments as *Chesapeake* glided through the night rain toward Point Alpha and her rendezvous with Ha Loi Trung. The office was squared away, the Plan of the Day printed and delivered, the desk neat. He sat before his typewriter, poised like a concert pianist, then slipped a sheet of yellow copy paper into the machine.

First, as always, a letter to his beloved mother and father, with separate enclosures to his two young sisters. Then a letter to Miss Pearl Koluczyk, his spinsterish eighth-grade English teacher who had once told him he had "the talent and sensitivity to be a real writer someday." Howie had his first crush on Miss Koluczyk, who was almost thirty then and subject to unpredictable outbreaks of hives. A letter would go to his old guidance counselor at Cleveland Heights High who had tried to change Howie's mind about the Navy when the time came to serve his country. And a letter would go to the editor of the Cleveland *Plain Dealer*, condemning the rash of campus demonstrations and antiwar protest marches in the Cleveland area. Two of Howie's letters from overseas had already been published in the *Plain Dealer*.

He felt refreshed and cleansed after his nocturnal visit to sick bay and the long hot shower before the ship left Sasebo. He poured himself some black coffee. If there was time tonight he might get one off to the President and the Defense Secretary on the great job they were doing.

And one would go to his congressman, Jarvis McCready. Congressman McCready, who liked to be called "Fireball," was the hottest hawk on Capitol Hill. Morgen had shaken his hand once, during an election campaign back in Cleveland. He liked sending letters to McCready because Morgen always got an answer signed by the congressman himself. Which was more than he ever got from the President and his Defense Secretary.

The night was young and the typewriter ribbon fresh and black. Howie Morgen made a trial run. *I pledge allegiance to the flag of the United States of America and to the republic for which it stands . . .*

The quick brown fox jumped over the lazy dog god dog god dog . . .

He rolled a fresh sheet of paper, crisp and white, with a carbon and copy sheet into the typewriter and set the margins. For a few moments he briskly rubbed the tips of his fingers until they tingled. He began typing with the smooth and deadly accuracy of an expert automatic rifleman.

Dear Mom and Dad ...

VI

The ship bore steadily southward. By the time she cleared Bashi Channel the skies had darkened. The following day she entered the South China Sea in heavy rain. Twelve hours before the scheduled commencement of Operation Wipe Out *Chesapeake* changed to a westward course of 270 degrees true, roughly halfway between Hainan's Cape Bastion and the Paracel Islands. It was an unseasonable rain, the aftermath of a freakish storm that had come out of nowhere and lashed the South Vietnam coastline and now headed north. The seas were running calm with a five-knot wind from the southwest. The night watch was set at a modified condition of readiness with all topside hands in foul-weather gear. Captain Damion devoted a two-minute talk to the crew over the PA system, describing the nature of the dawn operation. General quarters was set for 0500 hours. All was in readiness as *Chesapeake* rode the night sea toward Point Alpha.

At 0100 hours the OOD, a weapons lieutenant named Dace, awakened the captain. The duty officer in Combat Information Center had just reported a surface radar contact a point off the port bow, at a distance of twenty miles.

"Keep tracking," Damion said. He slipped a worn Chinese silk robe over his pajamas and went into the pilothouse and studied the radarscope repeater. Rain fell steadily against the canted windows. Fog enveloped the bow and floated past the bridge in wispy patches.

"How long have we been running in fog, Lieutenant?"

"Since I came on at midnight, Captain."

"Why wasn't I informed?"

"Thought you had been, sir. Sorry."

Damion settled irritably into his high bridge chair on the starboard side. He had been wakened from a dream about Mizu Yokaga in which Mizu and his daughter Angela were one. It was a troubling dream. Its shattering left tiny fragments clinging to his mind. The immediate business of his ship's safety thrust it from his thoughts. The duty officer in CIC was relaying data on the unidentified vessel. "Contact's barely moving, Captain, probably drifting. We're overtaking steadily."

"Is he pinging?"

"Sonar reports no ping, Captain."

"Give me an educated guess."

"Small craft in trouble, probably. A dead whale, maybe. If it's a surfaced sub, Captain, she isn't acting like one."

"We've no subs reported in this area. Keep tracking and advise me of any course or speed changes."

"Aye, Captain."

He scratched his chest, glanced at the bulkhead chronometer, frowned. Why Mizu and Angela? Dreams are weird. He was too rooted in logic to be swayed by dreams. Somehow this one troubled him.

He studied the sweeping arm of the radar screen, pale green and maddening in its impudence, revealing a glow of substance where no eye could see it. Was whatever lay out there in the fog-hung sea worth robbing his crew of three hours of sleep? Or robbing him of his dream? No radar was built yet to tell him that. He swung from the high chair. The watch crew stiffened to

69

attention, facing him. Only the helmsman remained intent on his duty. I'm sorry they do these things, he thought. We need a more comradely world at sea. But he knew it would never work.

"We may as well go to general quarters," he told the OOD.

"Aye, sir." Dace reached for the signal.

"I'll be in my sea cabin, changing."

Damion dressed quickly, abstracted in thought. A small boat adrift. A dead whale. The general alarm vibrated through his body as it did through the ship. *If I had a nickel for all the calls to general quarters I've obeyed....* He heard the familiar clatter of shoes in the passageways and on the steel ladders, Gruff voices, puzzled and vexed. He moved back to the pilothouse and settled in his high chair and stared at the luminous glow of the contact as *Chesapeake* closed the distance.

The PA speaker rasped. "*Plus One.*" Condition Zebra, a state of maximum watertight integrity, was set through the ship. In his mind he saw and heard the metal ringing of scuttles and hatches below decks. His talker, Morgen, panting from his hurried climb to his battle station on the bridge, handed him the phone. "The exec, Captain, asking what's up."

Damion understood the tension. He was jumping the scheduled GQ by more than three hours. "Something adrift out there, Mac. We'll soon know what it is."

The battle watch was relieving the duty watch standers. "*The time is Plus Five.*" The navigator came over strapping his battle helmet under his chin.

"All stations report manned and ready, Captain."

"Thank you, Willie." He saw the question in Wilcox's eyes. "Nothing much. Just playing it safe. Cut me in on the PA system like a good lad."

"Aye, sir."

Damion cleared his throat. "Men, this is your captain. Sorry to turn you out of your sacks before the scheduled GQ. We've picked up a surface contact. It's unidentified. We expect no enemy targets in this area but we want to be in a condition of full readiness. Operation Wipe Out is still our basic mission. We should know what's out there in a few minutes. Stand easy at your stations. The bridge will keep you informed. Thank you."

He turned to the navigator. "A range and bearing, Willie."

"Five thousand yards, Captain. Bearing is two-five-zero true, three-four-zero relative."

"Station extra lookouts in the eyes of the ship. They should wear foul-wather gear and caution them to use the life lines moving fore and aft."

"Aye, Captain."

"Prepare Number Two motor whaleboat with small arms and a .30-caliber machine gun. Have her swung out and the crew standing by for boarding or sea rescue detail."

"Aye, Captain."

"Any answer to our identification request?"

"No, sir."

"Keep asking. What's visibility, Willie?"

"Maybe seven hundred and fifty yards, Captain."

"Slow to fifteen knots."

"Aye, Captain." He passed the order. "All engines slow to fifteen knots."

"Notify ComTaskFor One we are slowing to investigate unidentified surface target. Give our position. Tell him we'll resume Operation Wipe Out and send along details as soon as possible."

Damion flipped a switch on the battle control console. "CIC from Battle One."

"CIC, aye."

"At fifteen knots what's the collision course to the contact?"

"Collision course, Captain. Two-four-seven true."

"Very well. Willie, steer two-four-seven true."

"Aye, Captain. Helmsman, ease your rudder left to two-four-seven true."

"Rudder is left, sir. Coming to two-four-seven."

Chesapeake's progress slowed. Damion watched the lookouts advance carefully along the slippery forecastle deck to their assigned stations. Blackness ahead.

"Slow to ten knots."

Wilcox passed along the order.

"Distance to nearest land, Willie?"

"A hundred twenty-eight miles, Captain, dead ahead."

"And to Ha Loi Trung?"

"A hundred forty, a few points to starboard."

The images coursed through Damion's mind. A sick or snoozing whale. Wreckage. A disabled Viet junk. A downed flyer from one of the Yankee Station aircraft carriers. He felt reasonably relaxed. In the darkened world of CIC, the total air, surface, and subsurface picture was under surveillance by trained electronics technicians. Anything that was not sea alone would be revealed to them with almost visual accuracy in time enough to respond as the situation demanded.

"Range to contact?"

"Fifteen hundred yards closing."

"Alert lookouts. Give searchlight officer range and bearing and orders to stand by for lighting up."

"Aye, sir."

The first sighting came from a lookout posted on the port wing of the bridge. He reported a dim light on a relative bearing of three-five-zero. Damion searched the sector through his binoculars. It was there, flickering weakly in the veils of mist.

"Slow to five knots."

"Engines are slowed to five knots, Captain."

"Weapons control, stand by."

Damion moved briskly to the port wing, tapped the lookout's shoulder. "Well done," he said. He returned to the pilothouse and wiped the lenses of his binoculars. "Light 'er up, Willie."

The powerful beam cut through fog and rain to reveal the shape of a battered coastwise junk. A single kerosene light swung in her gimbals somewhere amidships. Only half her mast remained and she drifted head on to *Chesapeake* with a bad starboard list. Damion could clearly distinguish the good-luck eyes carved and painted on her bow.

"Any crew visible?"

"None reported, Captain."

"All engines stop."

"All engines are stopped, Captain."

"Range?"

"Eleven hundred yards."

Damion went into the pilothouse and flipped the switch for Battle Two. "Commander McKim?"

"McKim here, Captain."

"Mac, would you please come to the bridge?"

"On the double, Captain."

Chesapeake with little way on rose and fell in the gentle rain-washed sea. Damion passed the word to cease all sight reports to the bridge. Commander McKim came into the pilothouse and followed Damion to the chartroom abaft the bridge. "I believe we can secure from general quarters in a few minutes, Mac. But before we do, I'm going to check out this baby."

"Why bother?"

"What do you mean?"

"You'd be taking a hell of a risk, Paul."

"How?"

"These gooks are tricky. That junk could be a Viet Cong booby trap loaded with dynamite."

"Any ideas?"

"I recommend we stand off, blow her sky high with gunfire from one of our five-inch mounts and shove off for Point Alpha."

"Suppose there's life on board?"

"What's a gook life or two compared to this ship full of our own kind?"

Damion's smile revealed nothing. "Thanks, Mac. I did want your opinion."

"You've got it, Paul."

"Have you had a look at that junk?"

"Of course I did."

"Notice anything special about it?"

"Just a plain ordinary coastal junk like a million others cluttering up the area."

"She's a Yabuta, Mac. Ours. Not the enemy's. She's modern with an up-to-date gasoline engine and fiber glass over her wooden hull from waterline to keel."

"So what? She still could booby trap us."

He shook his head. "We've got to board her, Mac, and find out what she's doing alone this far north."

"How do we do that?"

"I'm sending a motor whaleboat alongside."

"And if it's booby-trapped?"

"It's my neck. Not yours."

McKim wiped his red face and tightened his helmet buckle. "I have a feeling your mind was made up, my friend, before you sent for me."

"I like to encourage a free exchange of ideas and opinions among my officers, Mac." They went into the pilothouse together. "Order away the boarding party, Willie. We'll stand off at a thousand yards. Mac, get down there and give verbal instructions to the boat officer and chief boatswain to exercise every caution in boarding. Have 'em keep in radio contact and report back to you. Let me know what they run into. If no one's on board they're to get her papers and registry, and return to the ship. Emphasize minimum delay."

"Aye, Captain."

"Have the crew stand easy at battle stations. Secure the extra lookouts." He flipped the switch to the radio shack. "Advise ComTaskFor One previously unidentified contact is a disabled Yabuta junk. We are investigating for registry, crew, and seaworthiness. Request instructions for disposition."

He took a cup of steaming coffee Cesar handed him, and sipped thoughtfully. *Kill kill kill.* McKim never disappointed him. Yet any minute now might prove the wisdom of McKim's cold hard line and the error of his own more flexible reasoning. For an Oriental life or two, yes, McKim was right. It did not equal the risk to a thousand men and half a billion dollars worth of sophisticated hardware and the American taxpayers' money. But he did not intend to risk his ship and men. And the presence of a Yabuta junk this far north was worth looking into and warranted the delay in proceeding to Point Alpha. And he'd damned well be on station as scheduled.

The motor whaleboat cleared *Chesapeake*'s side and steered a course for the drifting junk a thousand yards abeam. The gun crew of the portside five-inch mount had the muzzle trained on the target. A messenger from the radio shack handed the captain a dispatch from the commanding officer, Task Force One. It read: *Take in custody crew and papers of Yabuta junk. Be-*

74

lieved stolen. Scuttle and resume Operation Wipe Out without further delay.

Damion called for Cesar. "More hot coffee, please. and bring a pot down to Commander McKim with my compliments. You'll find him on Number Two boat deck."

The squawk box came to life. "Captain, this is the exec."

"Go ahead, Mac."

"Boat is alongside the junk and boarding party reports one unarmed Viet with broken arm and bare-ass naked. No others. Mast and steering gear disabled. Gas engine okay but out of fuel. No arms or cargo. Requests further orders."

"Instruct him to take the man in custody, pick up ship's papers if any, open the sea cocks and let her sink. Then return to the ship."

"Aye, Captain."

Damion stretched. "Secure from general quarters, Willie. Secure the searchlight detail. When the boat's aboard, resume our course for Point Alpha at whatever speed's necessary to make up the delay. Send the man to sick bay in custody of the master-at-arms. I'll be in my stateroom below. I'll see the man there if the doctor says it's okay. General quarters as scheduled."

"Aye, Captain."

He went below. Thirty-eight minutes lost. Had it been worth the time? Admiral Pfeiffer seemed to think so.

Damion felt sad about sinking the junk. He had seen the Yabutas under construction in the Saigon yard and undergoing sea trials on the river. They were lovely craft for patrolling small canals and rivers, their shallow draft permitting passage where heavier steel-hulled boats could not go. Each one was custom-built by native craftsmen with adz and hand tools of the hard and durable sao wood of Thailand. Forty feet over all with her high transom and bow, she was as much at home in the open sea as she was cruising a muddy delta canal. It must have taken a brute of a storm to damage her so badly. Or a crew that did not know how to handle her.

75

He remembered the saucy junks with their brightly painted eyes from his boyhood days around Hue. He used to spend hours at the beaches in the Cau Hai lagoon listening with his school friends to the yarns the fishermen spun.

He shaved quickly and stretched out on the davenport to rest until they brought the single survivor to him. *Believed stolen,* the admiral's dispatch had read. . . .

VII

The master-at-arms and the captain's orderly assisted the rescued man in. Sick bay had loaned him a T-shirt and dungarees several sizes too large. He stood with his head bowed, a pitifully thin small man with sunken cheeks and a look of complete dejection about him. Yet he smiled and Damion knew why.

Scared. But you could never be sure with the shy smooth-skinned Orientals. "Sit him down. I'll talk to him alone."

He waited until they left. The man kept his eyes lowered. Damian offered a cigarette. The man shook his head. Damion lighted one for himself.

"I'm your friend," Damion said quietly. "Don't be afraid."

The man looked up, startled to hear his own tongue. His smooth brown face was badly bruised. Sick bay had patched him up efficiently enough but evidences of crusted blood still showed around his right ear. A large discolored welt covered the side of his cheek and head. His arm was thickly bandaged and splinted. His eyes still avoided Damion's.

77

"I was raised in Hue." Damion smiled. "Do you know Hue?"

The man nodded. "I have been there." He looked at the cigarettes. Damion offered the pack again and this time he took one. Damion lighted it and they smoked in silence for a while.

The man was in a state of near exhaustion. The medical officer had released him only on Damion's assurance that the interrogation would be brief and the man permitted to return to sick bay for rest and further treatment.

"What's your name?"

"Chu Tan Vinh."

"Your occupation?"

"Fisherman."

"Your country?"

"South Vietnam."

"May I call you Vinh?"

The man nodded and relaxed.

"My name is Damion, Vinh. I'm captain of this ship. Listen carefully to what I say. Then speak the truth. Do you understand?"

"Yes."

"We have little time so I will not delay. Your boat was a Yabuta junk. From its papers we know it belongs to your government. Did you steal it, Vinh?"

"This is true. We would have returned the boat when we reached home."

"We? Who are the others?"

"My two sons. My father. Also three fishermen from my village. All lost during the storm."

"Where were you going?"

"My father was village chief. The *ly truong*. He was old and dying. His wish was to be buried in our village."

"The boat didn't belong to you."

Vinh hung his head. "It is bad luck to die away from home."

"You had better tell me what happened," Damion said.

He had discovered the boat almost a week ago, Vinh explained. At the mouth of a river near Quang Ngai,

78

tied up for minor repairs. A crew of two stood by to guard her. Vinh said he and his family had been living in a nearby refugee camp where they had been sent from their village to the north.

"What is your village?"

"Ha Loi Trung."

Damion crushed his cigarette. "Go on."

"We were treated badly in the camp." He hesitated. "You have seen these camps?"

"No."

"Life is miserable. The food disgusting to us." His voice dropped to a whisper. "The province officials beat us. They hate us because we are strangers. They steal our government rice and pollute the water we drink."

"How long have you been there?"

"Two years and two months. My wife, my two small children are still there. They told us it would only be for a month or two, until the Viet Cong were cleared from our village." The words poured rapidly now. "Viet Cong agents not long ago came into a permanent resettlement village near us and burned down over two hundred houses. Do we deserve that?"

"Tell me about your village."

"They forced us to leave it. Our families have lived no other place for hundreds of years. Some hid in the jungle and returned after we left. We heard from them. We are told things are better now."

"You mean there are people in the village now?"

Vinh nodded. "They say the fishing is good and no one troubles them. We no longer believe what your people and the government soldiers told us."

"So you stole a boat."

Vinh shrugged. "There were only two crewmen. The others were enjoying themselves in Quang Ngai. We brought them food and got them drunk and were well out to sea before the others returned." He spread his hands. "It was the storm threw us off course."

"Perhaps the Yabuta was too much boat for you to handle."

Vinh shook his head violently. "It was a bad storm.

Swift and violent. There was less fuel than we thought. After that we were helpless."

"Now the junk is gone. You have lost two sons, your father, and your friends. And I must turn you over to the South Vietnamese government for stealing their boat."

Vinh gestured helplessly.

"Why weren't you picked up? The coastline from the DMZ to the Cambodian border is thick with Navy patrol boats. They board and search sampans and junks every day. If you manage to get by them, the radar picket boats would pick you up. And they fly patrol planes all over the area. Weren't you challenged?"

"We ran at night. Without lights. The second morning the storm struck. Yours was the first ship to reach us."

"You were lucky, Vinh. Now you luck's run out. It was a mistake to steal the Yabuta."

"We only wished to return to our homes, Captain. Is this a crime?"

"We'll let your government judge that, Vinh."

"Will I be allowed to return to my village?"

"I don't know."

"My wife and eldest son left by foot to go there with the wives and children of the fishermen who were lost. I would like them to know what happened."

Damion glanced at his watch. "You know, Vinh, that the Viet Cong have large guns near your village?"

"That cannot be true."

"It is true."

"I would have heard."

"How?"

"We get word back and forth almost daily."

"Just three days ago, many American Marines were killed and wounded by heavy artillery guns fired from the vicinity of your village."

"There were no Viet Cong there when we were taken away. That is why we felt it was safe to return. Those who returned first have rebuilt their huts and boats. If the Viet Cong were there, they would have killed them and destroyed everything."

"Why are you so certain?"

"My village hates the Viet Cong."

"How many have returned?"

"Perhaps two hundred. More each day. We hate the crowded refugee camps. We are fishermen. All we ask is to live in peace and fish."

He stared unblinkingly at his feet. Damion, after thinking it over, called for his orderly. "Help this man back to sick bay. His status is prisoner at large. See that he's treated with respect. No brig. No irons. When sick bay releases him, return him to my cabin."

He turned to Chu Tan Vinh. "Go with this Marine. He has instructions to treat you kindly. Let me know if this is not done."

Vinh hung his head. "I'm grateful for my life. I would have given it gladly for those of my father and my two sons."

Damion accompanied him to the stateroom door. "Tell me, Vinh. If your people who returned to the village were ordered to get out, would they do so?"

Vinh shook his head. "My people will not leave again."

"Why do you say that?"

"We have been betrayed too many times."

"You prefer the Viet Cong?"

"All we ask is to be left alone."

"Your village is in danger. I speak the truth, Vinh."

"I believe you, Captain."

"Since you left, the Viet Cong have brought in big guns. We must destroy those guns. Your village cannot escape the damage. Your people will suffer if they do not leave when they are told."

"We have suffered for thirty years. This time we will stay."

"For the last two days leaflets have been dropped from the air, warning your people to evacuate or risk death."

"We would rather die than leave our homes again."

"You are sure of this?"

"We have sworn to it with our blood."

"You swear it to me?"

"We have the same God, Captain."

81

Vinh left in the custody of the captain's orderly. Damion picked up the phone.

"This is the captain. Pass the word at once for the duty communications officer. Have him call me here in my cabin."

He hung up. Cold blood, he thought. He could not dispel the look he had seen in Vinh's eyes. A look he had seen in the eyes of the three Korean prisoners on Yong-hung-do. The ringing phone startled him.

"Captain Damion here."

"Ensign Folger, Captain. Communications watch officer."

"Folger. I want the following message sent plain language without delay to ComTaskFor One."

"Ready, sir."

"Sole survivor Yabuta junk claims two hundred civilians reoccupy his village, target Operation Wipe Out. Insists they will not repeat will not evacuate. Advise."

Ensign Folger read back the message.

"Highest priority, Folger. Plain language. Let me know when you hear." He hung up slowly. Had he said enough in the message? Had he kept the key details of the operation secret in the event of an intercept? Finally, was it any of his damned business?

The answer from Admiral Pfeiffer was delivered fifteen minutes later to Damion's cabin by a messenger from the radio shack.

From: ComTaskFor One
  To: CO/CGN-10

Subject: Operation Wipe Out

  1. Your source unreliable
  2. Proceed with subject operation as
      scheduled.

Damion borrowed the messenger's pencil and scribbled a second dispatch:

From: CO/CGN-10
  To: ComTaskFor One

Subject: Operation Wipe Out

    1. Strongly doubt target village
       evacuated
    2. Request permission delay subject
       operation pending report of leaf-
       let drop.

He had his answer in minutes.

From: ComTaskFor One
  To: CO/CGN-10

Subject: Operation Wipe Out

    1. Carry out your basic orders
       without further delay.

Damion dismissed the messenger. There would be
no more dispatches for the present. He relighted a
half-smoked cigar. His hand trembled. After all the
years of blind obedience to orders he should have
known better. That was the name of the game. That
was what McKim repeatedly told him and McKim was
an honorable man.

He stretched out on the davenport. His thoughts
drifted back to the encounter two days ago with Eric
Stevens. The bitter words still rankled. Why think of it
now? Why drag in Stevens and Yong-hung-do along
with Vinh and Ha Loi Trung?

Why not?

He was in deep trouble and for the first time was
willing to admit it. He sat up, irritable and unable to
relax. The cigar stank. He went into his bathroom and
flushed it away. For a long time he stood at the forward
windows watching the ship's bow nose the night sea.

All hands were recalled to battle stations at 0500.
Chesapeake at battle readiness by 0512 raced through
dirty weather and a murky sea to Point Alpha for the
commencement of her firing run. The storm's intensity
did not slacken. The ship aerographer's weather report

offered no comfort. Damion acknowledged with final resignation a routine dispatch from ComTaskFor One advising of the unavailability of air support either by plane or helicopter from the carrier force on Yankee Station.

On the bridge he felt the familiar waves of tension that precede considered acts of violence. Reports, terse, laconic, filtered to him over half a hundred sound-powered circuits from almost eight hundred battle stations through the ship. Each human, each machine, stood primed to perform its jigsaw fragment of duty when he gave the word.

Command at sea. A business like any other business, he reminded himself. But he knew it was not like any other business in the world. A factory, yes, and a power plant and the daily administration of complicated parts and people. But where on land could one find magic to match the magic of sea command, the single sweeping power over the lives of men and multimillion-dollar machines? A power at once frightening and exhilarating, whether aboard a tin can or a carrier.

How easy to play God, he thought, *how perilous. One must love and honor his fellow man to live with that power untempted.*

He glanced at tense faces under steel helmets in the crowded command post of the pilothouse. The navigator, Wilcox, ticking off with dividers a course leg on the large scale battle chart. His speaker intent on passing to Weapons Control in CIC the exact position from which the Terrier missiles would ride their radar beam to the target. DeMartini, the gravel-voiced chief quartermaster with the shrewd wizened features of an aging jockey, bent over the logbook. The narrow ascetic face of Morgen, the exec's yeoman, pallid and barely visible under the huge radio telephone helmet that carried the captain's battle circuit to all ship's stations.

Plank owners. Assigned to *Chesapeake* before her commissioning. The first team, Damion called them. Handpicked, he remembered with a touch of pride. More than two hundred were sprinkled through the ship's company—in CIC and Weapons Control, in the engineering spaces, in crew's mess during GQ where the nuclear, biological, and chemical warfare teams stood ready, should their highly technical skills be needed. He thought of the World War Two vintage five-inch guns amidships, two comic opera cannons compared to the sophisticated electronics weaponry on board. He smiled to himself. They alone had stood in readiness during the incident with the Yabuta junk. No other weapons on board could have served the purpose as well.

Commander Wilcox joined him. "Coming on station in sixty seconds, Captain, ready for the course change."

"Well done, Willie."

"We took her to forty-five knots without a quiver or a rumble. Held her there for a solid three hours."

"Someday we'll open her up all the way, Willie, and win the Indy 500."

"I'm with you, sir. All we need are wheels." He glanced at the bulkhead chronometer. "Fifteen seconds, sir."

"Very well. You've got the conn. First firing run is northerly. We fire to port."

"Aye, sir." Wilcox moved alongside the helmsman, his eyes on the sweep second hand of the chronometer. "Right standard rudder."

"Rudder's right standard, sir."

"Come to course three-one-five."

"Three-one-five, aye."

"All engines ahead full."

The man on the engine order telegraph thrust the levers forward. "All engines ahead full, sir. Main Control acknowledges. All engines are ahead full."

Morgen approached the captain, wires trailing from his radio telephone. "Weapons Control reports she is locked on target and standing by, Captain."

"Very well. I'll take the conn, Willie."

"All yours, Captain. Eight minutes on this course to Point Alpha."

"Steady on course three-one-five," the helmsman sang out.

Damion pulled the hood of his parka over his helmet and went out to the port wing of the bridge. A lookout grinned and gave way. Damion gripped the rail. Below him on the forward deck the slim taper of the upthrust Terrier missiles' deadly warheads glistened in the rain.

A thing of beauty, a warhead. Immaculate in grace of design. Splendidly functional. Automatically loaded from magazines below decks. Electronically trained, elevated, and fired. Propelled by two stages of solid fuel rockets to a target like a lover to a rendezvous.

Oh yes, beauty and grace and function, he reflected. *Like sea, sky, ship, and men.* Terrier, Talos, Asroc, Polaris. He had launched them all in their terrible grace and beauty. *But never in anger. Never to snuff out living things until now.*

Beyond *Chesapeake*'s rippling bow two hundred miles northward lay Yankee Station, an unmarked place in the heart of the Tonkin Gulf. The gathered might of Task Force One was there and in command the good Admiral Pfeiffer, who had not slept too well this night.

A scant ten miles off *Chesapeake*'s port beam, lost in mist and rain, the village of Ha Loi Trung slept. *But not for long,* reflected Damion. He pushed back the hood of his parka and pulled off his helmet. Rain slashed his face. His freed ears marked its steady beat against the steel deck. And the lookout who asked, "Something wrong, sir?"

"We'll know in a few minutes, son." He glimpsed a young face, a lock of dank hair. A new man. He wondered what the lookout's name was. He wanted to remain there, to talk. There was so much to tell him.

He entered the pilothouse wiping the rain from his face, feeling strangely remote from the scene. His actions and thoughts seemed no longer his own but those of a performer in a play, someone he watched with rapt and fearful attention.

Eight minutes, Wilcox had said. How many remained?

"Course, helmsman?"

"Three-one-five, Captain."

"Speed?"

"Thirty-eight knots."

86

"Point Alpha?"

"Five minutes to Point Alpha," Wilcox said.

"Thank you, Willie."

Now then, Damion, down to business. He flipped a switch on the battle console. "Weapons Control from Battle One."

"Come in, Battle One."

"Captain speaking. Report your condition of readiness."

"Readiness, sir? This station reported—"

"Report, please."

"On course to Point Alpha. Locked on target, Captain. Range is 19,500 yards, closing; bearing, two-seven-zero true, three-one-five relative. All systems GO."

"Very well. You will hold your fire."

"Repeat?"

"Hold your fire. Acknowledge, please."

"Captain, this is the gun boss. I receive you four-oh but do not understand."

"I repeat. Hold your fire. This will be a dry run."

"Aye, Captain. We will hold fire."

Damion unzipped his parka and peeled it off. All eyes were on him. To Wilcox he seemed withdrawn and oddly deliberate in his movements. Morgen took the parka and draped it over the back of the captain's high stool. Damion studied the radarscope repeater. The land mass of the coastline was clearly illuminated each time the search arm swung on it.

"Weapons Control officer on the JA circuit, Captain. He requests permission to speak with you on the bridge."

"Not granted."

The squawk box blared. "Bridge from Battle Two. This is Commander McKim. The captain there?"

Damion went to the squawk box and pressed the talk lever. "This is Captain Damion."

"Paul? Something wrong?"

"Everything's under control, Mac."

"The gun boss reports you're holding fire."

"Roger, Mac. This will be a dry run."

There was a pause, then McKim's voice, crackling with static. "Foul up somewhere?"

"You had better come to the bridge, Mac."

He released the lever and crossed to the console and cut in CIC. "Weapons Control, this is the captain. Keep tracking on target. Hold fire until further orders."

"Aye, Captain."

The bridge watch stood in silence not daring to look at him. Damion checked the compass repeater. "You're four degrees to starboard, helmsman. Steer a proper course."

"Sorry, sir."

Commander McKim, shaking rain like a drenched bulldog, burst through the door and saluted. Damion took his arm. "In the chartroom, Mac." He nodded to Wilcox. "Take the conn, Willie. At point Alpha steer a one-mile boxed course to starboard with ninety-degree turns until further orders." He glanced at the stiffened faces of the bridge watch and grinned. "Stand easy, men. The world's not coming to an end."

"What happened, Paul?"

"The fisherman we picked up. Ha Loi Trung's his village."

"So what?"

"He was on the way back there when the storm hit him. He swears it's not been evacuated and never will be."

"You can't believe these gooks."

"I requested permission from ComTaskFor One to delay until we could be sure."

"What'd he say?"

"Not granted."

"So let's get on with it."

"I can't cut loose with missiles on a fishing village full of innocent people, Mac."

"Innocent my butt! You told us yourself they clobbered a search-and-destroy Marine battalion."

"Charley guns did that."

"Who knows one from the other? They're all gooks. Slopes. Time's running out, Paul!"

"What d'you recommend?"

"Weapons Control open fire the minute we mark Point Alpha."

"I can't do that."

"Why not?"

"It's murder."

"Only if the gook's not lying. Which I doubt."

"He's not lying."

"We've got our orders. Destroy the village. *Orders,* Paul!"

Damion smiled faintly. "We've been over this before, you know."

"How do you mean?"

"Orders versus—other considerations."

"Talk, sure. Theories. This is the real thing."

"The real thing. Yes."

"I'm not about to let you hang yourself."

"It's you I'm worried about, Mac. If I don't carry out the order, they'll want to know why you, as second-in-command, permitted it."

"So carry it out."

"I'm turning command over to you."

"For God's sake, Paul, go back in there and give the order."

The ship heeled to port in her starboard turn. They grabbed for support. "Point Alpha," Damion said. "Relieve me, Mac."

McKim peered at the dim figures of the bridge watch, a tableau of stone images. He drew a damp sleeve across his beefy red face. "I can't do that to you, Paul."

"Then stand by me."

"What?"

"Back me up."

"If you'll carry out the orders, sure!"

"In good conscience, I can't."

"Screw conscience! What about duty?"

The nitty gritty of Nuremburg. "I'm asking once again, Mac. Stand by me."

"Sorry, sir." McKim's jaw stuck out, all God & Country. He settled his helmet firmly and tightened the chin strap.

"Very well. I'm relieving myself of this command—"

"Damn it, Paul, *don't do it!*"

"—and turning it over to you." His tone was gentle, not chiding. "Do your duty, Mac."

McKim stood fast, legs planted apart, all of him a study in suspended frustration.

"I'll make it easy for you." Damion took McKim's arm. McKim angrily shook free. They went into the pilothouse.

Wilcox behind the helmsman nodded. "We've executed the starboard turn, steadying on the first leg of the one-mile course, Captain. Steering zero-four-five."

"Thank you, Willie." He moved forward where they could see him. "I'm turning command of this vessel over to Commander McKim. You will take your orders from him. Quartermaster, please make note of the change in your rough log."

He saluted McKim who saluted in return and muttered, "I relieve you, sir." Wilcox simply stared.

"I'll be in my cabin below." Damion reached for his parka on the high stool. The last face he saw was Yeoman Morgen's, a blurred study in stunned disbelief. The last words he heard were McKim's, crisp and reassuring, ordering *Chesapeake* about, to resume her firing run.

VIII

He dismissed his Marine orderly at the staff elevator. Inside and alone, he pushed the signal for his cabin deck. He stared at the red emergency stop button. To push it, to stalk through the doors back to McKim, to abruptly announce he had changed his mind—that was his immediate duty. He clung to the rail, bent in pain. The harsh reality of what he had done loomed suddenly large and he drove his fist once against the steel elevator panel, gray regulation, unyielding.

Loneliness was an old companion. He had lived with it as a child and at sea and in the dead years after the divorce. But this swift loneliness shut in the gray regulation steel elevator of an abandoned command seemed unbearable. He believed for an insane moment he could not survive it. A man whose love is the sea, who is stripped of his ship, is as dead as any man can be. And Damion knew it. And he knew how weaker men sometimes dealt with it. He wished in that sinking moment to pray but he could not find the words. And he was content to lean back soothing the agony of his bruised knuckles.

He thought of his father, sea bottom now. To Stark Damion a dereliction of duty would be an act of unspeakable treachery, and for a Damion to commit it, impossible. He remembered the mock drills they would run through together—Manila? Hue? Tokyo?— it did not matter. He might have been ten or twelve then. *Abandon ship! Fire and rescue! General quarters!* His battle station was a tree house where his father had mounted an ancient and rusty machine gun salvaged from a beached river boat after the Chinese Communists were dislodged south of the Yangtze in 1936.

He recalled with sudden bitterness that night in Savo Strait when the stupidity of ships' captains and the blundering of admirals wrote in blood the blackest page of Navy history since Pearl Harbor. The impact of that memory calmed him. He found himself at his cabin's level, the elevator stopped, its door wide, and in a confused awareness of his sorry state he wondered how long he had been there.

Down the passageway to his quarters he almost stumbled over a damage control party, the men in their blue dungarees and battle helmets sprawled in various attitudes of rest along the deck outside his door. The men scrambled to their feet. Damion muttered, "As you were!" and went inside. It was clearly evident in their faces they had already learned what he had done. Some with eyes averted had made their judgments.

Somewhere he had read that military commanders should not be judged by the results but by the quality of their effort. *It will be interesting,* he reflected, *to know someday how the quality of my effort here will be measured.*

He had forgotten about Chu Tan Vinh. The fisherman was back from sick bay. He had removed his clothes and squatted naked on the deck in the center of the room. A lighted stub of cigarette hung from a corner of his blue lips. Damion snatched it away and killed it in an ash tray. Vinh sat unmoved with his head bowed and his splinted arm resting on his knees.

"Get up," Damion said sharply. "Put on your clothes."

Vinh rose awkwardly. He managed his dungarees

92

but could not pull the T-shirt over his broken arm. Damion helped him.

"What were you doing?"

"Praying."

There is much to pray for. "Why did you remove your clothes?"

"They are clumsy."

"This is a warship. Not a filthy sampan. Have they fed you?"

Vinh nodded, looking sullen.

"Has anyone mistreated you?"

"No, Captain."

"How do you feel?"

"Stronger."

"You still want to return to Ha Loi Trung?"

"Yes."

"The VC will kill you."

"My father is dead. The village needs me."

God help you. Damion waved him to a chair. His watch showed eight minutes past six. Any minute now the Terriers would fly. He went to his desk phone and dialed the radio shack. "This is Captain Damion. I want you to encode and transmit the following message to Admiral Pfeiffer, ComTaskFor One. His eyes only."

"Captain—"

"Message follows: Unable to execute Operation Wipe Out under existing condition. Therefore, I have—"

"Captain? *Sir!* I have orders not to accept or transmit any messages originated by you."

"Who gave that order?"

"Commander McKim, sir, from Battle One." In the breathing seconds of silence, Damion could almost hear the man's torment. "I'm sorry, Captain."

"Who is this?"

The answer was lost in a deafening roar of missile fire. A violent shudder ran through the cabin. Paint flaked and flew from the bulkheads. Chu Tan Vinh was flung from his chair to the captain's conference table. He cowered under it, his bandaged arm over his face. Damion gripped the desk.

The rockets thundered in steady rhythm. The

launching stations forward of the captain's cabin a scant fifty feet spewed golden streaks of flame visible in brilliant cascades through the forward windows in the gray dawn. The impact rattled dishes and gear, spilled books from the shelves. Eight and a half minutes behind schedule, Damion noted. *McKim will never forgive himself. But I forgive him.*

Ten minutes for the port run. Ten more to starboard. *They will drag like anchors,* he thought. He helped Vinh to his feet and pushed him to a chair and leaned close so Vinh could hear him. "There's nothing to fear. It will soon be over."

Vinh sat transfixed, his lips drawn tight and blue.

"I took away the cigarette because smoking is forbidden when the guns fire."

The rockets blasted westward to awaken Ha Loi Trung.

It's done, Damion reflected. *Finished.* He turned to Vinh. His eyes were sad. "Tell me about your wife and the small children," he said.

Commander McKim on the enclosed bridge conned *Chesapeake* with savage efficiency. The crew took his orders and moved about their duties with a sharpened awareness of some private drama, a gold-braid shenanigan behind this day's action. There was no return fire, no air opposition. Battle Control in CIC reported excellent accuracy. Wilcox navigating saw to the ship's steady helm and true course. *Chesapeake*'s performance that morning was faultless. She raced through the sea from Point Alpha to the end of her firing run as through a full dress battle exercise for points.

McKim stood with Wilcox near the door to the starboard wing of the bridge. He refused to sit in the captain's chair. The cadence of flaming rocket fire did not comfort him. Each deafening blast was a deathblow to his good friend and skipper. It filled him with an angry shame. He leaned close to Wilcox's ear.

"Any word from him?"

Wilcox shook his head. "Only that one call to the radio shack."

"I figured he'd pull some noble stunt like that."

"He'll be okay alone, won't he?"

"Hell yes. Steady as a rock."

"What fouled him up?"

"His damned integrity."

"His Marine orderly's standing by in the passageway, just in case."

"Good." McKim's brow was deeply furrowed. "Got to keep our cool, Willie, hear? Like nothing's happened. Every step counts. Department heads have the word. Soon as the firing run's completed, I'll go down to his cabin." He scratched his chin. "I know what's bugging him. I'll straighten it out."

"I talked to the bridge watch. They're with the skipper a hundred per cent."

"No reason why they shouldn't be," McKim growled. "Everything's squared away, the log, the firing routine. I'm worried about the rest of the ship, though. The word was passed like a shot the minute he went below." His eyes roved over the bridge watch.

"Think somebody yacked?"

"Who knows? Too bad he walked in and spoke up like that. No need for it. I'd have taken over smooth as silk. Could be he slit his throat, Willie. Right before our eyes."

"The crew'll stand by him to a man."

"I hope to hell you're right."

Wilcox checked the time. "In sixty seconds we reverse course for the downhill run."

"Okay. Pass the word." McKim heaved a sigh. "Wish to hell I never was born."

Chesapeake completed her second firing run without incident. McKim picked up the console battle phone and dialed the captain's cabin. "Firing runs are completed, Captain," he said loudly. "We're securing from general quarters and setting our course for Yankee Station. Feeling better, are you?" He hesitated, nodding. "Fine, Captain. Yes, sir." And hung up on silence.

The quartermaster made the necessary log entries. The rest of the bridge watch went along with the exec's loyal little game. All except Morgen. He remained aloof, his stony eyes unyielding.

McKim found Damion with his feet on his desk, a cup of coffee in one hand, a long black cigar in the other. It annoyed McKim to find Damion so relaxed. It seemed positively indecent under the circumstances. But he was also relieved not to find his skipper with a bullet through his head. Such things had happened before.

Chu Tan Vinh leaned against the Dutch door of the galley, probing awkwardly with Cesar for a common denominator of conversation. Their jabbering ceased and they stared at McKim. He felt like an intruder. Damion did not get up to greet him or thank him or congratulate him, as he had hoped the skipper might. Damion never seemed more a stranger and McKim, standing, saluting, thoroughly intimidated, wondered nervously who outranked whom.

"Pull up a chair, Mac. I won't bite you."

McKim glared toward the galley. "Shove off, Cesar. Take your Viet buddy with you." He watched them to the door. "Tell the Marine outside we're not to be disturbed." He turned to Damion, who had observed the proceedings with a faintly amused air. "We're in the clear, Paul. Everything's under control. You can relieve me now." Sweaty, irritated, he stood at attention waiting for Damion to resume the burden of command.

"Help yourself to some coffee, Mac."

McKim went to the galley and poured a cupful and added more cream and sugar than usual. He resisted with great effort a slice of cake on a silver dish. He was suddenly ravenously hungry. "Ready to turn your command over to you, Captain. Like it never happened."

"It's happened, Mac. No getting around it. A matter of record now."

"The record is four-oh." McKim could scarcely conceal his satisfaction. "Log entries read like they should. Operation Wipe Out successfully completed. We're en route Yankee Station."

"There should be an entry in the quartermaster's rough log at about two minutes after 0600 showing that I relieved myself of command and turned the ship over to you."

"It's there. Like you said. It reads 'temporary command' is all. Nothing wrong with that."

"The message I tried to send to Admiral Pfeiffer?"

"Like you never picked up the phone."

"It won't work, Mac. The bridge watch heard everything. The whole ship's got the word. I saw it on the faces of the damage control party when I came down here."

"So you were suddenly taken ill. Upset stomach. We had a routine firing operation and I handled it. No pain, no strain, Paul. All I ask is now is for you to relieve me and take over again."

"No, Mac."

"Damn it, I've just gone through hell for you!"

"Far beyond the call of duty. In fact—"

"Then let's get on with it. Relieve me—"

"—your loyalty to me, Mac, is a direct disloyalty to the Navy. You observed me in the act of disobeying an order. Your duty then was clear, as second-in-command, to carry out that order and you did. Now by trying to cover up for me, by permitting sentimental considerations to get in the way of your duty, you're risking your own good neck. Exactly what I've done, Mac, but for different reasons."

"I don't understand what in hell you're trying to do."

"Trying to protect you, Mac."

"All *I'm* trying to do—" McKim's angry eyes welled. He noisily sipped some coffee and then sat heavily in a chair. "You know me a damn long time, Paul. You know how I look up to you. I tore BuPers apart to get the exec post under you. God knows I'm no Einstein. But this much I know: I speak my mind and I'm not about to sit here and bullshit you about what's right with this world and what's wrong. I swore to do whatever the Navy asked of me when I took my midshipman oath. So did you. Today you made a mistake out there. You're human. We all make mistakes. I covered for you. You would have done the same for me. Now why in hell can't we just pick it up from there?"

"It wasn't a mistake, Mac."

"No smart sailor pisses into the wind, Paul. That's exactly what you're doing."

Damion shrugged. "I've been sitting here trying to dope it out, Mac. Only one thing is clear. Given the same situation, I'd do it again."

"Why crucify yourself?"

Damion stared at the dead ash of his cigar. "I don't know."

"You're home free, Paul!"

"Thanks for the try. There's no backing down now."

"What'll you do?"

"Report the facts personally to Pfeiffer. Like I tried, before you stopped me."

"That could mean a Navy court of inquiry. A court-martial, sure as hell."

Damion yawned. "I'm grabbing some sleep, no matter what." He swung his feet easily from the desk and walked with McKim to the door. "Steer us a straight course to Yankee Station, Mac."

"Have I a choice?" His voice was gruff with emotion.

"None that you'd take." He put his hand on the exec's shoulder. "It's a queer business we're in."

"Meaning what?"

"We're career Navy, right?"

"So what."

"I'm the big war hero. Inchon. Navy Cross. All that jazz."

"Make your point."

"I haven't the guts to kill in cold blood."

"You've guts enough to stand up and say so."

"Let me finish."

"Sorry, sir."

"You, Mac, are a proper Navy type. You obey orders. You kill without conscience."

"Doing my duty is all."

"Exactly. You're tough and dedicated. Everything the ideal Navy officer should be. Duty before anything else."

"Damn right."

"Then why are the tears in your eyes, Mac, and not in mine?"

He came awake sweaty and trembling, wrenching himself from another ugly dream. Daylight filtered through the port across the room. His wrist watch read 0935. He was fully dressed. The ship's vibrations indicated a moderate speed. From habit he reached for the phone to call the bridge, then changed his mind. McKim was in charge. Everything would be under control.

The dream about Angela had shaken him. She had phoned him in the dream and they had met in San Francisco in Ghirardelli Square. He was delighted she called (he was on leave and living in a downtown hotel) and eager to be with her again. She was lovelier than he remembered, fair hair streaming, legs slim and flashing. She kissed him before the world of smiling ladies and gentlemen, all of them nodding, approving, there in Ghirardelli Square. And stood back gripping his arms in her white-gloved hands and spit directly in his face. Held him and in loud harsh words denounced him. Called him filthy names. Between the vileness, she spat and spat again.

He could not break her white-gloved grip though he tried with all his strength. Hatred in her furious face had twisted it to darkened ugliness. Her teeth loomed large between spittled lips drawn in a smile as cold as death. The stylish ladies and gentlemen turned from their strolling and left the luncheon tables to watch with amused smiles. More than anything he felt a crushing shame and humiliation at Angela's performance. Angela who always adored him.

And wrenched himself awake.

He stripped and showered. The trembling eased out of him. A bad dream. That was all. He had stonier problems to face, more immediate in their urgency, but the dream had truly shaken him.

Dressing, he pondered the consequences of his act, to assess his conduct in the Navy's rigid scheme of things. Were I called upon to sit in judgment of a fellow officer, he asked himself, what verdict? His reaction was swift. No mercy. The accused acted deliberately, he would have explained to his fellow judges, committing this dereliction of duty while in full possession of his faculties and in direct disobedience of his orders, the United States then being in a state of war.

That final line amused Damion, always tacked on the tail of charges of Navy misconduct ranging from Silent Contempt to Mutiny on the High Seas. A state of war, *kind of,* he thought, this one not being a declared war, really. Many dead, oh yes, but no war.

He stared at his reflection in the mirror. A familiar face, neither more nor less criminal than before. He searched his eyes for guilt and found none. I could shave, he told himself, and did.

Shaving, he considered guilt. McKim had not hesitated in his choice of duty over conscience. His own feelings on the island off Inchon, when he had killed without hesitation, had been clear. There was no question in his mind about it then. Duty. A job to be done. He had never questioned that judgment since. Why now? After eighteen years?

Was my world so different then? A war was on, I was young and true blue and terribly serious about duty. Still am, he told himself, serious about my duty. But what, precisely, is one's duty in a *kind of* war?

He brushed his hair carefully and went into the cabin.

Cesar brought coffee. Damion sat at the small table and ordered breakfast. He searched the smooth brown face for a hint of change. There was none. Good Cesar. Loyal Cesar. I come to praise you, Cesar. We have cheated and violated and insulted your people for years and you bring me nothing but devotion and love, scrambled eggs and sausage, toast and coffee. *Gracias,* Cesar.

He studied the plan of the day and a copy of the ship's newspaper. The Orioles' Frank Robinson had hit two homers and it looked like student riots all over the nation were getting out of hand.

Cesar brought the food, but Damion was no longer hungry. He chewed some toast and finished the coffee and lighted a small cigar. He tackled the reports and communications on his desk but his heart was no longer in it. He stood moodily at the forward portholes.

A frightening dream. Angela would never behave like that. Angela loved him. He would not tell her about the dream.

Chesapeake slowed her course northward to time her arrival on Yankee Station for early morning. Captain Damion remained in his cabin. Commander McKim saw to the normal routine of a Navy man-o'-war underway. The crew settled down for the night watch.

Yeoman 1/c Morgen that day had labored through his desk duties with an impatience and haste surprising enough to draw whispered comments from his duty strikers. Even Chief Gurney, dropping by the exec's office to idle away an hour, was given short shrift. He retired to the chiefs' lounge muttering sour oaths and threatening punishments, threats that would dissolve like the foundations of his dream house in Redondo Beach.

Alone, Morgen wasted no time. He squared away the typing desk and spun a trial sheet of paper round the roller. This was the big one. It must be letter-perfect. It would speak eloquently of matters close to his heart. Love of country. Sacredness of duty. Loyalty downwards. He struck the keys. The typed words marched like soldiers to the left to the tune of the margin bell and carriage thrust. Straightforward and honest, reported in detail with exactness and precision, it would have warmed the brass heart of a Prussian general.

Morgen told it just as it had happened on *Chesapeake*'s bridge that troubled dawn. The words marched on. His fervor grew. His self-righteous wrath swelled. He was Nathan Hale regretting he had but one life to give for his country. He was the Unknown Soldier adored and mourned by a million mothers both Gold Star and plain. He was young Dreyfus vowing vengeance for the Hun rape of Alsace. He was the anointed avenger of Edith Cavell and Pearl Harbor.

He set it down and read it through. He tightened prose, slashing the outburst to a terse, powerful statement. He punctuated, added emphasis, and retyped a final draft. He sat back sipping hot black coffee and read it again slowly. It pleased and surprised him. It was better than he thought. He was Mark Antony and Edmund Burke. He was the outraged Zola of *J'accuse!*

He filed his carbon copy and folded the original in thirds, envisioning with a touch of nostalgia the flush of pride it would have brought to Miss Pearl Koluczyk's unkissed cheeks. He addressed the envelope and fitted the letter inside, pausing a moment before sealing it. What have I just done to the world of Captain Damion, he wondered. But what has Captain Damion done to *his* own world? *His* country? Morgen hesitated no longer. He sealed and stamped the letter. Marked *Urgent and Personal,* it was on its way to the Honorable Jarvis McCready, Senate Office Building, Washington.

IX

"Fife" Pfeiffer, commanding the American Navy's carrier force off North Vietnam, was one officer smart enough to beat the retirement purge that swept the service soon after World War Two. He rose from humble beginnings to his present three-star rank of vice-admiral while many of his classmates floated to obscurity or sank like stones. He was a shrewd judge of character. His round, cherubic countenance masked a brilliant intellect. He knew how to get where he wanted to go without making waves. Pfeiffer's weakness for cheesecake was Navy legend. ("It must have the consistency of wet cement," the admiral insisted.) His waistline was the Navy's constant source of concern.

Now in his spacious cabin, the admiral read the radioed reports of *Chesapeake*'s delayed action and frowned. He smelled trouble in *Chesapeake*'s command. His chief of staff, Captain Morris, had arranged a helicopter pickup to expedite Captain Damion's arrival on board. Pfeiffer agreed reluctantly. "No sense in stirring things up," he grumbled, "until we know a bit more about what happened." Now somewhat uneasily they awaited the helicopter.

"Paul Damion's not one to foul up," the chief of staff said for the third time. "I trust him completely."

"I trust no one completely," the admiral muttered. "Not you, Moe. Not myself." He tapped the sheaf of radio messages. "Something fishy went on out there. I want to know what."

The intercom console buzzed. Captain Morris flicked a switch and took the message. "Damion's on board and headed this way from the helo pad."

"Fine."

"The fisherman they picked up is with him."

"Treat him as a prisoner of war."

"A civilian, Fife?"

"Let Intelligence handle him and give me a full report."

"Aye, sir."

"I'm seeing Damion alone. Hold all my calls." He frowned. "Clamp full security coverage on all *Chesapeake* radio transmissions. Advise her intelligence officer to censor all outgoing mail."

"Half a dozen bags came on board in Damion's helo."

"Damn!" Pfeiffer thought for a moment. "Let 'em go."

"We could send 'em back to *Chesapeake* for censoring."

"It'd just start a lot of damned scuttlebutt. We still don't know what happened out there, Moe."

"I'll get the word out on the radio check and the mail." He paused at the door. "Want a yeoman here to take notes?"

"I'll call you if I need anything. Right now, no interruptions."

"Good to see you, Paul."

"Thank you, sir."

"The last time was—?"

"The War College in Newport, sir. Five years ago."

"You did well, I recall. I also recall a lovely wife and a leggy young daughter."

104

"Yes, sir."

"How are they?"

"Martha got a divorce four years ago."

"Sorry. The child?"

"Angela. Eighteen and in college. I hear from her regularly." The gentleness as he mentioned his daughter's name did not escape Pfeiffer. "Martha's remarried and quite happy with her new life and husband."

Pfeiffer shook his head. "Divorces. Student riots. Violence. Things happen too fast these days. Angela is where?"

"The University of California campus at Goleta."

"Goleta?"

"Santa Barbara. She's in her first year, studying art."

"You know what John Adams said about that?"

"No, sir."

"Adams said, 'I must study politics and war so that my sons may have the liberty to study mathematics philosophy and commerce so that their children may have the right and privilege to study painting, poetry and music.'"

Damion smiled. "I'm on the right track, then."

"We hope so." He gestured toward the galley. "Thought we'd want privacy. Dismissed my steward. Coffee's on the sideboard."

"None for me, Admiral, thank you."

"Okay, then. Down to business. Those radio requests to delay the mission."

"Yes, sir?"

"What exactly was on your mind?"

"I could not see the military advantage in destroying a village of innocent people, sir."

"The village had been evacuated."

"I had good reason to believe it had not, sir."

"So you opted to disobey orders to save lives."

"Yes, Admiral."

"A commendable attitude—for a Christian missionary, Captain."

"Yes, sir."

"You chose to be a Navy officer, though. Not a missionary."

"Yes, sir."

"Your duty was clearly to obey orders."

"I'm offering no excuses or alibis, sir. I disobeyed orders. I'd be grateful for prompt action in the matter."

Pfeiffer rubbed his jaw. "Relax, will you?"

"Sorry, sir."

"It's a bit irregular," Pfeiffer went on, "talking like this . . . unofficially and off the record. But you're not just any officer, you know. You're the man who brought off the Inchon landing. I feel an obligation to respect that, no matter what you've done since." He gestured. "The door's closed. We're alone. The cabin's not bugged. In other words, Paul, I'm here to help you."

"Thank you, sir, but—"

"I knew your father, you know." He studied Damion's taut face. "You resemble him. Rather startling, matter of fact. He was just about your age when he—was lost."

"I would prefer it, sir," Damion said, "if we could limit this talk to my dereliction of duty."

"Suppose you tell me, then," Pfeiffer said with a shade of annoyance, "exactly what happened out there."

Damion indicated the heavy manila envelope he had brought. "The rough deck log is there, sir."

"In your own words, please."

Damion told his story, omitting no detail. Pfeiffer paced the room for what seemed to Damion an interminably long time. The admiral occasionally glanced at him and twice muttered "Damn!" He lit a cigarette but immediately extinguished it. For several minutes he stared at a bank of closed circuit TV screens, completely absorbed in the carrier's flight deck and hangar space activities. "Big brother," he growled and snapped off the images. "This exec of yours. McKim. What about him?"

The question puzzled Damion. "Mac? Annapolis class of '52. Top quarter of his class. Nuclear program. Skippered a nuclear sub. Eminently capable at all levels. Why do you ask?"

"You threw him one hell of a curve."

106

"Mac behaved well. A true Navy officer all the way."

"Do I detect a note of sarcasm?"

Damion was honestly surprised and said so. The admiral filled a cup with coffee from the Silex at the sideboard. "You've also thrown yourself a curve, Paul. Why?"

"I thought I made that clear, Admiral."

"I refuse to believe an officer of your caliber would deliberately disobey an order. A Navy Cross at twenty-four, an unblemished and distinguished career so far, and one of five four-stripers being considered for flag rank—"

"I had no idea—"

"It's true, Paul. I warned you this conversation would be irregular. I expect you will treat it in confidence. You're highly regarded where it means most. That is why, damn it, I can't believe your action and I refuse to accept it."

"I'm grateful for your trust—"

"My trust, hell! It's the whole damned Navy's!"

"I wish I had a simple explanation for my actions, sir."

Pfeiffer caught the fleeting expression of torment in Damion's eyes. He went to the sideboard and brought out a flat box of cigars, offered one to Damion and took one himself. They unwrapped the fragrant casings from the dark Havanas and lighted up. Damion might have enjoyed the luxury of a forbidden Havana at any other time. Now he was too tense. It did not help matters to know the admiral was stalling to give him time to relax.

Pfeiffer slouched in his deep leather chair. "I'm going to talk about your father, Paul, whether you like it or not. It's because of my admiration for him that I'm taking the time to find out what the hell happened to you out there yesterday morning."

"It had nothing to do—"

"I'll do the talking, Captain. That's an order." He went on in a low, almost dreamy voice. "Stark Damion had everything. Looks, brains, money, a marvelous wit. He had few Navy friends. A social snob, I was told.

Some officers envied him, many snubbed him. To a corn-fed kid like me, from a piss-poor Middle West background, your father personified the glamorous Navy career officer. Diplomatic circles, society capitals, the exotic corners of the world. His career seemed to me a most exciting and desirable way of life for a professional Navy officer. I wanted to live that kind of life."

Smoke spiraled toward the ceiling. In the passageway the watch changed. Voices of the Marine orderlies came clearly to Damion's ears. Shoe leather scraped steel ladders. He tried to recapture the sound of his father's voice, dimmed in memory by the years. A deep voice, he remembered, its timbre blurred now with Admiral Pfeiffer's nasal drawl, indulgent and patronizing.

"We were in the same cruiser squadron. Your father with the flag in *Atlanta,* me aboard *San Francisco,* forward eight-inch turret officer. We met at an officer's club somewhere, Pearl or Noumea, I'm not sure, except it was early in '42. Before the Guadalcanal campaign. I don't know why Stark picked me out, a lousy two-striper fifteen years his junior." Pfeiffer sipped his coffee. "Lonesome, maybe. A bit scared. Like the rest of us." He avoided Damion's steady gaze. "He spoke about you. What a bright kid you were. How proud of you he was. How he missed you. I couldn't figure out why this big, good-looking four-striper in his custom-made uniforms with the chicken guts and campaign ribbons bothered to notice me, but I sure as hell didn't mind. Tickled pink, as a matter of fact. We became very good friends."

"He liked you for what you were. I can understand that."

"Whatever. Then along came Guadal and Savo Island and Ironbottom Sound." Pfeiffer tapped half an inch of ash into a silver dish. Damion shifted uncomfortably. Why can't they leave the dead alone?

". . . and then we ran into the Tokyo Express. November, let me see—" Pfeiffer was saying.

"Friday the thirteenth. In single column through Lunga Channel."

"You've done your homework," said Pfeiffer,

108

pleased. "But you cannot imagine what it was like unless you were there. Flares, star shells, blinding searchlights, flaming oil, screaming men. Half the time, there was no telling our ships from theirs. We were dead with fatigue, outgunned. Slugged it out toe to toe. Stopped the Nip and saved Henderson Field. At a price, of course, *Atlanta*'s flag bridge, where your father—"

Damion jammed the half-smoked cigar into a tray, sending sparks and ashes flying. He stood, his cheeks flushed. "Is this necessary, Admiral?"

"To explain my feeling of obligation, yes."

"I know how my father died. I've read every action report a dozen times."

"He died a hero, Paul. That's precisely why I bring the matter to your attention."

"Why, damn it!"

"How could you, a Navy hero's son and a hero in your own right, fail to carry out a direct order?"

"And how can you sit there and ignore the truth of what happened in Ironbottom Sound?"

"What do you mean?"

"It was *San Francisco*'s main batteries that took *Atlanta* under fire. Your own guns, Admiral."

"Nonsense! *Atlanta* was surprised and hit and left dead in the water early in the action. Salvos from Jap ships at a deadly close range. Scott and most of his staff were wiped out. Much later—"

"Those aren't the facts, Admiral."

"I was there, damn it!"

"Why did Callaghan order 'Cease firing own ships'? Why were eight-inch projectile fragments picked up later aboard *Atlanta* with *San Francisco*'s green dye color?" His voice rose sharply. "Why are you so eager to help me, Admiral? Because you were my father's friend? Or his executioner?"

The color drained from Pfeiffer's cheeks. "That's impertinent, damn it! Your attitude borders dangerously on insubordination."

"You said we'd talk off the record. I'm taking you at your word."

"I'm trying to help you, damn it! You're in trouble,

109

man! Damned serious trouble. Raking up a pack of nasty lies isn't helping one bit."

"My father wrote me almost every day during those early months after Pearl Harbor. He wrote long letters in remarkable detail. You're right when you say he was a snob. And he *was* lonely. But not once in those letters—and I know them by heart—did he mention meeting or knowing you. I suggest, Admiral, with due deference to your rank and excellent record, it's your conscience at work, not any sentimental memories about my father."

It seemed to take Pfeiffer a long time to get out of his leather chair. He picked up *Chesapeake*'s rough log and flipped through it. A light glowed above a push-button on his intercom. He ignored it. After several moments he returned the log to its envelope. His round face, paler now, revealed no emotion.

"We will proceed on an official basis, Captain. Everything on the record. Understood?"

"Yes, sir."

"I find no difficulty in distinguishing duty from sentiment. I'm still your senior officer and I'm not about to stand by and watch a fine Navy officer's career go down the drain."

"Thank you, Admiral."

"Aside from your missionary zeal, could there have been other reasons why you chose not to open fire as your orders demanded?"

"I recall none."

"Think back. Off course, perhaps?"

"We were dead on course. Fire control computers would compensate automatically for any course variation or error."

"Another target? Bogies?"

"All screens were clear, sir."

"Communications breakdown? Bridge to launching platform?"

"All systems were four-oh, Admiral."

Pfeiffer contemplated the end of his dead cigar with a fond expression. "Castro's best. Flown to me from Saigon."

"Sorry I smashed mine."

110

"Have another."

"I'd rather get on."

"You're not very helpful." He carefully relighted the cigar. "Were you feeling all right that morning?"

"Yes, sir."

"It was raining hard. You had taken aboard that Charley fisherman—"

"He wasn't a VC, sir."

The admiral appeared to be preoccupied with his cigar. "Fatigue? Tiredness from that long drive?"

"I had just completed two full days of R & R at Sasebo. The run from Hiro was routine, sir."

"There was that trouble at Sasebo."

"No problem, sir."

Pfeiffer stalked to the open porthole and stared moodily across the carrier's flight deck. Plane crews dressed like gaudy harlequins spotted sleek jets for later takeoff. Voices of the plane crews reached the flag bridge level like the shouts of schoolboys on distant playing fields. Beyond the carrier's deck in all directions warships on station trailed wakes to the horizon. Pfeiffer chose his words carefully.

"I ask you again, Captain, to search your mind for some acceptable reason for your action."

"Why prolong it, sir?" said Damion with some heat. "I've committed a deliberate dereliction of duty—"

"Don't say that!"

"What else can we call it?"

"It's not your responsibility to determine the nature of the violation! Do I make myself clear? I do *not* want to hear that phrase or any like it as long as you and I are discussing the matter."

"Yes, sir."

"I haven't thrown the book at you, have I? Don't throw it at me. When the time comes to sit in judgment, you can damned well be sure we'll go by the book."

The outburst must have tired him. He breathed more heavily. The rebuke had also unnerved Damion. He sat in sullen troubled silence like a punished child.

"What was it like out there?"

"What do you mean, sir?"

111

"The weather, damn it!"

"Overcast, a hard steady rain, wind velocity to fifteen knots. Visibility under five hundred yards. It's all there in the rough log, Admiral."

Pfeiffer picked up the log and reached for his glasses on his desk. He turned the pages slowly and carefully now, reading the quartermaster's penciled entries. The cabin was quiet. Damion went to the sideboard and poured coffee for himself and stood alone studying the pictures and souvenirs hung along the bulkhead. Hallowed names of men and ships. Trinkets dear to the hearts of fighting men. A jagged steel fragment framed in velvet. A Navy sword in its scabbard. He turned away.

"I see nothing here," Pfeiffer said slowly, still reading, "to indicate a skipper not performing his duties."

"Commander McKim saw to that, sir."

"You mean the log has been altered?"

"It's been deliberately written to relieve me of any embarrassment."

"Is it an accurate and honest log?"

"Technically, yes."

"A questionable kind of loyalty," Pfeiffer said, but Damion observed that he was not displeased. The admiral peered at him over the rims of his glasses. "Do you suppose an officer as dedicated—you said 'true blue'?—as your Commander McKim would go to such extremes to protect his commanding officer, if such a show of loyalty weren't deserved?"

Damion said nothing.

"And I presume," Pfeiffer went on, "a bridge full of officers and enlisted men at battle stations could not help overhear what went on."

"They know."

"And are ready to risk their rates and rank to cover for you."

"I suppose so."

"The log clearly shows it."

"A loyal crew, yes."

"Speak up!"

"I said, sir, they are a loyal crew."

"What about your loyalty to them?"

112

"I feel a deeper loyalty to my conscience."

"Where has that alleged conscience of yours been all these Navy years?"

"I don't know."

"Where the hell was it at Inchon?"

Damion thought about it. "It's only since Inchon, Admiral, that I began to feel anything like conscience."

"And why Inchon?"

"I never killed before Inchon."

"Would you kill now? Today? If this carrier were attacked and boarded by an enemy?"

"Are you serious?"

"Damned right I'm serious. I want to know what makes Paul Damion tick."

"I would do my duty without question."

"You would kill."

"I suppose so."

"You still have doubts."

Damion drained his coffeecup. When he spoke, it was with a fresh vigor that surprised the admiral. "Every moment of my adult like has been geared to obey orders without question. I still believe, given the circumstances you just described, I would not hesitate to kill."

"And could not give that order the other morning off the DMZ."

"No, sir."

"You're being inconsistent."

"Does that make me less a Navy officer?"

"Yes, damn it."

Damion searched the admiral's impassive face. "I can't believe in this day and age the measure of an officer must be his willingness to kill."

"Killing is the business we're in, Captain."

"Those were the demands of another day."

"Damn it, it's no different today!"

"The circumstances are different, sir. We're not officially at war. Here was this half-drowned fisherman. He'd been through hell. All he wanted was a chance to return to his village and rejoin his family. He was a living breathing human being like any number of Vietnamese fishermen whose kids I used to play with around

113

Hue. He assured me the village was occupied. I believed him. All I requested from you, Admiral, was time to make sure."

"We'll take that up soon enough," Pfeiffer said dryly. "I still refuse to fault you for a single error of judgment." He tossed aside the logbook. "Thanks to your exec, there's nothing in the record to warrant further inquiry. Your mission was accomplished—"

"And two hundred innocent civilians are dead or dying in Ha Loi Trung."

The admiral turned on his heel. At his desk he thumbed savagely through a thick file of dispatches, tore one loose, and thrust it at Damion. Damion read it, glanced at Pfeiffer, and read it again. He handed it back, badly shaken.

"We got there as soon as we had flying weather," Pfeiffer explained. "Because of your urgent messages and an unadmiral-like sentimentality, I requested extraclose photo coverage. The Viet Cong guns were wiped out. A few huts in the north portion of the village were destroyed. The rest of the village is intact. We found no evidence of life or occupancy anywhere in the village area."

"I find that hard to believe."

"My pilots don't lie."

"The village people could have been wiped out."

"This morning at dawn a search-and-destroy team went in on my orders to mop up. Eighteen dead VC at the gun emplacement—a well-constructed, far-from-temporary installation. No sign anywhere of the village having been occupied since we dropped leaflets."

"He really sold me," Damion said slowly. "Chu Tan Vinh. His father had died, he said. The village chief. He was going back—"

"A pack of lies."

"I belived him."

"Does he matter? One Vietnamese? A hundred? A thousand? Compared to the lives of our own American boys?"

After a long silence Damion said, "Yes. He matters."

"I begin to wonder about you," the admiral said.

114

"Human beings," Damion said slowly, "matter."

"Human beings? A filthy gook fisherman? An enemy agent? Whose life you saved? Who lied to you? Betrayed your trust? Made a fool of you?" He studied Damion's face. "Knowing him for what he is, would you still hesitate to carry out those orders?"

Damion took in the draped sword, the ribbons of chivalry and triumph, the brave faces in their frames of history, blurred and taunting.

"I don't know," he muttered. "I really don't know."

"When'd you have your last medical checkup?"

"Before we left the States."

"Your last leave?"

"Same time, Ten months ago."

"Where'd you spend it?"

"Aboardship. Pier Echo, Long Beach."

"You call that leave?"

"We had some complicated reactor work left over from the shakedown run." He hesitated. "I managed to get to Carmel for a few days."

"You have enough expert technicians on board and available from the yard to supervise any shipboard work. It's imperative commanding officers take Rest & Recreation when it's provided."

"Yes, sir."

"We *all* push ourselves too hard." He dragged on his cigar. "Remember those World War Two typhoons? Halsey lost a few tin cans, a lot of men, and there was hell to pay on some of the light carriers. Raised a big enough stink to call up a Navy board of inquiry. The board blamed it all on Bull's lack of judgment. Between you and me, he deserved it. The board ruled him guilty as hell but excused him on the grounds of battle fatigue resulting from the strain of his command duties."

"I'm under no such strain, Admiral. I was in full possession of my faculties when I issued the order to hold fire and when I relieved myself of my command."

"You sound proud of what you've done."

"Not proud, Admiral."

"Would you do it again?"

Damion thought about it. "Must I answer that?"

"You damned well must."

Damion remained silent for long seconds. "I'm not sure."

"It's a command decision," Pfeiffer said impatiently. "There can only be one answer. Either you would or you would not."

"I probably would," said Damion with a wretched look. "But it's something I must find out for myself."

Pfeiffer strode to his desk and flipped a switch. "Moe? I want the senior medical officer available immediately in sick bay for a complete physical on Captain Damion. The captain will be down there in five minutes." He turned scowling to Damion who stood at attention. "I'm authorizing a thirty-day leave, Captain, R & R, commencing noon today. Immediately following the checkup, you will return to your command. Your exec will assume duties as acting commanding officer until either a qualified four-striper replacement or you reports on board. Air transportation will be provided to the States. You're wound up tighter'n a tick, man. So grab yourself a good vacation."

Damion began to say something. The admiral held up his hand. "I've heard all I want from you, both on and off the record. I make my decisions hard and fast and stand or fall by them." He chuckled. "So far I've managed to stand." He took Damion's arm and walked with him to the door. "You a poker player, Paul?"

"Not really."

"One of the basic strategies of poker playing is to learn by heart the odds against winning with any particular hand. For instance, the odds against being dealt three-of-a-kind with a fifty-two-card pack, nothing wild, are about 46 to one. A full house, maybe 670 to one. A royal flush, about 650,000 to one. I make it my business to know the odds, the relative values of each hand, what sort of hand it will take to win the pot. And I study my opponents, learn their habits, estimate their probable strength or weakness from their tiniest actions and mannerisms. At the same time I try not to tip my own mitt."

"Yes, sir."

"I usually win. So much for poker. The odds on

116

Captain Damion's career are just as predictable. If we stick to the rough deck log, a clear and routine record, we have an even chance as far as your career is concerned. I'm willing to go along with that, if you are. For the same reason a Navy board of inquiry went along with Bull Halsey after those typhoons. On the other hand, should you tip your mitt and the word gets out to the newspapers and networks and that yelping pack of Navy critics both inside and outside the Pentagon on what really happened, then your career has less of a chance than a snowball in hell."

"If there's a choice—"

"You're not getting a choice. You're getting thirty days State-side leave and that's an order."

"Yes, sir."

"You're buying time to think. So am I. Admirals aren't suppose to be confused, you know. But you've done a good job on me this morning."

"Sorry, sir."

"There's more at stake than you may think. It's not only that I'm reluctant to throw a career officer of your caliber and background to the wolves. We've few enough top-rank men as it is. In this man's Navy, we protect our own. And deal with our problems as we see fit. The Navy's public image lately leaves much to be desired. An error of judgment like yours, in the wrong hands, can be blown up into a service scandal of major proportion." He paused for a moment with his hand on the doorknob. "Even the best poker players sometimes make errors of judgment, Paul. I made one this morning and I owe you an apology."

Damion murmured his doubts. Pfeiffer looked him squarely in the eye. "You were dead right about your father and me. I met him once, yes. A routine introduction in a large group. He was polite, that was all. But I did envy and admire him." He shrugged. "My old man ran a small slaughterhouse outside Des Moines. Lost it in the bank crash. I was butchering hogs when I was sixteen to work my way through school."

"Why make up a yarn like that?"

"We act sometimes without understanding why,

117

don't we? You've made that crystal clear to me. Which explains why you're getting thirty days of grace instead of an official reprimand or worse."

"I'm grateful, Admiral."

"It was no guilty conscience that prompted my stupid lie. Whatever it was, it was not that." A brusque formality stiffened his words. "It was unfortunate that *San Francisco*'s eight-inch guns raked *Atlanta*'s flag bridge. Regrets I have. But not guilt, damn it! It was not *Atlanta* we were trying to hit. It was a Jap ship the other side of her. With a short range and low trajectory—" He shrugged. "All I can say now is, I did my duty. That was all. So did you at Inchon. With honor. In this man's Navy, you're entitled to your own beliefs and precious few mistakes. It would be a mistake to allow those beliefs to stand in the way of your duty. Don't forget that." He ignored Damion's parting salute. "The Marine orderly will escort you to sick bay. Our flight surgeon is Captain Comroe. He's waiting for you. Your new orders will be cut immediately and on board *Chesapeake* within the hour."

"Thanks, Admiral."

"You haven't much to be thankful for," Pfeiffer said dryly. He rubbed his jaw. "Let's see . . . I'm notifying CinCPacFleet of your situation. When you're Stateside, Commandant, Twelfth Naval District, Treasure Island, should be advised of your whereabouts."

He nodded and closed the door. Damion stood in the passageway faced with a stiffly saluting Marine corporal. He bleakly returned the salute and fell in step behind the straight crisply pressed khaki back, his mind a sorrowing blank.

Pfeiffer in his cabin phoned the carrier's flight surgeon. "Paul Damion's on the way to sick bay, Captain. I want it to be a thorough physical, hear? Thorough enough to warrant a thirty-day R & R leave."

He lighted a fresh cigar and cut in the bank of closed-circuit TV screens. He stared moodily at the variety of shipboard activities. *Could have been my guns,* he reflected sourly.

118

Who the hell knew, once the shit hit the electric fan? All of those pitch black task force clambakes off Savo and Guadal that racking cruel summer and fall of '42 were laced with bloody deeds of courage and confusion. How the hell do they expect to sort out the pieces with half the men and ships in the mucky bottom of the Slot? No sooner a battle's done, the post-mortem historians move in like vultures to a freshly slaughtered corpse and gorge themselves on the tragic mistakes and costly errors and puke up their judgments by the gutful. Can they ever know what it really is like?

The dribbling fear. Gun thunder and men's screams. Torn flesh and spitted limbs. The bright-colored coils of insides in lamplight. The raw stink of fear mixed with the acid sweat and cordite inside a blood-splashed cement mixer of a turret with three eight-inch guns at 120 degrees. With three of your ship's sisters named *Astoria, Quincy,* and *Vincennes* already on the bottom, do you stick your head out into the starry night to see if the skipper has slanty eyes before you open fire? And crawling back to Pearl with fifteen holes ripped into your steel gut and empty spaces where men should be at muster, for whom do you grieve?

Except for the morbidly curious and a handful of widows and mothers, who the hell cares how it happened? *Why* is what matters. Which is Damion's point, damn it. And damn him. Ten more minutes of his smug all-suffering face and I'd be bleeding at the heart along with him.

Pfeiffer cursed. He peered into the empty galley, opened the small refrigerator, searched for a moment, slammed it shut. He dropped into a leather chair and drew hard on his cigar. He could not shake the image of Paul Damion's face, so much like his father's. That clear, unnerving gaze from two deep recesses under straight brows; the bony nose reddened by wind and sea; firm lines of mouth and jaw; the look of quiet strength and reserve. Respectful, yet forbidding intimacy. A strange breed of cat, this Damion. Too bad he was no poker player. A good man to match bluffs with.

The admiral sighed and thought again of food. He crossed the cabin and rang for his steward. He switched off the closed-circuit screens and snapped on the big intercom console panel. "I'm back in business, Moe. Open up your Pandora's box."

The lights blinked on like a pinball machine. From the galley came a clatter of the steward among his pots and pans. Pfeiffer glumly envisioned a wedge of soupy apple pie with a pale cardboard crust. He hastily changed the image to a lead-heavy slab of gritty and too-sweet coconut cake. The steward's specialties. Pfeiffer patted the ample arc of his stomach while he dealt routinely with the console of flashing lights. He snapped orders and acknowledged routine reports. The steward came in. Pfeiffer asked for fresh coffee and "something sweet."

"Apple pie, Admiral? Is delicious."

The admiral shook his head.

"Coconut pie, sir. Fresh out of the oven."

Pfeiffer closed his eyes. "Apple pie, thank you. Dry."

Whoever got the idea all Filipinos are great cooks? He winced. In a few months he'd be free of it. Back on the beach for one Stateside tour of duty in Dago before retirement. Then he'd let go. The hell with the pounds. There was one shop in all of California that knew a damned thing about cheesecake. Honest-to-God, creamy thick cheesecake with an honest-to-God crust, not made with those goddam graham crackers, its purity not mongrelized by sour cream or gooey fruit toppings. Just plain old-fashioned rib-sticking mouth-watering cheesecake, the kind his old Hessian grandmother used to make, back in Des Moines.

A fast chopper could get him from Coronado to Long Beach in less than an hour. The same for a fast Navy driver to Beverly Hills. If it was Sunday and the clean and sweet-smelling bakery on Beverly Drive was closed, he'd damn well order it opened. He'd done it once before, hadn't he? And he would sit at one of the small round tables with the big-breasted gaunt Bavarian wife of the morose refugee who baked the best damn cheesecake in California and wash it down with hot fragrant coffee laced with thick cream and admire the bad paintings of the Alps hung wherever there was room along the walls. Then a *Sachertorte* or two and a dozen *schnecken* for the trip back. Rank still has a *few* privileges, damn it, including the privilege of gluttony.

The steward appeared with coffee and pie. The admiral studied it as though it had just died. He grimly picked up his fork and began to eat. Rank also had its obligations.

An hour later Damion's helicopter lifted him from the carrier's deck and noisily threshed the air toward *Chesapeake* four miles dead astern. Damion ordered the pilot to take her up. "I want a real look," he said.

The helo climbed. In the blue Tonkin Gulf below, the sea might of America spread, slate-colored, bullet-shaped, an awesome armada. Tiny ribbons of bright color were signal flags flapping at the halyards. The formation swung into the wind, ships' wakes like egret plumes trailing. One by one with split-second precision the carrier's Phantom jets shot from her catapults, roared into the sky, and streaked toward the racked green land to the west. Damion watched them until they became specks too small for the eye to follow.

Above him the sun. Below, all that ever gave meaning and purpose to his life. He nodded to the pilot and the helo dropped toward *Chesapeake*'s fantail. Damion thought of Chu Tan Vinh who had betrayed him. Of all that happened, this pained most. In the face of Chu Tan Vinh he had seen the faces of his teen-aged schoolmates in Hue. Their code had been honor and trust. He had taken this for granted when he spoke with Chu Tan Vinh.

Trust? Could he trust the admiral again who had revealed himself in a foolish and vain lie?

Honor? Whom do you honor more than your father? If you love your father (and oh yes he had loved his father) you honor him by doing what you can to live in his image. Because that is what a father cherishes most, a son in his image. Damion had done that with joy, the boy dreaming of himself at his father's side. In the dream it was the sea, but it could have been anything, anything his father wanted it to be as long as

121

they were together, the boy and the man who was the boy.

But they put an end to that. In Savo Strait they brought it to a violent end, all of that boyish dream.

Eric Stevens had said it well. There is a difference that makes hopeless enemies of men. Damion was beginning to understand that difference every time a day dawned. Beginning to detect the enemy where he had never dreamed the enemy would be.

"We're down, Captain," the pilot said.

Damion climbed out of the helo. Whom can I believe, he wondered, except myself? The loner who risks all to serve some purpose more exalted than his own.

As I did at Inchon.

As I am doing now.

X

Angela in the cheerless attic room laughed and her voice gave brightness to the gloom. She dressed with the languor of a woman well loved. A thin square of blanket draped over the shadeless attic window blocked the afternoon sun. A man slept naked on a mattress on the floor. She watched him fondly, standing slimlegged, willowy, dressed to travel, pulling the brush through her long hair.

She went to the edge of the bed and gently rocked him. "Brown," she said. He slept on, his breathing heavy and full. Her hands moved over the hard-muscled body, curly hair matted with sweat. He stirred, groaned, and turning, opened his eyes unblinking, wide and steady on her face, sitting up as soldiers do, alert and ready.

"I'm going, Brown."

He reached with big hands and pulled her close. Her hair, so carefully brushed, fanned over their heads. Her lips grazed his ear, cheeks. He held her. "C'mon," he said softly. His hands moved over her.

"It's late, Brown. I'll never make it back in time."

"Don't go."

"Ah, Brown . . ."

"One more."

She pulled away laughing. "You're terrible."

"Love me?"

"You better believe it."

He sat admiring her, brushed her silken hair from his lips. Not believing his luck.

"It's a long drive, Brown. I better go."

"Drop me off near the campus."

"If you hurry." She retrieved her hairbrush from her bag. "I'll bring you a mirror next weekend."

"I can buy a mirror."

"Buy your books. I've practically moved in, haven't I? I'll take care of the knickknacks."

He dressed quickly. Soiled shorts, patched dungarees, a threadbare denim shirt, unkempt hair. GI boots. No socks. They went down the rickety stairs to her car. He carried a worn leather jacket slung over one shoulder. She swung her pouchy leather shoulder bag, happy as a schoolgirl.

She let him out at a garage near the campus while she had the tank filled. He looked forlorn. "You'll be back?"

"Next Friday, Brown."

"I need you," he said.

Her heart went out to him. She reached her face toward him. He turned away. "You won't be back," he said. He started across the street and did not turn to look again.

She drove south from the city toward the ocean and Monterey, following the narrow scenic drive down the coast, rather than the truck-rumbling concrete freeway. It seemed more in character with the weekend spent with Brown. It was their third weekend. Like being married, she told herself.

North of Salinas she swung west to Monterey and south on the coast road toward Big Sur. She had lived with her parents one summer at Carmel, when her father pursued postgraduate studies at the Naval School on the grounds of the old Del Monte Hotel.

124

A time now to remember. The brute surf. The transparent quaintness of the artsy-craftsy which her mother adored. Early morning walks with her father along the beach. Cold memories now. Her mother a strange Mrs. Coddington. Her father somewhere in the Pacific, more than ever a stranger. She did not like to think of that.

Skirting the Seventeen Mile Drive, she could not contain a tremor of apprehension. Somewhere nearby, her mother preened in her Pebble Beach paradise in her clique of garrulous and empty-headed peahens. Just my luck, Angela mused, to run head-on into Mother in her fake shooting tweeds, tooting back from some stupid social endeavor. The weekend with Brown had gone too well. Something must certainly mar it.

She truly believed it. Disappointment came often to Angela Damion. It seemed to have begun with the divorce, which in some pathological twist her mother blamed on Angela. "After all," Martha had said, between crocodile tears, "it's *your* happiness, *your* social future I'm thinking of."

To Angela it was like a death in the family. No one and nothing could replace the legal loss of her father. The widower Duane Coddington II proved a poor substitute. He was tony and bald, his old settler and whaling blood thinned by three generations of soft living and moneylending. His two teen-aged daughters were younger than Angela, overripe and insolent and already dating and mating in the swinging California way.

After six months of romantic fumblings and a week of hardnosed but cautious inquiry into her holdings and Navy allotments, Coddington married Angela's mother. He moved the two of them out of the prim Cape Cod in Kentfield into "Cypress Crotch," the Coddingtons' sprawling ancestral ranch house, not too distant from Pebble Beach's Cypress Point.

He figured it a good deal. He had a mother for his spoiled brats on the premises again. Following the departure of the fifth outraged housekeeper, he had given up in despair on the care and feeding of his flock. A pragmatic type, he recognized in Martha the qualities

125

he needed. She went well with his private banking practice. She adapted readily to the essential social graces and displayed a proper deference for capital gains.

In the morning glow of that second marriage there were brief moments of promising compatibility. But the ménage was doomed. The Coddington girls were long on lust and death on competition. Their initial curiosity rapidly faded into overt malice and a campaign of adolescent cruelties. Using their father's financial edge as a sword, they cut Angela from their cronies. They made it clear to the boys they bedded that laughing Angela with the smooth skin and lovely legs was like off limits. They intimated that her bra was like padded and her breath was like bad and anyone seen fraternizing with her would be like cut dead.

The mischief worked. Angela was snubbed. Tuned out, the Coddingtons called it. Martha in her rewed bliss was swept up in the social life she had always yearned for. She seemed blind to Angela's plight and bent backwards to coddle the Coddington brats. They were sly enough to deceive her and leave the impression that they and Angela got along just fine.

For Martha the new life was a convenient but not ecstatic change. Her husband made occasional business trips East without her. She sometimes wondered who was serving him at the other end. These were different from Paul's absences. She had really never suspected Paul of infidelity except with the Navy. Not even with the crippled Mizu. But that was Martha. After four years with no husband at all and one narrow escape from a meaty-handed golf pro who almost raped her, she was happy to settle for Coddington. Winning him was an ego-pleasing triumph. He was regarded as a prize in spite of his stuffiness and the added handicap of his two teen-aged swingers.

His talents as a bed partner left much to be desired. His preliminary love play invariably consisted of a dollar-by-dollar, deal-by-deal recital of the day's business. She realized with some regret what a good thing she had had in Paul Damion. But sex, she reassured herself, wasn't everything. Being Mrs. Duane Coddington

Two of Pebble Beach was as close to her dreams of an ideal existence she was ever going to get.

It was an upper crust hell for Angela, who hated everything it meant. After her mother's first few refusals to believe her, she kept her feelings to herself. She was like her father, incapable of self-pity, resourceful under pressure, a loner.

Her weekly letters to him revealed none of the Cinderella torment she endured. It was Angela's romantic nature to believe in the handsome prince and a glass slipper that fitted her foot alone. She wept for joy when she went off to the Cal campus at Santa Barbara. The red sports car was a gift from her mother, bought with the money saved from the allotment her father still provided for Angela's support, bought as well with a vague sense of guilt that somehow she had let her daughter down.

Angela roomed with a plump pot-smoking art major who had come to Cal on a sculpture scholarship from Beverly Hills High. Her name was Daphne Murdock. Her mother was a bit actress. Her father wrote telescripts for a sluggish daytime suds opera. Angela, in awe of Daphne's four-letter words and her airy sophistication, mistook it for budding genius. She allowed herself to be convinced that Daphne's sculptured creations in welded steel and found objects, and her experiments in such media as stale sourdough bread and twisted sardine cans, presaged a new dawn in the mainstream of three-dimensional art. She spent much of her spare time driving Daphne around city dumps and day-old bakeries as far distant as Santa Maria and Ojai to locate stale loaves and discarded cans (sild and brisling preferred). She told Daphne of her problems at home. She admired Daphne's casual views on premarital sex but could not bring herself, during the first months of freshman dating, to venture past "making out" to "making it." She tried pot once and had the courage to confess it did nothing for her except make her head ache. She was content to go along with Daphne's downbeat and brittle company of campus hippies. She needed friends. They in turn were attracted to her innocence and naïveté. She made them feel deliriously ancient and corrupt. Burned out. Totaled. She provided a convenient foil for their despair, reminding them of their own betrayed idealism and youth.

And suddenly Brown.

Two weeks before, she had been driving on the same road, headed north this time to Pebble Beach and another deadly weekend with the Coddingtons. She had stopped at a gas station near Morro Bay to check the oil and water before the winding and often perilous drive high above the sea.

Brown stood at the highway's edge, a chunky young man, his eyes unseen behind large round sunglasses. After a moment he came over. His voice was soft. "Going north, miss?"

She nodded. It was obvious.

"How's about a lift to Frisco?"

The forbidden word. She saw him clearly now. Eastern, urban, brash, dangerous. Risky business. You read about it every day. Her flesh tingled. She wanted to lie, to say she was only going another mile or so. He took off his glasses and wiped them on a soiled blue shirttail. His steady brown eyes unnerved her. "Never mind," he said.

"I'm sorry."

"Scared, too." His eyes were half-lidded, challenging. "Like—"

"Not at all—"

"—maybe I'll rape you or something?" Surprisingly he smiled, looked northward to the winding mountain road, squinting and not at all angry.

"That was uncalled for," Angela said.

He shrugged. "I got a little sunstroke standing out there, maybe."

"Have you been waiting long?"

"Two-three hours." He opened the small valise he carried and pulled out a finger-stained envelope. "I'm headed for college." She did not miss the edge of quiet pride and looked quickly into his face. "Brown's the name."

"Good for you, Mr. Brown."

She saw the letter from the admissions office of a San Francisco college. He folded it and tucked it back into its envelope before she could read his name. His anxious eyes looked to the south this time. Cars were approaching, headed north. The station attendant slammed down the hood. Angela handed him a credit card. Brown started to go.

"Been hitching long?" she asked.

"Left New York, let's see, a week ago yesterday."

"That's making very good time, isn't it?"

"Day and night, it ain't too bad." He looked at her with renewed interest. "Like I could help with the driving."

"I'm only going as far as Monterey."

She signed the charge slip and stuffed the receipt in her purse. Sixty dollars in that purse, she remembered. She regarded Brown thoughtfully. "Look, I really think you're okay but I just am too damn scared to take a chance. You understand?"

He shrugged. "I don't blame you, baby."

"Can I lend you bus fare?"

"Ever meet anyone on a bus worth talking to?" He reached into his jeans not angry, more like a man resigned to losing. He pulled out a thick roll of bills. It seemed silly at first to Angela, like a scene out of an old gangster movie. But again, the look of quiet pride.

"Never mind," he said. "I'll get there."

He took up his old stand on the highway. She started the motor, strangely elated, relieved to be free of him. She was safe. She had made a kind offer and she felt less guilty. But less guilty of *what* she was not sure.

Ahead lay deadly boredom. A weekend of her mother's prattling, the transparent plotting and vicious nipping of those two *caribes,* her stepsisters, and Coddington's tiresome elegies to capital gains. She had given up a beach house party weekend with Daphne's crowd. Daphne's motherly concern touched Angela. Her parting words had been, "Look, baby, you owe those ice water squares but nothing. Get smart. Start doing something for lil ol' Number One." She gave Angela a wet kiss reeking of grass. "Why go to *those* strangers for your fun?"

129

Angela swung onto the highway alongside Brown. "Get in," she said.

She never made it to Cypress Crotch. She spent the rest of Friday showing Brown the city sights. The idea amused her. He had never seen San Francisco. It pleased her to help, to see how truly he savored its strangeness. His delight in the Japanese Tea Garden surprised her. So did his familiarity with the habitat exhibits in the Science Museum. She began to respect him and he was not unaware of the change of mind. They had a few beers in Ghirardelli Square and he spoke of his love affair with the Museum of Natural History in New York and she began to like him very much.

They found him a room a mile from the campus in a cul-de-sac called Ransome Court. The weekly rent was barely within his slim budget and the room was three long flights up. Brown did not mind. He never had a room of his own, he told her.

She drove to the express office for the foot locker he had shipped. It was closed when they got there and would not open until the morning. She drove him out to Oakland for more beer in the First and Last Chance Saloon and back to a special pizza place she knew in Berkeley. She had never enjoyed herself so much, she told him.

She checked into a small hotel on Geary Street while he waited in the car, and then she drove him home. He said a shy good-by and touched her hand and left.

In the morning she drove him to the express office and they brought his foot locker back to the dreary attic room. *It needs so much,* she thought. They spent the rest of the day sightseeing and ate abalone on Fisherman's Wharf. He had no bed in Ransome Court, so Brown slept with Angela on Geary Street. They rose late in the afternoon only because it was time for Angela to return to school.

She drove him home. He stood awkwardly beside the car, his dark eyes squinting at her. "Nobody's ever done so much for me in all my life," he said.

"I loved it," Angela told him and meant it.

Their thoughts were identical though neither knew

130

it, each stunned by the good luck of their casual meeting. Each knew he was born to lose. Both hoped that together perhaps they would not lose so much.

Brown leaning against one of the campus oaks watched her go. This was their third weekend, the first time she spent it all with him and not on Geary Street. His hands, thrust in his dungarees, fingered the memory of Angela. His mind sorted the images with detailed and loving attention. He could not let go that memory. He could not shake her tactile presence joined in darkness making love. Darkness *is* love, he reflected. Black *is* beautiful.

Brown was a nocturnal man, a dweller always in dark places, a lover of bones and deep digging.

He walked to the campus bookstore and bought the books he would need in the morning. He had deliberately waited, never believing it would come to pass. Brown had a long history of disappointments. He was hardened to them and cautious even now.

He moved in dense afternoon sunlight to bleak downtown shadows, a man who loved walking. This city soothed him. He lingered for a while on Geary Street, studying the covers of his new schoolbooks. Two policemen in a squad car locked in the rush hour traffic stared too long at him. Brown shrugged and moved on. He wanted no trouble. He walked among the noxious cars piling up for the packed crawl to the ticky tacky of Daly City, San Mateo, Niles, Los Gatos, Atherton. How do people live that way? He hated the sun, the rat race vigor of daylight people.

As a kid in Manhattan, he had loved small animals. He was forbidden to keep one—a hamster—in the apartment. In those days with a city kid's longings, he would have settled for a lifetime job in Central Park Zoo taking care of the raccoons and ocelots. One rainy day he wandered into the American Museum of Natural History. Up to that time its grimy and forbidding façade had kept him away.

In the following months he covered every available exhibit in the thirteen acres of floor space and in the fifty-eight exhibition halls. He learned all there was to know about the habitat groups, from the Alaska bald eagle to the incredible upper Jurassic dinosaurs. The museum guards smiled at him. Staff docents indulged his tagging along and occasionally called on him to expand on their lectures. He was a nice kid, polite and shy, popular with them and useful when they had the large tiresome groups of Sunday afternoon visitors.

He knew then he would someday be an animal scientist. He would study fossils and travel to distant places with exotic, dust-crumbly names. He would reveal mysteries of the past that paleontologists had not yet uncovered.

It was exciting to Brown when his thoughts carried him off like that. But it was a hopeless dream. Brown was an only child. His father had spent much of his lifetime in a post office job. It was a respected pursuit, a safe and even honorable government career. It was already decided the son would follow in the father's footsteps. Brown's mother sold cosmetics door to door for a nationally advertised chain. A short and stocky woman, she dressed cleverly with a cruel girdle and looked slimmer and taller than she was. She favored ruffly lace collars over the jackets of her fitted suits. She smelled, in a rather disconcerting way, like the powder room in the cocktail lounge of a run-down midtown hotel.

Being a businesswoman, Brown's mother ran the family finances. Their combined salaries provided no more than a modest income. With the added expense of a small rented car used for transporting Mrs. Brown's bulky free sample kits, there was no possible provision for their son's college education. The Upper West Side apartment was tiny. Brown had to sleep on the Castro Convertible in the living room.

He was a dutiful son and resigned himself to it. There was a flurry of excitement when he was recommended for a $400 science scholarship. After a somewhat emotional family discussion, it became clear that, even if they gave up the rented car, there would not be funds enough to take care of tuition and board. A few weeks before graduation from high school, he took the civil service tests for the post office job.

Weeks passed with no word from Washington. The father resented his son's impatience. Brown's 1-A draft classification hung over his head. Idle daytime hours were agony. He drifted between the museum and the park, between the Labrador ducks and the Sunday morning junior executives in their well-cut work clothes playing touch football on the green.

He had it out with his parents one night. All the stored-up frustration inside him let go. His father slapped him. He spent the night with a school friend who lived on Central Park West. A few days later, in a recruiting office he just happened to be passing, he enlisted in the Army. It was the first decision he had ever made entirely on his own. From Fort Dix and the prison stockade he was sent to Vietnam.

He was twenty-three and home now. There had been girls in his life, long before Angela, kids really. After Vietnam, after the Purple Heart, there were women. Strange women, attracted by what the campaign ribbons told them. Women who had to know what the war was like. How it really was.

He would lie with them and brood about it for a while, turning it over in his mind slowly, as he did with all thoughts, all questions, wondering what business it was of theirs what it was really like. Christ, if you told them what it *really* was like, they'd gag and lose the heart to fuck, and that was all that mattered. So he would tell them about the rats as big as rabbits and the shattering nerve-shredding blast of Charley mortars and rockets and heavy stuff behind it like the bass section in a Lincoln Center symphony and how the mud sucked out of the holes in those special boots with the bottoms that thwarted the *punji* sticks Charley planted in the rice fields. Sometimes he told them about the chow, bolted down while he was dug in like a mole, crouching in a trench that stank of human filth while the slimy C-rations went down with the coffee so sour with ascorbic acid it tasted lousier than the rot-gut booze the boys guzzled in the back street Saigon dives. He told this only to the broads he really didn't care too much about because it took away his own appetite for the business at hand.

133

What about the killing, some would ask, stirring restlessly in minor bumps and grinds and touching his parts tenderly to get him up again. As though the gore and up were one and the same thing. The killing, they insisted. Was it like the writers said? Like the pictures showed? If he balked or seemed reluctant to speak of it, they drove at him, worked him over, grinding his eyeballs into his skull with devilish fondling and teasing. Riding over it always was the cruel relentless insistence on the intimate details, the color of bone splinters, the texture of spilled guts.

Finally he would tell them anything to be free of them. But he was too late. It drove them into frenzied acts of lust so urgent they needed all of him inside them all at once while they mouthed obscenities and behaved in every forbidden and shameless manner. So that in spite of his revulsion and the freshened memories of agony and despair, he found himself lost in his own craving, his own obscenities.

He would leave them quickly then, stalking early morning sidewalks in puzzled anger. As though some secret, male and inviolate, had been wrenched from him. As though men killed each other solely for the favors of women. As though women, well aware of it, dangled these favors like bait and climaxed in the telling. As though all women bedded shared this secret with each other.

Until Angela. Angela brought him innocence and rapture and restored his faith and gave him strength. Best of all, Angela begged no memory of how it really was.

His fingers touched the smooth ribbon of scar tissue near his groin. An Thei. That day he lay flattened in shallow cover hastily dug, until a Charley shell blew his five platoon buddies to nowhere and left him with a gaping hole inside his thigh. Chunks of bloody flesh covered him. His own wound miraculously bled little. It was not until later he learned these tokens of gore were all that remained of the others.

When the medics came he begged them to put a bullet through his head. He had seen the wound, a

134

mangled mess where they cut the fabric away. It felt as though all of it, penis and scrotum, had been shot away and he wanted to die right there. He was luckier than a lot of others. He came home intact and clean with an honorable discharge and money enough for a first year at college.

Intact. He remembered the night in base hospital when he dreamed of a woman and for the first time since An Thei he felt the muscle grow and stiffness out of the dream brought him awake smiling. He wept quietly and when the night nurse made her rounds he looked at her with different eyes.

Home clean is better than dead clean and the luck of Angela best of all. He began the walk back to his attic room. On campus, he passed knots of students gathered round several speakers. Some carried signs. Some chanted slogans and asked him to join them.

He kept walking. He wanted none of it. None of the asshole agitators or the hopped-up kids or the cool cats with crew cuts. He was here on business. He had a job to do. All the fighting he would ever do was already done and he had the Purple Heart to prove it.

She cleared Carmel without incident and headed south on the Big Sur road. She drove with care. Slides and fog could be risky here. She'd be late getting back but that didn't matter. She had nothing to look ahead to. After a weekend with Brown, life with Daphne and her freaked-out crowd seemed tame.

Brown. All the name she knew for him. Sometimes in bed he talked about his childhood. The museum, the zoo in the park. Never about his family. He spoke little when they walked. Passing students seemed to trouble him. He would turn his head to study them. When they were gone a puzzled look lingered in his dark eyes.

It was clear to Angela he was not one of them. He belonged to no group. *Like me. A loner.*

He would not tell her more than Brown. But he made love as though the world was dying, as though this time was the last time. It pleased Angela that the act of love came naturally to her. Brown praised and marveled and taught her ways. There will be other

135

men, she told herself, but he is the first and only one. When she wrote to her father, she could not write of Brown.

It was strange to compare Brown with her father, who was fair, smooth-skinned and lean, a cheerful man. Why had she chosen Brown, dark, sullen, and chunky? She recalled weird Freudian concepts she had listened to with amusement during the droning lecture periods in Psychology I (Introduction to Human Behavior; Professor Portulaca). Father image. Penis envy. Libido/mortido and the sacred nose-lore of Brschiss. I mean, why would a respectable medical doctor go around making up all these absolutely *wild* names for things. Some of the girls at Cal, the ones from around Beverly Hills and New York, had been going to shrinks since their days at the Dalton School and Westlake. Maybe that was what she needed. With a mother she despised and a father she adored and a crummy lecher of a stepfather who called her Angie. Silly thought. She was just as normal as the next girl, and she'd be damned if she'd throw away thirty bucks an hour to tell a dirty old man (or a dirty young man suffering just as much as she from that mixture of prudery, frustration, and desire), her intimate thoughts when balled. A smart chick could earn royalties for that kind of eminently publishable material.

Sillier by the minute. She should stop for coffee. Her crotch felt sore. Her thighs tingled. The rest of her felt marvelous. She began to miss Brown in the worst way. *Which is the best way. A gap filler, that quiet Brown. A joy and strength. Right here. Ah yes here.*

And he needs me.

She had driven with the car radio blasting from dusk to darkness, singing loudly and off-key Dylan tunes with words of wistful and biting social comment, the raw sound washed from her lips by the rushing night wind. Into the pale mystery of Bixby Bridge in moonlight. A gnarled Monterey cypress in the slash of headlights reminded her she had never made it home and how her mother had snapped and snarled when Angela had been good enough to call and say she was fine and not to worry.

Someday she would sit with her father before a cheery blaze in a stone fireplace like the one he had told her about in the Virginia house where he had lived for a time as a boy. They would walk a beach as they did that last time in Carmel, Brown with them peaceful and steady as she knew he would be. She would tell her father how much she cared for this lonely young man who had suffered much and who needed her love.

Or she could write it in a letter in the morning during the art appreciation lecture and send it airmail to his FPO. She would call Brown and tell him for sure she loved him and tell Brown she had told her father she was going to marry him. She smiled. Her mother would never know. It would never make the Bay area or Peninsula society pages.

She drove with thoughts like these, handling the car with skill. She raced from high macadam over the sea to the close roar of surf until a shimmer of light in the hillside at San Simeon told her she was halfway to Santa Barbara. Her spirits sank. What really lay ahead? A messy art studio, dull classrooms, Daphne in her weedy garden of grass.

She pulled over to the side of the road. A thousand years between now and next Friday. Between now and Brown. Daphne herself had said it. Take care of Number One.

She needed black coffee. There was a truckers' stop somewhere back along the line. And Brown in his grimy attic needed a mirror and curtains and a coat of paint and Angela.

She remembered a time when she was a small girl. Her father driving her somewhere in the Sunday hills (Carmel? Marin County?) came to a crossroads and leaned over and said, "Any orders, Skipper?"

"Hard left rudder," she shouted happily and he swung the wheel over. "All engines ahead full," she said, just the way he had taught her. And they headed back the way they had come.

And she did.

XI

Two passions ruled the life of Jarvis McCready (Rep-O). One was to attain the chairmanship of the House Armed Services Committee. The other was his wife Melba, whom he loved and loathed with an ambivalence intense enough for a lifetime of classic Greek tragedies. McCready also nursed a secret longing for enduring fame, but until Melba would give the word and wherewithal, the Presidency must wait. McCready was only thirty-five and just beginning to roll.

Baby-faced Melba was closer to forty and also rolled. Crippled by a congenital defect in her spine, she moved on wheels. She drove a big sports car as skillfully as she handled her sleek power-driven wheel chair. Melba was a well-formed woman from the waist up with a showy bosom whose cleavage she artfully featured. Her hands were deft, animate, and, like a magician's, fascinating to watch. She was robust and abrasive. She talked cleverly and too much, with a flashy well-fixed smile not entirely inappropriate—she was the sole heir to the richest self-made millionaire in Cuyahoga County. With such enviable assets, both per-

138

sonal and capital, it was easy to forget that Melba's legs from the knees down dangled like a rag doll's.

She was endowed with her father's brute drive and his genius for running things, and her mother's coarse greed. She held a master's from Western Reserve, a sharp tongue rarely in check, and a clever actress's control of her emotions. She could be charming or kind, or cruel as an empress. Jarvis at one time or another had suffered the ravaging touch of each. She ran him and his career like a privately owned puppet show. Everyone knew it, thanks to Melba. She was thoroughly pleased with her marriage and wanted no children. Children, she said, were nasty little scene stealers. In truth, she was secretly afraid she might produce another disaster like herself.

McCready's beginnings were seedier. He was born in a tin-roofed shack during the Depression and raised with three older brothers and a retarded sister in a variety of tenements and shabby rooms around the low flat sections close to the bridges and viaducts of the Cuyahoga ravine. His father when not drinking worked the docks handling cargo for the Great Lakes freight routes. During World War Two he was as close as he would ever be to steady employment in an airplane assembly plant until struck down one night on a payday drunk while crossing the railroad yards.

Jarvis's mother used the insurance money to see him through high school. The older boys had long ago left for the Army, to which their talents and appetites were well suited. Jarvis worked summers cleaning fish and enrolled in Fenn College to study business and commerce. He lasted one year. Studies were too demanding for a wisecracking redhead who preferred to get out where the real action was, where he believed his good looks and personality would bring him the big break he needed.

He soon learned how tough it could be. The best he could achieve after five years of job-switching was the title of assistant sales manager of the used car division of Cleveland's leading luxury car dealer where everyone not a manager was an assistant sales manager. In his late twenties, after a six-month stint at the Navy's

139

Great Lakes Training Station, he barely managed to stay in and out of debt and shoddy love affairs in scale with his meager salary plus commissions.

He joined a nasty little racist group called Freedom Force whose primary aim was to "protect the purity of our White American Christian society." The Force met privately twice a month to drink beer, chomp on pretzels, and to report and file incidents of Negro and Jewish transgressions. Much beer was consumed and the list of grievances swelled. Plots and schemes were hatched but no action was taken until a minor East Side riot erupted one hot summer. The Force members gathered at night in several cars and cruised hastily through the hostile Negro district. They wound up smashing a few windows in a Cleveland Heights synagogue and returned to their homes boisterous and purged. After a year or two of it, some special instinct of self-preservation kept Jarvis from further active involvement with Freedom Force. He quit the meetings but continued to pay his dues.

He enjoyed a special role in the early morning TV commercials sponsored by the dealer. He adopted the nickname of "Fireball" and developed a small reputation as a raconteur of ethnic jokes told loudly with gestures in suitable dialects and accents. His colleagues called him the life of the lot. Jarvis "Fireball" McCready never doubted that his big break would come.

Melba was the big break. It was lunchtime on the lot and Jarvis's good fortune he had brought along a bologna sandwich in a brown paper bag. He did not join the others for the businessman's dollar special at a nearby lunch room. He was called to the showroom to deliver Miss Melba Hoskins' new convertible with its specially built driver controls. She had wrecked the last one and after a two-week hospital stay was ready to roll again. Jarvis happened to be the only salesman on hand who knew how to manipulate the controls, and Melba wanted her $22,000 playpen right then.

In the days of driver instruction that followed, she began to feel in the strangest way, she wanted redheaded Jarvis as well. He talked too loudly and he

140

dressed like a tout, but he amused her. One night he boasted of his Freedom Force activities. She had to tell him it was her occasional contributions that kept it in business. It was good for a laugh. They found much to laugh about together.

He became a steady visitor to her parents' two-acre stone pile in the Heights. After the last driving lesson and a night of confused petting (the wealth of spare parts appalled him), Melba wheeled into her folks' bedroom and laid it on the line. She wanted Jarv for her very own and on a permanent basis.

The Hoskinses balked and asked for time. Ever since Melba was old enough to understand her plight, she had used it like a club. She gave them a firm deadline, after which she would elope. They made hardnosed inquiries into McCready's background, offered Melba a trip around the world with a titled dowager, considered a payoff to Jarvis. But they knew how useless alternatives were. Melba would have her way.

They could never say no. Filled with guilt and curiously pious in their late years, they suffered her traumas in silence. Her father blamed her affliction on his own gross sins of profit and plunder and gave heavily to the Church. Her mother was the former Gussie Ventrusca of Kansas City, the daughter of a blond Bavarian madam of the mining camps. Gussie herself achieved a kind of notoriety during World War One as a hootchy-kootchy dancer named Dew Drop until Hoskins came along and made a lady of her. Gussie blamed her dropped uterus for Melba's motor dysfunction and with Hoskins' reluctant consent stubbornly resisted surgery in favor of Science.

Their own social world was dying and barren. They mistrusted the new. Their entertaining was limited to the most essential business amenities. Plain Gussie at 240 pounds owned a solid gold Ouija board and subscribed to the opera because she drew comfort from the sight of fat Wagnerian sopranos. They wintered in Florida in a replica of the Heights mansion and avoided the sun. They waited with sour resignation for the day of their demise at which time Melba would inherit the steel foundries, wire mills, the nuts and bolts

141

empire, and all the new electronics subsidiaries she was helping them accumulate.

They made one last brave stand, denouncing McCready as a fortune hunter, and begged Melba to change her mind. The hell I will, she told them, and, like the good businesswoman she was, she listed his assets. Good Anglo-Saxon stock. Grass roots Middle West American family down on its luck. She would tone down his car-lot breeziness, fix his teeth, find him a tailor, and teach him canasta. She screamed down their final entreaties, threatened suicide, and set a date for the wedding.

She was free now to propose to McCready, knowing he would never screw up enough courage to do it on his own. Beneath the huge oaks that shaded the wide driveway to the carriage house, she offered him ample evidence she could be everything a woman need be to a man. Jarvis drove the borrowed company car back to his rooming house, locked the door, and bolted down a man-sized slug of the local blend. It would be the last taste of cheap whiskey he need ever endure.

He fell across his unmade bed and wept tears of uncontrollable joy. Later, because he was too charged to sleep, he went out to a bar and bought a bottle of bonded booze, went back to his room, and drank himself silly. Between giggles and hiccups he wondered what it would be like. How he would manage to breathe inside the clutch of Melba's powerful arms. How long it would be before he would miss the familiar clutch of a full woman's entwining legs.

They were married in the chapel of an old church, with its rich lawns and noble steeple overlooking the city and the big Lincoln Storage sign. The marriage contract read like the corporate merger of a multimillion dollar interlocking directorate with a store window dummy, price tags, and all. Which it might have been, happily forever after. But Melba was too clever, too ambitious to settle for that. Now wed, she put to work her grandiose plan and backed it with the hard cash it needed.

She had observed in Jarvis's style the diamond-in-the-rough qualities so many Americans admire in their

142

political idols. She calculated in votes the easy grin, the crinkle-cornered blue eyes, the well-pump handshake. There was groundwork to be done with the crude jokes, the oily flow of small talk, hangovers from his car-lot days and the two-minute TV commercials.

She undertook his schooling the moment they returned from their Bermuda honeymoon. A wing of the mansion house had been redecorated for the newlyweds. Jarvis got used to the ramps and handrails designed for Melba. It took a while longer to get used to the services of his own valet and the house staff. A speech tutor called regularly. So did professors of economics and political science. The custom tailor had no problems with McCready's wardrobe. He was a perfect thirty-six regular as long as he laid off the beer.

In the matter of a year, the voters of Cuyahoga County were presented with an attractive new candidate for the State Legislature—Jarvis "Fireball" McCready. It was Melba who insisted on keeping the nickname over Jarvis's petulant objections. "It's a vote-getter, Jarv," she reassured him.

She prevailed on Jarvis to renew his interest in Freedom Force and backed her faith in its vote-getting heft with a check for five thousand dollars. Jarvis attended his first meeting in over a year. He was nominated Vice Vigilante and Keeper of the Kurrency. He was sorely tempted, but Melba reminded him he would soon be caught up in a hot political campaign with the incumbent and would have little time for FF organization duties. He accepted an honorary title instead.

He was astonished to see how the membership had grown in his absence. He recognized prominent names and faces of citizens who traded their cars each year with his dealer, leaders of the suburban community, sponsors of charity drives, bulwarks of the church. Wine was served instead of beer and pretzels. Jarvis was treated with immense respect by members who had barely nodded a year ago.

The president and founder of a successful chain of cheap hamburger chalets ("You can't beat our meat or fake our shake") spoke for twenty minutes on Patriotism and Pikers. The list of subversive acts committed

143

since the last meeting was read and added to the prime list. The club oath was intoned and the victory song sung and the pledge repeated and the meeting broke up.

Melba and Jarvis joined the Prime Vigilante for coffee and brandy in his Gates Mills ranch home. He told them they could count on an all-out effort by each member of the Force and his family in getting Jarvis elected. It would be no problem, he continued blandly. The national organization behind Freedom Force, supported by private donations and its branch cells in major cities, had spent over a million dollars in the past year to influence legislation. Another million stood by to support the campaigns of deserving conservative candidates like Jarvis "Fireball" McCready.

The campaign got off to a good start. Jarvis's seedy beginnings in the slum of the Cuyahoga ravine were translated by Melba's campaign managers as "Simple And Honest Cuyahoga American." The SAHCA candidate, to his own surprise as well as his seasoned opponent's, landed in the State Capitol in Columbus with a whopping landslide vote.

That was ten years ago. In the intervening time, the Hoskinses died in a Florida-bound plane crash. What remained of them was ceremoniously installed in the family's marble tomb. Jarvis moved on to the Congress, a nontax-deductible business expense for Melba who shuttled by private jet between Washington, New York, and Cleveland, where she attended numerous meetings of numerous boards. She rented an opulent town house with its own garage and elevator in Georgetown and promised Jarvis a hundred-acre Virginia farm the day he was appointed to the House Armed Services Committee.

"It's up to you, Jarv doll," she told him, but by this time both of them knew better.

TAPE: 12 June: M to J: PERSONAL

". . . the way the cookie crumbles. Jarv. You've got to snap out of it and do something. I'm getting tired of carrying the whole load. Almost two years here and what've we got to show for it except bills bills bills. I beg your pardon. One lousy committee, the Select Small Business Committee. And low man at that. For God's sake, Jarv, I could buy out every damned one of those penny-ante pipsqueak small businesses you've been studying and investigating and not even show a dent in two per cent of my Hoskins holdings. You're bogged down there, Jarv doll, no chance to do the big things we talked about. I mean with our backing why settle for less? Why travel economy class when we're geared for deluxe first? What else was it but my do-re-mi that saved you from utter obscurity on that—what was it called?—House Administration Committee? If not for my stepping in and using a bit of muscle, they'd have locked you away forever in that Smithsonian swamp or you'd be correcting the Congressional Record maybe for the rest of your days here. You're built for bigger things, Jarv, and nobody knows that better than I. Not that what's happened is your fault entirely, don't get me wrong. These things take time. It's dog-eat-dog and God knows you're trying. At least you're on record for the right things. Vietnam and Sent/Safe and—well, yes, we bombed on the Falcon XII, even after you got the wonderful piece published that I had the man write, but I still insist it's one hell of an airplane. They've just been trying to rush it out before it's ready to please the chintzy critics who keep yelling it costs too much. What's a lousy seven million dollars a plane when our national security's being threatened? They just need time to iron out a few of the kinks. My God, look at the trouble they've been having with the Army's AH-56 helicopter and the M-551 Sheridan and look at the mess the Navy's in. So I think we've done damned well with our share of the Falcon XII, with a Hoskins module ejection escape system in every one that's built. Not that I'm about to allow personal considerations to affect my love of country.

"What I'm trying to bring out, Jarv doll, is you've got to get off your kiester and come up with a lovely gimmick of some kind that'll focus nationwide attention on you from the House floor. Something really big.

145

Something close to every American's heart like the assassination although I'm not recommending anything like *that,* ha ha, although I still think it's an inside job and good riddance. But the linage it got and the prime time, my God, if we could come up with some gimmick like that! Anything Tadsy could promote, or Mickelby and our other columnists could sink their teeth in, like they promised me they would. But we have got to give them something more than the deals you've made for those two-bit plastics people and the garment manufacturers you saved from bankruptcy. It's not what the public's interested in. The same for culture and fair employment and poverty and those other booby traps I've steered you away from. They swore to me, Mick in particular, they're ready to go with a big blast, not just the daily column, any time we come up with a big one. God knows they owe us something after what I pay them and all the booze they guzzle out at the house and dipping into your Havana cigars and cognac brandy by the box and case. Not to mention that drunken lecher Tadswell putting the blocks to the pantry maid Ella, that little sneak. I'm paying him to lobby for the Hoskins Foundation, not to prong the help. I'm ditching the little mink the minute I can get my hands on someone else light-skinned enough to take her place. The help situation here, my God, sometimes I wish I had stayed in Cleveland. If not for Greta, I tell you, Jarv—

"The truth is, I don't see the sense in being in Washington politics and not making it big, Jarv. Nobody got a bigger sendoff from Ohio since Warren Harding in 1920 than Jarvis McCready got two years ago and I might add not a single damned one of the senators or congressmen we invited or their wives so much as sent me a thank-you note and I'm not about to forget it when I'm calling the shots. And the time's coming, Jarv doll, you mark my words. Mother always said you get what you pay for and anything you get for nothing you earn. All we need is one break, Jarv, and we're on our way. Like the big stink you raised back home last Christmas on the abortion law. Have you been reading these letters? They're still coming in, telling you to

146

keep up the good fight. From nuns and bishops, no less, and just about every parochial school in the district. God knows we can use those letters and curry the Catholic vote next fall after the way that lush Maguire carried it. It really scared me until we bought our way out. But that's back home, Jarv, and it cuts no ice in the national scheme of things. Where we need clout is right here.

"Now we've set our sights on the Armed Services Committee and I'm ready to go all the way to get you there. How we missed out on the last vacancy I don't know, but if what Guilford tells me is true, we're first in line for the next. And if those damned left wing Democrats start screaming about conflict of interest again I'm really opening the whole kit and kaboodle on corruption in high places and the hanky panky that's been going on. I've got a scandal sweater knitted big enough to cover the Washington Monument and hot enough to burn the eyes out of Madame Defarge.

"The way I see it, Jarv, we have got to get you where the action is, the real hassle for power, and the right spot is in the nuclear game. Nuclear's where the big money is and where it's going to be by the time you're chairman of Armed Services and that's where *you got to be*. The Joint Committee on Atomic Energy's been fighting tooth and nail for an all-nuclear Navy and could be that's the star to hitch our wagon to. Hit it hard from the floor with a gimmick of some kind on nuclear power—something that'll shock the public and make the newspapers and networks take notice of you and your selfless and sustained and patriotic one-man fight to keep America Number One in the world. The military's with us, Jarv, and so's the right-thinking conservative middle class of America. All we need is that gimmick. I just read the other day that over two thousand officers, retired with the rank of colonel or Navy captain or higher, are now employed by the top hundred defense contractors in the nation. No need to tell you how close to the top Hoskins stands, is there, Jarv doll? Or the ex-generals and admirals on the payroll. And a hell of a lot of those Pentagon peacocks are retiring every month and I've yet to

147

meet one who doesn't know what side his bread is buttered on.

"I'd say that's our best bet, Jarv, and the sooner we get going the better. I'm running along now. Greta gets mad when I hang around here too long. She hates to let me out of her sight for even a minute, dear thing. Read those letters, Jarv. There's one from a sailor on one of those nuclear ships I think you ought to read. It gives me an idea and I'll talk to you about it tonight at dinner. Be sure to read those letters, Jarv. Gripes mostly, but you never know what comes of it. I'm putting the Navy man's letter, Morgan or something, on top. Be *sure* to read it. And don't erase this tape. Bring it along tonight so's we can discuss some of the things I've said. And get home by five, dear? Twelve for dinner, black tie, and we should have a drinkie and a chat first. 'Bye now. Oops, sorry. Don't forget to read the press release on those district kids to whom you haha awarded the National Science Foundation graduate fellowships so you'll haha remember their names when they call."

XII

McCready found the mail on his desk and the tape recorder nearby. He ignored them for the present. He had just returned to his office from the House floor where he had made the best speech of his life. There had been applause, not a thundering and not without an element of booing from the gallery. But with his party leader's nodding approval he had delivered a ringing denunciation of his dovish colleagues and he knew he had drawn blood. In a speech that was both spontaneous and theatrical, he denounced them as "Kremlin cravens inside our red, white, and blue walls," blocking passage of the nine-hundred-million-dollar Sent/Safe antiballistic missile defense bill ". . . to strip us naked of arms and leave us defenseless against their comrades, the peddlers of international communism." What had made the speech truly marvelous to Congressman McCready was that it came from his heart, not from scribbled notes or a taped directive from his wife.

During the noon recess in his office he basked for a few minutes in the warm salutations from devoted administrative assistants, secretaries, and staff members.

Hands were shaken, backs slapped, a few fake tears shed. Documents and mail were shuffled about, messages delivered, short-range decisions made. Two simpering schoolteachers from South Euclid were ushered in and introduced to him. McCready took it all in stride. He was filled with a heady joy. For the first time since his election almost two years ago, he felt good about being Congressman Jarvis "Fireball" McCready.

Everyone disappeared for lunch except McCready's private secretary, Wanda Berry. She carried in an armload of the congressman's monthly newsletters, just mimeographed, and the letters she had typed from Melba's earlier dictation.

Wanda was ash blond and bright, twenty-five, divorced from her soldier husband. She knew her job well. McCready trusted her and often confided in her. She had a secretary's crush on her boss and McCready knew it. He rarely touched her, much to Wanda's chagrin. Melba's spies were everywhere. One slip, he knew, was all it would take.

She told McCready that Melba's parting orders had been to make sure McCready read Morgen's letter and played back the tape. He assured Wanda he would do these things, ordered a lunch sent in, and watched with longing as Wanda's shapely legs under her miniskirt flicked out of the room.

Legs, he thought. Live flesh. All the way up.

He decided the tape and letter could wait. He wanted a few minutes in which to relish the pleasure of his triumph on the House floor. He tipped back in the deep leather chair with his feet on the desk and his fingers locked behind his head. Melba would be sore as hell when she heard about his impromptu speech. She hated to lose control. She demanded absolute obedience to her orders. Well, the hell with her. He was no chump. How long did she think she could pull him around like a toy puppy? He was sick and tired of being pointed out as the husband of the wealthiest cripple in the country. He showed 'em this morning who he was. Where he stood. His clarion voice over the turned heads of his colleagues had been heard all the way to the White House. The words had just poured out. That was the marvelous thing about it. They had just welled up inside him and he let them spill, remembering how to use his arms and toss his red thatch of hair. When he sat, the sweet waves of applause washed over him. He did not hear the booing.

Ten years had made some changes in the wheeler dealer. He still made good use of his car-lot gift of gab, adding to it a carefully controlled suavity copied from his more experienced Capitol Hill colleagues. He had progressed enough to enjoy the implications of his nickname "Fireball" and at no time discouraged a nationally syndicated female gossip columnist from describing him after a Melba-sponsored, five-martini interview, as "Marv Jarv." He had been twice voted "Best Dressed Congressman" by an obscure national guild of custom tailors in appreciation of the eighteen thousand dollars Melba spent annually on his wardrobe and accessories. His ruddy face was round and sleek but no less feral. His red hair, with some help from cosmetic additives, showed a distinguished touch of gray at the temples.

His disappointment until now was understandable. He had expected greater financial freedom when the Hoskins couple died. Instead, Melba tightened the purse strings and still directed his legislative career, which so far had middling to poor luck. No bill he introduced got past committee. No chairmen sought his counsel. What small reputation he had he owed to the columnists, commentators, and publicity people on Melba's payroll.

His best support came from Asa Guilford, the powerful House chairman of the party's Committee on Committees. Guilford had been helped in his campaigns by Melba's father during the early years. It was Guilford on whom Melba pinned her hopes for Jarvis's appointment to the Armed Services Committee. Guilford had piled up thirty years of seniority and headed numerous committees and subcommittees. His voting record showed him to have served the military-industrial interests with far more zeal than the lawmaking assembly to which his constitutents never failed to return him. He had much in common with Jarvis McCready.

Guilford had pointedly introduced the freshman congressman on arrival from Ohio to the Armed Services chairman and some of the ranking members. It was not an opportune moment. Jarvis saw the veto in their eyes and his heart sank.

He did not make it the first time around. Guilford's consoling "To get along, son, you got to go along," made him feel worse. Melba moved in on Guilford with reminders of his early years, and obligations relating thereto, which included several unpaid I.O.U.'s. Guilford promised to do better. Melba did not stop there. She arranged courtesy calls and faked constituents' letters describing Jarvis's selfless dedication to an armed and vigilant America. She needled her paid hacks. She threw the most lavish parties in town, inviting anyone who could remotely help her husband's career.

Jarvis became despondent, his ego badly deflated. He had come to Washington flushed with his triumphs in the State Capitol at Columbus. He found the seniority system rigid. He chafed at its "old fogyism" and the delays in recognition. He was politely ignored by his colleagues. He secretly suspected they ridiculed him behind his back. Capitol Hill bewildered him with its complex structure of formalities and traditions. He missed the easy pace of the state legislature, where in short order (and at considerable expense to Melba) he had become one of the most popular freshman members. The ready smile, the hearty handshake, worked as well as it did on the car lot. He had been happy enough in Columbus to spend the rest of his life there, assured of a possible term or two as state senator and of course a courtesy shot at the governorship.

He was sorry Melba opted for the Congress, but he had no choice. Melba called the shots. Her ambitions were rooted in pragmatic needs like defense contracts and smooth Tadswell, who ran the family "foundation," was the lobbyist who'd get them.

You had to hand it to Melba, he reflected. *She gets*

what she wants. And when she wants it, she goes after it first class.

The office, for example. Jarvis was crazy about his office. It smelled to him like the interior of a factory-fresh Cadillac. Melba had supervised each detail of its rich appointments. The deep pile carpeting and Oriental rugs, the custom furniture. There was no office like it on Capitol Hill. Melba personally had arranged for the paintings that hung from the paneled walls. The Gerard Terborch on loan from the Cincinnati Art Museum, the Gauguin from the Cleveland Art Museum, the Vandyke from the Columbus Gallery of Fine Arts. Jarvis admired the exquisite texture of Terborch's small, precise figures. He envied the aristocratic elegance of the Vandyke. But the Gauguin stank and he said so to any visitor who would listen. "If a kid of mine painted like that, I'd drown him." He jokingly threatened to use it as a dart board.

Jarvis spoke frequently of what he would do if he had a son. It masked a pathetic sorrow as much as a cunning move to future security. For several years after the wedding Melba's doctors had encouraged the idea. She was healthy enough and fully capable of bearing a child. Jarvis pleaded for it but Melba would have none of it. Now that she was forty, the doctors were less encouraging. It was possible, they told Jarvis, but dangerous. More mongoloids and retarded babies are born to women over forty than to younger mothers. Jarvis's hopes for a Jarvis the Second faded. He would never forgive Melba for stalling. Yet the possibility of a defective son in his own image was more than his vanity would allow. It never occurred to him that he might sire a daughter. Adoption? Jarvis dismissed the idea. Why bring in a stranger?

Since they had come to Washington, Melba had added a companion, Greta Ullbricht, to her staff. Greta was a large toothy blond physical therapist, a few years older than Melba, strong-featured and smelling of green soap and caraway. Her English was adequate and to Jarvis, often comic.

Jarvis at first welcomed her to the household staff. She took charge of things with no delay. She proved to

153

be capable, efficient, and entirely devoted to her job. She relieved him of numerous chores and he was able to devote more time to routine political matters. The two women soon were more like girl friends, Jarvis noticed with faint irritation. He was a late riser and often slept through the early morning therapy period in Melba's private solarium. Shortly after Greta's arrival he tried once to join her for the afternoon period from four to five. The solarium, he learned, was Greta's domain. Baring two rows of teeth, she made it quite clear it was off-limits to all men. Including Jarvis. Months passed. He soon became aware that Greta's arrogant rule encroached on the limited authority Melba parceled out to him as master of the household. His complaint to Melba was laughed off. Greta was the best thing that had happened to her since she married Jarvis, she told him. Greta was marvelous company, a superb masseuse, and Melba never felt better in her life.

"Before we know it," Jarvis said bitterly, "the old girl'll be crawling in bed with us." Melba, brightening, suggested it might be an amusing diversion. Jarvis suspected she meant it.

He returned from Capitol Hill one afternoon to female laughter and whisperings behind the solarium door. He listened, hoping to confirm his worst suspicions. Greta's voice irked him, a caress to Melba's soft purring. He pushed in the door, his imagining and dark suspicions at their peak. His prepared denouncement died on his lips. Melba, with a drink alongside her, was stretched out on the rubbing table covered by a thin sheet exposing her splendid neck and shoulders. An electric vibrator machine gently massaged her middle, its movements rippling Melba's breasts in a most provocative way.

His reaction was a study in shame and outrage. Shame for himself. Outrage because Greta witnessed what was so private to his married life. His outrage was short-lived. Greta, who had been reading aloud from a newspaper a short distance from Melba, threw it aside and advanced on him shouting harsh accusations in a hash of English and German. Jarvis raised a fist. Melba sat up from the table, the sheet dropping away. She stopped Greta dead with a hilarious shriek of "Rape!" And clapped her hands delightedly. Greta halted inches short of Jarvis, her underlip outthrust, cold fury in her eyes.

"Get out, yes?" she hissed. "Is private here."

"What the hell's going on, anyway?"

"He's jealous, Greta," Melba crowed and reached for her highball and drank. Her face glowed. "Jarv doll, you're green with jealousy!"

"I damn well want an explanation, Melba. All this giggling, you two, behind closed doors."

Melba wiped her mouth on the sheet. "Dark and dirty doings, Jarv. Greta's been reading Ann Landers to me—" Her coarse laugh rang out. Greta, relaxing, began to smile, though her glittering eyes never left Jarvis. "Those silly women writing about their troubles," Melba went on. "And in Greta's accent? You'd die." She waved her glass at Greta. "Read him the one about the husband who asked his wife to you-know what. Go on, Greta, read it."

"Never mind." Jarvis said in furious defeat.

"Now don't be sore just because Greta and I have a few laughs. Relax, Jarv. Foster'll mix you a drink." After a cold and what he hoped was a contemptuous look at Greta he turned to go. Melba called after him. "What you need, Jarv doll, is a live-in mistress to break the monogamy."

Jarvis left muttering to himself. The door closed on a gale of female laughter that chilled his marrow. He had seen nothing wrong. Worse, he had made a fool of himself in front of them. But he could not shake the creepy suspicion that he was being cuckolded by the big kraut dyke. Nor did it help matters that night in bed when Melba in harsh terms swore she would throw him out if he ever again stooped to such a boorish and cheapening performance. He promised he would not and after he swore to God on it she allowed him to fondle her and make what passed for love. But no kissing, just for punishment.

His lunch arrived. For several minutes there was no sound except the hum of the air-conditioning unit and the steady grinding and swallowing of food. McCready alone ate as though each meal was his last. He scooped in the food with his right hand. With his left, he turned pages of a copy of *Playboy*, kept in the lower left-hand drawer of his desk. Lunch over, he pushed aside the tray, closed the drawer on the Playmate of the Month, and switched on the tape recorder. Melba's crisp words came at him. McCready listened attentively, as though Melba were right there, as though his life depended on it. Which it did. When the tape had run its course he reversed it and ran it again. Three times. That was Melba's rule.

He removed the spool and put it in his briefcase and turned to the stack of mail and began to read Howie Morgen's letter. It was brief, he noted with pleasure, and easy to understand. But McCready was disappointed. He read the letter several times, trying to establish in his mind what there was about it that Melba found so extraordinary. He found nothing. He vaguely recalled other letters from Morgen (he remembered the odd spelling), but details escaped him. He received a lot of mail from the boys overseas. He insisted on signing the answers personally but rarely read what was written by his staff under Melba's direction.

He was too busy to handle the district cranks and the endless requests for small political favors. He agreed with Melba that most of it was beneath the dignity of a congressman with important national matters to occupy his mind. Certainly Morgen's letter seemed to contain nothing more vital than the usual gripe over some fancied petty grievance. McCready's admiration for Navy leaders was perhaps his most genuine conviction and not an attitude created for him by his ambitious wife. Melba was off-base making a fuss over the letter and he'd let her know that tonight. It was time he threw his weight about a bit. That speech he made ought to show her a thing or two about Jarvis McCready she never knew.

He heard Wanda Berry's high heels in the outer office. *Back from lunch early again. Oh you Wanda,* he thought. In his mind he embraced her firm thighs and grunted ecstatically at her squeals of delight. Someday. *Someday,* goddamn it, he'd show 'em who ran this outfit. He shuffled the papers on his desk and wiped his lips and rang for Wanda. She came in, closing the door.

"All done, Wanda. I read 'em all. They're okay. I got to study these damn committee reports before the session resumes."

Wanda removed the empty food tray with the letters and lingered. He yearned to touch her perfumed flesh, her thighs, breasts, all he desired in easy reach. He cleared his throat. "The letter on top of the pile, Wanda. From a sailor name of Morgen." His sleeve touched her and his voice trembled.

"Yes, sir?" She did not move, testing.

"Xerox me a copy like a good girl, eh?" Fondling her firm rump now. "I'll take it along with me."

"Take what, Mr. McCready?"

His hand dropped. "The Morgen letter, damn you."

She laughed coolly. "You work too hard. You should take time off. You know—all work and no play?"

"Play! The way the world is?" He fumbled for the flat edge of the handkerchief Foster stuffed in his breast pocket each morning, and remembered he had used it to wipe his shoes and had thrown it away. Wanda coolly handed him a paper tissue. "Damned air conditioning," he croaked. Their eyes met. "You crazy or something? I'd be out of my cotton-pickin' mind."

She shrugged. "You're a terribly attractive man, Mr. McCready."

"Get going," he said, pleased. "Lots of work to do around here. And leave the door open." He cackled. "Can't shoot a man just for looking, can they?"

His eyes followed her. Mint condition. But Jarvis knew a risky deal when he saw one. Wanda with all the factory extras and styling looked hard to beat, but she was good only for the short haul. And the trade-in cost could break him. A crying shame, he told himself, letting a cream puff like Wanda slip past. For real mileage and service she couldn't hold a candle to Melba. When you bought Melba you bought the whole bundle. Wanda, slick and smart as she was, would have to wait.

The afternoon passed quickly. He drowsed through a briefing from his legislative assistant on the next day's agenda and how he was to vote on the bills and reports before the House. He had resisted this procedure at first. After all, he was a seasoned state legislator, wasn't he? Melba and Asa Guilford assured him the most expedient way to handle a most complicated and sensitive procedure like his vote was to leave it to the pros. Once he was familiar with the ropes—

After a while, Jarvis simply gave in. There was so much else to do. And when the gut issues were explained to him, he did not really understand them, anyway.

It was time to go. He remembered that he had not read the release on the fellowship awards. The hell with it, he told himself. Why remember their names? Jarvis McCready never forgot a face. All he had to do in a case like that was say "Hi!" and smile big and shake the hand firmly and look them right in the eye.

A man could get to be the Vice President on nothing more than that.

XIII

Melba was informed of her husband's impromptu speech an hour after he delivered it. Now in her solarium for the afternoon workout with Greta, she had not yet decided whether to praise or scold him. She was pleased he had come this far, but resented his disobedience of her orders. No more impromptu speeches, she had warned him after a recent Fourth-of-July disaster still in the Congressional Record.

Big Greta, massaging Melba's neck and shoulders, prescribed a stiff scolding. Her concern touched Melba. The developing bitterness of the feud between her lovers intrigued her. She intended to do what she could to keep it flourishing and lively.

By the time Greta's expert fingers reached her lower back muscles and were kneading her buttocks, Melba's mind was made up. The spiciness of unguents and oils and Greta's openmouthed rhythmic breathing lulled her into a languid and mildly erotic state somewhat intensified by her second whiskey sour of the afternoon. She would give Jarv a nasty evening. Later in bed

159

when he was properly miserable she would relent and be forgiving and even allow him to kiss her.

Now the legs. Greta worked them gently in slow firm sweeps downward. Melba, prone, thrust her crotch sensually into the soft leather, exercising her sphincters. Her hand reaching touched Greta's white uniform and squeezed the flesh beneath.

"No tricks," Greta said amiably.

"Listen," Melba said. "I feel real good in the legs."

"Every day is better. Every day we do the exercises is better for the spinal column and in the legs more power." She swung Melba easily to a sitting position and rubbed her down with a large soft towel. "So." She lifted her and gently carried her wrapped in a huge terry robe to her bath. "You give the mister the devil, you hear what I say? Upsetting to you is no good for the muscle tone."

"He'll catch it, Greta," Melba promised.

Jarvis arrived home, showered and dressed for dinner, and joined Melba for a drink in her bedroom before the first guests arrived. She was in her wheel chair in front of a floor mirror studying her long polished fingernails. She wore a floaty scarlet chiffon, sheer as mist, with flowing sleeves and cut low enough to reveal half her breasts. "Asa's bringing Colonel Jillson," she announced.

"Who's Jillson?"

"A top aide to the Joint Chiefs. I asked Asa to arrange it."

"Do we need him?"

"He's young enough to be shaped our way and from what I've heard, terribly ambitious. Sure we need him. What we don't need is his cracker wife. But Asa asked them both and he's dragging his own along. She eats like a pig. So it's fourteen instead of twelve. We'll dine buffet instead of sit down. That way I can get off with Jillson and do some spade work." Her tone abruptly changed. "I'm told you made a big speech this morning."

"Not big, really. But the gallery applauded, long and loud."

"I was told you were hissed."

160

"There's always a few Commies, Melba. But Asa himself came over and told me it was a good speech."

"I've had a word or two with Asa."

"No kidding. I was great. You should have heard that clapping."

"One of these days you'll pull another Fourth-of-July fiasco and be a laughingstock forevermore. Have you forgotten that booboo? It's still in the Record. Read it some time."

"Damn it, honey—"

"Don't 'honey' me, Jarv. You took a hell of a risk." She went on sharply. "I warned you before. The speech you don't make can't keep you from being re-elected." She swung the wheel chair around. "Now zip me up."

"Where's the big kraut?"

"Checking the pantry and seeing about the wine."

"Why didn't she zip you up?"

"She does a million and one things for me every minute of the day."

"She's no damned good. I don't trust her."

"I'd be lost without her. So knock it off."

He zipped her up. "You going in there dressed like that?"

"Like what?"

"You're as open in front as a barn door."

"Colonel Jillson won't complain. Now let's go."

He wheeled her out of the bedroom down the long hall past the shut door of Greta's apartment. "A barn door," she muttered, "of all things." She braked the wheel chair and he stumbled.

"What I meant, honey, was—"

"They're lovely. My best feature. You want me to expose my shrunken legs? Is that what you want? Cover myself like a nun and light candles? Is that what you want?"

"Easy, honey. Don't shout. They can hear every word."

"Then don't criticize, hear? I left the zipper for you. Why? Because I missed you this afternoon. Very much. And what do I get in return? A barn door. You ignore my wishes, you criticize me, the help—" Her tears,

161

conveniently started, spread dark stains in the scarlet chiffon. He dabbed solicitously. She sniffed. "I need another drink."

"In a sec, honey." He dutifully kissed her and she reduced the rate of sniffle by a well-calculated half.

"Did you read the sailor's letter?"

He had intended to pass it off as just another GI gripe. Now he did not dare. "You were absolutely right. Terrific. We should do something about it."

"Exactly what I intend to do. Now wheel me in."

Melba's dinners never failed to achieve their improper ends. The buffet, following fresh caviar, its garnishes, and thinly sliced pumpernickel, included a jellied borsch, cold lobster Figaro, beef Wellington, a salad of fresh greens and a strawberry compote Grand Marnier. A case of vintage Bollinger and Chateau Margaux Médoc disappeared in the process. Colonel Jillson's initial reserve vanished with his second fifth somewhere between the strawberry compote and the cleft in Melba's décolletage. He was a ruddy, stiffly handsome man in his late thirties, cunning enough to mask his social insecurity with a running commentary of praise in a nasal Kansas twang for each dish and wine as he consumed it. By cigar and brandy time Melba's flattery had softened him like putty in her hands. Mrs. Jillson, a washed-out bit of Georgia fluff, seemed struck dumb by the opulence of the evening and had little to say except "Please, Mayam," and "Thayank you."

Despite his wife's overt prodding Asa Guilford fell into a snoring sleep and was discreetly maneuvered to a guest bedroom by Foster, but not before he passed along a bit of good news to Jarvis. Rumblings in the Bureau of the Budget over military spending were threatening to erupt into open warfare with the Congress's powerful committees holding high stakes in the Vietnam war. To counteract findings that might be forthcoming from the Bureau's preliminary investigations, concerned committee chairmen in the Congress were authorizing a subcommittee to look into current defense contracts, presumably to find the facts but actually to whitewash the expenditures. Jarvis McCready was one of five congressmen appointed to the subcommittee late that afternoon. Its first area of investigation would be several large aerodynamic industries on the West Coast.

Jarvis, with instant visions of freewheeling Wanda Berry three thousand miles from Melba's watchful eye, joined his wife across the drawing room. Melba was deep in conversation with Colonel Jillson. Jarvis in a jubilant mood was eager to boast of his new assignment but hesitated, not certain how it might involve Jillson. Melba glanced at his shining face. "I see Asa told you about the subcommittee appointment."

His smile died. "You knew?"

"My idea, darling." She beamed at Jillson. "Jarvis is off to the West Coast in a few days. Hush-hush subcommittee stuff, you know."

"Interesting." Jillson was reluctant to take his eyes from the point where Melba's chiffon ended and her flesh began.

"You *should* be interested," Melba said. "The subcommittee's single purpose is to preserve your office's good image and put a stop to all the bitching."

Jillson flinched slightly. "About what, Mrs. McCready?"

"Missile systems that fail. Planes that crash. Subs that sink."

"Accidents will happen, you know. Even in peacetime." But Jillson looked at McCready with more interest. "If there's anything I can do—"

"We certainly intend to call on you," Melba said. "Meanwhile we want your office to know there's at least one dedicated congressman fighting your battle on Capitol Hill."

"We need every friendly congressman we can get," said Jillson.

"Speaking of friends," Melba went on smoothly, "Jarv and I have just heard from a friend in Vietnam, a good friend, mind you, so I'm not about to disclose name, rank, or serial number, ha ha. But he tells of his

163

superior officer refusing to carry out his orders. Now what is that called, in military terms?"

"Outright refusal?" Jillson shrugged. "Just that—refusal to perform a duty."

"Is it like treason?"

"Hardly. Treason generally's an attempt to overthrow a government to which one owes allegiance. Not that refusal to obey orders isn't serious. It's damned serious. A lot worse, say, than neglect of duty." He frowned. "Are we talking about an actual situation? Because I'd prefer not to be quoted."

"It's just what this friend wrote us and we wondered."

"I've sat on enough general courts-martial, Mrs. McCready, to know what it's all about. Even studied military law for a while."

"Navy law the same as Army?" Jarvis inquired.

Jillson brightened. "If it's a Navy case I'd like to know about it." He puffed on his cigar and tried to look inscrutable. "Friendly competition is all. We like to put the other fellow down, Navy, Army, Army, Air Force, Air Force, Navy. You know?"

"A class-ring jerk," murmured Melba.

"Beg your pardon?"

"It would seem to me," Jarvis said, "deliberate disobedience by a commanding officer of an order given in wartime should be punishable by death or something."

"What was his command?"

"Now really, Colonel," Melba said.

"The circumstances under which the incident took place are of the highest importance in determining the seriousness of the act." Jillson on firm ground studied them alertly.

"We've said too much already, Colonel. It's just that Jarvis feels so deeply his commitment to his country, he cannot tolerate acts contrary to patriotism, loyalty, and such."

The logic of Melba's course of action was making itself clear to Jarvis. "There's enough of it around today without one of our own military leaders being guilty of it." He thrust out his jaw. "Let me get my hands on the facts is all I ask. I'll order an investigation

164

that'll rock the Pentagon from stem to stern." He stood, eyes half closed, the memory of the morning's gallery applause ringing in his ears. "The enemies of our great and good nation are everywhere, infiltrating within the very walls of government . . ."

"That's enough for now, Jarv." Melba's tone seemed casual but he recognized a familiar and ominous warning beneath it. He gripped Jillson's shoulder. "Just get in touch with me, Colonel. We're in this together. Trojan horse stuff."

After a puzzled look at Melba, Jillson nodded and poured a glassful of brandy and hastily drank it. Melba leaned toward Jillson.

"What you might do, Colonel, if you're interested, is keep an eye and ear open. This treason thing, I mean. The word's bound to leak out. Perhaps, while Jarv is on the coast, he can do a little checking, providing his subcommittee duties allow the time. As a taxpaying citizen, I'm interested myself in what's going on, whether our defense dollars are being used or abused by the military professionals like yourself whose salaries we pay. Nothing personal, you understand."

"I'm sure, Mrs. McCready."

"Melba, if you really want to be my friend."

"Melba? Gee. Swell! I'm Ted."

She sent McCready to the bar to fetch her special liqueur. "You see," she went on sweetly, "it's a Navy situation, as you suspected, you clever man. But knowing the Navy, not a word of it gets out unless they want it to." She inclined her head in a direction across the room. "The short man with the very big brandy snifter. Recognize him?"

"We were introduced but I don't recall—"

"Mickelby. The political columnist and commentator."

"I expected a much bigger man."

She squeezed his bicep. "We're not all as fortunately endowed as you, Colonel."

Jillson actually blushed and moved closer.

"Mick's always digging for a good story. He'd be the man to give the facts to, should we care to get them together." She leaned close, the arm of the wheel chair

165

barely separating them. "I've an idea we're going to get on very well, Ted. Together, we just might uncover something really worth while."

"Beautiful," Jillson murmured, feasting his eyes.

"We must meet again, Ted, and discuss progress."

Foster arrived bowing and announced a long-distance call for Mrs. McCready.

"Where from, Foster?"

"San Francisco, madam."

"I'll take it in the library." She smiled warmly at Jillson and excused herself and wheeled away. She returned a few minutes later smug as a fed cat. Guests began to leave and by midnight the McCreadys were ready to retire.

Melba propped nude against huge lacy pillows with her blond hair in two long glistening braids looked as seductive as a Valkyrie maiden in a boudoir setting by Horst. The silk coverlet draped over her thighs nestled an inch or so below her navel. Jarvis had drunk too much wine. She called for him. He lurched out of the bathroom and sat in a sullen stupor on the edge of the oversized bed.

"The way I see it, Jarv," Melba said, "the colonel will be stumbling all over himself bird-dogging the Navy story."

"Colonel?"

"Jillson."

"You kep' feelin' his muscles."

"Could be useful, Jarv, and I intend to use him."

"Yeah. I bet." He reached clumsily and cupped a breast. She seemed unaware of it. "Don't let it get too friendly, baby."

"I'll let him race his motor a while." She took his roving hand and absently helped it. "Those Pentagon characters are back stabbers. They'd tear throats for a scandal in one of the other services."

"You think Jillson'll get the facts?"

"He'll get nowhere. Navy brass protects its own like a mother lion. When his tongue's hanging out I'll give Colonel Teddy a jingle and feed him a few clues."

"Teddy already." Jarvis scratched his furry belly through a gap in his red silk pajamas. "Wha' clue?"

166

"The call from Frisco. I put in three calls this afternoon. Two paid off. I tried your friend here in Navy personnel. He shut up like a clam. Our man on the *Plain Dealer* helped some. He came up with the name of Morgen's commanding officer. A Captain Damion. They keep records of Cleveland boys serving in the armed forces and there was some publicity when Morgen enlisted. His ship's the *Chesapeake*—"

"Hell, I knew that from the letter."

"—and she's operating in the Tonkin Gulf. So I got in touch with Johannsen. He's Hoskins Industries liaison with Navy procurement on the West Coast. Very loyal. He found out right off this Captain Damion first of all is an authentic Navy hero. Something he did in the Korean War. Johannsen checked with the Navy brass in San Diego and the commandant of the Twelfth Naval district, people he's more than friendly with. Damion doesn't have a flaw in his record. Johannsen kept digging and finally hit the jackpot."

She pulled away from Jarvis's hands and read from a sheet of memo paper on the night table. "Emergency orders were issued five days ago to a Captain Brandt, a line officer, attached to a shore-based command in San Diego." She squinted at the memo. "ComCruDiv Nine, whatever that means. But this is it, Jarv. His orders were to report without delay to the U.S.S. *Chesapeake* to relieve the commanding officer. That would have to be Damion. Johannsen said he could smell something fishy just from the casual way everyone was acting."

McCready crawled into his side of the bed. "Take it up in the morning." He switched off the lamp and closed his eyes. Melba's elbow caught him below the ribs. He sat up scowling. "Goddamnit, Melba—"

"Morning, hell. I'm calling Johannsen now." She turned on the light and reached for the phone.

"You can't go calling people all hours of the night."

"It's nine-thirty out there. I'm not paying Nils Johannsen fifty thousand a year plus bonuses for half a day's work. He just better the hell be home, sitting by the phone waiting for me to call."

He was. While Jarvis snored Melba told Johannsen

167

precisely what she wanted. Captain Paul Damion was probably en route to some Navy shore station. It could be Tokyo or Pearl Harbor, Manila or home. "Find him," she ordered Johannsen. "Find out what happened out there and where he's going and let me know."

Melba lay awake for almost an hour after she hung up. It could be a juicy scandal. The letter from the sailor Morgen merely scratched the surface. Once she knew where Damion was, her plan would develop further.

A Navy hero. She found that tidbit of information strangely fascinating. It would be a challenge and a triumph to cut a Navy hero's legs from under him. Whittle him down to my size, she told herself. She nudged her snoring husband. He came awake blinking and whining. "Wha'? What's wrong?"

"This Captain Damion interests me."

Jarvis rubbed his red eyes, hating her, seeing no escape. "What's so in'resting?"

"According to Morgen's letter he refused to carry out his battle orders."

"Traitor to his country. Should be court-martialed and shot dead."

"A Navy hero from the Korean War. Annapolis man. Spotless record." She spoke dreamily and not at all to Jarvis. "It took guts to do what he did."

McCready was impressed. Flesh-and-blood hero. Envy stirred inside him. "Probably a Commie agent. Don't laugh, baby. They infiltrate everywhere."

"I find myself more and more intrigued by Captain Damion, Jarv. I'm going to the Coast with you."

McCready saw his fond dream of a holiday with Wanda Berry vanish. He knew the futility of trying to change Melba's mind. Now this damned hero. . . ! He was overcome by an urge to scream. Moments later his head was buried in the pillow and he was sobbing.

Melba seemed pleased. "Why Jarv doll, I didn't realize I meant so much to you." She stroked his heavy shoulders. "We'll have a ball. I love San Francisco. We'll eat at Jack's and shop at Gump's. I'll buy you the Golden Gate Bridge."

"Damn it all, Melba," he whined. "This is no junket! It's a business trip. Hearings. A congressional investigation. We can't go making pleasure trips on the taxpayers' money."

"It's a business trip for me, Jarv. I'll use the company jet and pay my own way." Her deft fingers loosened his pajama trousers.

"Hoskins?"

"Captain Paul Damion." Her husband's bewildered eyes and streaked cheeks brought a curious look of affection to her face. "He may be your savior, my dear. He just may be the man to make you the most talked-about congressman in the nation." She took a cigarette from an ivory box on the night table and lighted it.

He wiped his eyes. "Sometimes, Melba, I just don't figure what goes on in that head of yours."

"Don't try." She allowed him to move closer. "With me along, you won't be needing Wanda Berry."

His fingers froze. "Where'd you get a crazy idea like I'd be taking Wanda Berry?"

"Just a thought."

"A damned funny thought if you ask me." He abruptly turned from her and muttering tried once more to sleep. She smoked her cigarette thoughtfully until he jerked himself up from the pillow. "Will you for Chri'sake turn out the light so I can get some sleep?"

"Strange man," she said almost tenderly.

"What's so strange? I put in a long hard day—"

"Not you, Jarv doll. You Jarv, are a weak drunken pig. A vulgar slob. Insecure, cheap, scheming, ill-mannered. Why I ever married you—"

"You know damned well why."

"We all do stupid things in our lives, don't we? Like thinking we could get away with taking along Wanda Berry and those long lovely legs that go all the way up to her lovely ass."

His strong fingers grabbed for her throat and missed and clutched a thick braid of golden hair. A swift backward sweep of her powerful arm sent him reeling to the floor. Her expression was beatific. "Try that

169

again and I scream for Greta to beat the crap out of you. And that, believe me, she will be glad to do."

"You crippled bitch, you."

"River scum."

He staggered up from the floor, weaving, bleary-eyed, a hulk of faked outrage. "You and your dyke kraut can go to hell. I'm sleeping in the study."

He stalked out, a pajama string trailing. Melba ground out her cigarette, quite pleased with herself. She considered a call on the intercom to Greta down the hall but decided against it. She was fond of Jarv. She could have ditched him long ago. But the amusing diversions he offered were occasionally choice. Like the Wanda Berry bit. Small delights she was not yet ready to surrender. Nor did she care to give up the sense and actuality of power the management of his career gave her. She needed that power to sweeten the bitter cup of legless marriage, to compensate for the cruelties of nature. She thrived on it.

Jillson now. She knew he would come running should she care to nod. He carried an interesting scar along his throat and she must learn all about it. Had it been war or love or merely a goiter? Certainly his grits-and-pangravy wife would not have the nerve to object, should Melba care to make a thing of it.

Dull tools, she thought. Damion seemed an opponent worthier of her steel. What does one do to be a Navy hero, anyway? Sink an enemy submarine? Service the admiral's wife? One thing about the mysterious Captain Damion fascinated her: he had the guts to go against the grain.

Sleep came over her. The image of Paul Damion faceless in her thoughts possessed loins as sinewy and graceful as an El Greco. She dwelt on that image until it became sweetly erotic and in her half-awake curious way she dealt with it and in sinful bliss soon slept.

XIV

In accordance with his orders Damion flew to Saigon for further transportation. A sleepy-eyed chief yeoman at Navy Headquarters led him through a maze of makeshift passageways to the duty transportation officer. He was a slight, balding lieutenant commander with the faintly hostile look of a YMCA night clerk. Slouched over his desk, he glanced at Damion's orders, leaped to his feet when he saw the name and managed a bent salute.

"Yes, sir! Captain Paul Damion." He gestured toward his scrambled desk. "Sorry, sir. Big work load. Have a seat, Captain. Won't be but a minute." He moved away muttering "Damion. Captain Paul Damion," and disappeared at the end of a passageway behind a door marked ComNavForV.

Damion, puzzled, wondered if Commander, Naval Forces, Vietnam, was anyone he knew. What else could have galvanized the duty officer to such unusual behavior? He shifted about, staring through the duty officer's cubicle into the large outer office. Enlisted men sat at desks in rows fingering typewriters and noses, pretending to be busily engaged. He knew they were watching him. He felt tension in the humid air.

The duty officer returned and sat at his desk facing Damion. He cleared his throat. "We have your space, Captain. You're on a flight to Tokyo first thing tomorrow morning."

"Tokyo? That's two thousand miles the wrong way, Commander. I'm headed Stateside."

"Sorry about that, sir. That is the one morning flight Military Air Command makes. It's the only Navy transportation available to you at this time."

Available to you at this time. Something was awry. "I don't want to go to Tokyo. I'm willing to hang around a day or two for a direct flight east. Must be something going to Guam or Pearl."

"The orders are to fly you to Tokyo, sir." He fidgeted with the papers, threw a sidelong glance at the enlisted men who stretched to catch every word, and said quietly, "Of course there are commercial flights, Captain."

He was not being impertinent, Damion decided. He saw the oddly strained expression in the man's eyes and read it as the torment of a dutybound officer carrying out orders against his better judgment. He knew it firsthand. The recognition was shocking.

"Tell me something, Commander."

"Sir?"

"You were upset when you read my orders. Why?"

"Me upset, Captain—?"

"What's up, Commander?"

"Your name, sir. That was it."

"You've heard what's happened."

The face went dutifully blank. "Oh yes. It was at Inchon in 1950." His eyes sparkled, false as rhinestones. "I was there, Captain Damion. Only a chief quartermaster then. But I was on the open bridge of the lead destroyer in Flying Fish Channel when you signaled us in."

Some of the tension drained out of Damion. The man was stalling. He had heard what had happened off Ha Loi Trung. He was covering for his superior and trying to protect Damion from his own shame. A good man.

"Never believed I'd be meeting you face to face." He slouched before Damion's steady gaze. "Sorry if I'm out of line, Captain."

"It's good of you to remember," Damion said. "Now I'd like a word with your commanding officer."

"You mean, sir, my immediate superior?"

"I mean ComNavForV."

"That would be Rear Admiral Leo Fulsome."

"Very good. I'll speak with him."

"The admiral's on an inspection tour, sir."

"I'll wait."

"It'll be several days, Captain."

"Why?"

"He's north of here with Operation Game Warden, River Patrol Force."

"Well, I'm not about to fly an extra two thousand miles. Who'd you talk to behind that damned door?"

The duty officer cringed slightly. "My immediate superior, sir. Captain F. Vincent Garrison, Jr."

"I know Captain Garrison." Damion began to feel better. "You trot back in here and tell old Vinny Garrison Paul Damion's out here."

"Captain Garrison left orders not to be disturbed, sir."

Damion paused a moment before he spoke again. "Must I make my request an order, Commander?"

The man stared at the roomful of enlisted men and at the shut door and back at Damion "Please don't, Captain."

"Why not?"

"It could only embarrass all three of us, sir."

It took Damion a long moment to grasp fully what the duty officer was saying. The cold logic of it chilled his marrow. There was the door five degrees to starboard and astern of the duty officer's head. All he had to do was walk past and open the door and tell his classmate, "Vinegar" Garrison, what a gutless crud he was. Precisely what he had always been. At the Academy a cheat, a fawning, bootlicking excuse for a Navy career man. In the post-war years through Korea, a malingerer and graduate course-taker. And in recent years, with the Navy fighting for its independence and its autonomous life, a political plotter and back stabber.

He's got the word on me, Damion thought. *And hasn't the guts to show his face.*

"Sorry I blew my stack, Commander."

"That's okay, Captain."

Damion stuck out his hand. The man gripped it hard. "Sometimes I wonder what it's all about, sir," he muttered. "Whether it's worth the strain, is what I mean."

"It's worth it," Damion said. "Now write me that chit for the Tokyo Express. Like the man says. And check me into BOQ."

"Aye, Captain Damion." He signaled a yeoman and gave him the details. "Be ready for you in an hour, Captain."

"Thank you." He grinned. "Thanks for remembering Inchon."

"Any message for Captain Garrison, sir?"

"Any ideas?"

"I'd be delighted to tell him what a prick he is, sir."

"I'd be the last," Damion said, "to interfere with interoffice communications."

"Good luck, Captain," said the duty officer.

He walked into the hot blast of downtown Saigon, drifting along the sweltering streets, jostled by peddlers and whores, mindful only of the waste the side trip to Tokyo meant, a waste in time and money, a vengeful waste in terms of human decency. There were planes enough to Pearl. Whose idea was it, then? Hardly Garrison's. He lacked the courage. Pfeiffer lacked the bile. It didn't really matter. In the morning he'd be on his way. Roundabout, but pointed toward home.

The crowd swept him along the narrow sidewalk. It amused him to hear the Vietnamese jabbering in their native tongue unaware that he understood every word of it. Good people, sorely troubled, most of them, torn by conscience and greed in the fat shower of Yankee plenty. The endless traffic honked and clattered past, a jumble of cyclos, motor bikes, carts and taxies, cab drivers screaming contempt, schoolgirls on cycles, their fawn thighs gleaming. *A poor man's Paris*, he thought.

But if Garrison knows, so does the whole damned Navy. The word is out. The shaft awaits me wherever I go.

What he needed was a drink. He realized in his dispirited state it could only lead to more drink. There had been a few times in his life when his tight control faltered. The time on Yong-hung-do. That day when Martha had divorced him. One of those times, he told himself. Why fight it?

He stared through the open front of a saloon. From its dim recesses came shrill female laughter. He caught a whiff of perfumed flesh in the fetid air and the stale smell of drink. Nearest him at the bar a couple writhed in a shameless ritual of love play. A native soldier, drunk, turned suddenly and spat into the striped sunlight. The puddle of phlegm quivered at Damion's feet. Muttered words of apology were lost to him. His stomach heaved and he moved on, welcoming the tumult and babble of strangers in the street, drained of desire, in control once more.

The balding mustang was gone from his desk in Navy headquarters. As though he never existed. Had he passed along his message to Garrison? Damion would never know, but he felt better thinking about it.

A dough-faced yeoman handed him an envelope with his orders and the plane chit. Damion took a cab to a floating restaurant on the river, ate an excellent Chinese dinner, and rode a cyclo back to BOQ.

He showered and stretched on the bed naked and thought of the reunion soon with Angela. How she would look after his long absence. How much she had grown.

Long before the divorce his homecoming thoughts had always been of Angela. He remembered the uninhibited almost fierce way she would race to him across an airport waiting room and throw her arms around him, kiss him hard on the lips, hugging him, so that gently, firmly, he would hold her off and look into eyes teary with love and say, "Enough, enough," laughing self-consciously and enjoying every moment of it, but reacting oddly just the same. Not that it was wrong. Nothing like that. She was his daughter, still a kid and barely formed. Just that people sometimes stared too long and he was tempted once or twice to bunch a fist and tell them this was his own sweet kid and to mind their goddamn business.

The last time, though. It had come as a shock to him, to see how Angela had matured in the year he had not seen her. It had caught him unprepared and he had to unlock her arms almost immediately after she had embraced him. He caught the quick hurt look in her eyes and he asked somewhat lamely where her mother was. Angela said she didn't give a damn, *he* was all the family she wanted, and he realized all was not going well in the social environs of "Cypress Crotch," a genteel stone's throw from Pebble Beach's Cypress Point.

He stirred fitfully. His naked skin itched. He wished it were daylight and he on his way. The hell of it with Angela was she was no longer a kid. He was going to have to be a lot more aware of that and cautious in what he said and did. That last time at Carmel, walking on the beach, he had learned how bright she was and how concerned about the world.

They had got onto the subject of her college curriculum, which was mostly in the arts. She was more interested, she said, in ecology and the social sciences. She rattled on about pollution and the biosphere and before he knew it, they were into a debate on marijuana (No worse than booze and maybe better, she said), the Peace Corps (Did he think she should join it?), and of course Vietnam.

Angela made no bones about Vietnam. She was going to involve herself in the antiwar movement as soon as she could, once her studies were underway. Would he mind very much?

"No," he said, "as long as your studies don't suffer."

"I don't understand," she said, "how someone as warm and gentle as you got mixed up in the military."

"Gentle to you, Angela. Captain Bligh to my men."

"But to actually choose a military career . . ."

"It was chosen for me."

"By whom?"

"My father."

"You could have objected. Or resigned after you saw what it was like."

"It was different then."

"Different how? Wars don't change. Wars mean killing people in cold blood. People you don't even hate."

"It's doing one's duty." The words came hard to him.

"Whatever you call it, Dad, it's murder."

"It's loving one's country enough to go ahead with it."

"No matter how much you detest it?"

He nodded.

"Have you?"

"Have I what?"

"Killed."

"Yes."

"I mean—actually a person—someone?"

"Yes."

"You had to?" There was a trembling in her voice. He longed to take her in his arms and dared not.

"In line of duty. For love of country." The words rang hollowly in his ears.

They walked in silence, it seemed, for a very long time. She kicked the sand with the toe of her worn loafer. He admired the slimness of her ankles, faintly powdered with sand. She said, "I think love for one's fellow man comes first. Before duty. Before love of country." And seeing what her words had done to him, she held his arm tightly. "It should, damn it, shouldn't it?" He nodded, unable to trust his voice, thinking how much he loved this child of his and what a touching thing she had said.

"I'm annoying you," she burst out. "You must hate me."

He smiled down at her. "I love you even more."

"And I adore you." She hugged his arm. "The kind of man you are. It blows my mind."

"What a curious way to put it."

177

"I mean like what you did in Korea that time, when I was, I don't know, a year or two old, whatever it was. You never speak of it, do you?"

"No."

"But I heard it later from the kids at school, what a big Navy hero my father was, and I was the only kid who didn't know it. Whatever it was you'd done."

"It doesn't matter now."

"Except I have this ambivalence, this really crazy hang-up because here you are my father, the big Navy hero whom I adore. But there you are out someplace killing perfectly innocent people."

"And you hate me for it."

"I could never hate you. But I can try with all my heart to stop you from what you're doing."

"God give you strength," he said.

Now at eighteen with her freshman year well along, there was no way of telling how deeply she had involved herself in antiwar activity. In half-sleep he smiled. One thing was certain. She was not about to be crowned queen of one of those vulgar California pageants or festivals. Not for her Miss Cranshaw Melon of Fresno County or Date & Fig Princess of the Year.

He wondered what Angela would say when he told her what had happened off Vietnam and why he had been given this thirty-day medical leave. He would tell it like it really was. He could trust Angela.

He closed his eyes. They would be needling him with all kinds of questions, once the word was out. Navy brass. The press. The whole self-righteous pack of scandal hunters in full cry panting for a taste of Damion blood. Pfeiffer was an idiot if he believed the incident could be kept under wraps for long. Didn't he know he lived in a democracy?

Pull yourself together, old man. It's Yong-hung-do revisited. Survival. What you do to stay alive. You don't panic. You conserve strength. You outthink the enemy. You pull through. Meanwhile, just hang on and keep the faith. Take each kiss or blow as it comes. Trust in luck, but don't count on it.

178

What really matters, he decided in that vague twilight before sleep, is that none of it must hurt Angela. Because when you really get down to it, Angela is all that really matters. Angela is all I've got left.

XV

The public address speaker rasped its regrets. The early morning flight from Saigon was having its troubles. Damion checked in and stood apart from the others in the steamy waiting room at Tan Son Nhut. He discouraged the friendly overtures of fellow officers. *I'm a navigational hazard,* he told himself. *Steer clear.*

Some men slept. Others who had talked freely during the dawn hours now sat with the sullen resignation of men between battles, accustomed to foul-ups and delays, grateful to be alive. They would sweat out these final hours in stupefying heat with frayed nerves and hair-trigger tempers, still in the war zone, still vulnerable to violent death. But it could not defeat them. They shared one indestructible hope. They were going home.

New arrivals homeward bound continued to appear in a dusty stream of jeeps and command vehicles. The man behind the customs counter snarled instructions and orders. Weary GIs filled out the endless forms. A few girls clung to their departing lovers, their soft eyes searching. In front of the Pan Am ticket counter a roped-off area marked the spot where the enemy rocket had exploded a few weeks before.

Viet workmen sawed and hammered. Damion wondered where Eric Stevens had stood when the big VC 122-mm rocket smashed through the high roof. Men in sweat-soaked uniforms sprawled on their sea bags and duffels ignoring the noise and the mangled steel beams overhead. Most of them had been here since midnight.

The torn building's skeleton exposed to the morning sky reminded Damion of the Atomic Dome. It was barely a week since he had been at Hiroshima. It seemed longer. He thought of Mizu and the unfeeling flesh into which the cigarette burned. He thought quickly of Chu Tan Vinh, who had betrayed him. He thought of stout loyal McKim.

The 0805 took off at 1040, refueled at Manila and Okinawa, and arrived at the Tokyo airport without incident. He heard his name over the p.a. speaker and went to the information desk, where he was handed a dispatch from Admiral Pfeiffer ordering him to report by first available military air transport to Commander-in-Chief, Pacific Fleet, Pearl Harbor. His heart sank. Tremblay the Terrible.

A living legend. Four stars, each one dipped in sea bile and crusty with barnacles. Damion had hoped to get by without a confrontation with Tremblay. He had stood with Tremblay, side by side, on an earlier, happier occasion. Now he understood why he had been routed via Tokyo. Pfeiffer, faced with a painful decision, had needed the time to clear things with CinCPac. CinCPac took the conn and the screws turned.

He passed the next twenty-four hours in gritty airfield lounges catching catnaps on greasy plastic-and-chrome benches or aloft in bumpy and tedious flight. Time blurred in a ticker tape of confusing dreams and rude awakenings. He flew into rain squalls and blinding sun, through clouds and over endless blue sea. Strained metal creaked. The thunder of jet engines filled his ears until his head ached. Men snored, drank, groaned, wept, vomited. Old men now with boys' faces, foolish

181

and weak with the prospect of freedom. Or cold sober, stunned by the hell they had seen.

Silent or maudlin, my brothers, he mused. Yet he sat among them stubbornly erect and aloof, his thoughts on Angela.

The plane flying the last leg landed at Hickam field close to the Navy's air headquarters. A meeting was breaking up at a nearby hangar building. A young Marine major with a chestful of decorations and staff chicken guts draped at his shoulder left a group of officers and crossing the concrete strip met Damion at the plane's ladder. Damion, air deaf and sore, returned the smart salute with a token gesture and stood blinking at the lush green of the island hills. His summer khakis were hopelessly wrinkled. His tie hung loosely. He needed a shave and something to drink, something more substantial than rancid coffee in a plastic cup. His bones ached from the long flight.

"Captain Damion?"

Damion nodded, surprised.

"This way, please." The major started briskly across the cement apron in the direction of the building.

"Where we headed, Major?"

"You received Admiral Pfeiffer's dispatch, Captain?"

"In Tokyo. Yes."

"Then you know about meeting with CinCPac." He almost smiled. "You're in luck. He's here."

"I need a few minutes to clean up, Major."

"No time for that, Captain."

Damion felt too weary to argue the point. The Marine major was carrying out orders. The other passengers had drifted past and were gone. Damion took off his cap and wiped the damp sweatband. "My gear's still on board."

"I've arranged for it to be checked."

The major spoke with a curtness just short of rudeness. Damion did not miss it. "I'm cleaning up," he said firmly. "I'm not about to call on any admiral looking like this."

"No choice, Captain." The major pointed to a gray limousine parked alongside a hangar. "Admiral Tremblay's waiting." He saluted again. "I'll attend to your gear now." He turned, actually clicking his heels, and strode off.

Tremblay at sixty-plus was a scowling pockmarked bantam, his neck flesh wrinkled as a rooster's over the high collar of his starched dress whites. He sat alone in the rear of the car, dry and unruffled in the deadly heat, master of a million men and ships, imperious and unsmiling, a pocket-sized Caesar. His squinty blue eyes raked Damion from head to foot. Cold eyes, as indifferent to mercy as the sea itself.

Damion stood at attention. The admiral had just ordered it. A flow of cool air swept from the open door of the tonneau to the blistering concrete at Damion's feet. Beads of cold sweat ran from his armpits and coursed down his tired flesh. A Marine corporal sat at the wheel of the car and stared straight ahead. Damion envied him. It would be nice, he thought, to climb in and close the door and relax, in the soothing bath of cool air. He did not move, ramrod stiff, his eyes focused inches above the gilded peak of Tremblay's cap.

He reflected on the ordeals of others, ancient men who had suffered torture in the name of duty. Atlas, Hercules, Sisyphus of the classic myths. Flesh-and-blood heroes like Mindzenty or the death marchers of Bataan and Corregidor. Heroes, he reflected bitterly. The code of stiff lip, steel gut. So I stand at stupid attention in the blazing sun while every fiber screams to let go. Proving what a good officer I am? Justifying the cut of my bloody jib?

He caught the admiral's eye on him and met it without flinching. That, too, was part of the idiotic game, eye to eye without batting a lash, two grown men playing the silly kid game right out of Kipling and Richard Harding Davis. It was really very funny. In spite of himself and the torment in the sun and all it stood for and the good officer he truly was, Damion smiled.

"Wipe it!"

Damion wiped it. The admiral growled an order at his driver, who got out and left the engine running and walked into the cool shadows of the hangar.

"I'd invite you in," Tremblay finally said to Damion. "There is a small problem." He pursed his cracked lips. "To seat you forward where the driver sits would be an affront to your rank. To allow you alongside me would be an insult to mine."

Damion said nothing. His fixed jaw ached a little and he swayed slightly. The admiral scratched his nose, studied his fingertips, taking his time.

"However, to keep this eight-cylinder motor running and the door open and the air-conditioning mechanism on, is a shameful waste of the taxpayers' money. We can't afford waste these days, can we, Captain?"

"No, sir." His voice a croak.

"A bit of a dilemma, eh?"

Damion wilting clutched at a straw. "May I suggest, Admiral, turning up one of the jump seats?"

"And give you the benefit of our Navy's air conditioning? After what you've done to us?" He scowled. "More than you deserve. But the taxpayers come first. Get in."

Damion pulled down a jump seat and got in and closed the door. He wiped his face with a grimy handkerchief. The admiral regarded him without pity.

"Know why you're here?" He snapped his words.

"Not really, sir."

"To be reamed out. Pfeiffer's getting senile. You got away with murder. Medical leave, my ass! Know what I did?"

"No, sir."

"The minute I read Fife's report I notified Washington of the facts. Recommended immediate action. A full court-martial, Captain. No recommendation of mercy." He calmly lighted a cigarette. "They turned it down."

"Why, sir?"

"How the hell do I know why? It's a whiz kid Navy, run by computers! It used to be a sailor's Navy. A damned good one. Run by honest men who loved the sea." He snorted. "A yacht club full of lace pants technicians ass-kissing the push-button politicians in Washington."

He opened a thick briefcase. "Pfeiffer's report." He

shook a sheaf of papers under Damion's nose. "It stinks. You got some hold over him? He in love with you or something?"

His fist, large-knuckled and calloused, seemed surprisingly big and capable for a small old man who spent most of his time behind a desk. "A whitewash. He deserves the ax as much as you. For a dereliction of duty. For trying to protect a traitor in our midst."

"I'm no traitor, Admiral."

"You damned well betrayed a trust. You violated an allegiance to your country. You gave aid and comfort to the enemy. If that isn't being a traitor I don't know what the hell is."

He stared sourly past Damion at the activity on the runways. Damion shifted slightly. The cool air was worth every scathing word. The car engine purred soothingly.

"I was right there on 7 December '41," Tremblay said, pointing. "A hundred yards from where the first bomb hit the mess-hall roof. I watched A-20s and P-40s and B-17s and the cream of the battleship Navy burn or sink or die all around me." He drew on his cigarette and carefully tapped the ashes into a chrome tray. "Right here on Hickam and over the fence in the Navy yard, men wearing the same uniform you're wearing right now, gave their lives without question."

His raspy voice went on. "I haven't forgotten the day in Washington, young man, when I stood alongside you and the Secretary pinned a Navy Cross on your blouse. For Inchon. I was proud of you then. Right now I'd like to forget it. I'd like to forget I ever heard the name of Paul Damion."

He leaned back and smoked in silence for a while. Damion's underclothes clung to his body, greasy and chilling. A shoe lace had come undone. He covered it with his other shoe.

"You couldn't have picked a worse time," Tremblay continued. "Our public image is the worst in the Navy's history. Stupid accidents. Collisions. Sinkings. Desertions. Dirty politics. Budget cuts. Here we are in a nuclear age trying to meet wartime responsibilities and commitments with outmoded hulls and fossil fuel."

"Thank the Pentagon—"

"I'll do the bitching, thank you. We face disaster on all fronts. A single act like yours is as much a disaster as the sinking of a nuke carrier. Morale weakens. Leadership fails. Cowards take heart. Our enemies rejoice. The news media make a three-ring circus out of it. Our Army and Air Force friends pounce on it to pick up points for their own show. I ask for strong, loyal officers and what do I get? Traitors who disobey orders."

"All I did—"

"You were wrong! Tactically wrong, morally wrong—"

"What's wrong with trying to save human lives?"

"Lives?" Tremblay seemed to hear the word for the first time. "What's lives got to do with it?" Scornfully he said, "Where've you been hiding for the last few years, Captain?"

"Serving my country."

"Get one thing straight. Your country's a multibillion-dollar business conglomerate. The Navy's one lousy little part of it. A fourth-rate subsidiary. You and me? Budget items. Insignificant computerized code numbers with computerized jobs to do. And if we don't do those jobs, the machine knows it and the systems analysts in the Pentagon knock us off." He laughed, a brusque, nasty noise in the sudden quiet. "Lives?" he barked. "I don't know what the hell you're talking about."

"Hiroshima—" Damion said, himself surprised.

"Hiroshima hell!" The admiral's fist pounded the armrest. "You want *me* tell *you* about lives? Pearl Harbor? And Corregidor? Don't hand me Hiroshima. It's dead and buried. Forgotten. So's Hitler. And Guernica. And the Christian Crusades. And the Goths and Attila and your brother and mine, Cain." He jammed his cigarette into the ash tray. Sparks flew. "Lives!"

"People," said Damion. "Man."

"Man killed long before he prayed. You expect him to stop now?"

"It's got to stop sometime."

"That's the computer's problem. Not yours. Right

186

now in that uniform you're wearing, after what you did, you're a liability. The computer boys don't like it. And I don't like it."

"Are you suggesting I resign?"

"I've considered it."

"And—?"

"I don't dare. As a civilian, you could spill the Navy beans. And for a very fancy price. *Look* and *Life* would love your story. So would a dozen dove publishers and half the producers in Hollywood. In uniform, you're still under security regulations."

"At least I know where we stand."

"I'm taking no chances. I've enough problems out here without trying to analyze the nit-picking theories of my psycho sea captains." He frowned. "My God in heaven. We could've cleaned up this mess back in '65, when we first started bombing the North. Before they got their Russky SAM sites built. Could've wiped 'em out and been home for breakfast. Now we're in it to our eyeballs. Graft and corruption in Saigon. Nigger power back home." He fumbled for a cigarette, lighted it, and leaned back. "Steering a desk through a swamp of red tape isn't my idea of sea duty. But I carry on. I remind myself I'm a number like everyone else, with a job to do. That's all."

He sat in a huddled heap, arms and legs crossed, gnomelike and suddenly revealed. Damion could not believe it. This wizened tyrant in his fancy dress whites, surrounded by ribbons and medals and the aura of history, a number? Could this be all? A number?

Tremblay's shrewd eye missed none of it. "You learn to live with it, Captain."

"Maybe that's what's bothering me," Damion said, his own words an unveiling.

"And what's that supposed to mean?"

"It's not easy to explain."

"Try."

"I'm also a number. But there's a private man inside me. I respect him. Orders or no orders. Duty or not."

"I came here to humiliate you. Not to discuss lost causes."

"Humanity's no lost cause."

187

"I told you man killed long before he prayed. You said it had to stop, didn't you?"

"Yes, sir."

"Did you mean the killing or the praying?"

"The killing, of course."

"It's the praying should stop. People have lied to themselves about war and killing long enough."

"Governments make war, Admiral. Not people."

Tremblay rubbed his jaw. He stared morosely across the sun-baked concrete glazed with the oil of distant fields. "You're not the first line officer I've had mind trouble with."

"Nor the last, I hope, sir."

"I wish to hell I knew what's bugging the lot of you." He sighed deeply and glanced at his watch, all business now. "I've ordered a security lid clamped tight on you, Captain. Every public affairs officer and intelligence officer has the word. No interviews. No photographs. No statements to the press. Your destination?"

"San Francisco."

"Family?"

"A daughter, sir."

"You're not to discuss your status. Much as I hate to, I'm going along with Pfeiffer's handling of this. But I'm not through. I'm seeing CNO in Washington in a few days. You'll be hearing from us. Meanwhile—" He scowled. "—R & R's your official reason for leave, should anyone ask."

"Yes, sir."

"You'll get no sympathy from me. I intend to be damned hard-nosed with CNO about this—defection of yours. I've instructed the paymaster division to hold up pay from the day you quit your command. Understood?"

"You're making a personal and prejudiced matter of it, Admiral."

"Too damn bad!" Tremblay snapped. "The Navy's been my life for over forty years. I regard what you've done as a personal attack on me and I'm hitting right back!" He scowled. "You're familiar, of course, with the Military Code of Conduct."

"Yes, sir."

"May I remind you of the last clause. Roman numeral six, if memory serves me: *I will never forget that I'm an American fighting man, responsible for my actions, and dedicated to the principles which made my country free. I will trust in my God and the United States of America.*"

"The principles which made this country free also include respect for human life and liberty. And the pursuit of happiness. Each one of which we're violating—"

"Enough!" Tremblay shouted. He wiped his lips. "What were you going to say?"

"—violating in Vietnam. Scorched earth and slaughtered civilians. It was—that same respect for human life that got to me out there off Ha Loi Trung." He struggled for the right words. "The right to decide where duty ends and murder begins."

Tremblay glared at him. "What the hell's the use of talking? You're all alike. Down with America! You all spout the same Commie lies—the direct line from Moscow. Or is it Peking this time?"

"No use talking, sir. As you said."

"My orders stand. You'll fly commercial airlines. At your own expense. And get yourself cleaned up. You're a mess. A disgrace to the uniform you wear."

"Thanks to your personal routing via Tokyo."

Tremblay's face showed nothing. "Tamaris has your new orders."

"Tamaris?"

"The Marine major who met your plane. A Greek who could teach you a few things."

"I saw his ribbons."

"Fifty combat missions over North Vietnam. Seven MIGs. Twice 'punched out' of his Corsair II and hit by ground fire. Saved a wounded Skyraider pilot who ditched trying to rescue him. And coached the chopper crew to his life raft with a hand blinker." He glanced obliquely at Damion. "Still a few guys with guts around."

"I'm glad for your sake, Admiral."

"It was the skipper of an earlier *Chesapeake*, Cap-

189

tain, whose dying words were 'Don't give up the ship.' "

"David Lawrence," Damion said. "War of 1812, off Boston Harbor."

"Shame," the admiral said. He opened the door. "Now get out."

A blast of hot air swept in. Damion bent and kicked the jump seat up and stepped out and swung the door shut. Tremblay rolled the window down an inch. "Keep Commandant, Twelfth Naval District, advised of your whereabouts."

"Aye, sir." Damion saluted.

"Stay out of sight and out of the news."

"I'll try, Admiral."

"Try, hell. That's an order." The window rolled shut.

The driver came out of the hangar's shadows. Major Tamaris met Damion near the operations building and handed him the envelope of orders and a baggage check. Damion thanked him. For a moment he regarded the taut unsmiling face and with a pang recalled his own fine moment at Inchon. He wanted to say something. No words would come.

"Is that all, Captain?"

It was not all. He longed to tell the major how it had felt when he murdered his prisoners on Yonghung-do. That he forgave Vinh his treachery. That his hold-fire order was humane and no betrayal. There was so much he needed to tell Tamaris. But he had never seen brown eyes so pitiless.

"That's it, Major." He saluted. Tamaris returned a brief salute and without a word strode away.

Damion watched the broad-shouldered figure until the gray limousine in the shimmering sun swallowed it and disappeared from view.

He walked slowly into the operations building. You had to admire the sadistic genius of Tremblay. A real pro. Dredging up that old "Don't give up the ship" line. Decking himself out in his dress whites, knowing damned well the sorry shape a man would be in after thousands of miles of military air flight. But the cunning stab, the one that sunk deepest, was the Tamaris ploy, bringing Damion in shame face to face with a live young hero.

Did Tamaris get the jump seat? Or did he rate sitting alongside the Terrible himself, the Navy's Number One in the Pacific. What the hell was so marvelous about the major, anyway? Got shot down, didn't he? And snooty Tamaris was thirty if he was a day. He, Damion, had been a kid of twenty-four that time at Inchon. Won a war, damn it. And came home without a scratch. Match that, you salty old bastard.

He began to feel less sorry for himself. He collected his gear and took a taxi to the Honolulu airport. The sight of people going home revived his spirits. He understood and shared their happy prospect. Everywhere he looked he saw shopwindows sparkling with duty-free perfumes and liquors. Booths crammed with trinkets and piled high with gaudy souvenirs almost hid the pretty salesgirls from view.

He checked the mainland flight schedules, chose an airline, and took his place at the end of a queue. He found himself in the midst of a party of insurance company executives, a jovial lot accompanied by their wives, winding up a week-long sales conference holiday. They ranged in lines on both sides of Damion, a noisy cross-section of good-natured Americans in a jumble of luggage and expensive cameras, hand-painted coconuts and exuberant camaraderie. Their faces were too red. White fleshy arms and legs seemed unhealthy in contrast. Leis of fresh blossoms draped round their necks were paled by the florid hang-out shirts they wore. Their shorts were too long, obedient to the vogue of Bermuda or Nassau or whatever tropic island wore the current Seventh Avenue label. Garterless ankle socks, mostly black nylon, in the wrong shoes . . .

The wives were a chatty lot, self-conscious in shapeless muumuus, masking their shyness with much giggling and screeched greetings. Everyone having a marvelous time, thought Damion, touched with envy, resisting nausea.

He thought of the brochures and postcards of modern Hiroshima and his last evening there, spent with a friend of Mizu's, a college professor now in his forties who had survived the bombing. Guilt was corroding his spirit. The unhappy man's words were etched in Damion's memory.

"My love of fellow man, so Japanese in its innocence, was wiped out instantly by what I saw. People behaved brutally. They thought only of themselves. I was left unmarked, but with the strong feeling that human beings are nothing more than animals. Now that we have recovered from the Bomb and are prosperous, I feel it even more. I feel I, too, am an animal."

Damion looked at his fellow Americans on holiday—the noisy wisecracking, the winking and playful jabbing, the vulgar innuendoes. The luckiest people in the world. *For how long*? he wondered.

His spirits sagged. The line to the ticket counter moved too slowly. He thought once to bolt, to find a cool bar and in the semi-gloom settle his nerves with a tall drink until the crowds were gone. But he realized that crowds are never gone. They become worse. And he must learn to live with it. And the promise of Angela held him. That alone, though for a shaken moment even that had seemed a high price to pay.

The man in line ahead of him turned several times to stare at Damion's uniform and ribbons. Now he said, "Begging your pardon, Captain," saying it with exaggerated politeness. "I see you've been there too."

Damion nodded, trapped. The man's breath reeked sweetly of digesting fruit and island rum. He slapped Damion's ribbons with the back of his hand. "I was at Iwo. You know? Fourth Marines." He held out a long cigar and Damion, after a moment, took it. The ex-Marine stuck the cigar in his mouth and gestured at his fun-loving colleagues. "Fakes. Phonies. Right?" His voice a hoarse whisper, he leaned close, gripped Damion's sleeve. "Listen, Captain. I know, I *know*. The real thing is out where you guys are." He peered at Damion's ribbons. "You weren't on Iwo?"

"No."

"Listen. Lemme tell you what it was like. D'you mind? Green Beach on D-day, right smack under Suribachi." His bloodshot eyes gleamed. "Sure you don't mind?"

192

Damion looked past him at the waiting line. Four to go. He looked into the man's face, red-jowled and fleshy, the skin already peeling, the blue eyes pleading, a last flicker of hope there for a man drowning in a sea of middle-class mediocrity. Damion grinned. "Sure," he said and stuck the big cigar in his mouth. "Light me up like a good gyrene and tell me what it was like on Iwo."

XVI

It was past midnight when Angela came to the place where Brown lived. It was a gaunt green-shingled relic trimmed in clotted ivory, backed into a steep hill, its sheer façade ominous behind a high hedge and a snarl of untrimmed vines and shrubbery. It formed the bottom of a "U," in a cul-de-sac with a row of pastel structures on both sides, each a spurious variation on a Victorian theme.

No light showed in Brown's room. It was the attic front, a large, square window its only ventilation. Somewhere a record player ground out soul rock. Higher in the precariously angled street a dog howled, or a woman.

Angela climbed the rotting porch stairs. The flooring gave shakily beneath her. She moved gingerly. A dank graveyard smell rose from the soft earth beneath. She stumbled over a bicycle unseen across the open entry. Its loose chain clanked. Twisted spokes stabbed her flesh. A wheel spun, the rusty metal groaning.

Her body felt gritty and tense. Her bones ached from the long drive. She reached the stairs limping, not trusting the shaky banister. Her leather shoulder bag scraped the wall. *Any moment now,* she thought. *I'll scream.*

Brown in T-shirt and undershorts answered her knock. He peered over the chained door, his eyes squinty in sleep. He reached out and took her in. She clung to him. His arms felt strong and safe. She knew she was home.

The room smelled of marijuana smoke. He switched on a lamp. Clothes were strewn about or hung from nails driven into the rafters under the slanted eaves. The bed was a wide lumpy mattress on the floor. No sheets. A thin rumpled blanket once blue. Two fruit crates for tables or chairs, a beaded floor lamp, his army foot locker. Sardine cans for ash trays. In one corner an iron sink, a hot plate on a stool, some cracked dishes. Near the bed a pile of new school texts.

Brown with surprising tenderness helped Angela to the bed. She lay trembling while he covered her with the blanket and his old field jacket. He switched off the lamp. The room was bathed in the dim greenish glow of street lights. He sat at her side until she slept.

He remained there unmoving for several minutes in the semidarkness. He chose a stub from one of the sardine cans next to the bed, fitted a roach clip to it, and lighted up. He went to the window and sat cross-legged studying the pattern of car tops in the court below. Its rhythm fascinated him. The solid beat of soul rock had stopped. A rat shredding plaster inside the attic wall was the only sound that broke the night stillness. He took a long time finishing the joint.

Angela, he thought. *Home.*

He truly needed her. She steadied him. He had passed a nervous day buying the books for the courses he had registered for. The first class was scheduled for the morning. He had paid his matriculation and medical and lab fees. The tuition was paid. He had money in the bank for the first semester. He was all set.

It troubled him. Things had gone too smoothly. He was too long resigned to adversity. Its absence here confused him. He wondered how he would get along with kids younger and smarter than himself, hip kids

195

who looked on Easterners as squares or oddballs. And could he take the campus crap after a deal like Vietnam?

He had smoked two joints that night. He knew it was no good, to smoke pot alone in a depressed and nervous state. But he was lonely. That afternoon he had tried to talk with some of the other freshmen. Nothing came of it. They seemed eager to get away from him. It was between semesters and he was a stranger, out of the swing of things. The attitudes of unrest and hostility puzzled him. But he had come a long way and it had not been easy. He was determined to make a go of it.

He looked over the new books he had bought that day and put three aside. These were for his morning classes. He chose a shirt and slacks, fresh socks and undershorts, folded them neatly alongside the books.

His eye caught the gleam of Angela's shoulder bag. He sat scratching himself and studying it. He could spend hours on end sitting trancelike studying an object. He had got the habit when he was confined to the prisoners' stockade back at Dix.

He hurt now, remembering.

There were four grades of confinement. Maximum security prisoners were separated from the others and under constant supervision. Minimum and medium custody were less strict, differing from each other only in details like KP and the arming of the guards. The parolees lived outside the high barbed-wire-topped fence and were on their honor not to leave. Sometimes there were two fences and the space between was filled with coiled barbed wire they called concertina. To escape, a man would have to climb over both fences, but he'd get shot first.

The boredom of basic training, rather than its rigors, had got to him after the first two weeks and he overstayed a three-day pass. Brown caught minimum custody. His duties were mostly to rake the gravel yard in the center of the compound. He had no KP. He never knew why.

There were nine barracks in the compound and a mess hall. It was a dreary place. Everything was painted a sickly yellow. He raked from seven to eleven in the morning and from two until four in the afternoon. He worked slowly, deliberately, because there would have been nothing more to do with the rest of time. He learned much about a rake, the curve of its slender handle, the smoothness of grained oak in his palms and fingers, the wide smile of its iron teeth. The rake became his friend. He often talked to it.

Some of the "free" hours were spent watching films on first aid, venereal disease, field tactics, and training techniques. Except for these and the raking detail, his time was his own. There was little worth reading and only a token effort at organized sports activities. Nobody really seemed to care.

He did what the guards ordered and they left him alone. Most of the guards were fair, trying to do a job they had not volunteered for. One sergeant who took special delight in baiting Brown, who punched him "for fun," was transferred soon after Brown got there. He witnessed only two beatings in the three weeks he was confined.

Many of the men confined with him were conscientious objectors. He talked to them often and sympathized with their moral views. But he could not bring himself to join them. He was here for a purpose—to risk his life in order to become eligible for the benefits of a free education. If he continued to buck the Establishment, he'd end up nowhere. Once over the hill was enough.

He was determined to see his military service through. He swallowed pride and obeyed orders. He often sat by himself to stay out of trouble. He would concentrate on a building, a tree, a trash can, a fire alarm box, a siren, testing his control. He thought of it as a form of yoga all his own.

Later in the jungle swamps of Vietnam this same control saved his life. By the time he got there he had taught himself to do exactly what they said. It made no sense being a martyr. Like those CO kids back at the compound in Dix. Or the bunch that sat on the grass at the Presidio and sang civil rights songs and were charged with mutiny and drew up to sixteen years at hard labor.

He would go to college come hell or high water. Nothing would stop him. There was only one way to get there. You eat shit, he told himself. That's how you get there.

He had been watching Angela's shoulder bag for almost twenty minutes before he moved. He unclipped the dead roach and picked up Angela's bag. He unchained the door and went out through the hall to the dank bathroom shared with the tenants in the back room. He hooked the door shut and turned on the light. He flushed the roach down the toilet. Then he sat on the cracked seat and dumped the contents of the leather bag on the warped linoleum floor.

There was nothing unusual. A thin plastic folder of credit cards for a bank, a store, two oil companies. A key case, a hairbrush, a lipstick, five folded facial tissues. A small bottle of Empirin which he carefully sniffed. Contact lenses in a fitted case. A small leather purse with twenty-eight dollars and some change, a safety pin, two rubber bands, and a mini-pen. A tinted photograph of a Navy officer laminated in plastic. He sat for several minutes studying Damion's picture.

He returned everything to the handbag except the picture. He went back to the room and chained the door. He turned on the floor lamp so that the light shone directly on Angela's face. He shook her until she awoke.

She stared at him confused, blinded by the light. Her face was streaked with tearstains. Brown shoved the picture under her nose. She stared at it stupidly, still not awake. He shook her.

"Who's this guy?"

She took the picture and held it where her eyes could focus on it. Even without her contact lenses she knew.

"My father."

"That kid? You're lying."

She was awake now and stared up at him. "You took that out of my handbag."

"So what, damn it! Who is he?"

198

"That's cheating, Brown." She snatched the picture from his fingers. He slapped her hard across the cheek. She clutched the blanket, stunned.

He thrust his face close to hers. "Don't tell me who's cheating around here."

"Go away."

"Why'd you come back? What's the deal?" He stood over her, rubbing his knuckles.

Angela crawled to the far side of the mattress. Her eyes did not leave his twisted face. "You're crazy," she said, very frightened now. She reached for her handbag. He kicked it closer.

"Don't worry. It's all there. Count it. Every cent."

She slipped Damion's picture into the bag. Her loafers were at the foot of the bed. She wondered what he would do next.

"You gonna tell me?"

"I'd like my loafers, please." A whisper. No more.

"That kid's no father."

She watched his knuckled fists relax. "If you don't mind—"

"Okay, I'm sorry."

"I'd like my shoes, please." She dared not move closer.

"I said I was sorry."

"Could I please have my shoes?"

"God damn it, Angie—"

"Don't call me that. I hate it."

"You leaving?"

She nodded. He reached down and tossed the loafers on the mattress near her. She slipped them on her feet.

"You can't go out now."

"You just watch."

"This time of night—"

"I'll manage, thank you."

"It's not safe, Angie—Angela."

"This is safer—here?"

He sat heavily on the foot of the bed. *He looks pitiful,* Angela thought. She smoothed her dress and slung the bag to her shoulder. She was free to go now. The chain was in her fingers, off the door. She lingered.

"Why'd you look into my bag, Brown?"

"It was stupid."

"But *why?*"

"I'm afraid . . . suspicious."

"Of what? Te really *is* my father. I don't lie, Brown."

Brown did not move.

"That picture was taken years ago when he was a lieutenant and won the Navy Cross."

He looked up. "I shoulda known. It all went too smoothly, see? I knew it wouldn't work."

"You're yelling."

"I'm scared, damn it! Tomorrow's my first class. You hear me? You know what that means, after three shoddy years? To go to college?" He gestured hopelessly. "Aah. How the hell would you know?"

"You should be pleased, proud. Not scared."

"Gold braid scares me. Brass. I caught enough hell—"

"What that got to do with going through someone's personal belongings? Slapping me around for no good reason?"

"You better go," he said thickly. "Go on. Beat it."

"I mean, you must be high on something. Talking crazy—" She moved from the door. "No one's ever struck me in my life, Brown. Not my mother, no one."

"Leave me alone, will ya? Just please go."

"You dig through my personal things. Slap me like I'm some cheap floozy off the street . . ." She was beginning to enjoy her new strength. "Whatever you're on, Brown, you should swear off it if that's what the stuff does to you."

"I smoked a joint. Two. But that's got nothing to do with it." He regarded her cautiously with fresh hope. "When you left today, I got scared. I thought I might never see you again. Then I saw this picture. Your old man? Okay. But I got this crazy idea maybe they sent you—"

"Who's they?"

"Fort Dix. Where they kept me."

"You told me Vietnam."

"Dix. Before Vietnam. In the stockade for going AWOL. I went nuts there . . . off my rocker. I don't

200

want trouble, Angela. You got to help me. You understand?"

"It's so crazy," she said slowly.

"Look," he said. "You got to trust me. This once. Come here. Sit down." He yearned to reach out and bring her close but he waited.

"I don't know."

"I swear to God I won't touch you."

"I want to help you, Brown. It's important to me. If you're in some kind of trouble, tell me." She put the bag down. "No lies, though. I can't stand lies."

He groped in the sardine can for a butt and lighted it. His fingers were trembling. "I just panicked. All of a sudden. Like everything was going down the drain." He gestured toward his books, his neatly prepared clothes. He could say no more.

She went to him.

"Don't for God's sake ever hit me again, Brown."

"I could cut off my hand."

"Ah, Brown——"

They sat awake for a time. Brown kept a flat tin of marijuana cigarettes under a loose board in the floor near the head of the bed. He showed Angela how to turn on, inhaling deep breaths, alternating air with smoke, holding the smoke and swallowing it.

"You don't want to exhale. You'll gag and hack. Inhale real easy, see? Like this. A bit at a time. That way you don't wrench out your guts."

Angela remembered her first effort with Daphne's crowd. "Won't it make my throat sore?"

"The drug effect takes care of that." He watched her and grinned. "You're already a pro."

It was harsh in her throat but she said nothing. All that mattered was that she was with him. To have gone would have killed her. There was no other place she wanted to be.

They were like children in the quiet dark, lost and a little frightened and needing each other. The city sounds came muted through the open window. Late traffic hummed on the freeway. *We need curtains,* she

201

thought. *Dishes, some sheets, a bedspread. The walls could use a coat of paint.*

"You've got to talk to me, Brown. We're such strangers."

"Different worlds," he said.

"You really think so?"

"Like credit cards. I never had a credit card."

"You're funny," she said. "Talk some more." She listened to his New York voice, dreamier by the minute.

". . . so this notice to appear comes. From the draft board. I show it to my old man. He's civil service. Works for the post office. He hands me this crap about it's my duty to my country. My own father. Then my mother sticks her two cents in. How would it look to the neighbors if I didn't go."

"She actually said that?"

"Who needs parents like that? Pop lost his temper and hit me. So I walked out. I stayed with a kid I knew from school, a Jewish kid, real nice, a brain. His folks were in Rome or somewhere, on a buying trip. We stayed up all night turning on. He has a mind like a razor. Tops in math before they kicked him out of school—"

"Why'd they kick him out?"

"Wouldn't cut his hair was all. So he says. I think maybe it was pot but you never know. Anyway, I told him about my walking out and no job and the draft board breathing down my neck. He knew how I felt about college and how I didn't have the dough. He said the best deal would be to enlist and I told him he was nuts. He said no, you do a three-year hitch and you're sent home. Then you line up for the GI benefits you earned by risking your life for your country. It didn't sound so great. My Christ, three years! But I figured, what the hell. What else was there for me to do? God knows I had it to here with my folks. It'd feel good to get away from the rat race. Groovy. See the world." He said almost in wonder, "You know, the furthest I ever got from home before the Army was Bear Mountain, except for Jersey City once and once to Staten Island on the ferry."

"What did you do then?"

"I thought about it a while. One day I just marched right into a recruiting station and signed up."

"What happened at Camp Dix?"

"Fort. There was this one sergeant hated my guts. I took it. Lucky he got transferred. I would have killed him." He was quiet for several moments. "Then one night me and this kid from Paterson went AWOL." He told her about the stockade and the boredom and the beatings and the conscientious objectors. "But what I learned was that's the way things are—in the Army—in life. You got to eat it. If you want to get through the three years you eat it. And I ate it and that's why I'm here."

After a while Angela felt marvelous, languid and at the same time intensely aware of her surroundings. The sensations did not come to her in a stream. Each was like an entire movie lasting a long time and intricately plotted. Her thoughts seemed to drift as the movie dissolved and a new one took its place. Each image was steely bright. Her thoughts soared. Nothing was impossible.

Brown's rough hands. His smooth and hairy body. The texture of the blanket. The touch of her own skin. Each was a discovery, a sensation at once amazing and entertaining.

They made love and Brown slept. Angela felt free and relaxed. The lovemaking with Brown had never been so intense and satisfying.

And he needs me, she thought.

He fit no image of the American girl's ideal dream man, that composite of fairy book heroes, TV commercials, and Jesus. He was everything her proper upbringing had taught her to reject. She felt no guilt being with Brown, even though their meeting was an accident.

All life's an accident. She reflected on this with terrible clarity, envisioning a parade of horrible accidents, freeway smash-ups, train wrecks, the gore of jungles and bombed city streets. Mothers and fathers are accidents, she decided with a judge's sobriety. Give or take a missed period or pill, a divorce or three. Who are we

203

after all but our mothers and fathers and who will our children be but us?

It was so amusing. Life is Charlie Chaplin. A parade of sad and funny pratfalls. It was a revelation too dazzling not to share. She caressed Brown to wakefulness and then to ardor. She gathered him strongly in her arms and mothered him and when he was ready she loved him.

The right time at the right place is no accident. Morro Bay, she reflected. Here. There is a divine guidance to accidents. I must never regret one.

She whispered in his ear. "Who are you, really?"

"Brown," he said.

Ah Brown, she thought. *I love you, precious Brown, with your new books and your carefully laid out clothes. I must take good care of you.*

She was having trouble with the esses. All the lovely esses of the tongue. Sinking silkily to sweet slumber, she thought. Snuggling sweetheart . . .

And slept.

XVII

Brown awoke early. He shaved closely and scrubbed himself well in the chipped claw-footed bathtub down the hall. He dressed with care while Angela slept.

He stood around the bus stop outside the cul-de-sac, feeling very good with textbooks under his arm. In future mornings he would walk the mile or so to the campus or thumb a ride. This was the first day. The bus was a luxury well earned. He blinked into the morning sun and flexed his muscles, a long way from West Ninety-second Street. How good it was.

The bus rolled through the morning streets. People smiled and said good morning. The books in his fingers felt firm and clean, smelled new like a football for Christmas. He was lucky to be alive and whole, in love, and off to school. You're a lucky one, Brown, he told himself.

The bus slowed. The driver honked the horn. They were approaching the campus. Students in the street moved reluctantly from the bus's path. The driver swore softly. A woman alongside Brown stared at him and his books and shifted uncomfortably. Brown's easy smile faded. His jaw tightened. Policemen in pairs carrying riot sticks stood against buildings and stared stolidly ahead.

Brown pushed himself through the aisle to the seat behind the driver. The bus stopped, blocked by the knot of students in the street. They were chanting and marching with arms linked. He saw more of them on the roofs of buildings. They were shouting at the policemen. His stomach turned.

"I'll get off here," he said.

He walked toward the central plaza in the direction of the administration building. Demonstrators with placards and banners made it difficult for him to move. Spectators along the sidewalks had jelled into a solid mass pockmarked by blue knots of policemen.

Brown clearly heard the voices from the roof tops now—*"Pigs off campus! Pigs off campus!"*—an endless refrain picked up by the student protesters in the street. They carried rocks with their placards and copies of *Challenge*. Brown wondered if they were all students. None of them carried books.

He made it to the tree where he had stood the morning before when Angela drove off. He found a freshman student named Fisher whom he had met during registration week. Fisher's thick beard and long hair framed wide blue eyes.

"What gives, Fisher?"

"The Committee, man."

"What committee?"

"The fuzz locked 'em up. Goddamn pigs."

"Make sense!" Brown grabbed Fisher's arm. Fisher stared at him, surprised.

"Half a dozen cats and this one chick, man. They went in"—he nodded toward the administration building—"they never come out."

"Why?"

"The fuzz grabbed 'em is why. Won't let 'em out or talk or nothing. Like it's Hitlerville, man."

This kind of talk made Brown angrier. "Why'd they go in?"

"With the protest petition."

"What are they protesting?"

206

"Not they, man. *We*. You and me."

"Goddamn it, Fisher," Brown yelled. "I'm protesting nothing. I'm here to go to school." He tried to speak calmly. "Now what the hell's the fuss about?"

"Black studies, for one. Student control of curriculum."

"What about classes?"

"You got to be kidding, man."

"No classes?"

"You said it, man."

"What the hell right they got to do this to me?"

"You hear the speeches last night?"

"What speeches?"

"At the rally. Right here."

"She-it," Brown muttered.

Fisher began to warm up. His eyes were slightly glazed. "You see the morning paper?" Brown's fists shook and he could not answer. "Groovy, man! We let go with fire bombs. Burned the president in effigy. Totaled one paddy wagon. One pig got stuck. They threw thirty-eight cats and seven chicks in the Bastille. The governor's calling out the National Guard."

"They say anything about classes?"

"Get with it, man!"

"What about tomorrow?"

Fisher craned his neck, pointed through the crowd. "See him? With the bald head and the big sign? Economics prof. That one? Political science. Federation of Teachers is on strike. You want to fight city hall, man, go ahead."

"I want to go to class."

Fisher shrugged. "You cross that line, them cats'll eat you alive." He saw the look of despair in Brown's eyes. "This is for real, man. They can lock up our committee and bash in our brains, but in the end we'll get what we're after or level the whole friggin' works with the torch."

Brown looked beyond Fisher's wild snarl of hair to the barricades where the sheriff's deputies and police were deployed. He turned to go.

"Listen," Fisher said, grabbing his arm. "You holding?"

"I'm clean."

"Speed? Pot?"

"Nothing."

Fisher scratched.

"I been stoned all night. On an acid trip. I got to stay high."

Brown pushed his way through the crowd that had filled in behind him. It was hard going. The chanting voices mocked him. Pressure was strong against him in the direction of the barricades. He used his elbows, holding the books in each hand. There was a lot of good-natured jostling.

"Go home," he muttered. Some of them laughed at him. Others would not yield. "Go on," he shouted. "Out of the way, damn it!"

Remarkably, there was no anger except his. The books were torn from his fingers. They spilled, pages flapping, among dungareed knees, grimy toes in thick greasy sandals. And laughter. He tried to recover the books. Someone shoved him. He sprawled among the legs and feet. He could no longer see the books. He lay with his face scraping gravel and dirt and his thwarted fists dug into the earth.

Later, crawling to the outer fringe of the crowd, perhaps a hundred yards distant from the barricades, he was suddenly free. He got to his feet and stood there undecided, wanting to elbow, claw, and punch his way back to his books. A deep grief held him, the loss of something precious he could not explain. Something more than the books themselves. Dignity, perhaps, in the face of laughter. And faith. The old belief in his sorry destiny, for a time subdued, sprang up again. He stared across the sea of chanting, swaying heads. The signs and placards and the clenched fists of protest rode above them like lateen sails.

Hopeless, Brown.

He walked away, kicking bits of stone and broken glass, beer cans, Coke bottles. He barely saw them. A few yards away a fat girl, dirty blond, bra-less in a sweatshirt and tight flared denims, thrust a mimeo sheet in his hand and he saw for the first time that his hand was bleeding.

The announcement in blurry caps said that the Faculty Senate had passed a resolution calling for the removal of police, sheriff's deputies, and state highway patrolmen from the campus. It warned that the presence of National Guardsmen would only lead to more violence. It called for the holding of convocations and workshop discussions in lieu of regularly scheduled classes that afternoon and the following day and all the days after that until the harsh security restrictions were removed and the Protest Committee released unharmed and without penalty for their actions. It excoriated the governor and board of regents for their interference in campus affairs and labeled the college president a puppet.

Brown crumpled it into a ball and threw it away. His rage ebbed. He could not shake the deep awareness of his talent for failure. He had lived through too many hells for this moment. Its promise had sustained him against the cries of torn platoon buddies in the yellow country dust of Nam. This is how they paid off. All there was. All there ever would be. He was a fool to think otherwise.

He began the long walk home.

Angela had slept until noon. When she awoke, Brown was in the frame of the open attic window staring across the roof tops. She sat up.

"Hi!"

He did not move. She watched him for a few moments.

"Brown?"

Nothing. She went to him. Close now, she saw for the first time the bruises and his torn clothing. "Are you all right, Brown?" Touching him, puzzled, her fingers gentle. "You're hurt. Whatever *happened?*"

His flesh was clammy to her touch. She put an arm round his shoulder, worried because he sat close to the edge. She took his arm and tried to pull him from the window seat. He was as immovable as stone. What frightened her most were his eyes. They seemed out of focus. "Brown," she said again, terrified, "For God's sake, Brown, what's happened to you?"

Without turning he said in a low clear voice, "The largest of the three brontosaurs is seventy feet long, eighteen feet high at the hips. He's called 'The Thunder Reptile'—classic specimen of the Upper Jurassic Period." He went on with a terrible calm as though she were not there.

She panicked. It was too much. She dressed hurriedly, stuffing loose odds and ends into her bag. She hesitated at the door for a moment fearful and yet concerned. She hoped he would turn, come to her, say something. He did not move. She went out quickly.

Her red car was parked across the street. She began to unlock the door when she saw a traffic violation ticket under the windshield wiper. The sight of it dismayed her. Another threat to her security. She was too tense to drive, dazed by what had happened to Brown, vaguely aware of her own guilt in leaving him.

She walked down the cul-de-sac past racing, yelping mongrels toward the main cross street. She turned once and saw Brown at the window with his hands clasped over his knees, his eyes still fixed on some distant point in nowhere. At the cross street she turned right toward the cluster of shops two blocks away. Her mouth felt furry. She had not washed or brushed her teeth. She could not escape the sound of Brown's voice—so deadly matter-of-fact as he recited the statistics of the dinosaur.

What have I got into? she wondered. What have I said or done now to hurt him? The business of her handbag and her father's picture, the whole strange business of Brown from the moment he had asked for a ride back at Morro Bay seemed a bad dream.

She stopped for coffee in a narrow lunchroom and devoured three sugared doughnuts before she knew it. She paid and left. Next door a display of fresh fruit caught her eye. The oranges were fat, their flesh bursting through the rent navel. She stared at them, fascinated. The apples shone like polished glass. Oranges for girls, she thought. Apples for boys.

She moved on to the newsstand at the corner and scanning the headlines got her first inkling of what had happened to Brown. She bought the early edition of the afternoon paper and read about the troubles on campus. Poor Brown, she thought. She was ashamed of herself for running away like that.

She went back to the variety store. She took a basket and scooped up cheeses, meat, bread, beer, oranges, apples, milk. She chose a variety of the tiny cans of vegetables and a half-gallon jug of Napa Valley wine. She bought the yellowest broom she could find, soaps, cleansers and cloths, and an assortment of paper dishes. A boy from the store followed her home, wheeling the bags and cartons in a baby carriage.

Turning into Ransome Court she saw Brown at the window. His face and arms fixed above the green-stained copper ledge. He could fall, she thought, and hurried. The boy followed her to the top floor, depositing her purchases at the door. She overtipped him and hurried inside. Brown had not moved. She carried the groceries in, the heavy bags straining her armpits. She leaned the new broom against the wall behind the door and set about at once to prepare a meal. She glanced from time to time at Brown but otherwise ignored him. She heated canned vegetable soup on the hot plate, spread sliced chunks of sourdough bread with butter and covered them with slabs of jack cheese. She took the new broom and swept furiously while the soup came to a boil.

When everything was ready she carried it to the window where Brown sat. The steam rose from the paper cups of soup, fragrant and tempting. She sat at his feet but did not touch him.

"Now look, Brown," she said firmly. "I got to talk or split my skull. I don't give a damn if you want to hear me or not or even if you're listening. I just went through hell. I got to thinking what's happened between us. The way you suddenly turn on or freak out, and I can't take that kind of insecurity because damn it, I've got enough insecurity of my own. I walked out because it scared me. I got to thinking it was me. I was to blame. So I ate three doughnuts. I never ate three doughnuts at once in all my life, Brown. You hear? Never. Then I saw the headlines. About the campus riot. And I brought the paper home and a lot of gro-

211

ceries because I realize now what you've been through, wanting so badly to get to college and winding up with no classes. So it wasn't me at all. Not my fault, Brown, and certainly not yours."

She pushed the hair from her eyes, pushed sandwiches and soup closer so he could smell the goodness of the food. "I know one thing, Brown. After last night, you love me. We love each other. That's what matters, that we love each other and need each other. Nothing's gone wrong between us. Everything until now's been smooth, Brown. Groovy. We're very lucky, really. It's been a very nice relationship so far, you might say. But then this, this sitting here like you were dead or something. That scared me and I ran and I'm sorry about that, Brown, and I apologize."

She saw the slightest working of his jaw muscle, nothing more. She knew he heard her now.

"I'm glad I ran, Brown. Because I saw the headlines, after the doughnuts, and I felt like throwing up. I saw the headlines about last night's riots and what happened this morning, early, and how they threw a lot of kids in jail and burned a police prowl car and stuff. And that's what you walked into this morning, after what you worked so hard for and risked your life and all and your high hopes smashed. I know how that feels. I know how it feels damned well to lose something very precious. So I understand what you're going through, Brown. That's what I wanted to say in the first place. That I know what you're going through and I want to help you. I need you, Brown. I don't want to lose you. We need each other but I need you most. Because you're all I have in the world and I love you. I love you very very much, Mr. Brown."

He seemed to come alive slowly, the rigid inert form fracturing into moving limbs, fingers, eyes focusing, head turning, all of him stirring like a stopped film to life. He took Angela in his arms, precarious at the window's edge, but she did not care now. They rolled easily to the floor gasping tender surprised words, laughter in their happy tears, he muttering, "What a cruddy thing—a cruddy mess . . ." and her protests buried in

212

his kisses. Until Angela sitting up wiped her eyes and nose and announced that the soup was getting cold.

"I don't remember walking home," he said.

"There's a parking ticket on my car," she said.

"Let it rot," said Brown.

"Just need me, darling."

He tore the sealing ring from a beer can. "With this ring, baby." He slipped the metal band on her finger. Later he carried her to the bed.

"Pump me full of sunshine," she begged.

XVIII

Damion in the morning hubbub of the San Francisco airport changed bills for coin. He found an empty phone booth and pulled the door shut against the drone of canned music and the raspy reports of arrivals and departures. He placed a person-to-person call to Angela at college and leaned against the side of the booth thinking what a surprise it was going to be.

Angela at eighteen. Her mother had been a scant three years past eighteen when Damion married her. Martha too had been tall then, ambitious and greatly taken by the good Navy name and the prospect of diplomatic largesse. Her mother had checked out the Damion lineage on lunch hours between stints as the better-dresses buyer for a fashionable San Francisco store. The quiet young Navy officer was quite a catch, she told her daughter, and envisioned tours of duty for the three of them at the better world's capitals, state dinners included, everything laid on.

Damion stared uncomfortably around the airport corridor while the operator buzzed the number. A small doubt gnawed. Had he a right to expect a warm

214

welcome? Where did she stand on the role of absentee fathers? Had Martha poisoned her mind?

And what do I say now when Angela answers? Hello? This is your father? Do you remember me? We took a walk a year ago on a sunny beach. You told me what love and war is all about. Can you tear loose from your world to spend a few hours? I've a piece of good/bad news for you.

The operator cut in on his thoughts. She had reached the university switchboard. The call had been transferred to the freshman dorms. Miss Damion was not there, but the operator had her roommate on the line.

"I'll speak to her."

"That will be two dollars and five cents for the first three minutes."

Eight gongs and a tinkle.

"Hello?"

"I'm Angie's roommate. Who's calling her, please?"

"This is her father."

"Oh. *Hello.*"

"I'm at the San Francisco airport. I don't think she knew I was coming in."

"Isn't this Mr. Coddington?"

"I'm her father, Paul Damion."

"Her *real* father! Great! Well, hello! Angie's spoken often of you."

"Where is she, Miss—"

"Murdock. Daphne Murdock. Angela's not here."

"Can she be reached somewhere?"

"Well, that's it. She missed a few classes this week so I just figured she took off and was staying with— you know—her folks in Pebble Beach."

"I'll try there, Miss Murdock." He thought a moment. "Is Angela okay? I mean—missing a week's classes. Isn't that unusual?"

"Not really, Mr. Damion—"

"It's Captain Damion."

"Of course. Sorry about that. It's like this, Captain. Things, you might say, are kind of loose here. Like permissive, you know? And Angie takes off, sometimes it's Pebble Beach for a weekend or you know, a date maybe. Anyway, when she didn't show for classes last Monday—"

"You mean she's been away *all* week?"

"I'm sure she's okay, Captain Damion. Like she's with her folks up there, her mother, or maybe in the City, where a lot of the crowd goes for kicks."

"I'll check with her mother, then, and thank you, Miss Murdock."

"Daphne's the name, Captain."

He gave her the name of his hotel and asked her to have Angela call him when she returned. She seemed reluctant to let him go. "Angela never stops talking about you. A Navy hero and all that—"

"I'll be meeting you soon, I hope. And thanks again, Daphne."

He dug for more change and placed the call to Pebble Beach. He had hoped to reach Angela without involving Martha. Now it seemed unavoidable. He was troubled that Angela had missed a week of classes. Martha, a compulsive organizer, would scarcely permit it. He'd soon find out.

He dropped the coins into the slot and listened with growing uneasiness to the telephone's familiar litany. The only thing it doesn't know, he mused, is whether its chirp is a sad or sweet one. The prospect of a dialogue with Martha after so many years dismayed him. Command had drained from him the tolerance to submit to round-the-clock small talk of this garrulous neurotic who once had promised to love, honor, and cherish him. His household had become a ship of men who took his orders and carried them out.

He hoped he was lucky and Angela was there and it would be Angela who would answer the phone.

"Coddington residence."

"Mrs. Coddington, please."

"May I say who's calling?"

"Paul Damion."

Moments later Martha's cool voice floated over the wires and years. "Paul! What a lovely surprise."

"Hello, Martha." Funny how you feel nothing, he thought.

"Where are you?"

"San Francisco. Just in from Pearl for a few days."

"How marvelous!" She made it sound as though it really was marvelous, as though she really meant it. "Have you seen Angela?"

"Actually, it's Angela I'm calling about—"

"I'm not speaking to Angela, Paul. Right now I'm very angry with your dear little Angela."

"She's not there, with you?"

"She most certainly is not. She was expected for dinner a week ago last Friday—almost two weeks ago. Never appeared. We waited until nine with a roast beef dinner. Never called to explain. Nothing. I wrote her a firm note to school. Not even the courtesy of an answer or a call—"

"Isn't that odd?"

"I should say!"

"Think she's in trouble?"

"As far as I'm concerned, she's on her own."

"She could be hurt—"

"You're naïve, Paul, as always. She's mixed up with a filthy crowd of hippies. Have you seen that mess she shares a room with? Daphne something? My heavens! I will say this. I *have* had a phone call—two actually but I was out the second time—and your daughter's alive and well in San Francisco."

"Where in San Francisco?"

"I haven't the faintest. She calls from a phone booth in the City. I demanded to know where she could be reached. She just put me off. Oh no, Paul I've had it with our Angela."

"Does she have any money?"

"Your allotment, of course. Which isn't that generous, you know, what with inflation and all. Duane figured out—"

"If you hear from Angela will you tell her I'm in town?"

"I doubt it'll do much good. You've been out of touch, Paul, out there in the wild blue yonder. Have you any idea of what's going on with our younger generation? The drugs and loose sex and the hell-with-the-older-generation attitude?"

217

"You'd be the last one to allow a daughter of yours to get mixed up with anything like that, Martha."

"How do I stop her? She's eighteen with a mind all her own." She laughed softly. "Really Paul, you've got to catch up. Why not come for dinner one evening? You'll like Duane. He's often asked me what you're like. He's been terribly successful, you know, with his factoring."

"What's factoring?"

"Private banking. He's annoyed when I call it factoring but that's what it really is. Helping people who need money. You will come and meet him, won't you?"

"If Angela's there, yes. I'd be happy to come."

"I'll track her down, then. Where are you staying?"

He gave her the name of his hotel. She promised to call him the minute she located Angela. "I'm in the city often," she rattled on, "With my club work and volunteer charity organizations. I've a meeting tomorrow, come to think of it. At the Fairmark. I'll be staying over. Shall I call you for a drink later?"

He agreed and hung up. He gathered his luggage and found a cab and was driven to the City. He searched the faces of the young as the taxi crept along the crowded city streets. He felt sad and abused. The prospect of a drink with Martha did not help matters. What affection he once felt for her had dried to dust long ago. Except for the chance of a few hours with Angela, there was nothing here for him.

At the elevator after registering, he stood aside for a wheel chair exiting, propelled by a tall unsmiling woman with a jutting jaw and wearing coarse tweeds. But it was the occupant of the wheel chair whose presence attracted Damion. She was a striking blond, her hair in two coiled braids, her face curiously strong in spite of its delicate features. Her gray eyes, intelligent and alive, swept Damion with a commanding glance. He thought her lips had taken a cynical turn, but by then she was gone.

In the elevator ascending, the porter with his luggage grinned.

"Kinda grabs you, don't she?"

218

"Sad," Damion said. "A lovely-looking woman like that."

"And loaded." The porter whistled softly. "Best suite in the house. The works. I mean it's laid on, mister. And when her highness hollers, the whole joint jumps. Including the executive manager."

"Who is she?"

"Name's McCready. The Empress Suite's hers, anytime she's here. Somebody else in it, he gets out."

Damion smiled. "Husband must be an admiral."

"Worse. A Washington senator or something. Political jock-strap. Throws his weight around. You know the type. But she's the one calls the shots."

"Must be tough, married to a woman in a wheel chair."

The porter studied the uniform and Damion's face before he went for broke. "With such a bundle, Captain, and boobs like those, how tough it tough?"

In his room, Damion phoned the Commandant, Twelfth Naval District, and made his whereabouts known. He loosened his tie and stretched out on the bed and slept. The ringing phone wakened him.

"Captain Paul Damion?"

"Yes."

"Melba McCready here. My husband's the Honorable Jarvis McCready, United States Representative from the State of Ohio."

"Yes, Mrs. McCready?"

"Apparently you don't know him."

"I'm afraid not."

"We haven't actually met but you *did* notice me in the lobby, I'm sure. In the wheel chair. My husband's a confirmed military buff, Captain. House Armed Services Committee and all that. Having a Korean war hero like Paul Damion in the same hotel is too much for him to resist. Could you have lunch with us?"

"You're both very kind." Damion said slowly. He glanced at his watch. "I'm expecting an important call—"

"At what time, Captain?"

"That's it, I don't know."

"No problem, then. We'll lunch in my suite. Leave

word at the switchboard that's where you can be reached. One o'clock?"

"Well—"

"Fine, then. The Empress Suite."

He hung up slowly. She had cut right off.

XIX

Damion was glad he had come. It was an excellent lunch. Cracked crab, a quiche, salad of subtly flavored greens, a dry Napa Valley chablis. A Chinese chef prepared the dishes served by a uniformed butler named Foster. The tweedy woman introduced only as Greta abruptly excused herself when coffee was served. Damion observed her from time to time staring sulkily through the French windows of the salon visible through the dining-room doors. He had sensed her disapproval the moment they were introduced.

Melba poured the coffee herself. "Don't mind Greta. She won't hurt you."

A trained Doberman, Damion thought. "Have I done something to offend her?"

"She mistrusts men. You. Foster. Even my husband."

"A bad love affair?"

"Greta?" She seemed amused. "Just overprotective. If you'll stop feasting your eyes on my bosom for a moment, Captain, I'll explain." She indicated her legs. "Greta takes good care of me."

"You're an attractive woman, Mrs. McCready."

"Not from the knees down."

"You don't mind if I ask—?"

"Not at all."

"Polio?"

"Meningomyelocele."

"I shouldn't have asked."

"It's simply a failure of closure of the roof of the *spina bifida*—"

She went on. Damion saw at once that the recitation gave her as much pleasure as it pained him to hear it.

"—that's the bony vertebral canal, and the cord or its root adheres to a bulging sac of parchment-like skin and the meninges. The sac's filled with spinal fluid. Besides the sac, there's sometimes a dimple or an area of hyperpigmented skin or a tuft of black hair." Her smile was a bright child's. "I could say that by heart when I was twelve."

"An accident?"

"Congenital. I won't bore you with any more clinical details, Captain. Or the stupidity of parents who prefer faith to surgery." Her voice sharpened. "Care to see my little tuft of coarse black hair?"

"Terribly sorry, no."

She seemed to enjoy his embarrassment. "None of the usual vices are denied me, Captain. Except jogging and frugging. Cream and sugar?"

"Black is fine." A bewildering woman, he thought. He looked at his watch. "Your husband's delayed."

"He's not coming."

"You said—"

"You'll meet him in good time. He's terribly busy. They're holding congressional hearings here, you know."

"I didn't know. What hearings?"

"Congressman McCready's with an Armed Services subcommittee looking into alleged abuses by certain California defense contractors."

"It's about time."

"Meaning what, Captain?"

"Abuses."

"Such as?"

"Low bids that win contracts, then escalate into millions beyond the original estimate."

"You mean buy-ins?"

"That's the trade word, I guess."

"Blame rising costs of materials and labor—not the contractor."

"Reports indicate malpractice as well."

A pinched look came into Melba's pretty face. "I don't know what reports you read, Captain, or what columnists, but as a Navy officer who depends on the defense programs for your living, you should know what side your bread's buttered on."

"All I know, Mrs. McCready, is that in the process of commissioning my command, a nuclear-powered cruiser, I ran into costly delays, faulty workmanship, inferior materials, shocking cases of kickbacks and payoffs."

"What action was taken?"

"I reported it to my superiors through official channels. It's being studied." He shifted uncomfortably. "I'm glad your husband's doing something about it."

"Those reports are lies. Commie front malcontents trying to sabotage the defense effort."

"You don't really believe that."

"I damned well do," Melba said hotly. "It's an outrage. Here these companies are sacrificing the normal profits of private enterprise in a patriotic cause and these bastards scream for congressional investigations."

"Sorry I brought it up," Damion said.

"You should be. I run a business called Hoskins Industries—all of it—from this wheel chair."

"I know the company well."

"You should. Your command mounts twin Trident missiles amidships. You're familiar, of course, with their variable warheads, their fire control systems, and the sophisticated electronic hardware that goes with it. Don't interrupt me. I'm quite angry. If you're not familiar with it, may I mention Ordnance Contract # W64–089 ORD–6181, which the Navy awarded to my company three and a half years ago and which we delivered on schedule and which exceeded Navy performance standards and specifications—"

223

"—and which required an extensive overhaul ten months ago."

"We brought that in at $385,000 below estimate, damn it!"

"And made a fair profit."

"You bet."

"Then Hoskins did only what was expected of it. Congratulations. Too bad other defense contractors aren't as honest and as efficient and the Pentagon tougher in demanding delivery as contracted for."

"And ships' captains as dedicated as you to your command. Or should I say *recent command?*" She observed his surprise with immense satisfaction.

"How'd you know about that?"

"It's my business. I keep in touch."

"The matter of my command status is top secret material. How'd you get your information?"

Melba turned and called to Greta in German to bring Captain Damion's file from her study. Greta muttering bounded off like a hound after a flung stick. "Do you know, Captain, I've had every airline, train, and hotel checked for your arrival?"

"Why?"

"If you will take the helm, Skipper, and steer a course for the salon directly ahead, I believe we'll find a bit of sun and we can have a cozy talk."

He faced the harsh afternoon sun. Melba sat in shadow. Because of her wheel chair close alongside, he could not move. She regarded him fondly.

"In case your disciplined mind is considering the possible conflict of interest that may exist in the McCready household, let me say this about that. My husband Jarvis does not own ten cents worth of Hoskins holdings. Not a dime. My father was a shrewd man, Captain. A daughter crippled from birth doesn't generally attract the most eligible of suitors. Daddy knew it and wrote an ironclad and indisputable marriage contract in case Jarvis had any unlovely ideas. What Daddy didn't know were my special talents. Let me assure you, my husband has no complaints. In any department. I help him with his political career, as any

224

wife would. He is loyal and loving. And there is no more dedicated and patriotic public servant in all of the Congress than Jarvis McCready."

"The leak of classified information, Mrs. McCready."

Greta arrived with the files. Melba handed one to Damion. It was all there. His father's tours of duty, his own Annapolis graduation. His wedding, Inchon, the divorce, the commissioning of *Chesapeake*. He handed it back.

"The leak, Mrs. McCready."

"I'm coming to that. I particularly did not want Jarvis here when the letter was being discussed."

"What letter?"

"From the sailor on your ship." She opened a second file Greta had laid in her lap. "Morgen. Howard Morgen."

Morgen's face appeared at once in Damion's mind. Blue eyes in a narrow face, straight fair hair under the squared white cap, fingernails bitten down to hurt flesh. Prissy, he remembered, and damned efficient. McKim had said that once after Morgen had delivered some typed reports. Something else about him, however, McKim did not like. Damion tried to remember what it was.

He began to read the letter. Melba watched him closely. His face revealed nothing. When he finished reading he went back to the first page and reread the words *sheer cowardice and possibly treason*. The words shocked him but he was not about to let Mrs. McCready know it. He still was uncertain about where Mrs. McCready stood and what she was after. He handed back the letter.

"Nothing in it about relief of my command."

"Doesn't the letter upset you?" She seemed nettled.

"Any Navy man's entitled to write to his congressman."

"Is what he says true?"

Damion said nothing. It irritated Melba further. "It's got to be true, then," she said sharply.

"I'm sorry Morgen didn't come to me or to my exec before he wrote it."

"Oh, come now, Captain. You'd have drawn and quartered him."

"What does your husband think of the letter?"

"He hasn't actually seen it." Melba lied smoothly. "I've told him about it. In detail. I thought it best to have this little chat with you first."

"Do you always intercept his mail?"

"I do indeed. I keep a small staff especially for his personal mail. Mostly letters from all over the country praising him. And the usual constituents' requests, and always a complaint or two. Takes a huge burden off his busy shoulders. Morgen's letter seemed urgent and timely. Also dangerous. I felt my husband should hear both sides before taking any action."

"Action?"

"Protective action."

"Protecting whom?"

"You, of course."

"That's kind of you, but why?"

"I want my husband to help you, Captain. So I had to know all about you. I made inquiries, of course. I have an efficient organization, dealing as I do in multimillion dollar government contracts."

"Which accounts for the file."

"It has everything in it about Paul Damion from the day he was born until yesterday when his orders were endorsed in Pearl Harbor."

"Most efficient."

"It's what I pay my people for. And two hours ago you notified Commandant, Twelfth Naval District of your whereabouts. So I knew you were here, and in this hotel."

"A startling coincidence."

"Not really. There are few choices in San Francisco if one really wants a first-class hotel." She patted his knee. "I'm honored. It's a thrill to meet a real Navy hero."

Damion remembered what the cheeky porter in the elevator had said. How tough, really? With a mind like a computer and those twin turrets forward and all those millions, who needs legs? She was studying him.

"You *are* impressed?"

226

He nodded.

"I'm impressed too, Captain. Your good looks. Your tailor. Your fine record as a Navy officer. Your medals. All in the family tradition. It's what my husband admires and wants to protect."

"Thank you." Protect again. From whom? he wondered.

"And running the Navy's hottest nuclear warship, I'm sure you admire efficiency as we do."

"I get things done."

"So you see why I wanted this little talk with you. My cards are on the table. I've withheld nothing—"

"Except how you wangled highly classified Navy information."

"Clout, Captain. I have contacts in the Pentagon. I'm not ashamed to say so. Like you said, it gets things done. There are twenty-seven retired military officers holding top jobs in Hoskins and its subsidiaries. Among them, three admirals, two regular Army generals. A Marine general and two Air Force generals." She smiled. "My own Joint Chiefs. Their combined annual incomes, including salaries, bonuses and fringe benefits, approach but do not exceed a million dollars. Working for me, they earn every dime of it. That answer your question?"

He nodded. A low stubborn anger started somewhere inside him, a wariness in the presence of an enemy.

"How do you intend to help me, Mrs. McCready?"

"Obviously you're in some kind of trouble or this Morgen would not have written his letter and you would not have been relieved of your command. Am I right?"

"Go on."

"Jarvis, my husband, happens to be an ex-Navy man. He's not ashamed to admit he never got past seaman first class during the Korean conflict. The Navy's rewarded him for his efforts since on its behalf. Today he holds a reserve commission as a lieutenant commander. Once he knows the facts, he can go to bat for you, defend you as a Navy hero should be defended." She waved Morgen's letter. "From attacks like this."

"And precisely what facts must he have?"

"Exactly what happened out there."

Damion shook his head. "Impossible."

"Why?"

"I'd be violating my oath as a Navy officer."

"You weren't thinking of that when you did whatever you did out there," she snapped. "Whatever it was that got you canned."

"It's a matter only the Navy can decide." He watched her struggle to control her temper. "I'm grateful for your offer to help, of course."

"You're going to need help. Plenty of it. Friend Morgen could have written a dozen letters. Right now on Capitol Hill some left wing liberal could be yakking on how the Navy's covering up for something rotten one of its top sea captains pulled off Vietnam. Those peaceniks'd love to ruin a career like yours."

"I've got to go by the rules. You know that."

"I just don't get it. When it's to your advantage to let my husband help you."

"I'm not stopping him."

"You're certainly refusing to co-operate."

"What is it you're really after, Mrs. McCready?"

She eyed him sharply. "I don't know what you mean."

"Why should a busy congressman bother with a crank letter about an unimportant Navy officer?"

"Letters from constituents are important to him. He answers each and every one."

"There's more to it. You're not being honest with me."

Melba looked at him for perhaps three seconds. "I admire your directness, Captain. You're right. There's another very good reason for my interest in you and in this stupid letter."

"And what is that?"

"I want to make my husband famous."

Somewhere a phone rang. Greta loped off to answer it.

"And I admire integrity," Melba went on. "I'd hate

228

to see a man of your caliber get hurt. Could be, you're already doomed." She leaned forward, purring. "More coffee?"

"Doomed? That's an odd word."

"A cognac, then? Anything?"

"A cup of hemlock, if it's handy."

"I'm beginning to like you very much," she murmured.

Greta was back speaking rapidly in German. "The call's for you," Melba said to Damion. "Take it in my study. Greta?"

Greta led him down a wide hall hung with Fragonard prints to a spacious room of desks and files. He was surprised to find a busy office. A gray-haired woman fed sheets into a table-top Xerox. A girl in a miniskirt, with earphones over her streaky bleached hair, typed from a portable tape recorder. A word from Greta sent them packing. After a cold suspicious look at Damion, Greta followed them.

"Paul Damion speaking."

"Oh, Captain Damion. Great. This is Daphne, you know? Angie's roommate. I hope I haven't bust in on something important or anything."

"No, Daphne. Go ahead."

"Great. Well. Like when you called this morning? You must've thought me *stupid* or something, the way I behaved."

"Not at all."

"I mean it *was* stupid. Like I was stoned and it took me a while to pull myself together."

"Any news about Angela?"

"That's it. Being gone all week and no word, it's not like Angie. She'd have me cover for her, sign in, stuff like that, and I got to thinking, here's her real father in town and she's off somewhere and what I could do, I could meet you someplace in the city, like I'm free tonight, and we could maybe check around where the action is, like where she might be."

"Could you give me the names of some of those places?"

"It's the whole scene, Captain. Like there's Haight-

Ashbury or North Beach or Sausalito. You never can tell, she might be freaked out in somebody's pad—"

"I could just look—?"

"—or if I saw her red Mustang I'd spot it in a minute."

"Good of you to think of it, Daphne."

"It's beginning to bug me, see? So I thought if I called—"

"Call me again if you hear anything, will you?" He hung up.

In the salon Melba also hung up. Greta carried off the phone. Damion passed the two office workers chatting by the Fragonards. He nodded and they slipped past like sheep. In the salon he excused himself to Melba and asked for his cap. She regarded him thoughtfully.

"Won't change your mind?"

"No."

Her face tightened. "You're a fool, Captain. My husband winds up these hearings tomorrow and flies back to Washington. By then he'll have read the Morgen letter and prepared his statement. I'll see to it personally."

"Is that a threat, Mrs. McCready?"

"It's whatever you want it to be."

Greta handed him his cap and wheeled Melba to the door. Damion took his last look at the incredible décolletage, more like marble now than flesh.

Melba wheeled back to the salon. Her expression was thoughtful. "He's a tough one, Greta."

"Him?" Greta gestured with both fists twisting. "Like so I break him in two pieces."

"Big mean Greta. Damion in his own quiet way could make braunschweiger of you. In minutes. Now get me Johannsen in the downtown office. When I hang up, call that Colonel Jillson, Joint Chiefs in the Pentagon. The number's in my little blue book."

Jillson, she thought fondly. The big fool was full of simian surprises. Disgusting in a way. But right now in the right place to do me good. God knows, I'm ripe for some good after so much bad. She wheeled down the hall after Greta's hippy stride. "A cup of hemlock," she muttered, and burst into laughter so suddenly that Greta jumped "I *like* him. Greta. He makes me think."

"What is there to think?"

"The kind people left in the world. The pure in heart. Heroes. Martyrs. Not many left, Greta."

"Better you take nap and not think so much."

"Nietzsche you ain't, Greta. Move your big ass and get me Johannsen. And tell Molly to type up that tape. There's some stuff at the start I'd like to hear again." She slapped Greta's vast rump. Greta giggled and ran.

"Johannsen? This Captain Damion has a daughter somewhere loose in San Francisco. First name's Angela. Been in town a week or more, drives a red Mustang. She's probably on marijuana or LSD and shacked up somewhere. You know these kids today. Find her, will you? Try the hotels, the hippie hangouts. Those places. Use as many men as you need. I'm in a hurry on this one. I know. I know it takes time. You still have that police superintendent on the payroll, don't you? Well, use him, damn it. That's what we're paying him for."

"Colonel Jillson, please. Ted? Are you free to talk? All right, then. Give me a ring right back, collect." She gave him the number and hung up. She wheeled into the study and attacked a pile of correspondence. When Jillson phoned back she took the call in the salon.

"How's my great big teddy bear? I know. You were massaging the Chiefs' joints. I miss you, too. We've been held up a few days but I'm clearing out first. Monday, no sooner. Of course I will. Now look, sweetie. I need a small favor. A ship's log. I know you don't. I understand. But you do have Navy friends. Access. You do exchange small favors and other indignities, don't you? I knew you would. No. Not the log itself. That would be stealing. Just what it says. A couple of weeks ago, no more. There was a change of command. The *Chesapeake*, Captain Paul Damion was commanding. He isn't now and what Jarv wants to know is why he was relieved. The nitty gritty. Exactly.

Well, you know Jarv, always trying to save America from the Communists. Maybe this time we're onto one. Good. Lovely. I'll call you Saturday. You're sweet. Of course. Oh yes, you naughty boy. No. I'll call you. By-by now."

Greedy greedy greedy. More than they can eat. All of them greedy. Except Damion. Must be something he's got a sweet tooth for. She'd soon find out. She smiled. It was always such good sport, finding out. *Finding out ...*

She was almost fourteen before she found out her father hated her. Until then she had taken him, like everything else in her sedentary life, for granted. The Hoskins wealth (an asset she was reassured of too frequently by her conscience-stricken mother). Her shrunken legs. The ministerings and sympathies of servants, relatives, tutors, tradespeople, strangers. She soon accepted the fact that she was different and afflicted. It had not mattered in more than a wistful sort of way, perhaps when sledding children passed or the circus came to town. She grew wise to looks of pity in passing eyes. She learned to look away and not, as some instinct urged her, embarrass others with an impudent stare.

Her father changed all that.

It happened one summer afternoon. It was Hoskins's habit to be driven home for lunch and a long nap unless the workload at the office under wartime pressures did not permit it. The tide of war had begun to change, but not Hoskins. All that remained to engage his interest in his dour world was the accumulation of wealth and power. His women had failed him. Gussie had become a fat, pious slob incapable of producing a son in his image. And with a daughter crippled from birth there seemed no promise of a son-in-law worthy of his steel interests. He became a lonely man, cruel and bitter, green-gray splotches like lichen on his cheeks and the backs of his hands, the balls of his deep-set eyes like dirty hailstones. His mouth, pulled down at the corners, was rarely used either to speak or eat. His slow smile was quick death. As many men who dealt with him found out too late.

The noonday meal was done and Gussie slept. She ate enormously, to her husband's private disgust. She blamed Melba's misfortune for her eating habits, but the truth of the matter was she enjoyed eating very much. She would nibble daintily, it seemed, her small finger poised like a protective claw. But it was continual passage from plate to mouth until stuffed, she would excuse herself and stagger off to two antacid tablets and her bed.

It was the hour between Melba's German tutor and her piano lesson. The house was trapped in summer stillness. Melba had gone to her room, wheeling the new motor-powered chair like a racing Porsche. Her nurse was in the basement kitchen having her lunch with the rest of the staff. Hoskins, unable to nap, decided to visit his daughter.

He found her seated in front of the full-length mirror with her hands cupped under her well-formed breasts. It startled him. A merciless man in business affairs, he was awkward as a choir boy in the presence of women.

"What on earth are you doing, child?"

"Admiring myself." Her shameless eyes never left her reflection in the mirror. He roughly pulled her hands away.

"Admiring?" It was the tone of voice most dreaded by his executives. "What the hell is there to admire?"

Their eyes met. She saw then what she had never seen before. Open hatred, marbled with despair. In years to come she would garnish that memory with fancied lust and, after too many drinks, outright lechery. She was not beyond inventing a night or two of actual incest, its telling an aphrodisiac to Jarvis's clumsy fumbling.

But in that moment in the stillness of summer it was all there. The despair. The hate. Her young eyes, wild as a hawk's, missed none of it. Her heart pained as though rough hands squeezed it. "Are you blind as well as cruel?" she screamed. He stalked from the room. Before he left the house, strict orders were given

233

to dress Miss Melba in an adequate brassiere from that moment on.

She would not forget the look in her father's eyes. She never forgave him. It was clear now, she was alone. No mother or father, really. A parade of pet birds, dogs, even cats—anything except people with whom to share her dreams.

Her dreams. A ballet dancer, leaping, soaring like a bird, her marvelous legs the envy of a million eyes. A circus tightrope walker, toes curled to the wire and only her splendid legs in smooth silk between her and disaster in the sawdust a hundred feet below.

She was strong-willed and the dreams brought hope and as she grew and the bra cups swelled, she began to believe she would walk again. It was then she inquired about physical therapy and the exercises began. It was Greta Ullbricht, after a dozen others had come and gone, who came to stay.

From that girlhood moment of confrontation on that summer day, Melba's course was plotted. If there was nothing to admire, she told herself. she would use every wile within her power to attract. If they could not admire they could at least hate. She read all she could find in print on hate. It fascinated her. It was an emotion much closer to love, much dearer to her savage, spoiled heart.

Damion in his room below picked up the phone to call the district commandant. He might be interested in the luncheon meeting with Melba McCready. But a moment after dialing Damion hung up. What would he say? Certainly Mrs. McCready hadn't threatened the national security. And how much did the commandant already know? And whose side was he on?

He undressed and showered and lay in bed. Long afternoon shadows filtered through the curtains. Downtown traffic whined, a long-drawn mournful threnody. A mist from the bay hovered over the city. It smelled of the sea and saddened him.

Doomed, she had said.

A story teller's word. Melba, the big-breasted Scheherazade of the military-industrial caliphs, left him

234

with nothing to do but wait for the next episode. For the phone to ring. Daphne. Martha. Angela.

But please God, not Melba McCready. Her eyes had gleamed when he mentioned hemlock. He hoped he would never see her again. She could be spellbinding. Melba McCready's fantasies at short notice, he decided, could maim a man for life.

XX

Across town, Angela rose early in the morning and prepared a breakfast. Brown left with a kiss, a bit of egg on his chin, and the classified pages under his arm. Angela spent the morning shopping the neighborhood for pots, pans, and dishes. She needed material for curtains and someone to cut and sew them. Brown deserved something better than the ready-made stuff. She drove the car to a nearby garage and mailed in the money for the parking violations. She sat for a while in a park under the filtered shade of silk trees where children screamed at play and she yearned for a dozen of her own.

On the way home she bought ten yards of curtain material and left it in a drapery shop to be cut and finished. She bought two cans of latex paint, a roller and pan, feeling competent and useful and in love with the world. She ate strawberry yoghurt for lunch and a cucumber for dessert. She had one wall completed and another half-painted when Brown returned hungry and cross from his job-hunting day. Her high spirits wore down his glumness. They dined that night under plastic lanterns in a small Chinese restaurant. Brown promised to cook an Oriental dish for Angela one day, a concoction of fish, rice, and eggs he had learned to prepare in Saigon. They walked back to the room hand in hand.

The room smelled of fresh paint. Angela opened the big window and at one end of the window seat piled bright cushions she had bought that morning. She sat propped in a corner with Brown's head in her lap. One hand stroked the hair under his denim shirt. He smoked a joint, passing it to Angela from time to time. He had showered and smelt of soap and clove and she thought sweetly of the lovemaking to come.

"Brown?"

"Uh."

"In the afternoon paper, it said classes might be starting."

"Hooray for them."

"On the front page. The college president made a speech."

"Skip it."

"You want to read it?"

"Nope."

"Don't you think you should give it another try?" She bent close, brushing her cheek against his head. "You turned off too soon, Brown. You worked too hard for it."

"Today," he said, "I got offered a job."

"Doing what?"

"It looks good. They said to come back in the morning."

"What kind of job, Brown?"

"A job! Jobs pay money. What difference what kind."

"What about school?"

"Frig school."

"It's a stupid job, isn't it?"

"Why d'you say that?"

"You won't talk about it."

"It's money. Isn't that enough?"

"Remember what you said last night?"

"Last night I was stoned."

237

"You said a man can't get a decent job without a good education."

"So what!"

"So you'll take this lousy job for money and in a week you'll hate yourself and the job and me. You're too smart for that, Brown."

He sat up scowling. "So what do we use for bread?"

"If you stay in school, there's still the GI allowance—"

"She-it! It's not enough for one. Two of us?— Forget it!"

"I have my weekly allowance—"

"That I don't buy."

"Just for the first few weeks. Until you're squared away at school."

"You'd make a pimp of me."

"There are part-time jobs. Student aid—"

"Some aid! Riot sticks and Mace." He jumped to his feet. "I don't want a cent of your dough, you hear?"

"You want me, don't you?"

"You better believe it."

"Okay, then. Cut out grass and acid. Cigarettes. Beer."

"Why not just quit living, hah?"

"I want to live, Brown. With *you*. We'll split expenses right down the middle. Will you just read what the man says? Then we can talk."

"Where's the paper?"

He squatted down on the mattress and read the article.

The president had met with the student protest group leaders. He was not opposed to their right to demonstrate. He respected their right to speak out. But they in turn had the obligation to respect the other students' right to learn. He deplored the use of violence. It degraded everything the college community stood for. So did vandalism. He could condone neither.

The student leaders pointed out that the trustees and administration continued to impose rigid and unjust policies that were contrary to the realistic goals of the younger generation. Their demands were ignored. It left them no choice but to resort to violence to gain their ends. They recited wrongs of long standing. Wrongs, they said, that were responsible for the alienation of the young from our society.

The president agreed in part. Long quotes from his speech followed. It was true, he said, that some aspects of our world reflected a sick society. But understanding and analysis of social ills cannot be conducted in a boiler factory. Warped social mechanisms cannot be straightened with sledge hammer blows. Violence invites more violence.

Brown reached for a cigarette and lighted it while he was reading.

"What do you think of it, Brown?"

"I'm not finished reading."

He looked for a rebirth, the president went on, of great academic, civic, and political leadership. He hoped to see it spring from these youthful ideas and dreams. It was what America, in this time of deep distress, this agony of Vietnam, black and white, shameful waste and pollution, needed sorely. And without this leadership America would surely die.

But this vision could not become reality without justice. Justice would not be achieved without law and order, without real love between generations, without compassion among all men.

He called for his students and faculty and workers in the college community to meet the next night in a rally not of protest but as an act of faith in support of that vision, so that together they could attack the deeper problems ahead.

Brown put aside the paper and sat with the cigarette between his bruised fingers, his long barefoot legs thrust out, his dark eyes brooding. "You believe that crap?"

"I do, Brown."

"Nothing but gas."

"You got to believe him, Brown."

" 'The right to learn,' he says. Yeah. That's me." His voice rose. "I got one good look through a smashed office window before I left yesterday. Oil paintings slashed to ribbons. Files busted wide open. Papers, records, all over. Busted machines and spilled ink. Smashed typewriters—" He wiped his eyes. "You know what one IBM electric typewriter costs?"

She went to him. "Poor baby."

"I tried. Didn't I try?"

"Try once more."

"I'm taking that job."

"One more try, Brown."

"Try what?"

"The rally tomorrow night. You've nothing to lose."

"It's all lost. Everything."

"This once, Brown. For my sake."

"Will you go with me?"

"I could, I suppose." She stared at the open window. "Like we're in a glass house. I have really got to hang those curtains."

"Not that I can't take punishment," Brown said. "I found that out in Nam. But seeing those schoolbooks burnt and crapped on, it made me nauseous."

"I'm picking up the finished curtains at five tomorrow and I really want to get them up. If they're not ready, I'll go. But if they are, you'll be okay without me."

"We'll see," he said, and settled his head on her lap again.

"You understand, Brown? You won't mind?"

"Sure, I understand." He grinned up at her. "Your own pad. The very first time."

"Ah, Brown."

"That's what's so good, so goddamn wonderful, that we can talk to one another. I mean back and forth, a dialogue and no hate. Just your ideas and mine."

"No hang-ups."

"When I was a kid there was nobody I could talk to. I was talked *at*. Like my old man. Always a one-way monologue. He knew best. On his feet all day for Uncle Sam. The post office was God."

"What about your mother?"

"Always with her nose stuck in her account books. All we ever heard from her was the day's sales and how her feet hurt."

"They loved you, didn't they?"

"They never said so. Never a word like, What'd you

240

do today, son, what'd you learn at school? Never even an honest argument. They were too polite for that. Too scared." He crushed the cigarette with his heel. "I'd bring home library books on animals, biology, how a baby dinosaur got born once. They wouldn't look. Like it was something dirty or immoral."

"Poor people!"

He shrugged. "When somebody asks me someday what it was I remember most about my parents, I'll say it was their feet. They always hurt."

"When my parents got divorced, I wanted to kill myself."

"How old were you?"

"Fourteen. But I couldn't do that to my father. I'm all he's got in this world. My mother's hard as nails. Batty, too. Some people call her beautiful. Thank God I don't resemble her. I hate her, I guess. Stupid things are what she treasures most. Status. Her social clubs and charities, that junk. But she's a real phony. All she cares about is her picture in the paper and getting invited to the Pioneers Ball and the Velasquez Cotillion. That's the big deal where we live. She drools and fawns over the first families—that kind of jazz. But you should hear her haggle with the butcher when she gets the bill. Or over a few cents' worth of groceries. Or screaming when the help's been nipping at the booze."

"She marry again?"

"To this moneylender. Philanthropic usury, I call it. He talks through his nose and walks on the balls of his feet. Trusts nobody. When I was maybe fifteen and had scarlet fever, I had to chase him out of my bedroom one night. Thought I didn't know what he was up to. Won't come near me now, the slob. Scared stiff I'll tell my mother." She laughed. "As though I'd give her the satisfaction."

"What'd he try to pull?"

"The dirty old man routine. You know, let's play a little game, darling." She laughed again. "Funny thing is, I don't think—you know, he can get it up any more."

"How do *you* know?"

241

"I used to hear him and my mother trying to make it at night. Their bedroom's next to mine. I mean like animals. Then she'd start bawling and he'd call her the most awful names and go sleep in his study."

"He just didn't have it."

"My real father did. They used to have fun. I don't know what went wrong. She wanted something extra, I guess."

"Funny you can talk about your mother and father in bed like that. My parents, in bed and stuff—" He shrugged. "Anything they did together, they must've been ashamed of. I never knew about it."

"Parents." She stared across the roof tops at a sky misty with stars and wondered where her father was. "I try to see myself as a parent. The kind of mother I'll be. I mean, when you're young you're full of ideals and pretty silly dreams. But what happens to them when you're a parent?"

"Take the old beatniks," he said sitting up. "Like right here in Frisco. I used to read all about Kerouac and Zen and the Co-existence Bagel Shop. It's one of the things that brought me here, those guys. Ferlinghetti, Ginsburg. The Beat Generation. Like they folded up and passed away."

"They became parents."

"Now it's long gowns and love beads. Pot, acid, and rock. The flower children—"

"You know something? I don't feel I'm part of it."

"Something else'll come along. The acid heads'll wake up one day and find themselves Establishment parents—"

"With their own crazy kids, wondering what they did wrong."

"It'll blow their minds."

She rocked him gently in her arms. "I watched some kids down the street today. In that little park. So cute I wanted to rush down and grab them and hug them and play with them and I swore to myself I'd have a dozen kids of my own and then I got scared just thinking of one kid, *me,* and the kind of hell it's been sometimes like wanting to kill myself. What right do I have, I wondered, bringing a baby into a world that's sick and crowded, everybody screaming at you not to have babies, because there's not enough to eat as it is. And suppose it's a bad baby, malformed or something, and then I thought, What a drag it must be, having kids of your own. Being parents, when I see what happens to parents and how kids freak out and God, Brown—what becomes of people? Who are we?"

"We're us. Someday we'll be them."

"A dozen babies ... one baby. Insane! I mustn't look that far ahead. Right now is heaven, I could die, Brown, right now this very minute. Never in my life have I had so much to be so happy about."

She began to weep, softly. He held her until the trembling stopped, saying, "Okay, okay ..." his voice crooning.

"Aah, Brown, I'm so happy, I'm scared."

"I'll buy books again. At the campus bookstore. In the morning I'll go tell that garbage pickup man what he can do with his job."

"It was a job picking up garbage?"

He nodded.

"I love you, Brown."

"And when I'm home, woman—supper on the table, six o'clock sharp."

She lay quietly in his arms, her lashes wet, thinking, *For once I know who I am and where I am and what I want of life and I'm in love and that's true luck and as much as any woman can ask.*

243

XXI

The hotel where Martha stayed sat high on a fashion-able hill. Damion joined her in the cocktail lounge overlooking the bay and city. It was no accident she had chosen this spot to meet him. They had come here many times when they were in love. She was already drinking, seated in a corner he remembered, dressed in a knit suit and a five-storied hat of small fake flowers. She wore a sleek fur scarf round her neck to hide the wrinkles. Faint lines creased the corners of her mouth, but Damion found her bold good looks otherwise unchanged.

She studied him, approving, then kissed him after a moment's indecision, a dry peck somewhere near his lips. It was more than he expected. Except for brief businesslike notes concerning Angela's allotment for education, he had not heard from her since the divorce. It had not mattered to him except for losing Angela. During those proceedings, Martha had made it clear that, as long as he was away on active duty, nothing could be done to keep close ties with Angela and the judge had reluctantly agreed.

A long time gone. The wounds healed. The scars invisible. All that he missed now was Angela. Her absence worried him.

"Any luck?"

"Fantastic! We're getting financial support from three banks and worked out the details for a champagne supper. Fifty dollars a head."

"I meant Angela. Did you reach her?"

"Angela." She sipped her drink. "Of course, Paul. Laura's seeing to it. My housekeeper-secretary. Said she liked your voice. An absolute jewel. She's already contacted the college. They don't know a thing. Can you imagine that? Laura *really* told them off and they've promised to look into it. But the idea, with the tuition we—you pay, plus all those extras, you'd think they'd at the very least keep tabs on their students, on those freshman girls anyway, and Angela has this roommate, I mean *weird,* with floppy sailor pants and capes, green eye-makeup and all that heavy junk jewelry, you can hardly blame her, coming from around Los Angeles what can you expect, really, although I met her people, Hollywood types but I actually liked them. Anyway"—and she sipped her drink—"they named their daughter Daphne, can you *bear* it? and she told Laura you had called and she was wondering if she came in town if she could help by dashing about those horrid little dives where all these hippies hang around—"

"I need a drink," said Damion, and ordered one.

Martha's words fell around him like summer rain. He pretended to listen, nodding when the texture of her voice ordained it, wondering what next to do to find his daughter. It was just as well to sit here getting drunk with Martha as to race about the city looking for a needle in a haystack. It took small effort to nod and smile occasionally to the ceaseless droning of this prattling woman whose bed he once shared, whose flesh had yielded Angela. He wondered what it was about her he once loved. She dominated now as she did then, and he could not understand how he had submitted to it all those years. The Navy and his own self-discipline had taught him patience and coolness under fire, but

245

Martha challenged such sterling qualities to the breaking point.

After three more drinks and perhaps a hundred thousand words, twenty of which were his, he said, "Do you think we should notify the police?"

She stared at him fuzzily. "Oh. You mean Angela."

"I'm worried."

"You think it's that serious."

"Disappearing without a word? It's almost two weeks. That doesn't sound like Angela."

"You don't know her, Paul. She's impossible. She's already alienated Duane. She hates him. Sometimes I feel she hates me, too."

"She seemed sensible and reasonably happy the last time I saw her."

"My heavens, over a year ago—"

"Ten months."

"Well, she's changed. All these kids today, even Duane's. We've just given up trying to understand them." She spilled some of her drink. "What is it they want, anyway?"

"To live, maybe, before they die."

"How grim you are!" She dabbed at the wet table. "Calling in the police is a sticky business. Friends of ours, the Menendez-Clarks, he's CalBay Amalgamated, on the big board, you know? Well anyway, Carl and Chizzy, they're old *old* Monterey, and their son Deucey, that's Carlos Two, isn't that clever? just took off from this school in Ojai and they had no word for over a week and were frantic and they finally went into town and reported it to the police. I mean it broke their *hearts* but they had to do something or drink themselves into an early grave and they filled out this terribly frightening form like what wearing when last seen and they finally crept home simply drained and don't you know it, there was Deucey big as life and just as dirty and none the worse for wear. Seems he bummed a ride to Yosemite with a female friend—chip off the old block!—and they camped out for a few days and hitched back. First thing Chizzy asked was did she use the pill and Carl of course just hit the ceiling and right away called back the police to say that

246

Deucey was home and to forget the whole thing, which was damned sweet of him, I thought, but wouldn't you know, they had the nerve to notify him then and there that a missing persons bulletin had already gone out and Deucey's running away was a matter now of the police record and Carlos had signed the report and there wasn't a damned thing could be done about it. I won't trouble you with the rest of it, the wires poor Carlos had to pull all the way to Sacramento to get it wiped off, not to mention the money that passed hands, but if you want to drag *us* through that kind of mess—I know, *I know*, she's your daughter as much as she's mine—I just want you to know what you're sticking your nose in. And I'll have another martini, please."

"Don't you think you've had enough?"

"I don't. And this is my treat, my dear. My ex. One doesn't often get the chance to buy a drink for one's first love, does one?"

"The well-fixed Mrs. Coddington."

"You're still handsome. I should have ordered champagne."

"We'll give it another twenty-four hours. Then I'm calling the police."

"You're angry, aren't you? I'd forgotten those two bright spots of pink that pop out on your cheekbones." She leaned over and kissed one.

"God must've had you in mind when he made the first bitch, Martha. How come it took so long?"

"Breeding, darling." She gazed at him fondly, her slim fingers stroking her fur scarf. "I always found you most attractive, Paul."

"Thank you."

"I'll skip the last drink if you'll see me to my room. Got to freshen up. Behave nicely and you can take me to dinner."

She swayed as she stood but walked remarkably well for someone who had consumed four martinis. Her words were only slightly blurred. In the room she put away her hat and scarf and scaled Paul's white cap onto one of the beds. "Get comfy, Captain," she said. "The bloody war's a million miles away." She peeled

247

off her suit jacket and shook free her shimmering chestnut hair.

He went to the window and stared across the city of blinking signs and office roofs and housetops. A sailor's city. A sweeping strand of the Golden Gate Bridge arched over the channel and he recalled how good it always felt to be on a ship's bridge headed for the home port.

She came behind him silently and reaching round loosened the gold buttons of his jacket. The pressure of her breasts against his back in the strangest way reminded him of Melba McCready. He turned and kissed Martha. It was as good as he ever remembered. She pulled away slowly. "You still do it to me, you bastard. You know that."

Moments later she was stretched on the bed, her clothes in a small heap on the floor. He saw the long purplish scar from navel to pelvis, where Angela had come from, and he remembered the torment and trials of that pregnancy. She reached her long slim arms to him. "Hurry," she said. "I've waited too damn long a time for this."

He loosened his tie and kicked off his shoes. She rolled from the bed and, passing, kissed him. "Got to weewee, darling. I'll be in the john a sec, no more." She swept her handbag from the dresser and the bathroom door slammed shut.

He could hear her in there, urinating. He looked round the room. Nothing but her clothes in a loose, expensive heap, the fur piece and the hat, an elegant leather briefcase with her business of the day inside. He knotted his tie and put on his shoes and cap and slipped into his jacket and gathered up her clothes, all except the fur piece and the flowered hat. He left the room without a sound.

He hung the DO NOT DISTURB sign on the doorknob outside and walked down the hall until he found the housekeeper's pantry. He opened the laundry chute and let everything go. Shoes and stockings, bra and girdle, the lovely two-piece knitted suit, all disappeared with a well-bred silken hiss.

He took the stairs to the floor below where he tied

his shoelaces. The elevator hummed downward to the lobby and the street and he headed down the hill in the direction of his hotel at a brisk clip.

It was a lovely evening for a walk, the air fresh and smelling of blossoms and the sea. Angela was on his mind. But the image of Martha, stark naked except for her ridiculous hat and fancy neck piece and carrying her leather briefcase full of good deeds, gave him an immense feeling of satisfaction.

XXII

The hotel doorman saluted Congressman McCready
and assisted him from the chauffeured Cadillac hired
with the tax dollars of the People of the United States.
He was dog-tired, but passers-by stared, wondering
who he was, and he swung jauntily up the steps as
though he had just stepped out of a Turkish bath. Four
days of strenuous hearings marked by legal bickering
and political legerdemain had got his name on the front
pages of newspapers across the country. His press staff
had also helped. Right now, he thought, the way things
were going, he'd have that Armed Services Committee
billet in no time.

He nodded and smiled to people he did not know.
Passing the bar, he greeted two newsmen who had covered the afternoon hearing and at the desk graciously
condescended to grant an elevator interview to a
moist-eyed miss in a mini-skirt who wrote a column for
a local weekly. Melba had warned him about unmoni-
tored interviews, but he had not the heart to pass up
all that shapely leg flesh.

In the elevator, the young lady nervously consulted her notes.

"How does it feel, sir, being married to a lady tycoon?"

"Nobody's called me Mr. Hoskins yet."

"Do your separate careers keep you apart much?"

"It makes the moments together more precious than ever."

"What's your favorite dish, Congressman?"

"Pigs' knuckles and sauerkraut. Ha ha. Thought that'd get you. It's a specialty, see, of the wife's."

"A secret recipe, perhaps?"

"The secret's caraway. Just the right amount of caraway seed. This is my floor, young lady. You'll send two tear sheets to my Washington office, won't you?" He patted her rump and was gone before she could decide whether to thank him or scream.

Melba met him in the foyer. Her powered wheel chair faced an ordered pile of luggage. Portable files were wrapped in zippered canvas jackets and stacked for travel. Foster, in a long gray linen work coat, put aside his check list and took McCready's straw hat and hung it away. Melba ordered drinks to be served in the salon. McCready, wheeling her in, nodded at the luggage. "I thought you said we were staying till Sunday."

"Jillson called. Wants me in Washington tomorrow."

"What's the big rush?"

"He's lined up some hot dope on the Damion thing."

"Can't it wait? They're holding over the hearings until Monday noon." He settled her near the window and dribbled a fistful of macadamia nuts into his mouth.

"It can't wait."

"He could've given you the dope over the phone."

"He's afraid it's bugged. His, ours. Those Pentagon guys don't trust their own mothers." She took her drink from Foster's tray. "How come they're carrying over the hearings?"

"That idiot Acosta."

"Don't talk with your mouth full. What about Acosta?"

He swallowed and choked down a drink. "We were

251

down to the last witness. Prohaska. You met him once, he said. From Monarch Arms—"

"Acosta, damn it. What happened?"

"He starts asking Prohaska questions. Real sharp. Like somebody's fed him some inside dope. Turns out the son of a bitch is all dove and trying to make points. Before we could stop him he had Prohaska stumbling all over his words and yelling for his controller and he ends up taking the Fifth."

Melba laughed. "Good. He's a competitor."

"Then he calls back Pete Marley from Lynden Industries—you remember Pete from his Pentagon days? Now he's Lynden's liaison with his old buddies? Well, in twenty minutes time Acosta made mincemeat out of *him*. That little bastard's sharp, Melba—he fires his questions like bullets—"

"He was Rhode Island's attorney general for five years. Ask any Mafioso." Her humor had evaporated. "What'd he get out of Pete?"

"Blood. Before he was through, he got it into the record that Lynden's defense contracts jumped from $145,000,000 in fiscal '66 to $445,000,000 in fiscal '67. He had Pete practically admit his job was a payoff for the Pentagon business he threw their way. Made him give dollar and cents figures on cost overruns and accused Lynden outright of unfair 'buy-in' practices."

"Hell, we all do that."

"I got to a phone at recess and called Guilford out of the Senate dining room and he like to blew his top, he was so mad. He swore to me Acosta's through now. Washed up."

"There was press coverage, wasn't there?"

"A few portions of the testimony were classified info. Other than that—TV cameras all over the place."

"Then the damage is done."

"We had it figured as great publicity for our side. Until that idiot Acosta opened his trap." He took a long pull at his drink. "The media had a field day. Acosta had a stack of reference material a mile high and two aides feeding it to him. He didn't only finger Monarch and Lynden, either. Half a dozen West Coast

252

outfits he dragged in with charges of negotiated contracts instead of competitive bidding—"

"It gets things done, damn it! There's a war on!"

"—and the quasi-partnership between the Pentagon's procurement officers and their suppliers. 'One hand washing the other,' he called it."

"How'd he ever sneak past Guilford?"

"Then he ran through a list of the boo-boos—Snark, Rascal, Skybolt—I never even heard of them!"

"We had a piece of Skybolt. Air Force stuff. And Hound Dog-A, phased out before we got our teeth in it. Same with the Navy's Sparrow One and the Army's Nike-Ajax." She shrugged. "You tell 'em it won't work and they insist you build it anyway. Should I let somebody else get the contract?"

"Well, I finally got the guts to stand up and holler him down. I really did, Melba."

"Good for you."

"But his ugly dago puss'll be on every TV screen tonight across the nation."

"I've told you time and again, Jarv, tone down your talk."

"He's a—"

"Words like dago, polack, hunky. It's bad politics."

"It's only between you and I, Melba—"

"Someday you'll make a slip and lose an election. You've got every nationality under the sun back in the district."

"The ethnic groups're behind me a hundred per cent."

"Sure. But tell them the Virgin Mary was the first Jewish Mother and see who they send back to Washington."

"Sorry, Melba. So Acosta's a pure low-down, two-faced left wing ethnic traitor and I swear to God I'm going to get back at him."

"You tell 'em, Fireball."

"It was me the *Examiner* interviewed this morning. Big story, pictures, how a patriotic, redheaded freshman congressman stands up to his country's enemies within. I was riding high. Then Acosta has to open his

253

big mouth and steal the show." He drained his glass. "He's had it. Guilford'll fix his wagon but good."

"I don't know," Melba said thoughtfully.

"Hell! Asa'll run him off the Hill so fast his ears'll whistle."

Melba studied her drink. "I don't really know. There's been a lot of pressure lately, Jarv. You're not reading those reports and you don't know how sentiment across the nation is changing."

"Sure, against nigger violence and anti-American protests. And that's just what I'm about to—"

"People are tired of the war, Jarv, scared of inflation, fed up with taxes. I happen to run a clean business, cost plus. But people are sick of the political and military-industrial hanky-panky they read about in the papers and see on TV. It scares me. I'm taking a careful look around, Jarv. Could be the honeymoon's over."

"You're practically never wrong, Melba. That I got to admit. But you should've heard the booing Acosta got."

"Was it all boos?"

"There's always a few paid Commies around to make noise. It was mostly boos. I swear."

"Just the same I've got my people working out layoff schedules in Fort Worth, Marietta, and San Bernardino. We're holding off in Ohio. That's votes—now and for the future. But unless you make a big splash and make it soon, Jarv, time'll run out. We might be holding the wrong end of the stick."

"I'm not throwing the towel in yet, baby." He called to Foster for another drink. "Where's everybody?"

"I gave the girls the night off. They're sleeping on the plane tonight. Foster joins them soon as he gets the luggage and stuff ready. He's going along with it. Greta's shopping for me at Magnin's. She and I leave here at six in the morning. The plane crew's alerted for a seven A.M. takeoff which should get us to Friendship about four, Washington time. No sense in you getting up. You can use the extra sleep."

Foster arrived with the fresh drink. Melba told him

he was free to go as soon as the luggage was called for. She turned to McCready. "Johannsen was here."

"What's up?"

"He located the Damion girl. He didn't want to talk about it through the switchboard so I asked him up for a drink."

"How'd he manage to find her?"

"She registered one night in a Geary Street flea bag. No trace after that. But Johannsen's bloodhounds found out she had three parking tickets. They ran down the location of the car, the red Mustang I told Johannsen about. She came out once to shop, once to run the motor of the car. The tags check. They're pretty sure she's the one."

"She alone?"

"They only caught up with her this afternoon. Give 'em time. Johannsen's got a couple of men on it round the clock." She chewed on a macadamia. "Good man, Johannsen. I may transfer him to New York. Koenig's slowing down." She picked at a tooth. "It's a beat-up old rooming house in a dead end street. Full of hippies, which is what made it so tough to be sure it's her. The manager's an oddball artist, tanked half the time. Name is Flamm. Paints dirty pictures of his wife. About forty, wears a greasy turtleneck sweater and stinks—"

"I better clean up for dinner."

"Don't interrupt me!"

"Okay, okay."

"The hotel's sending up a menu at eight." She stirred her drink. "I talked to Damion today, you know. He won't crack, Jarv."

"I guess it's up to me to give it to him from the floor Tuesday, with Morgen's letter."

"You'll fall flat on your kiester. The letter's nothing without the actual details to back it up."

"I thought Jillson—"

"Can't count on it," she snapped. "Damion's our best bet and we can't get to him."

"Listen," McCready said. *"Listen!* We *can* get to him."

"How?"

255

"He's here, in this hotel. Right?"

"Brilliant, Jarv. Go on."

"He's looking for his kid, right?"

"Right." *Gotcha*, she thought, amused.

"Okay. He don't know where she is. But we do—"

"Jarv," she began wearily.

"We do, don't we?" His voice had become shrill, insistent. "Lemme finish, will ya?" He swallowed some of his drink. "Now follow me. We phone down to Damion."

"Gotcha."

"We meet him here, there, doesn't matter. We tell him plain and simple we know where he can find his daughter. Just like that." He waited for Melba's reaction.

"Go on."

"We hold it out for bait. If he really loves her, he'll tell us what we want to know. Then we tell him where she is." McCready sat back, very pleased with himself. "If not—at least nobody gets hurt."

"Sure," Melba said. "We can get John Wayne to play Damion and maybe Shirley Temple for Angela. You fool! Damion'd go to the police so fast your ear'll whistle."

"Why—"

"Because it's blackmail. Even if it wasn't, it wouldn't work. Not with Damion."

"Okay," McCready said, miffed. And nastily, "You'll be getting what you want from Jillson, won't you?"

She smiled, surprised. Could he possibly know about Jillson? "Jillson's double insurance, Jarv. An ace in the hole. Damion, though,—Damion intrigues me. I like to topple statues."

"It's my career you're risking," McCready grumbled.

"Listen to me, my fine friend. Any career you may have had you threw away by letting Acosta steal today's show. You've got one chance left. The Damion exposé. And damned if I'm letting that one slip away."

"It's beginning to smell, Melba—"

"What do you mean?"

"I checked him out. He's an honest-to-God Navy hero."

"So what?"

"He saved the Inchon landings. How can I get up on the floor of the House and attack a reputation like that?"

"You'll have the facts. And Morgen's letter."

"But I've voted along with every arms and defense bill—" He sucked his paunch in. "I'm a Navy Reserve lieutenant commander, Melba—"

"That's what's so beautiful about it. Your outrage against his dereliction of duty. It's so *sincere*."

"I don't know . . ."

"Look, Jarv. Damion's finished. If you don't blast him, somebody else will. The Navy can't hide this forever. Take that report we got this morning from Pearl. Tremblay carries a lot of clout."

"Damion's still one of them. They'll try to save face."

"I doubt it. There are enough rumblings in the Navy establishment to start another Civil War. It's time for a bloodletting and Damion'd make an ideal sacrificial lamb."

"And you picked me to stick the knife in him." He shook his head.

"It'll land you on every front page of every newspaper in the nation."

"Sure. Wanted for murder."

"And you'll be doing your Navy buddies a big favor. They can be ever so grateful with favors, you know."

McCready's eyes narrowed. "How come this guy Damion intrigues you, you said."

"Funny. I'd have offered him a top job with Hoskins if he'd talked, but not now."

"How come?"

"Not our type, Jarv."

"A deal with Damion—"

"If I so much as mentioned a deal, he'd have walked out on me."

"He walked out, anyway."

"I know, damn it. And he'll live to regret it." She

257

studied her useless legs for several moments. "We could play it straight, couldn't we?"

"Straight?" He perked up. This did not sound like Melba.

"A switch on your idea. Tell the daughter her father's in town. In some kind of trouble, we could say. Military secret. Confidential. You know. And you offered to help him and he turned you down."

"Why should she buy that?"

"Because you will call on her. Present your engraved card which identifies you as the Honorable Representative to the Ninety-first United States Congress and you charm her with your best used-car-lot technique."

"Why is your idea any better than mine?"

"Because it's honest, you fool. Yours was blackmail, plain and simple. This way Damion and the girl will believe you sincerely want to help him. There are sound reasons. You're a member of Congress and an ex-Navy man. A known hawk. You don't want a Navy scandal at a time when the Navy is in all the kinds of trouble it is. Show her a copy of the letter. If you play it right, she'll believe you. She'll certainly want to go to her father, talk to him, and convince him that you must know what happened out there so that you can defend his action and reputation and all that Navy jazz."

"When do I do all this?"

"After I meet with Jillson Saturday. I'll phone you Sunday morning from Washington."

"I kind of like the idea," McCready said carefully. He wondered what Angela's legs were like. Skinny, probably, with knobby knees. "How old'd you say the kid was?"

"Maybe eighteen. Damion should be grateful to us for steering his daughter to him." She took a long pull at her drink. "I really like this approach. It's so refreshing and honest, I could vomit."

"And when I have all the facts on Damion, I do a turnabout on the House floor and lower the boom."

"You do learn fast, Jarv doll."

Jarvis belched and looked unhappy. "I'd be happier tackling something else besides a Navy hero."

258

"Like what, Jarv? You've screwed up everything else."

"Well . . ."

He thought of the times in planes, looking down on Lake Erie at the scum waste of industry where it lay like mottled amoeba joined in huge patches, and beyond the downtown smog vast auto junk yards gleaming, brightly colored insects in the rolling verdant countryside. He thought of the Cuyahoga, along whose banks he had played as a kid, where today's industrial wastes corroded the Clark Avenue bridge and the trash was so rotted and thick it caught fire afloat and the firemen came round to put it out.

". . . like the environment issue, Melba. I could come out with a strong statement against air and water pollution—"

"Don't bite the hand that feeds you, friend."

"It's the big thing now. If we get on the band wagon early—"

"Forget it. I'm just as much against pollution as the next fellow. But I'm not about to throw God knows how many millions down the drain on a lot of idealistic dreams that'll never materialize."

"A lot of the big senators are behind it—"

"The hell with them! They expect me to shut down my plants and fire my help and go into bankruptcy to please a handful of do-gooders who never earned an honest dollar in their lives?"

"They're organized. They got injunctions out—"

"Just because I'm helping defend my country and dropping a few harmless chemicals in the lake. I call that damned un-American."

"I used to skinny-dip in that lake. It used to be clear as glass."

"Jarv baby, to make Lake Erie the way you remember it would take forty billion dollars and anywheres from fifty to five hundred years. Provided the pollution was stopped right now. I know. I read the survey."

"But what a way to get votes—a clean Lake Erie!"

"They have public swimming pools. What're they bitching about?"

"It's not the same thing, Melba."

"Just stick to this Damion thing and do as I say and you'll come out smelling like a rose."

"I don't feel right. A legitimate Navy hero."

"That's exactly his trouble."

"What is?"

"Damion's a hero."

"What's wrong with being a hero, for Chri'sake?"

"If you'd read a decent book once in a while instead of drooling over the bare-ass bunnies in *Playboy,* you'd know."

"What's that got to do with this Damion being a hero? My God, Melba!" He stood up, furious. "This land was built on the blood of heroes, from George Washington to Dwight D. Eisenhower—"

"Neither of whom spilled a drop."

"The guys who died on San Juan Hill and Anzio and Iwo Jima, they certainly spilled blood—"

"Save it for the district, Jarv. Next Fourth of July."

"You can't go around knocking heroes, Melba."

"Okay," she said wearily. She was secretly pleased. "If you'll shut your hole for a second and sit down, I'll give you a brief rundown on your star-spangled red, white, and blue fatherland."

Jarvis sulked while she sipped her drink thoughtfully for a few moments. He sensed this was going to be one of her Gotcha sessions. He knew what was expected of him. He sat erect and attentive as a schoolboy.

"In your job, Jarv, you've got to keep your finger on the pulse of the nation. Sensitive to what's going on in people's mind all over the country, not just on Capitol Hill. Got me?"

"Gotcha."

"I told you before there are all kinds of social changes taking place. Cheaper values, lower standards. Got me?"

"Gotcha."

"You want to stay in politics, you have to fit the new picture. Or you're out. Now I liked what you just said, coming to the defense of heroes, the American symbol of all that is true and noble and reverent and inspiring, getting mad about the idea that anyone could demean such an image. But in politics you got to be practical, Jarv. You live on votes. No votes and you die. Now where are your votes going to come from?"

"Cleveland, Ohio."

"Your votes in the years to come will be the votes of the younger generations. After all, this is your first term and we're looking forward to many more of the same. And whether we agree with their ideas just now or not, we have got to have those votes in our pockets when they go to the polls, come all those election days. Got me?"

"Gotcha."

"So that brings us to the subject of heroes. Nobody buys heroes today, Jarv. You could have peddled that jazz twenty, thirty years ago when everybody was crazy about heroes. It was a big thing. But not today. People have gotten cynical about heroes, especially young people. The big deal today is the antihero. Like the Poor Slob. The Loser. Or else it's the Villain, a Mafia type or a Hollywood heel. That's what the public goes for."

"May I say something?"

"Of course."

"I hold the greatest of respect for your brains, Melba, you know that. If I was a tenth as smart—well never mind; but on this idea I don't see eye-to-eye."

"Heroes are cornball. Out of style, Jarv. The biggest misfits in our society."

"What about the astronauts?"

"Sure. If you call a guy way out in space who knows how to push buttons a hero. A hero's a guy who's dying to bleed red blood for some cause he believes in. Like Che, for instance."

"Who?"

"Guevara. Not your district, Jarv. But that's a hero. A real loser, and believe me, he bled."

"The astronauts, they could've—"

"Know when they'll bleed? When the aerospace industry grabs 'em, and the Madison Avenue boys sink their claws into 'em. Wait and see what a few years and a few bucks'll do."

Foster appeared to announce dinner. Jarvis rolled the wheel chair toward the dining room.

"I'm afraid your hero Captain Damion's as absurd today as Don Quixote."

"Donkey who?"

"Is why I married you, Jarv doll. A hero you're not."

"Never had a chance to find out, really."

"It's not your thing. Believe me."

"If I ever got a chance—"

"Don't take it. Look what it's done to Damion."

"I still think it's a mistake, crucifying him."

Melba drained her glass. "He climbed that cross himself, baby. All I'm doing is driving the first nail."

XXIII

He could not sleep.

When he was a small boy living in the American Legation at Tientsin, he tumbled one day from a limber tree in a sudden spell of vertigo. High places since then terrified him.

During the midshipmen summer training cruises, the climbing routine meant a repetition of agonies aloft. He never flinched or failed to perform the chores assigned him. He taught himself not to look below, steeling mind and muscle to concentrate on the job at hand. He fought down fear and revulsion, sweating and praying, exerting every ounce of will power to control the urge to let go, sweet release that would plunge him to the holystoned deck or the sea. His outward calm revealed nothing of the terror inside him. His discipline paid off. No shipmate ever knew.

In the subsequent tours of duty, he dealt with his problem much as sea captains must who suffer from chronic seasickness, or victims of petit mal, or mates of alcoholics. They learn to live with it.

Now in a stuffy hotel room high over city streets, he

recalled that time he fell out of the tree. He had not wanted to climb it, but, taunted, he did and climbed higher than anyone. Each duty station since and each command demanding duties on a navigation bridge or perching him at a port or starboard wing aloft, triggered the old queasiness. It was why he chose not to pursue a naval aviator's career.

He remembered the abandoned lighthouse at the mouth of Flying Fish Channel and the puzzled look in Stevens' eyes when by chance he caught Damion in that moment of distress.

So damned silly, he reflected. A hotel is a fixed place rooted in steel and concrete deep into the rock. Faulted rock, to be sure, as they damned well found out in 1906. But not a shaky tree or the swaying mast of a full-rigged schooner or the dip and roll of a warship in a dirty sea. Yet here I am in sweat and fear, denied of sleep until morning.

We carry our own hell with us. Take poor Mrs. McCready. Let us dwell for several moments on the incredible Mrs. McCready. Wants to help me, she says. Out of the goodness of her heart. She can be most convincing and the forwarder she leans the convincinger she gets. More ample is the evidence of her true intent, shall we say? Nor is that remarkable frontal endowment all. There is her astonishing vitality. Because the legs are useless and nature compensates? Like the sharp-eared blind and sharp-eyed deaf? An old wives' tale. Is she talented in all departments, as she suggests? And will she reveal to me the hiding place of that coarse tuft of black hair?

Fort Knox with dead legs. What breed of man marries half a woman, gold and all? Saint or schemer? And if I never heard of Jarvis McCready, it doesn't mean he isn't a damned good congressman, a dedicated public servant doing everything in his power to make good on his campaign promises. Going out of his way to help a Navy officer out of a jam. More than my congressman has done. I don't even know who my congressman is. How many people do? Know who their congressman is. Mrs. McCready, I bet you. I bet you all the knocks in fool's gold Mrs. McCready knows who her congressman is.

Wants to make him famous, she said.

Let us examine the record, as the pundits say. Assuming the good congressman is on the ball, like all the other good congressmen. By now he has carefully weighed the political benefits deriving to him from the support of an aggrieved constituent named Morgen. (Why didn't the little twerp come to me? I'd have given him a fair account of my reasons. Why do those dumb kids write letters anyway? They always wind up losers.) Let's see. Benefits deriving from supporting Morgen's cause versus those to be gained whitewashing a spoiled Navy captain named Damion.

The good congressman claims I'm more important to save than Yeoman Morgen is to vindicate. She says. One, for sentimental reasons, the congressman having been a Navy man. (I should really check that out.) Two, political reasons. Save the Navy's face, prop up its image and at the same time his own.

A hawk, she said. What will a hawk think of a skipper who acted in direct disobedience to his orders? Who happens to cherish conscience over duty? Not much, with all the bloodspill in Vietnam.

Am I truly worth more to him than all those votes back in Someplace, Ohio? I doubt it. I doubt it very much. The Honorable Jarvis (he-has-got-to-have-a-middle-name) McCready has also got to have something up his sleeve beside his golden arm. If he wants to know exactly what took place off Ha Loi Trung, it isn't to benefit a charity case like me. There is nothing to be gained by telling him a word except a deeper loathing for myself, which, at this low ebb of self-esteem, seems impossible to plumb. Write off the good intentions of one McCready. What of the other? What's truly cooking on the back burner of Melba's wicked little mind?

Fame, she said. Reason enough to place in the hands of her ambitious young congressman/husband a bomb that would blow him unhurt onto the front pages. That's true fame. The front page. And what happened off Ha Loi Trung is that kind of bomb.

She has the clout. She has to have something to know where Tremblay stood less than twenty-four hours after he stated his position. And got her manicured mitts on my dossier. There seem to be brethren, bless their blue-and-gold hearts, who'd shed no tears to see me washed down the scuppers. They'd swing the mop. And look relieved and happy to see me go. And Mrs. McCready would know their first names, ranks, and serial numbers.

With a secret weapon like Mrs. McCready, who needs a Department of Defense?

He stirred restlessly, got up, searched for an air conditioner. There was none. He peered through a crack in the shade across a courtyard of blank wall and dark window at a square of night sky and shivering turned away and crawled back into bed.

What a dismal homecoming, he thought. Months at sea womanless. First day on the beach I'm badly tangled with two. Epitaph: *Here I lie with nothing to lay.*

He needed a woman now, a gentle one, not demanding. A warm and acquiescent one, like a few he had known. Not many, just a few. The ones you remember longest, tenderly, the submissive and grateful ones. The sturdy Catalan of his Med cruise, with her scrubbed face and tranquil eyes, white teeth and a marvelous chest. She cooked astonishing meals and washed his shorts and socks and woke him every morning with her lusty singing. When his leave was up she begged to sail away with him and care for him and, weeping, hung round his neck her only ornament, her dime-thin medal of a virgin.

The compact, satin-skinned Eurasian in Manila who bathed him in goat's milk and nibbled his toes and read him the penny poems of Joyce and fed him toasted salted insects. Her name was Jane. Her IQ 145 and she ran an IBM machine for a venerable British export firm.

And the understanding whore of Hue.

Women who lived and loved to pleasure men.

Not Mrs. Coddington. Granted, she had gotten herself stiff on martinis. Stretched out stark naked on the

266

hotel bed, she couldn't have had more than the fuzziest idea of how badly she was behaving. Not that he wasn't to blame. He'd had enough belts and was feeling no pain and indeed was contemplating a double pleasure—a remembered love and the pleasure of cuckolding the pride of the Coddingtons.

No one told him to look twice at her long belly scar. Or to think of Angela. It would have been fine. He damned well knew it would. He had been there before and it was first rate and it would be again, just this once, for old time's sake.

But she had to jump up and race for the john and that was what turned him off. My God, it was like a Percheron pissing. Damned if he could have made love after that, next door to all that plumbing.

And not Mrs. McCready, with her mind—and who knows what else?—a shining, step-right-in stainless steel trap. A predatory air about her you could actually smell. A smell he remembered in the tree at Tientsin. In all the high places of his secret fear.

Fine ladies. Armed to the teeth with the alluring scents of store-bought aphrodisia. Freudian trappings cling to their flesh like a "shroud of plastic gauze. Science has made them irresistible, orgasm-guaranteed or your money back. Nymphoneurosis, my love, and watch the gestalt.

In the moment of truth, their kisses are razors, the ritual no act of love but a cruel castration.

He was through with all that, except for the Catalans and the toe nibblers and the understanding whores. Women yes. But God save him from the ladies. And where there weren't women, there was the sea. A cruel mistress, a jealous love. But live with the sea and don't cheat and she'll pleasure you all of your life. Cheat once and you've crossed the bar. That's how it is with the sea. All or nothing. Not like some loves, a slow sick tearing, a dragging of chains for eternity. The sea's a cruel mistress. But not that cruel.

He got out of bed. He dressed in slacks and a loose shirt and loafers and went down to the lobby and took a taxi to Haight-Ashbury. He wandered in a strange afflicted world, gingerly and with caution though one would not know it, unflinching in the presence of blaring rock among the acid heads and gypsies. Pimply troubadours approached to beg, took in his steady eyes, and, thinking better of it, vanished. It was an *opéra bouffe* and a spectacle, a mad ballet of psychedelic posters he could not read, fright wigs grown from living scalps, the eye-shattering op and pop illusions of the garish electric light shows.

No Angela. All of them Angela. He was a hunter with blood-stained hands in a land of bereaved children. He turned away, lonely and unloved, into streets of chained stores and barred windows, walking in sorrow all the way. For the first time he began to believe that perhaps he had returned too late. Angela was already lost to him. She was there among the acid heads and troubadours and fright wigs, lost to him. To have found her there would have been more painful than if they had never met again.

He could have wept. But heroes are made of sterner stuff.

XXIV

McCready awoke late on Saturday morning and ordered a huge breakfast. He attacked it on the gritty balcony overlooking the bay, a huge napkin tucked under the silk collar of the robe he wore over his pajamas. He envied the casual elegance of people in travel photographs eating continental breakfasts on their balconies in Paris, France. Someday he'd work out a junket to get him to Paris and please God without Melba. His colleagues were always getting away with it and their private research reports dazzled McCready. He'd make it yet, in the name of one research or another, before he was too old to appreciate it.

He stabbed his way through eggs and sausage, soaking the yolks in the stack of pancakes underneath. A cindery dust settled into the syrupy yellow pockets. He did not mind, shoveling the food into his mouth, following it with noisy gulps of coffee.

He could not believe his luck. Melba three thousand miles away. Nobody to pull him around by his right ear. He gargled his coffee in delight at his freedom, lighted a cigar, stabbed the match and flicked ashes into the golden debris of his meal. At that moment there was no happier man in America.

He knew how brief a respite it would be. Melba had left him a tape of instructions and duties. Her absentee presence infuriated him. He would have loved to burn the tape or fling it like confetti from his balcony to show her who was boss. He thought of Wanda Berry. He could pick up the phone and call her and she'd fly right out and, strictly business, take his dictation and you-know-what-else. But Melba would soon know, damn her. There was no escape from the bitch embrace. Melba left nothing to chance.

He quit the balcony, belching his pique, and padded into the study, his jubilant waking spirits now at low ebb. The front page story of his subcommittee hearings depressed him further. Acosta was there in a four-column cut, his finger pointed at ex-General Marley in the witness chair. Disgusting, he thought. That chiseling Rhode Island turncoat must be paying an arm and a leg for that spread. Why the hell couldn't that lush Tadswell get him press coverage like that? Why wasn't that snotty Mickelby on the scene? Melba was paying those hacks a king's ransom to keep him in the public eye. He studied the photograph and found himself in a corner, half his face cut off. It made him no happier.

His legislative assistant had delivered a bulky mimeographed copy of the subcommittee proceedings before departing for the weekend. McCready slumped on a sofa and read the summary to see how many times his name was mentioned. It was Acosta's show. He threw aside the paper after a glance at the comics, relit his cigar, and turned on Melba's tape.

Her instructions as always were explicit. She told him to listen carefully to a series of cassettes she had received Friday morning, airmailed from a new communications service in New York.

"... a clever gimmick, Jarv. Summarizes the week's activities in the House and Senate and in the Pentagon. It cuts out all the junk you're not interested in and covers legislation and defense developments you're especially interested in. This'll save you hours of reading which you hate to do anyway, so give it a try and if you like it, we'll subscribe to the whole service."

He liked it. My God, it was made to order. It was ingenious, sitting and hearing the selected details of the nation's business that were his primary concern on Capitol Hill and not having to plow through all that legalistic gobbledegook. Oh, that Melba! No getting away from it. She was a bloody genius.

The phone rang. McCready chatted for a few minutes with Hurlburt, the subcommittee chairman. Steps must be taken in the Monday-morning session to repair the damage done by Acosta. Hurlburt had been on the phone for over an hour that morning catching hell from the chairman of the House Armed Services Committee for allowing Acosta to get as far as he did. He had spent another hour saying a meek *Yes, sir* over and over again while the irate chairman of the House Defense Appropriations Committee laid out the strategy for the final session. Not only were they steamed up over Acosta's surprising defection, but sentiment around Capitol Hill on the basis of a hasty survey revealed unexpectedly strong support for Acosta's attack on the defense contractors. It was not going to be as simple to muzzle him as they had first believed.

McCready hung up slowly, somewhat gratified that an important senator like Hurlburt of Georgia had called him by his first name and taken him into his confidence. But damn it, Melba was right again. She had called the shot. How the hell did she always know in advance? Always get the drift of things before he did?

He went to the small bar and was chagrined to find nothing but ginger ale and club soda. More of Melba's damned efficiency. He phoned room service for a fifth of bonded whiskey and a bucket of ice. He spent much of the afternoon sprawled in front of the TV set switching between a double-header and dreary summer replacement network shows, snapping the buttons of the remote control, sipping long draughts of whiskey in water, crunching chunks of ice between his teeth.

A hotel chambermaid appeared at three and began to make up the beds and clean. She was past fifty and black. She sniffed a lot. McCready's eyes followed her movements. He remembered his hotel room in Columbus when he had been a state senator. He had worked out a deal there with his floor maid, grabbing her when she came by, when they were reasonably sure the hotel housekeeper was elsewhere.

Anna. That was her name. She pronounced it Ahnah. It used to tickle him, saying Ahnah. Right now he felt proud of himself, remembering her name because mostly he remembered faces but rarely a name. She smelled of Clorox. At ten bucks a throw, she provided him with some of the hottest, fastest screwing he could remember. On again, off again, Finnegan. Ahnah. She was a scared little thing. Czech, with bad teeth and an accent that excited him sexually. Most of the time he hurt her, not wanting to, but she wiggled and twisted so damned much, the sweet little fool. When he was spent, she'd slip away flushed and panting, whispering her thanks through those bad teeth and in that aphrodisiac accent. She never complained about the rough way he handled her. Anna was used to rough treatment and the ten bucks she stuffed into her bra was a windfall.

McCready learned later what a windfall it was. Any hotel guest who wanted her could have Anna for free. Anna's whole life was a roll in the hay. Nothing else gave her such pleasure and pride. For McCready it was worth the price just to put something over on Melba. He figured it was the only time he had ever gotten away with anything on Melba and if that wasn't worth ten bucks a throw, what was?

The chambermaid was putting away the vacuum cleaner, bent into a closet, her thighs above rolled stockings exposed. He let his breath suck away. She was too old and fat and black. Anna had been white with a trim rear end and she didn't sniffle. The old woman said good-by. McCready got up and thanked her and gave her a dollar and walked with her to the door, telling her who he was and how the Negroes in

272

his district loved him and he would be leaving on Monday.

The woman left in faint bewilderment as the great congressman patted her behind in the friendliest way to prove he was a man without prejudice. Alone in the apartment he did a surprising little jig, kicked his heels once, and collapsed in a chair helpless with laughter, a little drunk and surprised he felt so lonely and missed the others, even Greta.

He napped for fifteen minutes, arose in a sour mood, mixed himself another drink, and went into the study and played Melba's tape through, checking to see that he had done everything as she had directed. The tape ended with a reminder that she would be calling him Sunday morning just as soon as she had the dope from Colonel Jillson. Then she would advise him what to do about the Damion girl.

Jillson. McCready had not missed the look in her face when he suggested she was getting everything she needed from Jillson. How dumb did she think he was? How blind? Sure. Maybe he had not meant it exactly that way, but the second that sly smile stole across her lips he realized what he had said and what she was thinking. She couldn't keep her hands off Jillson that night of the party. He saw right then what a gold-plate lecher Jillson was. Takes one to know one, damn it.

Right now she expects me to believe she's back there yakking to Jillson on the phone but why should she phone? Jillson could come calling, and with that big apartment to lay around in and the kraut dyke egging them on and in love with the idea of Melba cheating on me, they'd be having a ball. And if three's a crowd for Brother Jillson, Melba sure as hell'd send her to the movies.

He could see Greta Ullbricht in a movie house slumped down in a seat next to some polack or hunkie with hot pants trying to make a pass and getting his fingers crushed bone by bone, not daring in his alien accent to make a sound and terrified of this brutish broad whose thighs had touched his once too often. McCready rolled the image round his mind and poured himself another whiskey with a lot less water.

273

Trouble with Melba, she treats me like a pet, like I got to be led around on a leash and told to sit up, beg, jump over the stick. Like I'd get my kiester paddled if I didn't. . . . *"Don't bite the hand that feeds you,"* she had the stinking nerve to tell me to my face.

"Fed up with it," he muttered to no one. The whole bundle. The whole damned Damion mess smelt bad from the word Go. Melba's idea. Christ, he'd have written that sailor, what's his name, a routine letter saying thanks, he would look into it and go on defending your country, lad. That would have ended it. That's all there was to it. Why the hell go stirring up a hornets' nest? The Navy's got troubles enough as it is and the Pentagon Navy brass he came in contact with in Washington had always treated him four-oh and taken good care of him, making planes and ships and Navy stuff available when he needed it. But does she bother to ask first or check on whether he wants to get himself involved in this crazy idea of crucifying Damion? No. *She's* got to call the shots. *She's* got to be the brains and run the show.

Here was this Captain Damion in the same hotel where he, Congressman Jarvis McCready of the House Armed Services subcommittee, now sat, and all it would take was a phone call and a man-to-man talk, dropping the names of a few admirals he knew and a few sincere and modest words on how much the Navy meant to him, the way Asa Guilford might do it. In no time he'd have Damion eating out of his hand. Then he'd tell Damion where he could find his daughter and the three of them'd go out and eat a damned good steak, bloody rare, and he'd order one of the French wines on Melba's list and in no time at all Damion's tongue'd be looser than a slippery shoelace.

What he'd do with the dope Damion gave him, later on the floor of the House, was a different matter. Something he could take up with Guilford. Maybe he could put something big across without doing to Damion what Melba had in mind for him.

He lifted the receiver to call Damion's room and dropped it. Melba would have the phone bugged. He

274

cursed vilely and sat staring at the darkened TV tube while he finished his drink. The thought of a steak reminded him he had not eaten since breakfast. What he craved right now was one of those thick corned beef sandwiches on Jewish rye bread, half-sour kosher pickles, and a plate of potato salad on the side, washed down with a couple of bottles of beer.

Where the hell do you get a good Jewish corned beef sandwich in San Francisco? In Cleveland, in Washington, in Chicago, he knew where. He could fly there like an arrow. But in San Francisco?

He grabbed the phone book, flipped the yellow pages, found several listings. He felt much better. He shaved and took a leisurely shower. Images of salamis hung in delicatessen windows in his favorite deli in the Heights engendered a mood of well-being. He could almost smell the pickle spices and the steamy frankfurters. Perhaps a second sandwich, pastrami or rolled beef, to follow the first. He cackled. Melba detested Jewish delicatessen food, forbade it in the house. This was another one-up on her, as good as Anna and a hell of a lot cheaper.

By the time he was dressed his mood of the early morning had returned. He felt marvelous. He remembered that Melba was going to call him in the morning to tell him what to do about the Damion kid. He was going to have to see her, wasn't he, one way or the other?

He paused, holding the ends of the tie he was knotting before the mirror. Why not tonight? Why not steal a march on the old girl? No harm in that. And who knows, the kid might be gone by tomorrow and Melba's slick little scheme goes up in smoke.

Goddamn it, he had to talk to somebody.

He wrote down Angela's address and put his card case in the right hand pocket of his jacket. He was dressed in a dark navy Dacron-cotton summer suit over a medium blue silk shirt with his woven monogram disappointingly hidden from view. His neck-tie was striped rep silk in red, blue and yellow, held down with a jeweled gold tie clip. His shoes were shiny black

275

slip-ons and he wore a colored handkerchief in his breast pocket. It was ten minutes before eight in gathering twilight when he went down the elevator to the street in search of, he told himself, his supper.

XXV

Angela did not go to the Saturday night rally with Brown after all. The finished curtains were delivered and she was eager to get the rods and brackets up and the job done by the time Brown got back from the rally. She had finished painting the walls flat white that morning, using the pan and roller and touching up with a small flat brush. The room looked cleaner now and rather severe. The curtains would add the right touch, she decided, admiring the rough woven cloth, blood red and bright purple in broad vertical stripes.

Brown had left at eight saying he would be back no later than eleven, no matter how long the rally went on. She kissed him. "I'll wave from the window," she said and watched him marching briskly in the lingering twilight. He never turned. She waved anyway. He was like that, shy in public places, almost ashamed to be noticed.

She washed the supper dishes and stacked them on the drainboard to dry. She carried the small bag of garbage down four flights to the covered cans where Flamm kept them at the side of the house. She hesitated for a moment on the way back.

277

The Flamms were at it again. She stood fascinated by the violence of the quarrel somewhere in the back kitchen of the manager's apartment. On the rickety front porch a shade was up and, glancing in as she passed, she was confronted by one of his huge paintings, a shocking closeup of a clitoris in garish pink and red acrylics. She hurried up the stairs dismayed, angry at herself for peeping. She mistrusted Flamm. His eyes were worse than roaming hands and he smelled like a bearded goat.

She went to work at once on the window curtains. She pulled the rods and brackets out of their container and sat on the floor and studied the instructions for installing them. She was neat and well organized, armed with yardstick, hammer, screws and screwdriver, and an awl to start the screw holes in the wood frames of the window.

Somewhere in the house a record player ground out The Creedence Clearwater Revival's "Proud Mary," so loud she could not hear the Flamms below or the barking dogs of Ransome Court.

The night was humid and still. Angela changed to her shortest shorts and a bra top and swept up her long hair into a loose Renoir knot. She propped the instruction sheet against a cushion and standing on the window seat carefully measured the distances where the curtains would begin and end. She marked points through the bracket holes and started the screw holes into the wood with the awl. She consulted the instruction sheet from time to time to double-check her accuracy and soon was totally absorbed.

She delighted in work of this nature—measurements, figures, getting details so precisely that the finished job would be a source of pride and fulfillment. Balance, she thought. Because I'm a Libra.

When her mother had wanted to change Angela's name legally to Coddington, Angela had raised such a violent fuss that the project was hastily dropped, though not without ill-feeling from the family. She didn't give a damn then. The freeze between them had already set in. It wasn't the idea alone of playing a dirty trick on her father (she would have died first); it

278

was the six-letter balance in Angela and Damion that would be violated. Brown, now. He'd just have to add an "e" to his name if they ever married.

One thing she knew; she would never become a club snob like her mother or the crowd her mother ran with—the smug, well-groomed, glittering types, shallow and vain, married to their well-oiled executive money-making machines.

She frowned. Married. *What diff does married make?* She had read somewhere there were as many divorces as marriages in this country and at the present rate the divorces would soon outnumber the marriages. She had no way of knowing how things would go between Brown and herself. She knew this much: if Brown got turned off on their relationship, she'd leave him. At least they'd have given it a try. She'd never be the one to turn off, to call it quits. Right now she was the happiest she had ever been and she meant to squeeze each sweet drop of it while it lasted.

How lucky I am, she thought. All the hang-ups people have in this world. My mother, with everything she's wanted out of life, still bitches. Daphne. Blowing grass and dropping acid, turned off and tuned out on life. And the Flamms. Can you scrape up anything rottener from the bottom of the human barrel? I think I know why Daddy likes the sea, and it isn't just because his father chose it for him.

What are my hang-ups? she wondered. Besides these curtains?

She had the brackets aligned and firmly bedded. She rigged the traverse rod and fitted it into place.

All my life, she reflected, I've had a tough time trying to make serious talk with people. Nobody expects a nice-looking WASP female in her teens to be capable of putting together a whole sentence without saying "like" and "y'know" and "groovy," not to mention having an intelligent opinion about something, or an original idea. Half the battle is to get them to listen seriously and then to understand what my values are. Even Daddy. Even Brown. They're kind enough and gentle and listen to what I'm trying to say, but they're still thinking, This is a female and that cuts down nor-

279

mal communication by half. Others are just hopeless, I mean adults, male or female. They stare first and then try not to look amused and sometimes they get angry and change the subject as though to say, What right've you got, you smart-ass kid, to *think!* So that after a while I just stopped talking about my feelings to anyone except Brown and, if Daddy is around, to him.

Trouble with me, maybe or perhaps, is that I've been raised to believe in the Judeo-Christian concepts of good and evil and lately it's gone out of style and like a lot of other kids I'm groping around for something like it, something I can safety-pin myself to, and not feel totally ashamed.

Mother, oddly enough, drilled some of those ideals into me. With the Girl Scouts and those three fabulous camp summers on that lake in Maine, the water so clear you could see bottom out in the middle ... With all her other failings I'll always be grateful for that.

But Daddy. God, how I love to look at him, read his thoughts, hear the sensible words he speaks. I hurt him that day in Carmel on the beach. I could see the hurt pass through his eyes and out and never a flicker of change in his beautiful face. And how proud he was of me for saying what I truly felt about war and I know in my heart he will never forget it.

He must be as sick of hate and killing as I am, sick of humans run amok, and yet he cannot freely speak his mind. Poor man! Like me he cannot cope with cunning, or malice or greed. All we ask is to feel sun, breathe clean air, smell growing things, love and be loved, live out our lives in peace. It seems so hopeless, sometimes, I wish I were dead.

The curved curtain hooks snapped one by one into the eyelets of the rod. She tested the drawstring, gently tugging the plastic knob. The red and purple curtains smoothly kissed.

Somebody knocked.

It startled Angela. Flamm, she guessed. She had not locked the door.

"Miss Damion?"

Not Flamm, thank heavens. But who knew her

name? She faced the door, suddenly afraid. "Who is it?"

"Congressman Jarvis McCready, Miss Damion. A friend of your father's." A smooth voice, the accent flat, Midwestern. She went to the door and cautiously opened it. McCready waited, cautious too, his best car-lot smile gleaming.

Angela apologized with a relieved laugh. "It wasn't even locked. Do please come in."

"I'm not intruding?" In now and more confident.

"I'm just hanging some curtains." She looked at his clean-shaven ruddy face. Daddy's age, she guessed, ex-Navy trying to look Establishment. He *looks* perfectly respectable. "You know my father—?"

He nodded, handing her his card, "I would have phoned beforehand, but of course, no phone."

"We've only been here a week or so." She gestured vaguely. "Place is a mess. You could sit on one of those orange crates, I think."

"I'll only stay a minute."

She was studying his card. "Ohio. You must be an important man, Congressman McCready."

"Duty, Miss Damion, is how I view the public service."

"This war," she began.

"Heart-rending," said McCready. "We must stand foursquare behind our President." And, seeing the odd steady way she looked at him, he shifted his eyes and waved at the curtains. "You go ahead with whatever you were doing. My business can wait."

"But you're using your office, I hope, to bring this horrible war to an end."

"Of course I am," McCready said. "Indeedy."

She believed what he said. He smelled of a male cologne and spices tinged with garlic. And what would his business be at this hour? "Is—my father all right, sir?"

"Your father?" He laughed heartily. "Splendid man."

"I mean—not hurt or anything?"

"Fit as a fiddle, Miss Damion."

The ball of her thumb ran across the surface of the

card before she put it aside. A thin card of excellent
quality, engraved in a delicate script. Angela knew.
Her mother made a thing of calling cards. "I'm done
with the curtains, really," she said and worked them
once to show him. "First time we'll have any privacy
up here."

"You live with someone, do you?"

She nodded. "How'd you ever find me?"

"Wasn't easy. As a congressman, I have certain—
ah—privileges. Resources, you might say."

"You're sure my father's all right?"

He smiled. "Your concern touches me deeply. He's
fine and what's more, he's right here in San Francisco."

"Daddy *here*! Can I *see* him?"

"I don't see why not."

McCready could scarcely contain his delight in the
way things were progressing. He was encountering difficulty only in keeping his eyes off Angela's exposed
flesh. "In just a moment, my dear, I'll tell you all about
it. There's one small problem." And seeing her expression hastened to add, "Nothing serious, I assure
you."

"I can hardly believe it, Daddy here in San Francisco." She tried to sit still. "I'll just shut up and let
you tell me about it."

"His ship. You know—the, ah—"

"*Chesapeake*. Golly, she—"

"Right. Nuclear cruiser."

"—was here en route to Vietnam the last time I saw
Daddy—" Should she have said that? A congressman
and security measures and all that?—"at least we
thought that was where he was headed."

"She's still out there, Miss Damion. Your father,
however, has been relieved of his command."

"Why?"

"The exact circumstances are still hush-hush."

"Did he do something wrong?"

"I am privy to certain confidential material, being
I'm with a subcommittee of the House Armed Services
Committee. You may have read about it in the Chron-
icle, with my picture, page three, last Thursday. Un-

fortunately as to what transpired, the exact details aboard the USS *Chesapeake*, I'm not at liberty to divulge."

He paced about, his eyes shifting from the bright striped curtains to the white walls, to the sorry mattress bed, anywhere to keep his gaze from where his instincts directed it. "This is the situation," he went on briskly. "Your father has been the victim of attacks by certain parties wishing to destroy his career. A hero like your father, I don't have to tell you the jealousies a man like that can attract, Miss Damion, from higher up, even from his own ship. Vicious and untrue, to be sure, but nonetheless damaging, and once made public, it could ruin his career."

"How awful!"

"When this was brought to my attention I of course made a most thorough search into your father's background and the charges and in my opinion they are groundless. Now I want to protect your father, Miss Damion. I want to speak out from the floor of the Congress to which I am a humble and duly elected Representative, to defend your father. To stop dead these—mm—scurrilous attacks."

"I can't believe anybody'd want to do anything like that to Daddy. He's such a—nice man."

"Your father, my dear, is a loyal and honorable Navy officer. A gentleman by the most exacting standards." The sound of his words rolling freely over his loosened tongue gave McCready strength. He looked directly into Angela's face. "A patriot and a genuine hero. We've talked with your father—"

"We, sir?"

"My colleagues. Others like me interested in preserving the good name of Captain Damion and the United States Navy as well."

"But it all sounds so—weird!"

"These are weird times. As you well know," he said, looking round the room. "We talked to him. We want to protect him, keep his name and the good Navy reputation unsullied." He liked the word. "Unsullied, you understand." And his eyes took her in.

"Yes. Oh yes." Poor man, she thought. So jumpy,

kind of, the burden of the nation's problems on his shoulders. Or is it only Ohio he takes care of?

"But your father is an unusual man, my dear. Shuns publicity. He's most reluctant to disclose anything of what took place. He feels that the Navy is capable of dealing with its own problems in its own way."

"Isn't that the right way, sir?"

"Ordinarily, yes," he said smoothly. "But your father has enemies in high places. In the Navy establishment itself. To protect him, steps must be taken by a member of Congress, the true and elected representative of the people. Or he's finished. His career ruined. Everything he's done in the service of his country could be wiped out." McCready dabbed at his face and neck with his fancy handkerchief. "Your roommate's out, I take it?"

She nodded absently. "It doesn't seem fair. After all Daddy's done for his country." She hesitated. "He won the Navy Cross in Korea. Did you know that?"

"That's exactly why we—you and I, my dear—must help him."

"But *how?*" I'm just his little girl, she thought.

"I want you to go to your father and convince him he must cooperate with us."

She sat down to think about it. A strand of loose hair fell over one eye. McCready drank in the smooth lines of her outstretched legs, tanned and shapely. Oh God, he thought, help me.

"I really should, shouldn't I?"

"It's your duty, you might say."

"Being threatened like that. After all he's done . . ."

"You must help us, Miss Damion."

"Can't we go to him now?"

"Actually, tomorrow would be better."

"I'm really terribly concerned. And of course with Daddy right here in the city, you know—excited. Can't I just go and see him?"

"Well—"

"Where's he staying?"

"At a downtown hotel. Ah—incognito—"

"I could phone. From down the street."

"Can't risk it, Miss Damion. His phone could be bugged, you know."

"I want to see him," Angela said with surprising firmness. "My own father. In trouble. I want to see him right away."

McCready had not planned on that. McCready had not planned anything. He had acted on impulse and out of pique for Melba's arrogant authority. He pretended to think for several moments, trying to control his heavy breathing.

"It's a rather awkward situation," he said. "For me, a man in my position, I mean." He looked directly at the well-filled bra top and away to long immaculate thighs down to Angela's feet, narrow and delicately arched. Ten toes. As though he had never counted toes before. Live and pink. Delicious as nipples, each one. "On such short notice," he went on. "Wouldn't your roommate miss you?"

"I could leave a note," Angela said, dying to go.

McCready spread his hands wide. "You're such a lovely-looking thing, Miss Damion. How can I refuse you?" He had fingered her bra top before she knew it. "But you can hardly go like that."

"I'll change," she said rising. "Won't take a minute." His brief touch dismayed her and for the first time she wondered about him. "If you don't mind—could you wait in the hall, please?"

"I promise not to look," he said with a brittle laugh and turned his back.

"Come on now, Mr. McCready." Uneasy now.

"I swear," he said and chuckling, covered his eyes.

"Let's not play games." It's Coddington he reminds me of. Laughing nervously and not wishing to offend, she said, "You're rather old for that."

"You're young enough to be my daughter," he protested shrilly.

"But I'm not your daughter." She pushed him toward the door. "Go on, now. Please?"

He turned and brusquely took her, his damp cunning hands swift in knowing where to go. She gasped and tore free.

"Now look—" she panted, backing off in terror.

He moved toward her, his smile pleading.

"—I'll scream."

"Oh no! You—got me wrong ..." and grabbed for her. Lost now, all reason gone.

For a moment in the jungle of their thrashing, in the play of outstretched hands and arms, there was a terrible grace. As though each, imploring, sought in the other some sanity in this mad embrace. Lunging to shout for help. Angela stumbled. The edge of the window seat spilled her heavily across the sill. The yardstick between her flashing legs snapped like a toothpick. Off balance, her momentum sent her headlong over the edge between the parting red and purple curtains. Her fingers clutched and lost them. A single low bewildered cry and she was gone. McCready heard the thud of flesh and bone on metal and, seconds later, a final fainter thud.

He could not believe it. There and gone. Like that. He rushed toward the window, a step, no more, and in panic backed away. He stood transfixed for a confused moment, foolishly patted his hair and adjusted his tie. His fumbling fingers stuffed his sweat-stained handkerchief into his breast pocket. He looked about wildly.

Got to get the hell away from here. Fast. Hat. No hat. Didn't bring a hat, dummy. Doorknob. Never touched it. Go. *Go*, damn it.

He pulled his handkerchief from his pocket and wiped the doorknob and started into the dark hall and stopped short. Calling card. Christ! He went back.

The room was strangely still. The red and purple curtains hung awry. He looked away, sickened. The snapped yardstick. Forget it. Yardsticks snap. The calling card lay on the orange crate Angela used for a night table. He slid it gingerly into his pocket and went out again, down the stairs, cautious and terrified, his fingers touching nothing but the stale inside air.

He frantically reassured himself. She would be out there stunned, perhaps knocked cold. An arm or leg broken, nothing worse. Any second now she might start screaming bloody murder. He would deny everything. Once he was clear of this dump he'd swear on a hundred Bibles he had never gotten further than the

Jewish deli on Geary Street. Let her rave. Out of her mind, he'd say and swear to it. Stoned on pot. You know these crazy kids today.

Last flight. Thank God. Why do they play their goddamn music so goddamn loud? But thank you, God, just the same and please for sweet Jesus' sake get me out of here just this once.

Down the porch steps with the briefest of glances where Angela sprawled senseless in a coarse tangle of deep weeds. He made it to the narrow sidewalk and stopped. A faint groan carried over the hedge. He stood still, his breath bubbling like a squeezed balloon. He went back.

Angela lay face down, a crooked arm outstretched. Her bra top had torn loose. McCready could see the lower curve of her breast. A man's hoarse voice in anger came from somewhere in the back of the first-floor rooms. McCready bolted.

He hurried down the pitched sidewalk in the shadows of parked cars to the end of the cul-de-sac. A dog whined. He ran and turned into the main street. Sweat coursed freely over his body. He thought at any moment he might faint. He kept his head down and walked until he found a street he recognized and he made his way to the hotel.

There was dinner dancing that Saturday night. The happy couples, young and old in ball gowns and white dinner jackets with ruffled shirts and gleaming jewels. Their sleek cars waxed and shiny. McCready used to love dancing. Christ, the affairs he used to crash at Wade Park Manor. The free booze and fancy canapés. Now with Melba—

Oh God, Melba

McCready passed the party people unnoticed. He pushed into an elevator to the Empress Suite and double-locked the door and poured himself two straight shots of whiskey. Two minutes later he threw it up and with it his deli dinner. He staggered into the bedroom and tore off his ruined clothing and kicked off his shoes and fell on the bed.

In his elasticized socks and slim line undershorts, Congressman Jarvis McCready stretched out on the

Empire bed in the rank odor of his own vomit and terror and thought only of what Melba would say. She would know. She would damned well know.

His body heaved with each noisy sniffle until he dropped into sleep.

XXVI

The turnout for the rally encouraged Brown. Two thousand, he heard someone say. They had it tuned in on a transistor radio one of them carried. Neat, he thought, to be right where the broadcast was coming from. He pushed his way across the packed quadrangle. A good-humored mood prevailed. The students were animated and friendly. Brown talked to several as deeply concerned as he over the disruption of classes. The exchange of views gave him strength and hope. He was in a buoyant mood when the college president got up to speak.

There were cheers and boos, the cheers louder than the boos. He got off to a good start, most of the crowd with him until he introduced the first speaker, the dean of students. As though on cue, impromptu speakers jumped up, using anything as a platform to thrust their heads above the crowd. Their harangues brought shouts of protest from most of the students who had come to listen to what the administration had to say. The president's voice from the platform could no longer be heard. A student leader scheduled to speak grabbed the mike and begged for order, to no avail. The voices of the others boomed, scratched, bellowed, screeched, distorted by feedback over amplifiers and mobile bullhorns. One accused the president of being a paid puppet without a shred of authority. Another deplored the tactics of hard-core militants for breaking up classes. A third speaker pleaded for "the right to learn."

Brown pushed his way with difficulty in that direction. He was caught up in a tussle near the platform of a speaker exhorting the crowd to take action now to avenge the dismissal of a black sociology professor and the withdrawal of credit for the course. Brown elbowed past, desperate now, determined to see the business through. He had promised Angela he would. He truly wanted to, for his own sake.

A fist flew in his face.

"Let me by, damn it!" He had to reach the speaker who stood for the right to learn. *Had* to reach him. His life depended on it. And watching him assaulted tumble from his perch, Brown went berserk. Slugged flesh. Kicked bone. It felt good. It mattered no longer who caught it.

Campus guards moved in. A sullen roar rose from the crowd, an ancient sound. Obscenities erupted. The city police department's tactical squad, instructed by the administration not to interfere, hovered on the fringe, uncertain of its role. Window glass shattered. Stones found flesh and blood ran. Panic swept the crowd like a grass fire.

The college president was hustled to safety. Tears streamed down his lined cheeks. The campus guards were in complete rout and the city police on signal moved in six abreast. They met a shower of bricks, glass, and curses with tear gas and clubs.

Brown carried a student with a bleeding scalp to a quiet place. "What's it all about?" the dazed boy kept mumbling. His face was drenched in blood. Brown said he didn't know. He stayed to the end helping others until the area was cleared.

He was glad he stayed. In the aftermath of the riot, amid torn posters, shredded paper and clothing, whiffs of gas, beer cans, glass, and the whimpering wounded, he found the leader of the group who had spoken out for the right to learn. Brown talked to him over coffee for almost an hour. It was the first time he had found anyone willing to listen to what he had to say. Brown wrote down the leader's name and gave his own name and pledged his support. He left the campus feeling strangely elated, prepared to fight for a cause he had almost abandoned. Thanks to Angela. It would be the first thing he would tell her.

It was almost eleven when he turned into Ransome Court. His shirt was in tatters. He carried a bruise under his right eye and a quart of chocolate and pistachio ice cream under his arm for Angela.

Flamm was stretched on the top step of the warped porch. His head lolled against a paint-flaked column. His feet were bare and grimy. He sucked noisily from a beer bottle. Brown started up the steps. Flamm wiped his mouth with the back of his hand.

"Hey, you!" His beery eyes gleamed in the reflection of the street light. "Been waitin' for you."

Brown paused. He usually avoided Flamm. The man's bad art, his aging hippy patter, offended Brown. He took in the wild tangle of greasy curls round a balding center, the matted bristle of unshaven cheeks. Flamm belched.

"I been up there, man. You been out."

Brown felt a cold knot of fear inside. He stared up at the attic window. The red and purple curtains hung limp and awry.

"Where you been, anyway?"

None of his goddamn business! But Flamm had something to tell him. Brown could feel the awful pressure of it. "A campus rally," he said slowly. "Nothing—wrong, is there?"

"Your chick is all." He nodded toward the garden. "Stoned, man."

Brown whirled. Flamm chuckled hoarsely. "What you cats smokin' these days? Carbon moe-noxide?"

Brown went to Angela, dropped his package of ice cream, touched her, gently turned up her face. He had seen the look too many times. Flamm was grinning. It was too much. Brown sprang to the steps. Both hands

291

grabbed Flamm by the throat. "What happened, damn it!"

The bottle fell from Flamm's stiff fingers. "Like I said—" he choked. Brown let go.

"She's dead, you drunken bastard. *What happened?*"

"How would I know, man? I come out for a breath of air is all and there she was . . ." He belched again. ". . . you say *dead?*"

Brown slapped him hard. Flamm's head struck the warped porch floor. He crawled to the door cursing and fell into his apartment. Brown went into the garden again. He touched Angela's cheek. "Still warm," he said to no one and numb with shock, he thought, *No medic to call. No Cong to kill . . .*

He heard Flamm's thick voice shouting into a telephone. A million miles away. The ice cream began to leak into the thick weeds.

XXVII

Midnight.

Damion faced a police sergeant across a scarred desk in a huge room smelling of Saturday night drink and violence.

"I want to report a missing person."

The sergeant reached for a yellow printed form. Tiny pouches under his eyes twitched with fatigue. His gaze shifted from Damion to the drunks, muggers, and whores in various attitudes of apathy and sullenness round the room, back to Damion and the yellow sheet, stabbing a ball point pen into oak to make it write.

"His name?"

"It's my daughter. Angela Damion." He spelled it.

"Address?"

"I don't know."

"She don't live with you?"

"She's a student. She attends a college in Santa Barbara—"

"That's a job for Santa Barbara, Captain." He scowled at Damion. "You got to file there."

"She's here in San Francisco."

"Don't matter. It ain't our jurisdiction."

"But she's here—"

"Captain. We got us maybe fifteen hundred, two thousand minor females drifting around this city—"

"I'll speak to your superior officer, Sergeant."

Their eyes met briefly. The sergeant shrugged, outranked. He regarded Damion's ribbons with a curious eye. "We can file an Outside Missing if it's an emergency."

"What's an Outside Missing?"

"Somebody from another city we put out to our men here." He stared past Damion's head at a noisy group of students herded in by two police officers in crash helmets. "You're going to have to wait a while, Captain."

"Can I look at that form meanwhile?"

The sergeant scratched his head. "Don't see why not."

Damion took the sheet to another part of the room. Students looked at his uniform with contempt. One of them muttered "Pig!" and was instantly rewarded with a rough shove from a policeman. They were lined along a wall near the desk. The sergeant began to book them. A girl in torn jeans wept tear gas tears. She was heavier than Angela and her ankles were thick. Damion felt sorry for her.

He looked at the form. Nickname or Alias. By Whom Wanted. Who Last Saw Person? Mental Condition. Personal Habits (Hvy Drinker, Gambler, Etc). Et cetera, et cetera.

He filled the blanks where he could. When he came to Identifying Marks Including Dental Work, he went to the desk and handed the sheet to the sergeant.

"I'll have to call her mother. There are some answers I don't have." He looked around. "Is there a public phone?"

The sergeant pointed down the hall, but his eyes were on the sheet. "Damion. . . ?" He looked up. Damion had started down the hall. "Just a minute, Captain." His eyes blinked almost lazily. "You *Paul* Damion?"

"It's down there. Yes."

The sergeant came round and opened the gate door on the railing that separated his desk from the outside. "You're in luck," he began and stopped.

"Luck?"

"What I mean, Captain, we just got some word on your daughter. You won't have to file in Santa Barbara after all." He bowed Damion through the gate. "If you'll step this way," he said, polite as a wedding usher, "the lieutenant'll see you. Name's Chandler."

He's being terribly kind, thought Damion.

XXVIII

Sunday.

McCready awoke bathed in sweat and filth. He phoned the lobby for the local papers. He piled them on the bed and searched the pages for a report of what had happened. One paper carried the story, a brief one-column piece in the back of the first section, unrevised from the night desk through the composing room and shop in order to make the last city edition. The headline was all that mattered to McCready. She was dead. He was safe.

STUDENT DIES IN 4-STORY FALL

The body of Miss Angela Damion, 18, was discovered late last night in the front yard of a rooming house at 12 Ransome Court.

Miss Damion, a freshman student at the University of California campus at Santa Barbara, is believed to have fallen from the fourth floor window of the attic apartment where, according to the building manager, J. Flamm, she has been living for the past ten days.

City Medical Examiner Branson gave as the immediate cause of death a broken neck. Circumstances surrounding the tragedy were not readily available.

Miss Damion is the daughter of Mrs. Duane Coldington of Cypress Crotch, Pebble Beach, and Captain Paul Damion, United States Navy.

McCready read the piece several times. He studied each sentence for possible clues. How much did they know? What were they keeping back? Would there be an autopsy? He thought of Captain Damion. Here in the same damn hotel. Had he read the article? Did he know his daughter was dead? And why shouldn't Congressman Jarvis McCready of the big compassionate heart call to offer his sincere and deepfelt sympathy and regret?

He shed his soiled drawers and socks and took a shower. He ordered a breakfast and carried the comic pages to the balcony. He wondered what happened after he left Angela in the yard. Who found her? Was she already dead? One thing was certain. He sure as hell wasn't asking any questions. Calling Damion though, that wasn't asking questions. That was being neighborly.

He was halfway through his breakfast and rehearsing his conversation with Damion when the phone rang. It startled him. He ran to the bedroom to answer it. It was Melba. He had forgotten her promise to call.

"You're out of breath, Jarv."

"I had to run all the way from the balcony."

"Where've you been?"

"Right here, I swear."

"I mean last night. I had some smashing good news and tried to reach you."

"What time?"

"Eight-thirty your time. And again at nine."

"I went out for a bite."

"What's wrong with room service?"

"I wanted a breath of air. I been working over those committee reports and before I knew it was past dinnertime and so I went out to grab a bite. You could've left a number," he said, feigning pique. "I'd have called back."

297

"I was tied up with Jillson. Listen, that's the best part of it, what I wanted to tell you. He gave me all the rope we need to hang Damion. Xerox copies of every dispatch from Admiral Tremblay to the CNO. Tremblay's here in Washington right now. Jillson tells me a meeting's set up very hush-hush with the Pentagon brass and Tremblay's screaming for a showdown."

"What about the ship's log?"

"Extracts word for word, but no true copies. We'll print it, anyway. It'll be up to the Navy to deny it."

"Sounds great, Melba."

"I got it all from Jillson. Last night."

I'll bet you did, he thought. To the last drop.

"But that's not the only reason I called, Jarv." She began to laugh. "Something else broke our way. On the Damion girl."

He held his breath.

"Johannsen—get this—called me a little after eleven. Eight your time." McCready shut his eyes and prayed. "His night man Lucas finally got the whole picture on sweet little Angela Damion. This'll kill you, Jarv—" She heard a rustling of the receiver at his end. "You there, Jarv?"

"Yeah."

"Get *this*: Angela Damion's been shacked up, all right. But with a nigger."

"A nigger?"

"Lucas saw him come out last night and she waved to him. How does that grab you?"

"You mean they've been watching the house?"

"Of course, dummy. You knew that."

"All last night?"

"I had Johannsen lay him off after he spotted the jig. Lucas, I mean. We had all we needed. Why run up the extra expense?"

"Good."

"You get the drift of what I'm trying to bring out, Jarv? This lily-white daughter of your Navy hero, shacked up with a common nigger."

"Melba—"

"I can just see the good captain's face when he finds

out." She burst into laughter. McCready held the instrument away from his ear and looked wildly at the balcony where his breakfast gathered dust and the funnies flew.

"You may as well give Damion a ring now, Jarv. Call him and give him the address where she's shacked up with this nigger. And my regards."

"Will you repeat—"

"*Call Damion*. Tell him where his *kid* is."

"That's all he told you?"

"Who?"

"Johannsen."

"Damn it, Jarv. You loaded or something?"

"All I'm asking is, didn't Johannsen—"

"What are you picking on Johannsen for? He's done a hell of a good job!"

"He could have called me. I was right here."

"So that's what's bugging you." She laughed again. "Now don't pout, baby. Sure, I could've given him word to notify you, Jarv doll, but why involve you any deeper in my personal skulduggery? We want our fighting congressman with clean hands. For that big speech you'll be making on Tuesday. Listen! I've already talked to Guilford. He's very high on all this. Everybody is. The timing's perfect. Guilford's clearing it with the Speaker so you'll be recognized. Not easy, Jarv, but it's being done. Asa's sent me his two top speech writers. They're right here this very minute. I refused to let the material out of my hands. They're in your study roughing out what you're going to say. In your own words, of course. Tadsy's coming by later to see what he can promote out of it and of course we'll give Mickelby first crack at it for his column."

"Melba—"

"You'll have to study it the minute you get here tomorrow, Jarv. We're canceling all appointments. It's going to be the speech of your life. This I guarantee." She began to feel generous, almost loving. "A shame you're not here now to help write it, but time's of the essence." A bell rang. She shouted something to Greta. "Sorry, Jarv. Someone at the door. Now listen—"

But he was not listening. His mind raced. She would

299

learn soon enough of Angela's accident. *(It was an accident, I swear to God, Melba, may I drop dead on this spot)* and put him through one of her ruthless interrogations.

"Melba? Melba. . . !"

"In a minute, damn it! When the speech is set, we're running off press copies and releasing it to the wire services, networks, and press corps. With a firm release date here of Tuesday two P.M., by which time you'll have made the speech. Actually, if the media jump the gun a few hours, no harm done. But I want to give the West Coast papers time enough to put the whole story together—text and comment. We got to make up for that beating you took from Acosta. Then—"

He cut into her words loudly with desperate calm. "Melba, the Damion kid is dead."

"Damn it, you always interrupt!" There was a long silence. It gave him a strange glow of satisfaction. "When?"

"I just happened to pick up the morning paper—"

"When!"

"Last night Late."

"What happened?"

"She fell from a window."

"How did you find out?"

"I told you!" His voice shrilled plaintively. "It's in the morning paper."

"You sound funny, Jarv."

"What do you mean, how did I find out? You think—"

"What happened? My *God!*"

"It's only a few lines. A little article on the back page."

"Read it to me, Jarv."

He read it, a little boy reciting for his teacher.

"She must've jumped," Melba said softly. "Damned kids. Stoned on hard drugs. Shacked up with trash. Berserk."

"You alone, Melba?"

"Of course I'm alone."

"I mean I heard the bell ring. When you called Greta."

"It's Tadswell. He's out front mixing himself a hangover." She remained silent for three or four seconds. "Does Damion know?"

"Why ask me? You told me to talk to nobody, call nobody, do nothing without your okay. So how would I know what Damion knows?"

"You're too charged up, Jarv. Relax. I'm thinking."

Me too I'm thinking—what a friggin' mess you got me into. So sweat a little bit yourself, you bitch, and get me out of it. Get me a hundred million miles the hell out of it.

"I better catch a plane for home," he said.

"Why?" Her sharp tone warned him to be careful.

"It's got me down in the dumps, Melba. This whole bit. Crucifying this poor guy with his daughter dead—"

"One's got nothing to do with the other," Melba said in her crisp business conference voice. "It's not like you, Jarv, feeling sorry."

"I'm tired is all."

"Well, pull yourself together."

"I did have a couple of drinks last night. I was lonely—"

"You stayed clear of Damion?"

"Of course!"

"And the girl?"

"Swear to God!"

"Because it could be sticky if you didn't."

"I did like you said, Melba."

"Well, go to your hearing tomorrow morning like nothing happened. And get back here as fast as you can." She paused. "I miss you, too."

He knew she way lying. Sentimentality from Melba was a danger sign. It put him on his guard. "I'll be on the first plane," he said.

"Your speech'll be all ready for you."

"I still don't like it. The way things are going."

"We'll discuss it when you're here, Jarv." She laughed so suddenly it startled him. "He's a damned sight better off."

"Who?"

"Damion. How would you like a nigger for a son-in-law?"

301

He hung up slowly. On the balcony he poked a fork through the remains of his ruined breakfast and gathered up the scattered funnies. Damn her, he thought. She can say nigger and nobody stops her. But let me say dago or polack just once and the roof falls in.

He smoothed the Pogo page and tried to read it. It was no use. He had had his fill of politicians for the day. Even Pogo could not snap him out of the gloom in which Melba had left him.

XXIX

At dawn of the morning of this sorrowful Monday, Damion followed empty streets to the rocky promontory called Land's End. Gentle waves piled sand in rhythmic layers against the graywacke cliffs beneath him. The tide was low, the air dank. A fragment of the tanker *Frank H. Buck*, wrecked in 1937, poked skyward in gray tulle mist like a swollen periscope.

He had come here often and always alone. In the winter the wind blew hard and the sea hurled icy wet thunder against the offshore rocks. In eary morning hours he had spotted dens of gray foxes cleverly hidden in the chaparral of the cliffs and once caught sight of a sea otter sporting among the sea stacks. There was a fine view of Golden Gate Bridge and the Mile Rock Lighthouse. But that was not why he came here.

This was a pilgrimage of sorts, as one goes to a shrine or sanctuary. Near Land's End stands a forbidding steel monument, the shell-riddled bridge of the heavy cruiser *San Francisco*. A useless rebuke to man for his hatred, Damion reflected, for his capacity for violence. Like the gaunt Atomic Dome at Hiroshima.

Like Berlin's skeleton of Hun reverence, the Kaiser Wilhelm Memorial Church off the Kurfürstendamm. Like war memorials anywhere.

Damion stood for a long time contemplating its proud battered lines. From this bridge in that deadly November night the orders had issued to open fire on *Atlanta*. This relic may well have been the last thing his father's eyes looked on.

He felt hollow, as though everything inside him had been scraped clean. The old grief and the new grief cut like sharp dry bones.

At eight o'clock a Navy color guard showed up. Damion stood at attention and saluted while they raised the colors. And left.

He arrived at the cemetery in Monterey a few minutes before the service began. They buried Angela in a large plot among the Coddingtons on a rise of green earth that bordered a generous sweep of the sea. It did not trouble Damion that she was laid to rest among strangers. Angela could not know, and she was all that mattered. Bereaved, he had shut himself in from his surroundings. Loneliness and silence were familiar companions in his private despair.

Martha in black leaned heavily on the arm of her husband, whose two daughters, subdued in the presence of real tragedy, appeared fresh and pretty. Perhaps twenty mourners were present when the minister began to read from his Bible, half of them sad-eyed young people in their strange and colorful dress, wearing headbands and love beads.

A band of minstrels on their casual way to Camelot. He supposed Daphne was among them.

Martha wept brokenly and her grief so affected Damion that he soon had to control his own tears. He had not believed Martha capable of such deep emotion. He remained standing across the open grave until the minister finished reading the prayer, and turned away when the shoveling began. It was too much to stand and watch. The simple ritual for burial at sea he understood. A flag, a splash, and it was done. This show of tassels and fake lawn grass, the ornate casket, the obscene flowers, the death rattle of stones—

Someone touched his sleeve. It was Chandler, the detective lieutenant who had seen him at the police station when he reported Angela's disappearance. He again expressed his regrets. Damion was curious. What was he doing here? The detective nodded in the direction of the young people.

"You never know," he said. He confided to Damion that another detective in plain clothes mingled with the mourners. Damion moved away.

Brown was there, holding a small bouquet of white carnations. He stood apart, his eyes steady on the grave as it filled. He had shaved off his beard and trimmed his hair short. He wore a neat dark suit and looked sombre and clean.

Chandler sidled over to Damion. "Know that one?"

"No."

"He's the one shared the attic with your daughter."

"I'd like to meet him."

The detective looked hard at Damion, shrugged and almost said, "Okay, it's your funeral." What he did say was, "No harm, I guess. He's clean."

"Clean?"

"We frisked him."

"For what?"

"He could've had something in that bunch of flowers."

Coddington assisted Martha to a limousine, daughters trailing. Others drifted off, whispering, casting glances at Damion. Brown approached the fresh mound and placed his bouquet among the others near the head of the grave. He stood quietly, his head bowed. The detective went to him.

"Brown. This is Angela's father."

Damion put out his hand. Brown, expressionless, took it.

"Sorry we have to meet like this," Damion said.

"Yeah." Brown stared down at the fresh grave.

"Can we talk for a minute?" He saw Brown's quick suspicious look. "Only about Angela."

Brown's eyes were rimmed in red and bloodshot. He

305

had not slept since Saturday morning. His bruised face looked swollen. He glanced from Damion to the detective. "Does he have to be around?"

"No," Damion said.

The detective moved off. Brown watched him go.

"Give you a hard time?"

"There was no need." He studied the tips of his black polished shoes. "I wasn't even there."

"When you left the house, Angela was okay?"

"Full of joy. All set to hang them new curtains she bought."

"She liked doing things like that?"

"She wanted a home for herself. Never had one, she said." His eyes found Damion's. "This was it. For the both of us. I'm black, sure. Made no difference to her."

"Or to me, Brown."

"I needed her, see? That's what was important to her."

"Someone who needed her?"

Brown nodded. "Someone she could unload all that love on. She was all love. Angela. I mean clean love. She had it to give and nobody gave a damn. I was lucky, I guess, being there."

"Were you going to get married?"

"If she'd have me, ever. We didn't know each other except maybe a couple of weeks. But she wanted everything just right. The place. It wasn't much, see? A dump, really. But it was hers—ours—and she loved it." His lips trembled. "She said she'd wave from the window when I left. I never turned to look."

"Why, Brown?"

"For her sake. You know how people think."

"She was happy. That's what matters."

Brown wiped his eyes. "She must've leaned too far, hanging those curtains."

Damion looked across the rolling green slope of headstones and crypts to the sea. "I hardly knew Angela."

"She loved you, sir."

"She did, really?"

"Looked up to you."

"She didn't approve of—what I do."

306

"You were the whole world to her just the same."

Damion stared down at the mounds of flowers so artfully, so tenderly arranged. "That's good, Brown. I'm glad you told me that." They walked toward the gate road. Another funeral party was approaching. The air smelled sweetly of turned earth.

"What are your plans, Brown?"

"Without Angela—?" He shrugged. "I was all set for college, see? It was Angela gave me the guts to go back." He fingered the cheek bruise. "Now—"

"Yes?"

"I got a good chance to re-enlist."

"The Army?"

"I'm grabbing it."

"You had the Army, Brown. You know what that's like."

"Sure I know. Is it any better on the outside?"

"You're a free man on the outside."

"Like Lieutenant Chandler let me know I was a free man?" He spat. "Who needs it? Or the college crap I got caught in? Or what happened to Angela?"

"But Vietnam—"

"Last night when they finally let me go, walking home from the police station, a twelve-year-old kid tried to sell me horse."

"What's horse?"

"Heroin. And when I said no, she offered me her sister." He looked out across the bay. "Who needs it? With Angela gone, everything here can plain go to hell."

"Life can hurt, Brown."

"The Army don't hurt me if I don't hurt it. Mean, yeah. And cruddy. But a man knows where he's at. Today that's not a bad deal."

They stood at the big gates. "Can I drop you someplace?"

"I'm okay," Brown said.

"Keep in touch with me, will you?"

"I'll try."

"Good luck, Brown."

"Thank you, sir." He hesitated. "God bless you." He took a few steps, changed his mind and tagged along with Damion to his rented car. "You ever get to New York City, sir?"

"I might, someday."

"You ever do, be sure to drop in at the Museum of Natural History. Up at Central Park West and Seventy-ninth Street."

"What's there, Brown?"

"Things you won't believe, sir. What life is all about."

Damion smiled. "Sounds marvelous."

"I promised Angela I'd take her there one day. I'll take you instead."

"You won't be there, though."

"Some day I will."

"You're an odd one, Brown."

"I know every exhibit," Brown said, "like the palm of my hand."

"If I'm ever in New York, I'll go there."

"Angela would have loved it," Brown said.

A message awaited Damion at his hotel. Eric Stevens had telephoned, expressing his regrets on Angela's death. He hoped Captain Damion would have time to see him. He was driving in from Bolinas where he lived and would arrive in San Francisco about four that afternoon. It was one-fifteen.

Damion removed his jacket, shoes, and tie and stretched out on the bed to wait for Stevens. Odd it should be Stevens, he thought.

Without Angela, Brown had said. An epitaph for a lonely black. Would they scratch it on his wooden cross in some booby-trapped rice paddy? Or on a stone small enough to bury with his dog tags in the wars to come? Brown is okay. Brown knows where he's going. A hell of a lot more than Damion knows.

He slept. The way sleep comes at sea, tissue-thin and restful. The phone awakened him. It seemed only minutes later but his watch read three-thirty-five. He reached for the phone, expecting Stevens.

"Captain Damion?"

"Yes."

"Hold for Captain Vesey, sir."

"Who's Captain Vesey?"

"Chief of staff to Commandant, Twelfth Naval District, sir."

"Captain Damion? Joe Vesey here."

Damion did not recognize the name. No matter. The Navy, lately, was full of strangers.

"Sorry to read about your daughter this morning, Captain."

Damion waited.

"A terrible blow to both you and Mrs.—Coldington."

We'll let it go at that, Damion thought.

"Hello?"

"Right here, Captain."

"Yes. Now then, the commandant got a dispatch from Washington maybe an hour ago. Phone call, really, and then this dispatch for the record. He feels maybe you should drop in for a chat."

"What's the dispatch about?"

"The commandant'll discuss that with you, I'm sure."

"If it's important, I'd like to know now."

"The dispatch is stamped *URGENT* but we felt after what you've been through—"

"I'll come over right away." Thinking, he had turned in the rental car and Stevens would not mind driving him to Treasure Island.

"Tomorrow's time enough," Vesey said firmly. "We'll provide transportation, Captain. A car and driver'll be at your hotel say 0900, if that's convenient."

"That'll be fine."

He stripped and took a shower and was ready when Stevens phoned from the lobby and he went down to meet him.

XXX

Steven was no thinner, but he seemed more relaxed than when Damion had seen him in Hiroshima. He wore a faded blue denim jacket with a loosely knotted foulard scarf, tan drill slacks, and a pair of worn sneakers. The business portfolio under his arm looked silly.

"I know it's not the best of times to come calling."

"No matter."

"I owe you a drink and an apology," Stevens said in a blunt voice.

"Suppose we start with the drink."

The afternoon saloon rush had not yet begun. They settled themselves at a corner table in the small men's bar. Stevens shouted for a waiter. It surprised Damion who saw no need for shouting. "You want anything today," Stevens explained, "you got to holler for it or they despise you." He grinned. "Arrogance is one of our most precious civil rights."

The waiter hurried over and Stevens ordered drinks. "I'll try to speak my piece, Damion. It won't be easy."

"You're troubled by our last talk, I suppose."

310

"Right."

"Forget it."

"Obviously you haven't." Stevens frowned. "Since that time, I've learned a few things about you."

"You said what you truly felt at the time. I can't fault a man for that."

Stevens shrugged. "You're sure a sucker for punishment."

Damion waited, wondering how much Stevens knew. The drinks arrived. Stevens held his for an extended moment. "Okay. My apology's accepted. We'll write off my cavalier conduct to battle fatigue. The sour aftertaste of Vietnam. My nasty New York upbringing." They drank. Steven fumbled with his portfolio. "I read about your daughter Sunday morning. Very sad. I'm terribly sorry."

Damion said nothing. Stevens waited a moment and went on. "I didn't know you were in town until the obit this morning said so. I didn't know about the divorce, either. Anyway I didn't phone and I may never have phoned. You weren't what I'd call a close friend. But—" He dug out a sheaf of papers and handed it to Damion. " —this news release from Washington is why I tracked you down."

Damion saw on the left top, the Seal of the United States followed by the words *Congressional Record* in Old English script and above that a statement reassuring taxpayers that it was not printed at government expense. A release date appeared below it in boldface type. Damion caught Jarvis McCready's name in the headline. He began to read.

Stevens snatched it from Damion's fingers. "Finish your drink first. You'll need it."

"How can they do that?"

"Do what?"

"How can this be part of the *Congressional Record* with tomorrow's release date on it? McCready hasn't made the speech yet."

"It's phony. You're right. Not a true record at all. It's a press release from his office decked out to look like an excerpt from the record. A lot of the stuff that gets into the record was never said in the Congress.

And some of the spoken remarks strangely disappear when the record comes out."

"Why is it permitted?"

"Congressional license. Caution." He grinned. "If it wasn't edited and revised, the *Congressional Record* 'd look sillier than a comic book." He swallowed some of his drink. "This is a transcript of a speech the Honorable Jarvis McCready of Ohio will deliver on the House floor at about ten o'clock." He glanced at his watch. "Maybe fifteen hours from now."

"McCready's right here in this hotel."

"How do you know?"

"His wife invited me to lunch—a few days ago."

Stevens went to the bar, picked up the phone, and called the front desk. He came back unsmiling and took a long pull at his drink. "He left at noon today. She checked out early Saturday morning." He signaled the waiter. "You a buddy of theirs or something?"

"Hardly."

"Why should Melba McCready invite you to lunch?"

"You know her?"

"I know what happens to military people she takes an interest in."

"What happens?"

"Suppose I ask the questions now. Why'd she call you?"

"She offered her husband's help—" He hesitated.

"Nothing to hide," Stevens snapped. "I know you're in a jam with the Navy." He tapped McCready's speech. "It's all here. I'm curious to know just what she offered beside her husband's help."

"Whatever it was, I turned it down."

The waiter stood by and Stevens reordered drinks. Damion looked puzzled.

"How does he get his speech written and printed if he just left here a few hours ago?"

"One of his Washington stooges—or hers—wrote it for him. Standard procedure. McCready couldn't write a speech like that. He's an idiot. It's also standard procedure to send out advance copies with a release time."

"How'd you get hold of a copy?"

"Luck. I've been on vacation since I got back from Saigon. Leave of absence, sort of. I'm writing a book."

"About what?"

"Vietnam. What I saw and how I felt." Stevens fidgeted. "Anyway, I got a call this morning from my managing editor. The McCready speech had come in on the wire. This copy was on his desk airmail special delivery. That's no cheap service the McCreadys run. The military affairs editor thought it a kind of odd speech for a hawk like McCready. He remembered I knew you—"

"How'd he know that?"

Stevens flushed. "I got maudlin one night over a few drinks. Told him about our meeting in Hiro. Told him the background. This morning he called me out in Bolinas and asked me to come in and take a look at the speech. He thinks there's a hot story behind it So do I."

"Bad, is it?"

"For you—murder."

"A letter from a sailor named Morgen?"

"Verbatim."

"What else?"

"Extracts from your ship's log are mentioned but for security meansures not released. Says McCready."

"That's what his wife was after."

"And you told her?"

"What do you think?"

"Where else could they get such accurate information?"

"A Department leak. The Pentagon, probably. She said she had—what's the word?—*clout*. That was the word she used." He reached for his fresh drink. "She's got *something*. To get anything of a confidential nature she had to get to the top."

"No strain for Melba."

"You seem well acquainted with the lady."

"I've got a file on Melba Hoskins McCready as thick as her husband's skull. She is clever and she makes great copy. There's a hell of a story in Melba if anybody can back it up with proof and wants to risk a libel suit and maybe his skin. Nobody's had the cour-

313

age to try—yet." He picked up the speech. "This looks like Melba's work."

"Why me?"

"You happened to be available and vulnerable. Melba's a ballcrusher. She leaves a trail of ruined generals, bank presidents, corporation caliphs, wherever she goes."

"It explains the call I just got from the commandant of this district." He told Stevens about the dispatch from Washington. Stevens nodded.

"The Navy's got the word, then, right from Melba's hot little lips."

"I had better read that speech, I guess."

"In due time. If you care to risk another wife's invitation, mine's asked you to come out for dinner."

Damion shook his head.

"Look," Stevens said, "I know what you've been through. You're as low as I was when we met in Hiro. A change of scenery might help. I know it will."

"Some other time, Stevens."

"A ride through the country. A home-cooked meal. I happen to have a small cache of Havana cigars." He grinned. "The only real risk is a burnt roast."

"It's awfully kind of you—"

"Hell, I'm after a story. And dying to take a crack at Melba. Come on."

Damion considered it. He drained his glass.

"Genuine Havana—?"

Stevens paid the check. "You'll want some easier clothes. In the next half hour a small army of my less alert colleagues'll be ringing your phone like a three-alarm fire."

While Damion changed, he related the details of his lunch meeting with Melba McCready.

"That's classic Melba procedure," Stevens said.

"Once the speech is out, I don't see how the Navy can deny what I did out there."

"If you had gone along with Melba, it wouldn't have mattered. You'd be a rich retired Navy officer."

"Let's go to the country," Damion said.

Stevens handed him the news release. "May as well

read this on the way." The phone rang. "Don't answer it," Stevens said.

They rode the service elevator to the garage and left the building. Stevens drove his low-slung car through city traffic over the bridge into Marin County. North of Sausalito he took the road west leading to the coast. Damion settled into the bucket seat and began to read.

A Warning! Dry Rot in Our Navy Command

SPEECH
OF
HON. JARVIS
McCREADY
OF OHIO
IN THE
HOUSE OF
REPRESENTATIVES

Mr. McCREADY. Mr. Speaker. About a week ago there arrived in my office, directed to me personally, a letter from one of our fine young men who are serving their country overseas. This particular young man, I am proud to say, is from my own Congressional District. His name is Howard J. Morgen, and he is doing his patriotic duty as a yeoman first class in the naval service of the United States, a duty for which he gladly volunteered in preference to rioting or marching in protest on any of a number of college campuses across the nation. I beg your indulgence for the next few minutes while I read this brief but poignant letter and in

conclusion offer my own humble comments. I quote now from Yeoman Morgen's letter:

USS Chesapeake
FPO San Francisco
Dear Congressman McCready, I wish to report an incident which I'm sure you, as a patriotic American with your strong interest in our nation's military affairs, should know about. It hurts me deeply to report this to you, but I feel it is my duty to do so.

Early this morning, under battle conditions, our commanding officer failed to carry out his battle orders. In doing so, he risked the lives of his crew and our ship. In my opinion, this is an act of sheer cowardice and, for all I know, treason.

I witnessed this with my own eyes, as did several shipmates, some of them officers who are probably trying to "cover up" for

315

him. How can we, the enlisted men, be expected to do our duty out here when the skipper of a United States warship, a commissioned officer many times decorated, a captain, USN, behaves in such a shocking and un-American manner?

I regret that I am prevented by my conscience and security reasons as well as Navy Regulations from telling you further details. I am sick at heart. Only my shame at this act and my love for my country prompted me to go even this far. In my humble opinion, sir, this is a situation that should be made known to the proper authorities. I am asking you, as my elected representative to the Congress of the United States, to take whatever action you deem necessary to investigate this matter so that the lives of American boys will not be risked again by such a shocking act. This is an insult to the traditions of the United States Navy and must not go unpunished.

> Yours respectfully,
> Howard J. Morgen
> (Y1c, USN)

P.S. Thanks for answering my past letters so promptly.

I call your attention, Mr. Speaker, to key words like *cowardice* and *treason*. I call your attention, Mr. Speaker, to the foul word, *un-American*. Each of these words strikes anger in my heart, outrages my deep love of country. And I call your attention, Mr. Speaker, to the simple and eloquent sentence: *I am sick at heart.*

I too am sick at heart. Sick at heart to learn that we in blind faith in our military structure have entrusted the lives of brave young men like Yeoman Morgen and his shipmates to a commanding officer unfit to command; to unworthy leaders who do not lead but run. To cowards and traitors, Mr. Speaker.

The lives of our fighting men are priceless and it is with reluctance, I assure you, that I speak in the same breath of so crass a consideration as cost. But speak of it I must. The dollar cost to construct a nuclear-powered cruiser like the U.S.S. *Chesapeake*, Mr. Speaker, comes to $400,000,000. It takes another $100,000 a day to operate her. Yet, if we are to believe Yeoman Morgen's words, we entrust this multimillion dollar vessel and its precious, nay, priceless cargo to a coward and a traitor.

But what of Yeoman Morgen's words? Are they to be believed? Does he speak the truth? Or is his letter the ranting of a vengeful malcontent, perhaps himself a coward, a traitor, determined to undermine with the insidious cunning of our avowed Communistic enemies, all that we hold sacred in these great United States.

The answer, Mr. Speaker, is a resounding NO. I have at considerable personal expense investigated the background of Yeoman Morgen. I am proud to report my findings. Yeoman Morgen's Navy record is unblemished. He was born in my district and is a registered voter there. His father, though foreign born, is an American citizen who has distinguished himself in his community and throughout the length and breadth of our Buckeye State with his selfless generosity in support of many public philanthropies. His is a love of country that any one of us here assembled, with generations of native-born forebears, might well envy. And Yeoman Morgen's mother, bless her, comes of pure and devout Lutheran stock that settled the shores of Lake Erie a hundred and fifty years ago and tilled its rich soil. So we may put aside for all time any questions of Yeoman Morgen's loyalty to his country. But what proof is there, to support his serious charge?

Mr. Speaker, I hold here in my hand photostatic copies of excerpts from the quartermaster's rough log —the actual record of what transpired on the bridge of the U.S.S. *Chesapeake* that so outraged and shamed the loyal instincts of Yeoman Morgen at his battle station that heinous morning somewhere off Vietnam. I regret, because of the classified nature of this information, I am forbidden to reveal its contents. But I will be more than willing to do so in closed session to those of my qualified colleagues or others with proper security clearance. What it reveals, I assure you, Mr. Speaker, leaves no doubt as to the accuracy of Yeoman Morgen's charge or the gravity of his commanding officer's dereliction of duty.

In conclusion, I realize full well the damaging nature of my statements here. They reveal something sick and rotten in the proudest branch of our armed forces. My feelings for the United

States Navy are well known to this distinguished assembly. I have spoken often in support of it. I served my country in that Navy. I am proud to say I still serve as a reserve lieutenant commander. It is solely because of my dedication to our Navy's ideals and traditions that I dared to bring before you this shocking example of what can happen here if once we relax our vigilance, if once we weaken the chain of steel that surrounds and protects us—our first line of defense against the godless forces who are sworn to destroy us.

Mr. Speaker, the commanding officer of the U.S.S. *Chesapeake* is a weak link in that chain. I urge that steps be taken immediately to repair that weakness. I urge the brave men of all branches of our armed forces to display the kind of vigilance Yeoman Morgen displayed. It took courage beyond the call of duty to risk censure and punishment as he did, to expose what he believed to be a threat to us and a comfort to the enemy.

In these troubled times, Mr. Speaker, with our nation's ideals sorely threatened, with our sacred institutions in grave danger from within as well as from without, we cannot, we must not, relax our vigil. I vow here and now to redouble my own efforts so that this great nation's integrity, its strength, and its beauty remain unsullied. I stand shoulder to shoulder with each of my distinguished colleagues who deems himself a true American. Together we cannot fail to provide the beacon that will guide our Ship of State through the enemy waters of godless aggression safely to her cherished harbor.

Damion returned the press release to Stevens' portfolio. They were following the Panoramic Highway, the road climbing toward Mount Tamalpais and the giant redwoods of the Muir preserve. Damion recalled with sadness this countryside. Stevens negotiated the passage with reckless skill. The air was cooler here, the sky swollen with clouds. Damion caught flashes of the sea. Minutes later the descent began and they regained the coast.

Stevens glanced curiously at Damion. "Any comments?"

"They build a $400,000,00 ship that costs a hundred thousand a day to run and they pay a man a lousy thirteen thousand a year to run it."

"Look at the fringe benefits."

"Thanks a lot."

"Hell of a speech, isn't it?"

"He doesn't say where that cherished harbor is."

"That's your own death sentence you just read."

Damion smiled faintly. "They prepared me for emergencies of that nature a long time ago."

"Why'd you do it?"

"It was long overdue."

"I didn't have to read between the lines. You were fed up with war when we talked in Hiroshima."

"It showed?"

"When you said you'd gone there to visit some *hibakusha*, I knew you were going soft."

"I always prided myself on my poker face."

"Surprised me, because the Damion I remembered was a gung-ho Navy bastard who murdered three helpless prisoners in cold blood."

"A long time ago, Stevens."

"Like yesterday to me." He skidded round a turn. "I understand a little more now."

"What do you understand?"

"You had a tough job to do under real pressure. And a young head full of Navy derring-do."

"I was scared out of my wits."

"You got the job done. You got us home free. I just hated your guts for killing those three guys."

"If they had got loose they could have fouled up the whole Inchon invasion." He glanced quickly at Stevens. "I'm not offering alibis."

"We could've taken them with us."

"It was too risky."

"So you murdered them and you haven't been able to live with it since."

Damion watched green boughs flash past sundrenched fields, warped fence posts silvery with age. "You ever had to kill anyone, Stevens?"

"No."

"A dog? A cat?"

"Never."

"You should thank God."

"I've seen a lot worse since Inchon. Compared to it, what you did on Yong-hung-do is child's play. If that's any comfort."

"It's no comfort."

"That's what my book's about."

The road at sea level passed fishing shacks and bleached docks. The shoreline had an abandoned look, a gloomy seascape in grays and greens. A scattering of tourists and sun-baked locals gaped as the swift car hissed by. Baskets and fishing tackle draped the fronts of seedy bait stores. Across a reedy stretch of shallows graced by swans and ducks, Damion spied the plain roofs of buildings in a cluster of old treetops.

"Bolinas." Stevens stretched his fingers on the wheel and his knuckles cracked. "We take the long way round. After supper, we'll sit down and see what can be done to help."

Everybody wants to help, Damion mused. McKim. Melba. Now Stevens. And nobody can help, really.

"You don't seem too troubled by that speech."

"After Angela—?"

"Sorry."

"But there's much to think about."

Stevens' wife handed him a tall drink and suggested he call her Julie. She was a cheerful and robust woman with merry eyes. Her country kitchen smelled of fresh-baked bread and roasting meat. A mixed fragrance of flowers blooming in the overgrown garden enveloped the rooms of the house.

It was a two-story clapboard affair in need of white paint and much repair. Tools and garden implements lay about everywhere. Out back a badminton court lacked a net and needed weeding It was a scene of comfortable disarray foreign to a ship's captain's eyes. The Stevenses seemed not to mind. They sat with Damion on ancient wicker rockers on the cluttered verandah drinking icy vodka. Two sons were off to a ball game.

"Ten and twelve," Julie Stevens blithely explained.

"We had 'em late and that's the end of it. I wanted a daughter so badly—" Her husband's warning look confused her for a moment. "Oh dear," she said and looked so miserable Damion went to her and kissed her cheek.

Peaceful, he thought. There was a bit of a sea view through the foliage beyond the entrance gate. Across the road a small restaurant with round tables al fresco flaunted bright-checkered tablecloths. It reminded Damion of the seaside cafés along Spain's sunny coast south of Barcelona. In the other direction the narrow street became a dirt lane ending abruptly in a stone wall. The chimneys and roof of a beach house jutted above its spiked top. The Stevenses gossiped about town trivialities. In the kitchen the big iron kettle bubbled. Two loaves of bread and a huge pan of brownies cooled on a window sill. A home, Damion thought. Angela's dream . . .

"If you have a lawn mower," he said, "I'd be happy to work for my supper."

He mowed until dusk. A lawn mower, he marveled. A simple and uncomplicated mechanism to delight a mind preoccupied too much of the time with the performance of a reactor plant and a steam plant and fission produced when Uranium 235 is bombarded by neutrons to create the essential heat to drive the main propulsion turbines that turn the screws that drive the ship to launch the missiles—

—to cut the grass. That was what mattered. To cut the grass to give the earth the food to grow more grass. Fresher and greener. In all his life he had never pushed a lawn mower.

It was almost eight o'clock before the Stevens boys returned from their ball game. It took an anxious phone call from their mother to get them home. They arrived late, raucous and sweaty, were introduced as Adam and Josh and sent off to clean up. Everyone sat down to supper. The boys chattered freely and without awe for their elders, telling how the game went and who stank and who made the greatest one-handed catch in baseball history. It was a lively meal. They ate like trenchermen and cleared the dishes. After half a

321

dozen brownies and a quart of milk, they excused themselves and raced for the upstairs TV set.

Julie Stevens retired to the kitchen and her stacked dishes. Stevens led Damion to his study and delivered on his promise of Havana cigars. He loaded a pipe for himself and set out a brandy bottle and two glasses on the low table between them. It had cooled since the sun set. The boys had laid a small fire and Stevens touched it off. Outside the crickets chirped. Damion and Stevens sat by the fire in sagging corduroy lounge chairs sipping the good brandy. They smoked in silence for several minutes until Stevens realized that Damion was having trouble.

Damion began to cry softly at first. Stevens closed the door and stood at the window puffing on his pipe. He was at a loss for something to do or say. The drawn-out weeping continued uncontrolled for two or three minutes. It wrenched at Stevens' own troubled heart. He thought of where he had been and what he had seen and heard at different crises in his life. A dying machine gunner near An Thei. The three riddled bodies on Yong-hung-do. His mother's dying curses. Things you remember. What the hell is it all about? Why do we do this, God's children, to ourselves?

After a while Damion got up and put aside the cigar and blew his nose and wiped his eyes. He finished the brandy in his glass and Stevens offered the bottle. Damion shook his head.

"I had better be getting back," he said.

"We were going to talk," said Stevens.

"No use," said Damion.

"Tomorrow may be too late."

"It's already too late." He went into the kitchen and thanked Julie Stevens for his supper. The boys came down the stairs two at a time and he thanked them for the use of the lawn mower and they gravely shook his hand. Julie Stevens walked out with them to the car and when it was time to leave hugged Damion and begged him to come back to Bolinas and he promised he would. Stevens tooled the car toward San Francisco. Damion relighted his dead cigar.

"You're a lucky man, Stevens."

"You mean the warm loving wife, the splendid sons in my own image?"

"Without the sarcasm, yes."

"Not luck, Damion. Or sarcasm. Family's too precious a thing to me to leave to pot luck."

"It was to me—once."

"It's a full-time job, Damion. I learned the hard way." He swerved to avoid a dead rabbit in the road. "Never knew my old man. He took a powder a week after I was born. We used to live in Hell's Kitchen then. The asshole of Manhattan. My mother was knocked down by a hit-and-run driver one night on Death Avenue. I was fifteen. I sat holding her hand, bawling like you did a while ago, until she died. It took seven hours. The few times she could speak she cursed the old man and the world at large. Filthiest words I ever heard. There were three of us at the cemetery in Jackson Heights. Me, the gravedigger, and a young Catholic priest from the neighborhood who felt sorry for me. I never cried again. I swore I'd have a family someday—the family I didn't have as a kid."

"You have it. A lovely family."

"This time I'm home for good." He grinned. "Which is why Julie's so damned cheerful."

"What's the book about?"

"It's a novel. Sound crazy?"

"Your war experiences—the pictures and the story—would seem more likely."

"People don't give a damn any more. I used to think if I showed them war as it truly is—pull all the stops—they'd be shocked into doing something to stop it." He shook his head. "They look at the pictures and read the words and it's no different to them from any blood-and-guts TV serial."

"What makes you think a novel'll be any different?"

"Nobody remembers the journalists who covered the Napoleonic Wars or what they had to say about it. But they sure as hell remember *War and Peace.*"

"Good luck."

"I'm no Tolstoi, God knows. But I have to take a crack at it." He was quiet for a few minutes. "I came home for another reason. I don't like what's happening

323

here. I want to be close to Adam and Josh until it blows over."

"You mean campus protests?"

"I mean the whole bag. Social upheaval. Hate. The Big H. We teach kids the Christian ethics of love and peace and then we pump 'em full of hate and send 'em halfway round the world to kill. Christ. I've seen these kids out there. They don't know they're being conned. They haven't had a chance to live yet, to make love—"

"You're driving too fast."

"Sorry. What the hell. You read the papers. You know what I mean. So I want to be around my kids. Live with 'em. Fight with 'em. Love 'em. I want them to know where I stand and I want to hear their side of it and we'll kick it around. I can't manage that too well from Southeast Asia." He glanced at Damion. "Still driving too fast?"

"You're doing fine."

"After I called you this morning, I got to wondering what makes you tick. Your whole life's been geared to military discipline and duty. It took a hell of a traumatic experience, to go against all that."

"It was building up. Since Inchon I've been walking a hairline between conscience and duty. I never really faced up to it, though, until the decision I made—at sea."

"You won't say where—even now?"

Damion smiled. "Funny, isn't it?"

"I'm not about to knock the time-honored traditions of loyalty and duty, sir. But duty to whom? The McCreadys? Loyalty to what? The corrupt Saigon government? They're the ones you're serving. Not the American people. They're the ones responsible for this divided country."

"You don't believe there's a real threat?"

"There's nothing but fear. Escalation by fear and propaganda. Armies and navies need wars or they're unemployed. Or worse, ignored. Most people realize it but they're too damned lazy or too scared to speak out. This country's turning into an idiot's paradise. I owe my kids a decent world, Damion, and I'm devoting my few remaining years to give it to them." He slowed for

324

traffic. "We're at the bridge already. I talk too damned much."

"It makes sense, what you say."

"Hell of a lot of good it does, with the world on its merry way to hell."

Damion stuffed his cold cigar into the ash tray. "Call me when you start building your ark. I'll be glad to lend a hand."

Stevens parked the car a block from Damion's hotel. "The press boys'll be looking for you in the lobby. Use the service elevator. I don't think they'll spot you in those clothes unless a bellhop or somebody tips them off." He held the car door a moment. "I'm going directly to the office and get a story off to New York. It may not help much, Captain. They've stacked the deck against you. But I've an ace or two up my sleeve. The McCreadys for one."

"It's not the McCreadys I'm worried about. It's a few of my brother officers."

"Can't help you there. But there's something in my files on the McCreadys tie-in with a hate group back in Cleveland. I want to check the files. It may come in handy."

"Does it matter?"

"You fight fire with fire. The FBI'd love to have a look at it."

"You're going to a lot of trouble—"

"Anything that makes this a cleaner place to live in, benefits my kids. They've got to live in it a hell of a lot longer than you and me."

"Good enough."

"For some cockeyed reason we've been taking dirty politics, graft, and corruption for granted. Like it's part of the cost of living. It's time we did something about it." He stuck out his hand. "I'll be in touch."

"Take it easy going back."

"Listen," Stevens said, looking thoughtful. "Whatever happened to Lee?" He saw Damion's bewildered look. "The tough little Korean on the island with us."

"Lee Sung Nam. My God." He stared at Stevens.

325

"Lee was killed in action soon after he rejoined his outfit. What brought him to mind?"

"I got to thinking what might've happened if you hadn't shot those prisoners. Lee would've shot them anyway."

"True. With one difference."

"What's that?"

"Lee would've enjoyed it."

"It sure as hell made no difference to the three prisoners." He raced the motor. "Good luck with the commandant."

Damion made it to his room undetected. The phone was ringing. He removed the receiver from the hook and put it aside. He was exhausted and it was almost midnight. And who is there in the whole damned world who'd have anything to say I want to hear? He undressed and got into bed. He thought for a while about what had happened to him in Stevens' study. Embarrassing in a man who never showed much, but he had to admit he felt much better for it. Like opening the sea cocks.

There's a first time for everything, he told himself and soon slept.

XXXI

Foster at the National Airport met the congressman's plane when it arrived in Washington. It was a gloomy night. Rain fell with the rustle of musty silk. McCready directed Foster to wait for his baggage and proceeded to the car.

It was out front, the motor running. It was one of the nice things about being a congressman. Park anywhere you please and nobody makes a fuss. Some of McCready's lost arrogance returned.

He got into the seat alongside the driver's. He knew it would make Foster unhappy. Foster was a stickler for form. It amused McCready who usually sat in back to please Melba. He wondered what Foster's real feelings were. Did this breach of etiquette offend his sense of dignity? Or did Foster merely resent being so close to him.

McCready felt awful. He had drunk the limit allowed on the plane and added to it the contents of his pocket flask. He had waved off the advertised gourmet supper aloft. When the evening snack arrived he was fuzzy-minded and famished. The stewardesses kept eying him and he resented it. Normally he enjoyed their attention, but the last thing he wanted now was to be noticed. He cleaned his plate of finger sandwiches in a matter of seconds and drank two cups of black coffee. He hungered for the taste of the beef filets he had earlier refused. Just as well, he grumpily decided. He was queasy from the whiskey and food he had just devoured. And there was still the damned aftertaste of the Saturday night before.

He squirmed round on the car seat. What the hell was keeping Foster? He really hated Foster. He wondered why it took him so long to admit his hate for the man. He had recognized Foster's disapproval of him ages ago. Foster was firmly entrenched in the Hoskins family when McCready first started courting Melba, and he felt it then. Everything McCready knew about butlers he had learned from the movies and for too long he mistook the man's attitude for the natural behavior of the breed. He had never met a live one until Foster.

It confounded McCready that Melba trusted Foster with everything. He knew how untrusting Melba truly was. Why Foster? McCready was not about to buy that old family retainer crap. He suspected that Foster was stealing Melba blind and had been doing the same with her parents when they ran the household. Behind their backs, of course. Kickbacks on the booze and fancy groceries and the gratuities that were never passed along and all those juicy little service items. It could add up to quite a sum. Why the hell did a smart broad like Melba let him get away with it?

Maybe Foster had something on Melba. Caught her in the act. Doing something she wasn't supposed to be doing when she was a kid. She sure as hell gave him plenty of opportunities, racing around the Heights and up to the lake and the club in that special job she drove before McCready came along. The Cleveland society notes often had a snide word or two about the antics of that racy Hoskins girl.

Who the hell knows? Maybe Foster was tearing off a piece of Melba long before little ol' Jarv came on the scene. That could damn well be it. Knowing Melba.

328

Sitting in the car he began to think about Foster now in a much more personal way. Just what does he have for equipment down there? A silver-plated silent butler to sweep up the crumbs? Does he murmur, "If you please, madam," as he slips it in? You never think about a butler doing anything but butling and there he was tearing off a steady piece in the pantry of the fashionable Heights rock pile while the folks were off to the opera. Who knows how long he serviced old Nellie herself before she cracked up? He's well into his fifties now, McCready estimated. It surprised him to hear how many men in their fifties still got it up. His colleagues spent half their time in the cloakrooms bragging about it. No reason why a careful liver like Foster wasn't getting all he could handle. He never touched the booze. McCready knew. He often checked. Son of a bitch's getting plenty, McCready decided.

Maybe he's banging Greta. McCready snickered. There's a couple for you. Who does what to whom? What's Greta's armament beneath those iron bloomers? What's she got down there, anyway? Tusks? A bear trap? A live octopus? Or a nail-studded swastika? He'd ask Melba sometime, when she's in a fun mood. You could bet your bottom dollar Melba'd know. But she'd sure as hell have to be in a fun mood for anyone to find out. Which she hasn't been in much of lately.

Friend Foster will bear watching. The way things are and after what happened in Frisco, he damned well will bear watching. The bloody cheating limey stud.

Foster appeared through the rain under his umbrella, followed by a porter carrying McCready's luggage. Now why the hell can't he carry it himself? Two lousy valises and a garment bag? What the hell are we paying him for? He watched with sour disapproval while Foster supervised the stowing of the luggage. And the dirty look I'm getting, for sitting up front. Well, screw him. I'm in the front seat for a damned good reason, Friend Foster. You so much as open your yap and I swear to God I'll stuff my foot into it.

Foster got in and cleared the airport and headed toward town. McCready lighted a cigarette. He knew how much Foster disapproved of smoking. Foster

329

turned the air conditioning up. McCready turned it off. He began to feel wonderful.

"Everything's okay at home, Foster?"

"Oh yes, sir."

"Mrs. McCready?"

"A bit tired, sir."

"On the go all day, I suppose."

"A board meeting this morning in Chicago. An executive conference at the steel plant most of this afternoon. Another board meeting in New York tomorrow."

"Drives herself too hard."

"Always did, sir, if I may say so."

If you please, madam. He smirked at Foster, whose eyes were straight ahead. "I'm going to lay the law down, Foster. Both Mrs. McCready and I need a rest badly. Nassau, Jamaica. Something like that."

"It would be nice, sir. Very nice."

"She's resting now, I hope."

"Awaiting your arrival, sir."

McCready frowned. Was there a faint ominous note in Foster's voice? Or was it his imagination? He was badly rattled. He needed a drink and more solid food to settle his nerves.

They were passing the Pentagon, ablaze with light. *Cooking Damion's goose, no doubt.* He thought about Angela and how he had bolted from the front yard of the rooming house. His stomach turned. He killed the cigarette. *Poor damn Damion. Talk about troubles ...* He thought of the speech someone had written for him, the speech he was going to deliver in the morning. A copy had been delivered to him at the airport by one of Johannsen's hard-faced boys. He had stuffed it in his briefcase and had not looked at it since. There'd be plenty of time for that tonight.

He wished to hell Melba had stayed out of this one. It was Melba's fault it had turned out so badly. Her own damned fault for trying to run everybody's lives. He resented her staff's easy familiarity with her business affairs, that part of Melba's world to which he was an unwelcome stranger. The board meetings. The coming and going of officers and directors, fifty- to a hundred-thousand-dollars-a-year men, none of whose

330

names he remembered two minutes after they were introduced. He swallowed Melba's explanation that it was best that way. It gave his political enemies no opportunity to level charges of conflict of interest against him. Melba was adamant on that score. He had to admit it made sense, but it burned him up all the same. They were sure as hell cheating him out of his interests, though it wasn't clear to him exactly how it was done.

Damn it, he couldn't even use her private plane or train or any of the company cars. . . .

"The flight back was okay Saturday?"

"Quite smooth, sir. A bit bumpy over Cleveland."

That tone again, faintly patronizing. *Like he knows something I don't know. If this son of a bitch is pulling my leg . . .* "Nothing serious, Foster?"

"Mullins did mention a new starboard jet engine, sir."

"That's quite an item. Does Hoskins build that engine?"

"I wouldn't know, sir."

Mullins was Melba's private pilot. Another bit of Melba's world off-limits to him. He had seen Mullins once or twice. Handsome brute if you like your men hairy and thick-lipped. McCready wondered if it could be done in a plane while the plane was flying, this thing called automatic pilot. My God, he thought, how horny can you get?

Foster swung into the McCreadys' street, signaled the automatic garage doors open, and drove in. "I'll leave you here, sir, and fetch the luggage up the service elevator."

"Very good, Foster." He got out feeling angry with himself. He had meant to pump Foster with questions. Had there been any calls from Johannsen? From anyone on the coast? Something in Foster's manner prevented him from doing it. He wondered just how much Melba knew. He would sit alertly and watch for a sign. She was tough but she wasn't invulnerable. He'd made it, hadn't he? He sighed. It was too bad he hadn't got some inkling from Foster beforehand. But twelve years of saying thank you to the man had taught him the futility of such a course. Foster was the original silent butler. The crumbs he gathered disappeared from sight and were never seen or heard from again.

Melba held out her arms and McCready believed everything was going to be all right. He kissed her warmly, kissing her lips and cheeks and hair while Greta openly sneered. He kneeled by Melba's wheel chair and presented her with a gaudy package containing a bad jade necklace for which he had been grossly overcharged in a shop in the San Francisco airport. Melba opened it and admired the oval stones and put the strand round her lovely throat. McCready threw a triumphant look at Greta. He mixed himself a drink and sat with an arm round Melba's shoulder until it was time for bed. McCready was just tight enough to feel amorous. He dismissed Greta in spite of her protests and carried Melba in his arms and settled her gently in bed. Melba seemed pleased. It was normally Greta's last chore of the day. He had not displayed such devotion in years.

A curious passivity had come over Melba. She seemed shy and almost childlike in her submissiveness. McCready in a rapture of reprieve barely took notice. He had replenished his own drink and mixed a stiff bourbon highball for his wife. He settled against her shoulder. Melba was propped comfortably on several soft pillows. Jarvis regarded the swell of her chest with proprietary fondness. His searching fingers met hers. For a moment she seemed to halt their progress, then guided them to their twin objectives. He squeezed his eyes shut, caressing her.

"Melba honey. . . ?"

"Yes?"

"Driving in from the airport, I was thinking—"

"Good, Jarv. *Good.*"

"—we both have been knocking ourselves out. Both of us can use a rest and I got to thinking, a second honeymoon. Bermuda, maybe. Remember Bermuda?"

"I sure do remember Bermuda, Jarv."

"Soon as we get this business over with, a little holiday'd come in handy, don't you think so?"

"I sure do think so, Jarv."

He returned to the fondling. His mind took up the idea and fondled the bliss to come.

"Jarv?"

"Mmmmm . . ."

"What happened out there?"

". . . mmm. Out where, honey?"

"The Damion girl's apartment."

With difficulty he kept his fingers moving. "Poor kid took a tumble."

"Jumped?"

"Paper said 'fell' . . . It was in all the papers."

"What's your theory?"

"Hopped up on drugs. Fell, probably."

Her hand found his and kept it moving.

"You don't suppose someone could've pushed her, Jarv?"

"Nah. The poor kid took a tumble."

"How do you know?"

"It's what the papers said."

"What really happened, Jarv?"

"I just told you—" He hated to open his eyes. He knew when he did, hers would be steady on him, calculating, and his first false words a target. "Even the police don't know."

"But you know, don't you, Jarv?" Her hand still encouraged him, but he knew the jig was up. That languid, purring quality was too familiar. She wasn't guessing. "You're in real trouble, Jarv, and that can include me. I want you to tell me everything exactly the way it happened."

She waited. She knew the man she had married. She could spot a lie in his eyes by a look, on his lips by a smile. She could tell when he lied over the phone. He never had a chance and no one knew it better than he did.

"How'd you find out?"

"Johannsen's man happened to be driving out of that dead end street when you walked in."

"He never saw me before in his life."

"He saw your committee picture in the paper. He was leaving to phone Johannsen about the girl being

333

shacked up and Johannsen sent him home. He never gave you a second thought. Not until he read about the kid being found dead. He had the good sense to call me here and not say a word to Johannsen."

"It was an accident, Melba. I swear to God." He told her what happened in the attic room.

"Did you try to help her?"

"Happened too fast, Melba. There one second, gone the next."

"I mean after that. Where she fell."

"I started to. I heard someone coming and—I got the hell out."

"She could have lived."

"I thought only of you—"

"You're lying."

"My God, Melba, the publicity could ruin you!"

"Sweet of you, Jarv. Noble. You know damned well you were saving your own skin."

"There was no time to think—"

"There was time enough to make a pass at her."

"She was half naked, wearing this nothing bikini—"

"So you had to grab. You couldn't go out and rent yourself a fifty-buck whore. You had to get yourself something for nothing."

"I went there strictly on business."

"You're lying again."

"You said you wanted her to help us!"

"I said to wait, Jarv. Not to go until I cleared with Jillson. And I did. And I phoned you. And where were you? Out after a bit of charity ass. Well, you bought it this time, baby."

"I never laid a hand on her."

"We're through, Jarv."

She had never said it before and it frightened him. He moved his hands urgently over her body, caressing and kissing. Melba lay still, neither resisting or responding. When he tried to kiss her lips she turned away.

"Take a look in your closets," she told him.

"What's in my closets?"

"They're empty."

"What's the idea?"

"Foster's packed your things. Suits, shoes, shirts, the works. Good man, Foster. Reliable and discreet. Rare qualities."

McCready got out of bed and slid back the closet doors and pulled drawers open and slammed them shut. "I'll kill that limey bastard—"

"Quiet," Melba warned. "Greta's outside the door with orders to come in if once I raise my voice." She reached for her drink. "Get back in bed. We're not through talking."

"You got things all wrong, Melba—" He crawled back, his mind spinning.

"Lucas—that's the investigator who spotted you—is asking for a lot of money. I don't blame him and I'm paying it. But I'm taking it back from you month by month."

"I've got some rights!"

"You lost them Saturday night."

"The hell I did! No court in the world—"

"Courts?" She laughed harshly. "Don't tempt me."

"Now look, Melba. We've been together a long time—"

"The separation papers are in the works. So is a reasonable financial arrangement. You have, after all, performed certain services. Unless you object to receiving support from a physically handicapped woman."

"Damn it, Melba—"

"I suggest you hire an attorney to represent you. To avoid any future embarrassments."

"You're treating me like a business write-off."

"I am a businesswoman."

"Why can't we talk this over man and wife?"

"We could." Her laugh was chilling. "If you were a man. Now then. Foster's reserved you a small suite at the Roger Smith. You're welcome to spend the night here. Tomorrow you're on your own." She handed him his drink. "Relax, Jarv. Beginning tomorrow, you'll probably be famous."

"You mean you've already spilled this to the press?"

"I mean the response to the advance mailing of your speech is fantastic. Beyond our wildest hopes. Your office staff's been working round the clock handling phone calls, invitations to speak, requests for your photograph, newspaper and TV interviews. Which reminds me. There's a message to call the White House first thing in the morning. Lem Packard. He's a top adviser on domestic affairs."

He sat up. "And you're letting me down. Just when we make it big?"

"My mind's made up, Jarv. It's in the works." She looked pleased. "I'm going to miss you, Jarv."

He drained his glass and hurled it across the room. "Damned right you'll miss me. Who else'd put up with a crippled old bag like you?"

"Flattery'll get you nowhere, Jarv doll." The doorknob rattled. "It's okay, Greta. Everything's okay." She watched the terror come and go in her husband's face. "I've always been rather fond of you, but now you're a luxury I can no longer afford."

"Talk sense, for Chri'sakes."

"You let that Damion kid die. You might have saved her. You didn't even try. That's the same as murder. How do I know you won't do the same to me someday?" Her fingers moved almost absently over his body. He did not respond. "Come on, Jarv. Relax and enjoy it." She smiled. "You may as well leave on an upbeat. How about one for the road?"

I've made love to a lot of types, she thought later while he snored, but never to a murderer. It definitely adds something, she decided. I should look into it sometime.

McCready left early, about an hour after dawn. Greta in the hallway sagged in sleep, her huge thighs spread like two oak limbs before her. One kick, McCready thought. One swift farewell boot into that miserable stony crotch. He passed it up. With the troubles I've got, he thought sourly, who needs a broken foot?

He was not unhappy about leaving. The last tango with Melba was more disaster than upbeat. He had bruises to show for it. It was hard to believe she could behave like that and throw him out. But he wasn't

336

through with Melba. Not by a long shot. As she damned well soon would find out.

He walked through the empty corridors of the old House Office Building. His deserted front office looked like vandals had struck. He shuffled through telegrams, invitations, stacks of letters and memos. Everyone wanted McCready. He went into his private office. Mail and messages with higher priorities were neatly stacked and marked on his desk. Wanda, he thought, brightening. Life without Melba won't be too hard to take after all.

He put up water for coffee and sat at his desk and read the speech they had prepared for him. Terrific, he thought. Sensational. How wonderful it must be to sit down and write a speech like that. No wonder the mail was heavy and the phone lines jammed. No wonder everybody in the world suddenly discovered what a great guy Jarvis McCready was.

Well, screw 'em. Screw 'em one and all.

He waited for the water to boil. *Famous, she said.* She goddamn well knew what fame meant to him, how sweet it must taste to a have-not from the Flats. His name in the paper, his picture in the magazines. She knew damned well what it was like. She had lived enough with him to see what fame meant to him. What it would mean to anyone who came where he came from.

Where he came from . . .

At twelve he was flabby with unsteady eyes and a weak foolish smile. As a kid he learned to run faster than the rest of the gang. He had to or suffer their cruelties. He learned guile and smooth talk and how to make the boys laugh. He could clown his way out of danger with the nimbleness of a toe dancer. At seventeen, with his three brothers off to the Army and his sister in a charity ward, he was transformed by some miracle of adolescence into a self-assured young dandy in shoplifted clothes, attractive to girls, his red forelock trained to flop loosely over his eyes. His wisecracking style and his gift of gab made him his high school's most popular student. He could organize anything from a block party to a gang bang and gather the benefit—

337

the receipts and the choicest of broads—while the others did the dirty work.

He was the apple of his mother's eye. She slaved and stole for him and swore he'd be the President of the United States before she died. She gutted lake pike for the Star Fish Company under the bridge. She waited tables in Joe Kindler's and slung hash at the Flat Iron Café. Some nights she ended on her back in any number of the shacks along Riverbed Road. But in the morning the money went into the bank each time for her darling Jarvis's college education.

It got him a year at college—no more. It was a business college in downtown Cleveland. He learned one thing—to hate office routine and business machines. It was no life for a man who dreamed of his name in lights, his photo along with Kirk Douglas and Marilyn Monroe in the Sunday supplements. He knew how it would go, picturing himself sporty and confident in the TV interviews with the Hollywood columnists who came calling. He could not miss. His mirror never lied.

They found his mother dead in a lot alongside the Canine Crematory. The running gag that made the rounds of the beer joints along the Flats was that they should have buried Aggie McCready where she died. It couldn't be fitter. He realized after a short Navy stint (he had a chronic mal de mer) that at twenty his mirror had failed him. No glamorous life lay ahead. Not a hope of it, at least, until Melba came along. And that hope shriveled when it became clear to him the driver's seat was hers.

He poured the boiling water over a spoonful of instant coffee and let it cool. Congressman Jarvis McCready by the grace of God and Melba Hoskins McCready . . .

Murderer, she had called him. He remembered another time when she had told him, *A hero you're not.* Words you don't forget. *If you were a man,* she had said. It took a man, it took a goddamn hero, to live with a bitch like that. How the hell *could* he forget?

Would he forget Angela Damion sprawled in her dark garden of hopeless weeds? And how long would it

338

take to forget her father, the Navy hero he had never met? Whom he would murder in a couple of hours on the floor of the House.

... *the same as murder,* she said. The memory chilled him. He sipped the hot coffee.

What've they got against heroes, anyway? I love heroes. What are they trying to do to this poor guy whose only mistake was to refuse to carry out an order? What the hell was the order, anyway? Drop the Bomb on the Kremlin? And why did that stupid kid have to write his letter and get me into this goddamn mess I'm in now?

He finished his coffee and picked up the speech again. The murder instrument, he thought. You had to hand it to those guys. You had to be a genius to write a speech like that. A speech that could kill a man. You had to go to the right college and read all the egghead books and write doctorates, whatever the hell those are, and study literature and talk like a Harvard professor. You had to be Tadsy and Mick. You had to piss perfume and wipe your ass with silk. You had to be all the things Melba McCready adored and fawned over and paid through the nose for. All the things you, Jarvis McCready, are not.

"Screw 'em." His voice, hollow in the silent office, startled him. He looked around aggressively, scratched his thatch of red hair. Some murderer, he thought.

He pushed back the incredible piles of mail and messages, Wanda Berry's neat valentines, and pulled a pad of yellow ruled sheets from the drawer above the *Playboy* cache. With a thick black pencil in his fingers, he began to write a speech of his own.

He came out of his private bathroom, freshly shaved. Wanda Berry was bent over his desk, reading what he had written. He came behind her.

"Yi!" She spun around.

"Hi, Wanda."

"I took the liberty—"

"I changed the speech a little."

"A *little?*"

"You're looking great, Wanda."

"I'm a wreck. They're calling for you all over the place. Packard from the White House. Shall I put the call through?"

"Anybody else in?"

"We worked until after midnight. I told them to come in late—"

His arms went round her. He kissed her lips hard and wet. She stayed right there.

"What a way to start the day," she murmured.

"We got us some unfinished business, young lady. But right now you call back Mr. Packard. You tell Mr. Packard anything he wants to say to me, he can say after the morning session."

"You can't do that to Lemuel Packard, hon."

"I sure as hell can." He chuckled. "Don't worry. He won't call back." He looked at his watch. "Session opens in fifteen minutes."

"Why won't he call back?"

"His boss isn't going to like my speech."

"But it's already out."

He kissed into her words. She pulled away. "What's got into you, anyway?"

"It's what I got out of." He grinned and slapped her bottom. "Get this shop cleaned up. It's a hell of a mess and we want to look our best when the media boys come banging on the door." He started to go.

"Would you sign a few letters before you get snowed under?"

"My successor'll sign 'em."

"Successor. . . ?"

She ran after him but he was gone.

He took his seat. The big hall hummed with talk. Secretaries and aides scurried about with last-minute notes and memoranda and the Representatives of the People settled down for another expensive morning of frustration.

Some of them came over to McCready and shook his hand and commented on his speech. He kept an easy smile on his lips, nodded and wisecracked. His insides were churning. He regretted not having bolstered himself with a presession slug of whiskey.

340

He looked around. Tadsy and Mick had done their work well. The gallery was jammed. He thought, too bad Melba's not here. With luck she might have had a heart attack. Not that it would do him a damned bit of good now. It would have been nice just to be around while it happened.

Asa Guilford in the front row, half out of his seat, turned in McCready's direction and beamed at him. McCready beamed back and Guilford held up two fat fingers in a victory sign.

You know where you can shove 'em, McCready thought.

The Speaker rapped for order. And rapped again, and again and finally the hall was quieter than it had been before and the great democratic process got underway. McCready heard his name called. The final murmurings ceased. McCready got to his feet. One of the seven official reporters moved in close, his open shorthand notebook ready, his relief standing by. McCready cleared his throat.

"Mr. Speaker." The big hall fell silent. "Mr. Speaker. You have seen or have before you a copy of the speech I'm about to deliver. This speech has been given wide advance circulation, as is the custom with this august legislative body. As a result of this advance publicity, my office in the last twenty-four hours has been inundated with telegrams, airmail and special delivery letters, and phone calls. It is a heart-warming reaction from the good people across the face of the nation who print the news and I should be deeply gratified. I guess, with a reaction like that, it must be a pretty good speech, full of patriotic catch phrases and some pretty highfalutin' grammar. Now I must go on record, and I regret the confusion it may cause. But I want the record to read that I did not write that speech, Mr. Speaker. I never saw that speech. I never approved of it. And I'm not about to make it."

The hum of voices swelled. Several reporters hurried from the hall. The speaker pounded the desk with his gavel. Asa Guilford, beet red about the jowls, rose heavily. "Will the representative from Ohio yield?"

"I will not yield, sir." he shuffled his yellow sheets

341

and glanced about nervously. All eyes were on him. He thought he might sit now, and give up. He thought of Melba's scorn and suddenly the weakness was out of his legs. His fingers no longer trembled. "You're going to get your speech just the same," he went on. There was a ripple of laughter. "Maybe it won't hold a candle to the other one, but at least it's my own words and out of my own head." He heard a few snickers and grinned. "After I wrote it, I realized I didn't have to put it down on paper at all. It's what I really wanted to say, not some faked-up mess of words half of which I'm not sure how to pronounce." The laughter this time was genuine and warmed him. "It's how I really feel. Deep in my heart. Nobody has to write down a thing like that."

Someone in the gallery applauded and the gavel fell. McCready went on. "I didn't come here to praise or condemn Yeoman Morgen for the letter he wrote. He too said what he truly felt. I admire him for having that kind of courage. But I also don't understand why he didn't have the extra courage it took to say what he had to say directly to Captain Damion, his commanding officer.

"Captain Paul Damion. Skipper of the *Chesapeake*. The Navy officer in Yeoman Morgen's letter whose name my highly paid—but not by me—speech writers refused to mention, while they set him up for murder."

Guilford was on his feet beseeching the chair. "Mr. Speaker . . ."

"I have the floor, sir," McCready said clear and loud. Guilford fuming sank back. "Maybe none of you here ever heard of Captain Paul Damion. We never get to know the names of our generals or admirals unless there's a world war on. Or one of them commits a boo-boo. Well let me tell you who Captain Paul Damion happens to be. He's a hero. An authentic, living Navy hero who, when he was a lieutenant, junior grade, carried out a dangerous and hazardous mission. Without him, we never would have taken Inchon. We would most certainly have been defeated in the Korean conflict. That's who Captain Paul Damion is. But you would never hear it from him. All he did at Inchon, he

342

would tell you, was his duty. And that is the Navy officer my highly paid speech writers and the people who pay them stabbed in the back when they wrote that speech I'm not delivering.

"But every newspaper and TV and radio station in the country has that speech and Captain Paul Damion's name will be heard on every newscast tonight and his picture splashed on the front page of every newspaper, labeling him a Navy coward. A Navy traitor. The ugliest American since Benedict Arnold.

"That's why I'm here, Mr. Speaker. To protest that label if it's the last act I do as a representative to the Congress of the United States. Why? Why risk my career? Because I know in my heart how this man has suffered, both in his career and in his private life, from forces over which he had no control and was helpless to deal with. Somebody said a little while back, someone who should know better, that American heroes have gone out of style. Nobody in America believes in heroes today. They're a laughing stock. Objects of scorn and ridicule. Well, in my humble opinion, if we had a few more heroes around like Paul Damion, this country wouldn't be in the sad situation it now finds itself. This is a time for heroes like Paul Damion, a time to put down the enemies who would destroy him."

Guilford was on his feet shouting. McCready raised his arm high. "I will not yield, sir. I have but a few more remarks to make and will burden my distinguished colleagues no longer."

The gavel pounded. McCready went on. "It is not a time to murder our heroes, Mr. Speaker. It is a time, rather to call on them for their strength and courage. The courage of a Captain Damion. And the courage of a Yeoman Morgen, who is young, Mr. Speaker, and unseasoned, but who has the true makings of a hero because he has the courage to speak out. I wish I had that kind of courage. I regret that until now, I did not. And all I can do now is the decent thing. Which is to save one hero's life. It's sad enough we send our heroes out to die for us. We shouldn't murder our heroes as well.

"That is about all the speech I have to make, Mr.

343

Speaker. I didn't write that phony speech but if any one of my colleagues or anyone else is interested in knowing more about it, I'll be holding a press conference in my offices right after adjournment of this session."

He sat down. In the din that followed, the Speaker's gavel pounded uselessly and Asa Guilford's shouts for recognition could not be heard. It would not be accurate to say that strong men wept. But an unusual amount of bourbon traveled over lumpy throats the balance of that remarkable morning.

To the north and east two hundred and fifty miles, Melba McCready in her best wheel chair, wearing a Rudi Gernreich basic with a nothing front, barely stifled a yawn. She was presiding over a meeting of directors in the stone, steel, and glass Hoskins Towers high over Park Avenue. The agenda she had weathered this far covered the quarterly reports of the Hoskins Electro Corporation (industrial components, control systems for complete machine automation), Hoskins Machinery (self-clamping drill jigs, gearless and gear train drill heads, feed and cam units), and a Hoskins subsidiary that manufactured electric brakes and clutches, and ball-bearing screws. Except for this last item, in which Melba displayed unusual curiosity and about which she asked innumerable pointed questions, the proceedings were boring her to death.

At the moment, the controller of Hoskins Forge & Foundry, a producer of electrical connectors, was trying to explain the current fiscal's near-million deficit by evaluating a New England competitor's trade manual and price list. Melba tapped a gold pencil and dreamily debated his future worth to the organization. His gravelly voice dug his grave deeper.

Greta Ullbricht let herself as quietly as her bulk and chafing tweeds permitted into the conference room. Melba usually forbade such intrusions. This time she welcomed it. She had stationed Greta in her study down the corridor to receive any word from Washington on the reception of Jarvis's speech.

344

"Is a man outside," Greta whispered. "Wants to see you."

"Any word on the speech?"

"Is nothing yet."

"Tell whoever it is I'm in a meeting."

"I told. Is important, he says."

Melba frowned. "How'd he get this far?"

Greta shrugged. "Is very important, I think."

"What's he want?"

"You. Only."

"Who is he?"

"From the government."

"Tell him to make an appointment."

Greta shook her head. "He don't move, he says, till he sees only you." She seemed impressed. "He showed license."

Melba repressed a smile. "License to what?"

"FBI."

"Tell him to leave his card."

"Already I told him. So he will wait."

"Let him wait, then." Melba winced at the droning tones of the controller she would be firing next morning. She touched Greta's coarse tweed sleeve. "What's he like, Greta?"

"Big shoulders. No mustache. Your type."

Melba rapped her solid silver gavel. A Christmas gift, she recalled, from the grateful executives of Hoskins F & F. "An urgent matter, gentlemen. Please excuse me and do carry on."

A change was welcome now that she had thrown out Jarvis. She would miss him for a while. A bit of dalliance might well relieve the boredom until she came across someone to fill Jarvis's shoes. She had heard reports on the Treasury swingers. And tales on the prowess of the FBI studs. Some of the reports were fascinating. If they came anywhere close to the talents of the CIA types she knew, it could be a barrel of fun.

Greta wheeled her away. Halfway down the corridor, Melba signaled a stop. "No word from Washington is funny, Greta."

"No word," Greta said.

"Because that session's almost over. You don't suppose—"

"What is?"

"Never mind." Melba relaxed. "He wouldn't have the guts."

She smoothed the décolletage where Jarvis's cheap jade beads nestled in the glistening crevice. A diversion, anyway. She moistened her lips with her tongue. Who knows what FBI really stands for? What these fun things in life could lead to?

She smiled at the young man who rose to greet her. He smiled back. Greta was right on. Her type, all right.

"Mrs. McCready?"

"Yes?"

He identified himself. "We want to ask you a few questions."

"About what?"

"An Ohio group called the Freedom Force."

"Sorry. I'm in conferences all day." She liked his hazel eyes, his smile. "Can you drop by my hotel later? Perhaps we can discuss it over a drink."

But he had opened his briefcase and was taking out some papers. And he no longer smiled. "See my attorneys," Melba said coldly and Greta swung her about.

"We'll do that, ma'am," the young man said, smiling again, watching her go.

346

XXXII

The gray Navy sedan slowed at the Treasure Island main gate for the routine sentry check. Newsmen and cameras seemed to spring full blown from the green grass and shrubbery and like a strangler fig enveloped the car. Two duty Marines advanced, flushed and angry, not certain of their roles. A corporal inside the booth barked into a telephone. Damion told the driver to pull over to the side. A newsman with a TV mike fired the questions.

"You heard Congressman McCready's speech, Captain?"

"I read it—"

"He called you—"

"I know what he called me. I read the speech. Now if you'll be good enough—"

"Certainly you'll make a statement, after a speech like that."

"You read the speech. You know all there is to know."

"Was your daughter on drugs, Captain Damion?"

Cameras. Flash bulbs. Questions so idiotic, so personal. He wanted to lash out at the lot of them. He rolled up the windows and thought of the demonstrating mob outside the gates of the yard at Sasebo. He sat trapped until a flushed-looking Navy commander arrived and waded into the crowd. "C'mon, you guys. You know the rules. There'll be a regular press conference inside at ten o'clock." He turned to Damion. "I'm Gilchrist, base PA officer. Sorry I'm late, sir. You'll be able to talk to these guys later."

The sedan started up. The Marine corporal saluted. The newsmen got into their cars and followed.

Treasure Island looked hostile to Damion. All Navy shore installations affected him the same way. He longed to be clear of them and back aboard ship. He wondered if he would ever make it again.

The car wound slowly down the wide drive past technicians and workmen on their morning coffee break quarterbacking the war, figuring time-and-a-half and how much to demand the next time their union contract came up for grabs.

He hated these places. Too bad the Navy could not run without them. He had suffered the agonies of new construction, civilian contempt for the uniform, the slowdowns and stupidities of repairs and overhaul. In spite of Melba McCready's protests he had endured them too often to believe the delays were unavoidable and the errors accidental. Only accidents were accidental. A shipyard was not a ship; a shore base was not the sea.

Captain Vesey met him, crew cut and spare, and introduced him to the commandant, Rear Admiral Lodge Rockingham. He had a direct, no-nonsense air about him that appealed to Damion at once. The last thing Damion wanted now was more sympathy. He sat where the commandant directed and was pleased to accept the cigar offered. Vesey took a seat near the window. Rockingham lighted up and sat behind his desk. It was clear to Damion the admiral had small taste for the unpleasant duty he had to perform.

"No sense beating about the bush, Captain. Washington's handed me a real dilly." He waved at some papers on his desk. "Lot of scuttlebutt, as usual. Hard

348

to know what to believe. They tell me some congressman made a speech this morning, upset the applecart." He shrugged. "I missed it—"

"He jogs mornings," Vesey explained.

"I heard about that speech," said Damion.

"Whatever," said the commandant. "This dispatch is what I go by. It's from the CNO himself. For my eyes only. He wants you here Monday morning at 0900. Seems CinCPac's called up—well, it's a court of inquiry, Captain. It's my job to set it up. Million details, y'know." He frowned. "You're not attached to any command in Washington, are you?"

"No, sir."

"Then would you mind telling me what the hell this is all about? I mean, I'm a Med sailor, Sixth Fleet most of my life. But I know about you. The Korean thing. What the hell's going on?"

"They want to investigate the details of an incident aboard *Chesapeake*, my last command."

"Something fouled up?" He waved his hand. "Never mind. I shouldn't have asked. It's just, each day it gets harder than hell to know what's going on." He glanced at Vesey. "May as well tell him what we know, eh, Joe?"

Vesey nodded. Damion studied his cigar. The commandant heaved a sigh. "The Department's in an uproar. Tell him, Joe."

"There's been a leak of top secret information, Captain. This congressman's speech this morning, this McCready of Ohio, it apparently contained material known only to the CNO himself and maybe two of his deputies."

"You have any idea, Captain," the commandant interrupted, "how tight security is back in the Department?"

"Very tight, I'd expect."

"I served my time on the CNO's staff after I ditched an *SOC* at Salerno, flying off the old *Savannah*. Let me describe that security, Captain. After each meeting, an officer and a chief petty officer from a special destruction unit empty the secret wastebasket into a paper bag. I know because I was that officer for six months.

We'd tear off the doodling on the staff's scratch pads, the top three or four sheets, because the impressions from sharp pencils show through. We'd catalogue the material and seal it and store it in a safe for a week. Then it went to basement incinerators and was burned. Then the ashes were pulverized to dust, and a destruction statement, signed by the chief who did the work and by me as supervisor, was turned in." He leaned back. "How could there be a leak, tell me?"

"That was wartime, Admiral," Vesey said.

"So what? Everybody handling those secret wastebaskets is screened for top security clearance."

"Somebody talked, then."

"It's this damned unification," said the commandant, "Pentagon politics. Ruining the Navy. The Joint Chiefs, the Department of Defense, outside civilians instead of Navy-trained personnel, everybody with his nose in everybody else's wastebasket."

"No love lost there," Vesey said.

"And you got aides and deputies and secretaries swapping favors back and forth." Rockingham sat straighter. "You can bet your bottom dollar the leak isn't in one of our Navy's wastebaskets."

"The speech this morning confuses matters, Captain," Vesey said, "because I'm told it wasn't the speech that was sent around in advance."

"I didn't know that," Damion said surprised.

"And we didn't happen to catch it on the news this morning. I got a man monitoring it. No word so far."

A steward arrived with coffee. The commandant complained in lengthy detail of the routine problems of a shore command. Damion smoked his cigar patiently and sipped black coffee. Finally, Rockingham pushed his coffeecup aside. "Now I must inform you that your R & R is canceled as of 0900 this morning. You are requested, but not ordered, mind you, to take up temporary residence here on the base. A security measure, I assure you, to protect you from the press and publicity hounds. Of course, you're free to talk to whomever you want, but I recommend you let the PA officer handle it. He knows the ropes. We'll provide suitable

350

quarters, of course. We're proud of our lash-up here. Every comfort a shore-based man could want."

"Thank you."

"It's been requested that you remain on call until the court is convened and the inquiry completed. Let's see—" He consulted a desk calendar. "That gives us six days. Any questions?"

"No questions, sir."

"None at all?"

"No questions, Admiral."

Rockingham shrugged. "Officers' club chow's the best in the county. Cheap, too. So's the booze." He glanced at Vesey. "Anything else, Joe?"

"I'll handle any requests you may have, Captain," Vesey said. "The base PA officer is Commander Gilchrist."

"I met him."

"You may need legal advice. Our staff legal officer is Commander Lizarraga." Vesey tapped his skull. "Very savvy for a Filipino."

I know Filipinos, Damion thought, annoyed, twice as savvy as you and with much better manners.

"The new orders are being processed," Vesey continued. "When they're endorsed, I'll send along your copies. I suggest you arrange transportation of your gear from the hotel as soon as possible."

"Everything's right here," Damion said. "I figured this was what it was all about."

He was settled by noontime in bachelor officers' quarters, in a room on the second deck with a view of both bridge and bay. In spite of the commandant's recommendations, he chose to eat in a small dining room off the lobby, not caring to risk the camaraderie of the club. He was preparing to go to lunch when the phone rang. It was Stevens.

"You're a hard man to track down, Captain. Nobody on that base ever heard of you."

"How'd you get me?"

"The public affairs officer's on the ball. You hear about McCready?"

"What now?"

351

"He never made that speech."

"I heard something. Clue me."

"He pulled a Sydney Carton. True martyr type. Disclaimed the printed speech. Never wrote it or approved of it. Spilled his guts to an army of news media people for two solid hours this morning."

"You're kidding."

"Scout's honor. You've no idea what hell it's raised with city editors and composing-room foremen. But that's not the big news."

"What could be bigger?"

"He called you a hero. Right there on the floor of the House."

"I have a medal to prove it," Damion said. "If anyone cares."

"McCready cares. It was a hell of a speech. Nobody knows what inspired the poor slob."

"His wife?"

"Hardly. But something's happened there. I'm trying to find out. Because he dragged a few family skeletons out of the closet." He chuckled. "This should swing a lot of public favor your way."

"But not Navy. I'm up for a court of inquiry next Monday."

"You don't suppose, after what McCready said for the record, they'll call it off?"

"It doesn't change what happened off Ha Loi Trung."

"It casts a different light on things." Stevens was silent for perhaps three seconds. "Ha Loi Trung. Thanks. You don't think it'll go easier for you now?"

"Read the Military Code of Conduct."

"That's for prisoners of war."

"We'll see how it goes."

"That file I kept on the McCreadys—remember? Well, the FBI grabbed it. Loaded with details they've been tracking down for years."

"Kind of a dirty trick on McCready, isn't it? After that speech?"

"You kill me," Stevens said and hung up.

XXXIII

Damion had two visitors during his stay on Treasure Island. He had told Gilchrist he wanted no more press interviews and no visitors. Gilchrist promised to handle it. He called Damion one morning. A visitor was at the gate and refused to leave until he had spoken to Captain Damion. The Marine sentries had notified Gilchrist. Gilchrist had spoken briefly with the visitor.

"A polite little guy," Gilchrist said apologetically, "but firm. Says he's a citizen and demands a visitor's pass."

"Another crank. I'm getting a lot of weird mail lately."

"This one claims it's a matter of life and death."

"A dangerous crank."

"I can't figure him out. Says it's about his son."

"What's his name?"

"Morgen."

Damion met him in the lounge. Harvey Morgen was pink-cheeked and obviously agitated. About fifty-five,

353

neatly dressed in cashmere and gabardine, his sparse hair brushed to cover a bald spot.

"It's very kind of you to see me, Captain."

The accent told Damion at once what it was that had troubled McKim. Yeoman Morgen was a Jew and to McKim it would always be a consideration. Damion had never given it a thought. Funny world.

"I'm glad you came," Damion said.

"Planes." He shuddered. "Twice in my whole life I flew in a plane. The other time also out here to say good-by to Howie when he went overseas." His worried blue eyes sought Damion's. "What a terrible thing my son's done to you, Captain!"

"He saw it as his duty."

"He couldn't ask first?" He looked nervously around. "What a time they gave me until I could convince them I had to see you."

"What is it you want, Mr. Morgen?"

"Can we go someplace and have a bite? A drink maybe? My hotel? They maybe got a good restaurant here? You're my guest. Name it."

"You can have lunch right here with me."

"Impossible."

"No choice. This is all Navy."

"I'll choke on every bite."

They ate a quiet lunch. Morgen did well on roast beef hash, a salad, and coffee and talked about his business successes, talking quickly and nervously as though at any moment he expected to be told he must go. He avoided any discussion of his son until they were in the privacy of Damion's quarters.

"He's a good boy, my Howie. He means well. This you got to believe. He loves his country. He'd gladly give his life, God forbid it should happen. But a good kid, Captain Damion, clean through and through. You hear what I'm saying? Not like these kids today, these hippies. I swear to God, I don't understand what's got into them, with their drugs and long hair like a girl's. A shame, and right in my old neighborhood, hippies on Coventry! You ever hear of such a thing? My old synagogue—I haven't the heart to tell you what they use it for now."

"Tell me about Howie."

"Howie. The way I raised that boy, Captain, you wouldn't believe. What was I? An immigrant, a green-horn. Twenty-six years ago America opened its arms to me, took me in, an orphan, a refugee, a Jew. A no-body. I made out okay, knock wood. I can never pay back what America done for me. Except with—with loyalty, like giving my only son. Gladly. You know Howie enlisted? He didn't wait for the draft. He quit high school. Because he knew I wanted it. Because his country needed him." He wiped his eyes. "You know Howie, Captain? Personally?"

"He stood his battle station on the bridge alongside me."

"Which is exactly what brings me here, by plane yet, to explain a little this crazy thing Howie went and done. I could've dropped dead on the spot when they called from the *Plain Dealer* and told me. Since then I can't sleep a wink. Then I had to read this morning in the *Plain Dealer* how they're going to court-martial you—"

"Not a court-martial, Mr. Morgen—"

"Harvey. Please." He gestured with his hands. "It used to be Chaim. Now it's Harvey." His smile was impish. "That's America for you. You knew right off. I could see you knew I was Jewish."

"—It's a court of inquiry. To determine the facts."

"But my wife—? Howie's mother? A saint! Raised on an Ohio farm, it happens she's not Jewish. So what? With us it doesn't matter. Our two daughters, God bless 'em, they had some religious training. But whoever they marry—America comes first. You hear what I'm saying? First—America. So what does Howie do? He goes and writes this—you'll excuse the ex-pression—*farshtinkener* letter and they're going to court-martial you."

"It's only an investigation, to ask questions and de-termine what actually took place out there."

"So they're flying Howie in, special. He phoned last night from Honolulu. Collect."

"It figures."

"So it's a serious business, Captain. I want to help you out."

"What do you mean?"

"You're in trouble? I happen to know a smart Cleveland lawyer he could do you some good."

"There's a Navy lawyer here. He'll handle it."

"How can he be on both sides? Look, I got in mind a big man, making easy a hundred thousand a year—"

Damion smiled. "I'll be all right."

"A loan? You can pay me back any time or never."

"Why should you do this?"

"Why? Howie is why. My son. He did this to you. His guilt is my guilt."

"Nobody's guilty of anything, Mr. Morgen."

"So why is there this, this trial, all this hate, flying people from God knows where to punish you? I read all about it. You hear what I'm saying?"

"There's nothing to be done."

"You're absolutely positive?"

"Yes."

"I don't understand," Morgen said slowly, "how you can take such a thing so calmly. It's a shame, a big man like you, a national hero, they should go and do such a thing." He shook his head.

"You're a good man, Harvey. A decent man. Howie's a lucky boy having a father like you."

"Coming from you—praise like that—" He could not go on. He stood up and wiped his eyes again and with Damion's arm across his narrow shoulders walked down the hall.

"I'll be meeting Howie when he gets in. I'll have a little talk, father to son—"

"Don't be hard on him."

"My own flesh and blood?"

"I'm glad you came," Damion said. "It helps me understand why Howie did what he did."

"I'll never forgive myself," Morgen said. "Not helping you. Nothing."

"You helped, Harvey, I'll be fine."

"I couldn't even buy the lunch," Morgen whispered, barely audible. He clung to Damion's hand for a moment at the door. Damion watched him go, straight-

cked among the flower beds and green-trimmed
alks until he was lost from sight. Damion went back
 his room.

Guilt, he thought. The little man made him sad.

The other visitor was Commander Lizarraga. Lean,
nned, good teeth, the strong grip of a tennis player.
hey talked for several minutes about Manila. His
mily had originally been Spanish nationals, sugar
owers for generations. As a child during World War
wo he had been imprisoned in Santo Tomás. His
ack bore the scars of Japanese machine-gun bullets,
e told Damion, received in the last fiery days before
Ianila was retaken.

Lizarraga zipped open a thin briefcase and put on
is glasses. "You understand," he told Damion, "you're
ntitled to choose any other legal assistance you may
ant."

"You'll do fine," Damion said.

"Then let's get down to business." He thumbed
irough the papers. "I've been doing a lot of Damion
esearch since I took you on. That citation when you
on the Navy Cross, for example." He smiled oddly.
You were a pretty nervy kid at twenty-four."

"Lucky, I guess."

"One small matter there I'd like to clear up."

"Shoot."

"You took prisoners, right?"

"Three."

"What happened to them?"

"We shot them."

"Escaping—?"

"They were bound hand and foot to trees." He
owned. "Why bring this up now, Commander?"

"So that we're prepared to answer questions that
ay be raised about your record. Frankly, this one
oubles me."

"It happened eighteen years ago—"

"They'll dig back to the day you were born. In your
ase, Captain, they'll leave no stone unturned." He
hifted uncomfortably. "Just bear with me, eh?"

"Go on."

357

"Did you report how you disposed of the prisoners?"

"It's in the official record. Operation Choptan
Might take some digging in the archives but it's
there, exactly as it happened."

"I already dug. I read your Operation Choptank r
port."

"Then let's get on."

"In a moment, Captain. When you took the prisor
ers, did you try to get information from them?"

"Lee Sung Nam, the ROK lieutenant with us, trie
So did I."

"What results?"

"The usual. Name, rank, serial number."

"Did you torture or mistreat them in any way?"

"Just what the hell are you getting at?"

"The truth, Captain. For your sake."

"Lee wanted to. He felt they were more his enem
than ours and the information could have been usefu
I refused permission."

"Can I get hold of this ROK lieutenant?"

"He's dead."

"Did you consider torturing the prisoners?"

"It was a temptation. Their leader was a nasty cu
tomer. Lost face being captured, cursed us—" H
smiled faintly. "—spit all over Stevens, who tried
feed him." His smile faded. "He'd have probably go
ten away if we'd have left them there."

"At no time was there mistreatment or abuse."

"We stuck to the rules."

"And shot them before you left."

"The success of that landing at Inchon, for whic
thousands of men that night would be risking the
lives, hung on the secrecy of our presence there." H
looked away. "So I shot them."

"You, personally?"

Damion nodded.

"Still bothers you?"

"Yes."

"A final question, Captain. You're familiar with A
ticles 79 to 81 of the Geneva Convention rules on th
treatment of prisoners of war?"

Damion knew now what was coming, what Lizarrag

358

had in mind. He wondered why it had taken so many years. "Yes."

"Then why," Lizarraga said carefully, "was no action taken against you for shooting the three prisoners?"

Damion did not say anything and Lizarraga went on. "I've searched the record. Your report does indeed give the details. But in the reports of immediate command over you, in the entire Inchon operation, there's no mention of this violation. How come?"

"I don't know."

"An oversight, perhaps?"

Damion shrugged.

"A cover-up?"

"By whom?"

"Some well-meaning friend, perhaps, higher up?"

"You know damned well that's not likely, Commander."

"But not impossible."

Damion ran his hands wearily across his eyes. "It troubled me for a long time. The shooting was in the report, exactly as it happened. I expected a reaction. There was none. After a year passed, I felt it should be brought up. I wanted to keep my record clean. Defend my action. I started asking questions through my immediate superior. A few weeks passed. He called me in one afternoon. Very paternal, I remember. Told me what I was doing was commendable. True Navy spirit and all that jazz. But he recommended I forget all about it. 'No sense glorifying three dead gooks,' was what he said. I never forgot that."

Lizarraga walked to the window and stared out across the busy base to the tower of the 1939 Golden Gate Exposition Building.

"He said 'gooks'?"

"Yes."

"You have any idea what it's like to be a gook—a special kind of Filipino gook in Navy gold braid?"

"I can guess."

"There's a retired admiral drops in at the club every now and then. I try to avoid him but he manages to pounce on me. Calls me 'boy' every time he sees me.

359

Swears he knew my father, a stewards' mate in the riverboat days on the Yangtze." Lizarraga swore softly. "My father was never in the Navy. He was the spoiled son of a sugar grower. He went to Hotchkiss and Yale and never did an honest day's labor in his life. But he owned the finest private collection of Oceanic art in the Orient. Second finest in the world."

"What happened to him?"

"The Japs killed him in Manila. He was helping a captured American pilot to escape." He turned abruptly from the window with a rueful smile. "You know what your great American author says? Henry Miller? He says that combatting the 'system' is nonsense. There's one aim in life and that's to live it. Shall we get on?"

"By all means."

" 'Scrap the past instantly,' says Miller."

"It has curious ways of reviving itself."

"We're about to deal with that now." Lizarraga sat again and adjusted his glasses. "I'm satisfied that what you did at Inchon was in the line of duty. Should the point be raised we can defend it. Actually, the Navy approved of your action. The record and the Navy Cross support it. Now, a few weeks ago off Ha Loi Trung, you behaved like a human being. In doing so, you broke the rules. That, they don't approve of. But in this band of brothers your father was a hero and you're a hero and the Navy sometimes looks the other way. Everything would have been all right. The worst that might have happened after the R & R would have been a light reprimand. But the word got out. Congressman McCready's speech—either one of them—left the Navy no choice. The cat was out of the bag." He studied his notes for a moment. "Tell me this. How much did the shooting of those prisoners affect your decision not to open fire off Ha Loi Trung?"

"You're being too clever, Commander."

"A man's conscience at work?" He shrugged. "A sure winner with any jury, given a smart defense lawyer."

"A Navy court won't buy it."

"Depends on who sits on that court. If it's the old

360

guard, we may have trouble. If we draw a couple of young admirals, we'll do very well indeed."

"You really believe that?"

"The Navy's changing fast, Captain. This new breed of bright youngsters kindles hope in the breast of even a cynical, second-class minority gook like me." He smiled. "The kind of admiral you're going to be."

"You think I'll make it?"

"You practically have. From the scuttlebutt I hear. Look. Last year alone we processed more than thirty-five hundred legal assistance cases right here. Many of them are kids who'd rather take a prison rap than fight a wrong war. You should sit in sometime. Their pleas are eloquent. And unrehearsed. The younger admirals sitting on these courts aren't blind. Or deaf. They're getting the message. They discuss among themselves what might have to be done about it. They're hip to the changing social order. They're a part of it themselves."

"That's damned encouraging, Commander."

"I know a few like you, Captain. Young, intelligent, extremely capable, who would not have opened fire on a defenseless village. They're the ones I'm counting on."

"We'll know Monday morning, won't we?"

"I feel our position's fairly strong. No matter who sits on that court."

"Won't Tremblay pack it?"

"He'll try. But he's got his enemies, too."

"In either case, it doesn't alter the fact that I disobeyed orders."

"No matter what you did, the record shows that the orders were carried out. The mission accomplished. You disobeyed for a sound moral reason. The worst they can come up with might be impairment of military morale and discipline. You'd still catch a reprimand, but no more."

"You make it sound easy."

"Disobedience of orders is a delicate subject, Captain. It's been argued in Navy courts for a hundred years or more. Certain orders, for example, are absolute. They cannot be disobeyed."

361

"A Polaris sub skipper's orders, for example?"

"Exactly. He can't fire his missiles on his own, no matter what situation he faces."

"And he can't refuse to fire when he gets the order from the President. I know," Damion said. "I was there."

"In your particular situation, off Ha Loi Trung, you decided not to carry out your orders. No damage was done." He spread his hands wide. "One of the penalties we pay for the privilege of command is the risk of making decisions like that." He began to stuff the papers back into his briefcase. "There were mitigating circumstances. The fisherman. Your conscience. Points I'll make. And I'm not ignoring the political aspects of it. There's a lot of pressure on this court from both sides. Navy brass is determined to brighten the tarnished image. Have to, now that the story's out."

"They're bringing in some of my crew, I hear."

"Anyone with a real grievance against you?"

"I don't know of any."

"Well, the truth will be heard and that's what it's all about. I'm counting on strong public opinion to support us."

Damion walked with him to the lobby. "Grateful for your help, Commander." His thoughts seemed elsewhere and Lizarraga spoke to reassure him.

"I'll be right there with you Monday morning. You've got nothing to worry about."

"I was thinking of the prisoners of war."

"Ancient history now," said Lizarraga.

"I was thinking of all of us."

XXXIV

It was a Sunday to remember. The sun shone. The bay sparkled. The summer dresses of pretty girls brightened the flower-lined walks. Damion at attention admired a snappy color detail of the Treasure Island Honor Guard swinging along to its duty station. At Building 291, clear young voices of the choir in rehearsal filled the morning air. In the main chapel just inside the main gate, a mass was said and done. Scrubbed Catholics stood cleansed and happy-looking and talked about the Giants and Dodgers.

Eric Stevens drove in from Bolinas that afternoon. They walked in the hot sun across the causeway to a shady slope on Yerba Buena where grass and trees framed an unimpeded view of Alcatraz.

"No omen, I hope," said Stevens.

"It's deserted."

Stevens had worked all night writing his syndicated articles. They would run in more than a hundred major papers across the country. He would cover the court of inquiry in the morning, he said, supporting Damion's action at sea. But the general tone of the series would be pessimistic, dealing with the deteriorating state of the nation, the Damion case its most recent and damning example.

"The way I see it," Stevens explained gloomily, "Man's a creature flawed by hate. Brilliant, but self-destructive. For all his genius and skill, he's not yet come up with a system to keep him from killing his own kind. To punish you for an act of compassion is typical of the flawed structure. Kill, they told you. It's your duty. If you don't kill, we'll punish you. What kind of creature is that?"

"It's always been like that."

"In man's brief stay here, yes. But whatever phenomenon created him, say God, realizes he's flawed and is doing something about it. Like Detroit pulling back a model for replacement of a faulty part."

"Man's no product of an assembly line."

"Science thinks so. Me too. Somewhere along that line we lost love and compassion. A shame, because man as a reasoning creature was a lovely experiment. Now his time's run out. Hiroshima was the warning. Vietnam? The beginning of the end." He plucked at the grass, studied a fistful, threw it aside. "Maybe next time she'll come up with something better."

"She?"

"Nature. Whoever's pulling the strings."

"God?"

"Man invented God." He got to his feet. "Even that didn't work. Come on," he said. "I can use a drink."

Damion took him to the officers' club. They finished a drink each before Damion realised he had been recognized. He knew he should not have risked it. They started to leave.

A young ensign detached himself from a group and followed.

"Captain Damion?"

Damion paused. "Yes?"

"Ensign Smith, Captain. Elmer P. Smith." He was straight and slim, confident-looking in his dress whites and cold sober. Stevens was reminded at once of Damion the first time they met. "I just want to say to your face what a stinking thing you did out there. You're a disgrace to the uniform you wear. I hope to God it won't be for long."

He wheeled and marched back into the shadows of the bar. Damion walked with Stevens to his car.

"A pompous ass," Stevens growled. "You should've slugged him."

"He should have saluted," said Damion.

A message awaited him at BOQ. His old exec, McKim, had phoned. He was with his wife across the bay. Would Captain Damion return the call? They would love to have dinner with him.

Damion went to his room and thought about it. McKim. That would be the true test. It would be great to talk it over with McKim, just this once. It was tempting, telephone number and all. He tore the message into small, pained squares and flushed it down the toilet.

He skipped dinner that night. He undressed and showered and stood at the window looking across the island. They had dredged up some four hundred acres of bay bottom to make Treasure Island and join it with Yerba Buena. He wondered what it had been like before man laid hands on it. Yerba Buena. Anything. Nice, probably. Everything man touched, it seemed, turned to crud.

I'm beginning to sound like Stevens, he reflected.

Below his windows were the officers' tennis courts. He had awakened that morning to the thwack of tennis balls and cries of "Deuce!" and "Love!" It saddened him a little. He had never played tennis. He had never played golf, either. It was a funny way for an American to grow up, never playing a set of tennis or a round of golf. Or running a lawn mower.

He stretched out on his bed with his arms under his head. There had been a weed-choked tennis court once, that boyhood time in the winter countryside of Virginia. Snow covered it much of the time and anyway, it was useless. No net or lines and all those weeds. It had been a show place once, of Federal charm and dignity, but its paint had flaked and its timbers sagged and it was poorly heated.

365

The Damions used the fine old fireplace, eight feet long, in the front sitting room. One day his father drove him to a planing mill and they brought back a long slab of clear pine, the rough bark still on its sides. He helped his father sand it, smooth as a clipper deck. "Properly holystoned," his father had said. Then, using a flat brush and black paint, he lettered in Old English script:

Round This Cheery Hearth, Speak Ill Of No Man

Together they put the varnish to it in thin veneers, stroking in steady sweeps and drying well between each gleaming coat. When it was ready they centered the slab on the stone mantel and lighted a fire. Paul sat with his mother and father, their faces glowing, their smiles warm, and had his first sip of hot mulled rum. Full of love and warmed by the rum inside him, he would remember it as the happiest moment of his life. Outside dry leaves rustled on the dead tennis court.

And where is *your* son, Paul Damion?

He stirred restlessly. Last of the Damions. A title out of Zane Grey? And who was the Henry Miller Lizarraga thought so much of? Damion had never heard of him.

Martha fled. Angela lost. No son to bear the Navy Cross. How does a sane man in his mid-forties advertise his desperate loneliness? *Spoiled Navy officer seeks second wife. Has medals. Wants son. Will travel.*

Doomed, she had said. Seeress McCready with her private hot line to tomorrow.

Tomorrow would be all right. Lizarraga had practically guaranteed it. But even Lizarraga with the best of intentions could not count out the Elmer P. Smiths.

XXXV

A simple room as courtrooms go. A dais, desks, hard chairs, the proper flags. Colored prints of naval sea battles on the walls, each bearing a motto identified with the American warship engaged. Among them, Lawrence's dying words on the riddled quarterdeck of an earlier *Chesapeake*.

In the outer waiting room and offices of Building 218, civilian secretaries went about their duties with a somewhat harried air. The *Chesapeake* court of inquiry was front-page news, attracting more press and channel coverage than expected. A large crowd of base personnel and visitors idled about the building entrance. Two stone-faced guards wearing white helmets and belts with sidearms checked passes at the door. Sunshine streamed through the windows, promising another hot and dry California day.

Damion sat alongside counsel at a varnished oak table. They were separated from the witnesses in the front rows by a long wood railing. Behind them the spectators and journalists filled the remaining seats in the crowded room.

Damion looked at the dais where four members of the court sat. One seat was empty. Damion knew the four admirals. Their chests gleamed with battle ribbons. Tremblay had done his work well. He wondered who the fifth admiral would be. Not that it mattered. There was weight enough already to give him the deep six.

Lizarraga leaned close. "Not too bad," he whispered.

"Murderer's Row," said Damion.

"Cleaves is without prejudice. A very fair man." His voice lacked conviction and Damion heard it.

"He remembers the *Maine*," he said.

Admiral Cleaves was the presiding officer. A baby flattop skipper at Leyte Gulf. A stickler for the rules, with the judicious look of a seagoing Solomon.

"That's LeBecque on his right. He could be tough."

Damion looked at Rear Admiral LeBecque. Over sixty, with cherubic cheeks and the demeanor of a sadistic monk. The man who had sailed a destroyer squadron into the teeth of a Pacific typhoon to prove to the world our Navy could take it. Two destroyers and twelve hundred men could not, Damion recalled.

Rear Admiral Biswell sat next to LeBecque. A hollow-eyed desk admiral from CinCPac's command, with an undistinguished record and chronic hives, squirming out his retirement day.

On the left of Cleaves sat a craggy-faced Scotsman from the Amphibious Command. Rear Adam Gordon. He had spent a poor night, his eyes circled like a raccoon's, his head already nodding. The fifth admiral had just arrived and Damion was stunned. "That's Hank Chapin out of BuAir," he whispered. "How'd he ever get past Tremblay?"

"We still have a few friends."

"I served under him, right after Inchon. A good sailor and he ran a happy ship."

"He's in line for CNO someday."

Chapin, crew cut sprinkled with gray, had deep-lined cheeks and intelligent eyes. He glanced Damion's way and grinned. Damion nodded and looked away. He was sorry they had chosen Chapin. It was an unexpected

challenge, having Hank Chapin up there to contend
with.

The courtroom was noisy. Turning, Damion saw
McKim and Morgen among a half-dozen familiar faces
in the front row. McKim, looking like his ulcer was
killing him, red-eyed and fierce, raised a clenched fist.
It startled Damion and pleased him. He loved McKim.
Morgen, a seat away, seemed nervous and avoided Damion's eyes. Damion was not surprised. Between
McKim at sea and his father ashore, the poor kid must
have gone through hell.

Admiral Cleaves was rapping for order.

"Here we go," Lizarraga said with a tight smile.

"Relax," Damion said and Lizarraga stared at him.

The morning's business passed in lazy sunlight.
Witnesses were called and dismissed. The questioning
of the bridge crew was brief and direct. They answered
the questions and gave their testimony in clear and
simple statements. Damion could not repress a smile.
McKim had done his work well. Morgen alone had
trouble telling his story. He was flustered and often
contradicted himself. Chapin in particular gave him a
hard time until Cleaves dismissed him and Morgen,
close to tears, shambled from the stand.

There were no more witnesses to call except Damion. "We're doing fine," Lizarraga whispered.

"So far," said Damion.

Admiral Cleaves squinted at the big clock on the
back wall. His gurgling insides told him it was almost
time for the lunch recess. He envisioned the club's
celebrated roast beef hash. He'd have it in the Garden
Room with a cold brew this time. He gently blinked his
eyes at Damion. May as well start to cook the goose,
he thought. He nodded at the court clerk. Damion's
name was called.

"Here." Damion raised his hand. The admiral
cleared his throat.

"Will you rise, please, and identify yourself."

Damion stood, steadying himself against the table.
"Captain Paul Damion, United States Navy. Serial
Number 149128."

Cleaves's smile was indulgent. "Serial number's not

necessary, Captain. Now then, your last command was U.S.S. *Chesapeake*, was it not?"

"Captain Paul Damion. United States Navy. Serial Number 149128."

"Yes, we have that, Captain. Your last command now."

"Captain Paul Damion. United States Navy. Serial Number 149128."

Cleaves looked puzzled, smiled gamely, whispered a few words to LeBecque who shrugged. Cleaves motioned to Lizarraga. "Counsel, is there anything—?"

Lizarraga leaned close to Damion. "Just answer the question, Captain." His voice had a bewildered and pleading tone. On the dais, Admiral Gordon's mouth sagged open, paralyzed in mid-yawn. His tense colleagues exchanged glances. Cleaves ignored his stomach's hunger rumbling and forgot to smile.

"I'll repeat the question, Captain." He stressed each word. "Was *Chesapeake* your last command?"

"Captain Paul Damion. United States Navy. Serial Number 149128."

The spectator section hummed with loud whispers Lizarraga tugged at Damion's sleeve. "You're crucifying yourself. *Just do what he says!*"

Hearing his own words, he was shocked at their meaning. No one could help Damion, he realized, last of all Damion himself. Puzzling fragments of Damion's conversations came to mind, making terribly clear what Damion wanted to tell the world.

He let go of Damion's sleeve. The scrape of his fingers on the coarse gold stripes galvanized him to his sworn duty. He was on his feet.

"If it please the court—"

Cleaves rapped the gavel several times sharply on the desk. "The witness will answer the question!" He glared down at Damion. "I shall not tolerate open contempt for the dignity of this court."

A sudden commotion erupted in a seat near the back of the room. All heads turned. Eric Stevens had leaped to his feet, his jowled cheeks cherry red.

"What the hell's wrong with you bastards? Don' you understand what he's trying to say?"

Two marines had him by the arms, their white helmets bobbing. They dragged him from his seat. Damion caught a glimpse of the faded blue denim and an arrogant flash of red foulard. For a moment Stevens tore free of his captors. His powerful voice shook the room, shook Damion's calm.

"He's a prisoner of war . . . what you made him, you bastards! What you make all of them—"

The guards were in control again. Stevens' words were lost in the machine gun thumping of Cleave's gavel.

Nice try, Eric, thought Damion and faced the court.

"Admiral Cleaves—sir?"

It was Chapin, half risen, his good face serious. He stretched his lank frame across confused Gordon's chest of rumpled ribbons. "I submit, sir," he went on in a firm voice, "that the witness may be overwrought—"

"All I'm asking, Hank, is that he answer a simple question!"

"He's capable of that, Admiral Cleaves, I assure you. I can personally vouch for it. Perhaps a brief recess and a few words with counsel. . . ?"

Cleaves turned to Lizarraga, grumbling, "If counsel for the witness wishes a brief recess, the court will grant it."

Lizarraga spoke a few words to Damion who shook his head. Lizarraga faced the dais, spread his hands in a hopeless gesture and sank into his seat, unable to speak. Chapin addressed Cleaves.

"May I ask the witness a question, Admiral?"

Cleaves nodded. Chapin came round the dais and stood squarely in front of Damion. Their eyes met. "You all right, Paul?" There was no answer. He moved closer and spoke softly. He knew Damion heard him. "You have friends, Paul. With you all the way. Just see this through."

A stillness seemed to swell the room out of proportion. All eyes were on Damion. "Just answer the question, Paul." Chapin pleaded. Damion took a breath. His glance wavered before Chapin's steady one.

371

The gavel pounded. "Enough of this," Cleaves rasped. "I order the witness to answer the question."

Orders, Damion thought, and stiffened. What it's all about.

Lizarraga covered his face with his hands. Chapin went back to his seat on the dais. Damion felt sorry for gallant Lizarraga, for brave Chapin—fellow officers he would gladly die for. And loyal deluded McKim behind him. But for Ensign Elmer P. Smith. . . ?

Round This Cheery Hearth, Speak Ill Of No Man

What Angela had said: . . . *with all my heart to stop you from what you do . . .*

Thwack! went the gavel.

"The court's waiting," Cleaves said.

He stood a little straighter. "Captain Paul Damion," he said, proud, "United States Navy. Serial Number 149128."